DOLLARS FOR THE DUKE

He put his arms round her, then slowly, very slowly, as if he was still afraid to frighten her, his lips found hers.

As he kissed her he knew, just as he had expected, her mouth was soft, sweet and innocent and gave him an ecstasy he had never known before in his whole life.

To Magnolia it was everything she had wanted and longed for, and which she had thought she would never find.

Bantam Books by Barbara Cartland
Ask your bookseller for the books you have missed

Barbara Cartland's Library of Love Series

Dollars for the Duke

Barbara Cartland

BANTAM BOOKS
TORONTO · NEW YORK · LONDON

DOLLARS FOR THE DUKE
A Bantam Book / June 1981

ISBN 0-553-14650-5

Published simultaneously in the United States and Canada

Bantam Books are published by Bantam Books, Inc. Its trade-
mark, consisting of the words "Bantam Books" and the por-
trayal of a bantam, is Registered in U.S. Patent and Trademark
Office and in other countries. Marca Registrada. Bantam
Books, Inc., 666 Fifth Avenue, New York, New York 10103.

PRINTED IN THE UNITED STATES OF AMERICA

0 9 8 7 6 5 4 3 2 1

Author's Note

As I have related in this story, the long line of American heiresses eager to marry titles, in the late nineteenth and early twentieth centuries, started with Jennie Jerome, who married Lord Randolph Churchill in 1874.

Historians estimate that by 1909 there had been five hundred marriages in which the bridegroom might have been dissolute, feebleminded, homosexual, or brutal, but so long as he appeared in *Debrett* or the *Almanach de Gotha* he was readily acceptable.

The wedding ceremony was always bizarre, lavish, and vividly publicised. At Sherrys, a restaurant in New York, an immense bird was exploded to shoot ten thousand roses over the guests. In the circumstances, in which the girls themselves had no say, it was amazing that the brides adjusted themselves to the Society into which they had been married.

As a child, the loveliest person I ever saw was the Duchess of Marlborough, who had been Consuelo Vanderbilt and who, despite being desperately unhappy, was adored by everyone who knew her. Her biography, *The Glitter and the Gold* describes her sufferings and the way in which her dominating mother used threats and even violence to compel her to marry the Duke.

Chapter One

1882

"I have set out the whole amount, Your Grace, **as** you asked me to do."

The Accountant put a sheaf of papers down in front of the Duke.

He looked at them, then stiffened, as if he could hardly believe what he read.

There was a long silence as he turned over several pages before he asked:

"Is it possible, Fossilwaithe, that my father could have run up such a mountain of debts without you or anyone else remonstrating with him?"

"I assure you, Your Grace," the Accountant said respectfully, "both I and my partners spoke to His late Grace on several occasions, but he brushed us aside. Once, he even informed me that I was to mind my own business!"

The Duke sighed.

He was quite certain that the Accountant was telling him the truth, and he remembered that his father had always been exceedingly impatient when anyone argued, let alone opposed him.

He looked down at the figures again as if he

thought that by some miracle they might have changed. Then he said:

"Well, Fossilwaithe, what do you suggest we do about it?"

He had no idea that the elderly man had been watching him with an expression of compassion in his eyes.

Now he made a helpless little gesture before he said:

"It is a problem that has kept me awake for nights, Your Grace, and quite frankly I do not know the answer."

The Duke sat back in his chair.

"Let us put it more bluntly—what have I to sell?"

Again Mr. Fossilwaithe, Senior Partner of the Solicitors' firm which had looked after the Otterburn Estates for many years, appeared to have no ready answer.

As if he felt the situation was intolerable, the Duke rose from his desk and walked across the room to stare out with unseeing eyes over Park Lane towards the green trees in Hyde Park.

Otterburn House in London was large and impressive and was a fitting town-house for the Dukes whose name it bore.

But the present and fourth Duke of Otterburn was thinking of the Castle and huge Estates in Buckinghamshire which he had inherited unexpectedly and to which he had returned from the East only a month ago.

He had never expected to find himself in the position of being the Duke of Otterburn, since he had an elder brother besides a father who had seemed a young man at fifty and likely to live for at least another forty years.

However, the late Duke had been stricken down in what he liked to call "his prime" by an epidemic which had swept the country last winter, taking its toll of more lives than were usually lost in any one of the small wars in which Britain was regularly engaged in one or another part of the world.

When Seldon Burn learnt of his father's death, he was only just recovering from the blow of learning that his elder brother, of whom he had been extremely fond, had broken his neck while hunting.

The information when it reached him had been much delayed because he was fighting a bitter campaign against the treacherous tribesmen on the boundaries of Afghanistan, and he was not in a position to communicate with his father as he wished to do until he returned to Peshawar.

It was there that he found waiting for him a telegram to inform him that his father also was dead and that his presence was required in England as soon as it was possible for him to return.

He easily obtained compassionate leave.

At the same time, as he journeyed back across the hot plains, sometimes by train, sometimes by slower but much more agreeable means on horseback, he faced the fact that his life in the Army had come to an end.

As a younger son it had been very clear to him as he grew to manhood that he could expect to receive nothing but a small allowance from his father and must make his own way in the world.

Later he had become aware that although his father had lived in a flamboyantly extravagant manner ever since his grandfather's death, there were obvious signs that the Estates did not pay their way and that debts were accumulating.

However, it was nothing to do with Seldon, and he joined the Army, taking part in several skirmishes in parts of the world like the Sudan before he was posted to India and found that there, at any rate, was a life after his own heart.

Because he was an excellent soldier in every way and a born leader of men, he commanded a company of soldiers who survived the perils of war by being unremittingly courageous and quick-witted.

It was what Seldon Burn was himself, and he soon earned the reputation of being a daring, if slightly unpredictable, officer on whom the Higher Command could rely in a crisis.

There were always crises on the North-West Frontier, and in that part of India there was always an enemy lurking behind every rock and every boulder.

The fact that Seldon and his men could outwit those who were supplied with Russian guns and activated by Russian treachery was a reward in itself.

Yet now, as he steamed through the Red Sea and into the Suez Canal, Seldon knew that a chapter of his life was closing and a new and very different one lay ahead.

He was not sure what he felt about becoming the fourth Duke of Otterburn.

When he had last been on leave three years ago, he had discussed the position with his brother.

He had been quietly confident that Lionel, at any rate, would uphold the dignity of the name and somehow manage to repair the damage that their father was doing to the family finances.

"The old man is spending money like water," Lionel told Seldon.

"Where does he get it?" Seldon enquired curiously.

"God knows! As you well know, he will never discuss his private affairs with me."

"Does he really need to live in such an extravagant style?" Seldon asked. "I notice that we now have twelve footmen in Buckinghamshire, six in London, and the stables are so full of horses that one can hardly put a pin between them!"

"I know," his brother groaned, "and Papa is determined to extend his racing-stable at Newmarket.

He has not had a win this year, and it infuriates him!"

"And apart from the horses," Seldon remarked, "there are the pretty women who are the prerogative of every rake!"

The two brothers laughed. They were both aware that their father was an extremely handsome man and had an eye for a pretty woman.

"You should see the latest," Lionel remarked. "She really shows off the diamonds he gives her to advantage!"

"Who is she?"

"One of the famous Gaiety Girls. She cannot dance, she cannot sing, but she looks like a goddess, and Papa keeps her cornucopia filled to the brim!"

The brothers laughed again. Then Seldon said more seriously:

"You know, Lionel, it is going to be very hard on you when you do inherit."

The Marquis shrugged his shoulders.

"It is no use worrying," he said, "and as Papa is strong and healthy, there is every likelihood that he will outlive both of us!"

Thinking of his brother now, Seldon could remember his saying it carelessly, and yet at the same time, as far as he was concerned, it was to be a prophecy of what actually happened.

Now Lionel, who had never married, was dead, and so was his father, and Seldon, who had never expected for one moment that he would become the Duke, was left with a mountain of debts which were even greater than he had anticipated.

He turned from the window.

"We have to find a solution, Mr. Fossilwaithe."

"I agree, Your Grace."

"I suppose there is no chance of our selling this house?"

"It is entailed, My Lord, otherwise your father, if

you will forgive the impertinence, would have sold it a long time ago."

The Duke sat down again at his desk.

"I suppose that applies also to the contents of the Castle, especially the paintings?"

"Almost as if the first Duke, your great-grandfather, Your Grace, anticipated that something like this would happen, they too were entailed by him, and your grandfather tied up everything else in such a manner that it would be almost impossible to have anything released."

Mr. Fossilwaithe paused before he added:

"There are, of course, five hundred acres on the north-west of the Estate which belonged originally to Your Grace's grandmother."

The Duke's eyes lightened.

"What would that fetch on the open market?"

"Not very much, Your Grace. And I think I should remind you that not only are the Alms-Houses situated on that particular land, but also a great number of the cottages occupied by your pensioners."

The light faded in the Duke's eyes.

He knew only too well that if he sold the land to speculators or even to other conscientious landlords, the pensioners could be turned off and the Alms-Houses emptied and filled instead with tenants who could pay a reasonable rent.

He stared down at the paper in front of him as if once again he could hardly credit that Mr. Fossilwaithe had not invented such a preposterous figure.

Then he said:

"I think the best thing for me to do is to read very carefully through these papers you have brought me, and I would also like to study the survey of the Otterburn Estates which I understand your firm made when my father died."

"There is a copy of it at the Castle, Your Grace,"

Mr. Fossilwaithe replied, "but I have another here if you would like me to leave it with you."

"Thank you."

Mr. Fossilwaithe produced the copy. Then he said respectfully:

"I wish, Your Grace, I could have brought you better news and given you a more optimistic forecast for the future."

"You have told me the truth," the Duke replied, "and I know you will agree that only by knowing exactly where I stand can I have a chance of finding my way out of this mess."

There was a sharp note in his voice as he said the last two words, and looking at him the Accountant realised how much he disliked the position in which he found himself.

He was in fact feeling that because the debts were so astronomical, the family name was being dragged through the mire.

"You know, Your Grace," Mr. Fossilwaithe said quietly, "that my firm will do anything in its power to help you."

The Duke rose to his feet and held out his hand.

"I am aware of that," he said, "and I can only thank you for all you have done so far, and your tact and understanding in what I know has been a very difficult situation."

"I thank Your Grace."

Mr. Fossilwaithe shook the Duke's hand and bowed himself to the door.

Only when he had gone did the Duke sink back in his chair, almost as if he was exhausted by the mammoth task which lay ahead of him.

It was as if the question, like the beat of a drum, repeated itself over and over in his mind:

"What the devil am I going to do?"

In some ways he was glad that it was he who had to cope with the problem rather than Lionel.

Lionel had never been a hard man, and he would have found it impossible to be as ruthless as the Duke now felt he might have to be.

First, the Castle had to be closed.

He was aware that this in itself would horrify his Burn relatives who had always looked on it as the focal point of their lives.

It was to the Castle that they flocked on every possible occasion that called for a gathering of "the Clan."

They gathered for weddings, funerals, anniversaries, festivals like Christmas and Easter, the christening of their children, and discussions of all the problems that they could not solve individually. They stayed at the Castle so that somehow with the help of their other relatives a solution could be found.

The Duke knew that to close the Castle would make them feel as if they were deprived of the central point of their existence.

"What else can I do?" he asked himself. "It is a huge place and needs a fortune spent on it."

He had gone to the Castle as soon as he arrived in England. He found that in the last five years the best rooms had been redecorated by his father regardless of expense, but the kitchens, the sculleries, and the pantries were a disgrace and the servants' quarters would not have seemed out-of-place in a slum.

There were no modern facilities, and his father, because he was quite content to have the water for his bath brought up two flights of stairs and along endless corridors by stalwart young footmen, had no idea of the inconvenience lesser mortals had to endure in order to keep clean.

The gold and silver plate used in the Dining-Room was priceless, but the cracked crockery from which the household ate and drank was only fit for the dust-bin.

The peach- and orchid-houses were in excellent

repair, but the gardeners complained that they were short of tools and the roofs of their houses leaked.

As he looked round, the Duke had thought it was as if he was afraid to turn over a stone for fear of what he would find underneath it.

The horses must be sold, that was obvious.

The racing-stable was still as unsuccessful as it had been three years ago and he doubted if he would get very much for it.

Although the horses at the Castle were certainly spectacular animals, the amount of money they would bring in when they were sold would be a "drop in the ocean" against the sum total of his father's debts.

As if he felt he could not bear to sit at his desk staring at the figures which Mr. Fossilwaithe had just put in front of him, the Duke put the papers in a drawer.

He walked from the Library, with its exquisite leather books, along the passage to the Drawing-Room which overlooked the garden at the back of the house.

Here his father had employed one of the most expensive decorators in London to cover the walls with silk brocade and to pick out the cornices and the frieze in gold-leaf.

He had also imported an extremely expensive artist from Italy to paint the ceiling with an allegorical picture of Venus surrounded by cupids.

It was extremely beautiful, and the room was undoubtedly a show-piece, but nothing in it was sale-able, and the paintings, while undoubtedly outstanding, were of course entailed.

The Duke looked round the room in a depressed manner, then walked to the grog-tray standing in one corner, which, on his father's instructions, was always to be found in every room.

This was not because he drank a lot himself but because if he wished to talk to one of the pretty ladies with whom his life was surrounded, he did not want to be interrupted by servants bringing in drinks, and he preferred to pour them out himself.

The Duke noticed the bottle of champagne which stood in a golden ice-bucket bearing the family crest, the decanters of brandy, whisky, and sherry, and a plate filled with pâté sandwiches.

Thinking back over the years, the Duke never remembered seeing anyone eat any of the sandwiches which his father ordered to be placed, fresh, in every Living-Room every morning and every evening.

He only hoped that some member of the household enjoyed finishing them off when they were taken away at the end of the day, only to be replaced the following morning with a fresh batch.

He had just poured himself a very small brandy and was filling up his glass from the soda syphon when the door opened and the Butler announced:

"Lady Edith Burn, Your Grace!"

The Duke turned round in surprise to see his cousin, who, nearing middle-age, was not only still extremely good-looking but also very smartly dressed.

"Edith!" he said in astonishment, putting down his glass. "This is a surprise! I thought you were abroad."

"I came back especially to see you, Seldon," Lady Edith answered. "In fact, I only docked in Southampton yesterday morning."

"Then you were in America?"

Lady Edith nodded.

She walked across the Drawing-Room to sit down on a blue brocade sofa and regarded her cousin from under the brim of her elegant hat which was decorated with ostrich-feathers.

The Duke eyed her with a faint smile. Then he asked:

"Well, what is the verdict?"

Lady Edith laughed.

"You are not so modest, Seldon, that you do not

know you are extremely good-looking, and in fact so handsome that I am sure hundreds of British hearts will start to beat faster at the first glimpse of you!"

"I doubt it," the Duke replied drily.

Lady Edith raised her eyebrows.

"What does that mean?" she asked.

"That a Duke without a penny to his name, and debts which will prevent him from playing an active part in the social life you enjoy, is not a particular asset."

There was a sudden softness in Lady Edith's voice as she replied:

"I was afraid, dear Seldon, that that was what you would discover when you reached home."

"I knew things would be bad," the Duke said. "It was something that Lionel and I both accepted, but we had no idea that it would be so catastrophic!"

Lady Edith sighed.

"I liked your father. He was one of the most fascinating men I have ever met in my life, but he never could deny himself anything he wanted, and the more expensive it was, the more he was determined to possess it."

"I am glad he enjoyed himself!" the Duke said wryly. "But the truth is that I have somehow to pay his creditors, which as far as I can judge will take the rest of my lifetime, and while I am doing so I must find a job, unless I am prepared to starve!"

There was no doubt now of the note of bitterness in his voice, and Lady Edith said:

"I am sorry, Seldon dear."

"So am I," the Duke replied, "and I daresay you will all be sorry when I close the Castle and this house, but there is nothing else I can do, and the sooner the family accepts it, the better!"

"I think it will break their hearts," Lady Edith said quietly.

"I was sure you would feel like that," the Duke said. "But Fossilwaithe has just left me, and the sum

11

total of my father's debts could buy this country several much-needed battleships or supply an Army with at least two Regiments!"

As if he could not bear to look at Lady Edith as he spoke, he walked once again to the grog-tray to ask when he reached it:

"What will you have to drink'?

"A small glass of sherry, please," Lady Edith replied.

When he had poured it out, the Duke was thinking he was glad in a way that the first to hear the bad news was his cousin Edith.

She had always been one of the most charming and sympathetic of his relatives, and he had thought that she had more common sense than most of the others.

Her history was a sad one, for she had become engaged when she was eighteen to a charming man, rich and titled, who had fallen in love with her at first sight, and she with him.

He was several years older than she was and had spent many years travelling round the world, sometimes just for amusement, and sometimes because he spoke a great many languages and acted as an unofficial but very talented Envoy for the Government.

They became engaged, but, as was to be expected, Lady Edith's parents insisted on the conventional six-month wait before they should be married.

Then her fiancé was asked to take part in some very tricky negotiations that were taking place between the Foreign Secretary and the Sultan of Morocco.

It was difficult for him to refuse, so, taking a fond farewell of Lady Edith, he told her that he would carry out his mission as quickly as possible and be back at least two months before the wedding was arranged to take place.

He left, and Edith busied herself buying her trousseau, while writing every day to the man with whom she was desperately in love. But when the time came for his return, there was no sign of him.

It was only when another month had passed that she insisted on her father getting in touch with the Foreign Office.

It was then that he learnt, to his consternation, that Lady Edith's fiancé had reached Morocco, then inexplicably had disappeared.

It took some time for him to get in touch with the British Consul and then for the Consul's reply to reach England.

As the months passed, the only information Edith received was that her fiancé had been seen with a tribe hostile to the Sultan, and he was thought to have been taken prisoner by them.

The authorities imagined he was being held captive somewhere, but nobody could work out where it was likely to be.

Because there could be no official statements, it always seemed to Edith that the Foreign Office dragged its feet even to find him, much less to insist on his release.

The months went by, a year passed, and still there was no news.

On her father's insistence, the Foreign Office sent a representative out to Morocco to make enquiries.

There were rumours that Lady Edith's fiancé had been seen in the interior of the country, that he was kept closely confined, that he had escaped and all traces of him had vanished into the sand, and a dozen other stories, none of which seemed to be true.

But whatever was said, the fact remained that he had not returned, and the Foreign Office, intent on not displeasing the Sultan, did not appear to press the matter as urgently as they might have done.

Time passed, and still Edith waited.

Then when her parents and everyone else said there was no hope and she must assume her fiancé was dead, she still went on waiting.

It was ten years later, when some explorers coming back from the unknown parts of Morocco told of a tribe who had kept a white man their prisoner until he had died, that Edith finally accepted that there would be no return of the man she loved.

After this, she made some sort of life of her own, but she never married.

Being comparatively well off, she began to travel, first with her parents, then with a Chaperone, and finally, when she grew older, with just a lady's-maid.

She was thirty-five when she published her first book, *Travels in the East,* and followed it the next year with another, *Travels in the West.*

As Queen Victoria's subjects were interested in the world of which the British had appropriated a great amount, the books were popular and Lady Edith became a celebrity.

Her independence brought her a lot of criticism from those who believed that women could not survive without the protection of a man and should be content to stay at home with their children, if they had any, or to devote their lives to good works, if they had not.

But Lady Edith merely laughed and enjoyed her fame, and the Duke thought, looking at her now, that because she had through her wide experience become wise and sensible, she could help him with what would be the inevitable protests and arguments from the rest of the family.

He handed her the glass of sherry, then picked up the brandy and soda he had poured for himself when she had arrived and took a sip of it.

"That is the position, Edith," he said, "and there is nothing I can do about it."

"On the contrary," Lady Edith replied, "I have an alternative, if you would like to listen to it."

"Of course. I am prepared to listen to anything you have to say," the Duke answered.

As he spoke, he had the feeling that the alternative that Edith would suggest would not be a practical one.

Lady Edith set her sherry down on a table beside the sofa before she said:

"It is quite simple, my dear Seldon. What you have to do is to marry money!"

Her answer was certainly not what the Duke had expected.

He stared at her as if he felt he could not have heard her aright.

"I have just come from America," Lady Edith explained, as if he had asked the question, "and New York is full of ambitious women determined to marry their daughters first and foremost to English aristocrats. The French, the Italian, and other nations are close runners-up, especially if the men are Princes."

"You cannot be serious!" the Duke exclaimed.

"I most certainly am!" Lady Edith replied. "Ever since Jennie Jerome married Lord Randolph Churchill in 1874, the matrimonial ambitions of the hostesses on Fifth Avenue are to see their little girls wearing a coronet, and strawberry-leaves have an attraction all their own."

"If what you are telling me is the truth," the Duke said, "the whole idea is disgusting and makes me feel sick!"

"That is what I expected your reply to be," Lady Edith smiled, "but because you have been out of England for so long, you have no idea that a great number of Englishmen find that their title is a very pleasant exchange for several million dollars."

"I can hardly believe what you are telling me," the Duke said, "and let me tell you now that any suggestion that I should sink to that level will receive a categorical 'No!'"

Lady Edith picked up her glass of sherry.

"Of course, dear Seldon, you are right," she answered, "and I admire you for it. But after what you have just told me, and what I knew only too well before I came here, there are just a few questions I would like to ask you."

"What are they?" the Duke enquired in an uncompromising voice.

"Your great-aunt wrote me a letter, which I received just before I left New York, telling me that she has not, since your father's death, received her pension."

She waited for the Duke to speak, but as he did not do so she went on:

"Your father made her an allowance of seven hundred fifty pounds a year, which is now all she has to live on. Of course she has a house on the Estate, which I understand is badly in need of repair, but she is nearly eighty, and I doubt if she could manage on less money with the two old servants who have been devoted to her for many years."

The Duke did not speak, and Lady Edith continued:

"And there are quite a number of other elderly people who have always been looked after by the family. I have a list of them, and they start with your old Governess. You must remember Miss Chamberlain? She only receives two hundred pounds a year, but she is sixty-seven and crippled with rheumatism, so it would be impossible for her to work even if she wished to do so."

As she spoke, Lady Edith had been drawing a piece of paper from her hand-bag, and now she looked up at the Duke to see that he was scowling.

"The servants," she went on, "and other employees who have been pensioned off come, I understand, in a special category which has always been seen to by the Solicitors who manage the Estate, but it was considered indiscreet to let them know what our actual relatives receive."

She held up the pieces of paper.

"I have a list of them here, and it comes to just over three thousand five hundred pounds a year, and quite frankly, Seldon, they have a struggle to exist unless the sums can be increased."

"Increased!" the Duke exclaimed. "How do you think for one moment that I can find three thousand five hundred pounds a year?"

Lady Edith sighed.

"I know it is impossible, but what do we do with these old dears? Without any money they will all end up in the Work-House."

The Duke of Otterburn again walked across the room to the window.

"It is intolerable!" he said furiously. "When I think of the money my father spent on actresses and on horses that never left their stables for the race-course, and on an army of unnecessary servants."

"It is very hard to think of it," Lady Edith said sympathetically, "but we cannot put back the clock, and what is done is done."

"I know that," the Duke said. "The question is, what can I do about it?"

"Unless you intend to all intents and purposes to murder the people on this list, there is only one thing you can do."

"Marry for money?" the Duke questioned. "It is degrading, obscene, a solution that I consider worse than the bartering of slaves or the buying of a woman's body in a brothel!"

His voice sounded harsh and raw, and when there was silence behind him he turned to say:

"Forgive me, Edith, I should not speak to you like that."

"I understand, Seldon," she replied gently. "For anyone with principles and as straightforward as yourself, it does sound an unpleasant traffic."

The Duke made an inexpressible sound and she went on:

17

"At the same time, it is something which has happened in English Society since the beginning of time. Look at every family we know and respect. They have always at one time or another brought in heiresses to fill the family coffers, and I cannot help suspecting that a little red blood mixed up with so much blue must improve the species!"

"That is an impractical remark if ever there was one," the Duke said impatiently.

"I prefer to think of it as a practical one," Lady Edith replied, "and because I have spent quite a lot of time in New York, I think I understand the feelings of the New World mothers who want their girls to have the best of the Old World."

. She saw the expression on the Duke's face and said:

"Some of the American girls are very attractive, very well educated, far more so than our girls, and have both personality and character."

She thought the Duke looked sceptical, and she continued before he could speak:

"American men are different. They start off when they are young by concentrating all their energy, their strength, and their ambition on acquiring money. Very few of them are at all cultured, and very few, when one thinks of it, have any interest outside their own subject—finance!"

"I do not want to listen to this!" the Duke exclaimed.

"Yes, you do!" Lady Edith replied sharply. "I am telling you, Seldon, that your only chance of saving the family, the Castle, and the lives of those who are dependent on you is to marry a charming American wife who will bring you an enormous fortune which you will spend as you like, while in exchange she will be content to bear your name and be a Duchess."

"You sound exactly like an Eighteenth Century procuress!"

Because he was angry he meant it to be an insult.

Lady Edith laughed.

"If you are trying to hurt me, Seldon, you are not succeeding. I know what you are feeling, but even idealistic people like yourself have to accept the world as it is, and not as they would like it to be."

Her voice softened as she said:

"I consider marriage is your duty, and you will find, once you take the plunge, that it is not as disagreeable as you anticipate. I promise you, the wife I choose for you will be both attractive and adaptable—two things which it may surprise you to know are something the Americans have, and which we usually lack."

Lady Edith paused for a moment before she went on:

"You have to marry sooner or later. If you look at the English girls when they first leave the School-Room, where they have been chaperoned by Governesses and never allowed to appear in public until the moment they make their debut, you will find it depressing."

She gave the Duke no chance to reply but continued:

"They will have spoken to no men except for the local Curate, and it is impossible to believe that they will become the charming, witty, sophisticated women you doubtless found very alluring when you were far away on some unknown battlefield."

There was laughter in her voice as Lady Edith spoke, and she added:

"Your life will be one long yawn if you choose an English girl as your wife. Instead, I am offering you someone very different; and apart from her physical attractions, you will be many million dollars better off."

"I will not do it!" the Duke said positively. "I am damned if I will!"

19

Lady Edith did not answer. She merely drank a little more sherry.

"You heard what I said, Edith?" the Duke demanded.

"I heard you, Seldon," his cousin answered, "but you will marry, because there is nothing else you can do."

Chapter Two

Magnolia shut the door and hastily thrust the note she had been reading down inside her gown.

Then she stood with a tense and wary expression in her eyes as her mother came into the room.

Mrs. Vandevilt, who privately was known as "The Dragon of Fifth Avenue," was an extremely handsome woman.

She carried herself like an Empress, and the ropes of perfect pearls she wore round her long neck and the huge diamonds in her ears made one think of some Eastern Potentate.

But her eyes were hard, and there was no smile on her lips as she regarded her daughter with a steely glance.

Magnolia felt herself tremble and there was a long, uncomfortable silence before her mother said:

"I understand some flowers were delivered here to you an hour ago. Who were they from?"

"I ... I do not ... know."

It was a lie, but it was not a very successful one, and it was impossible for her to look her mother in the face.

Instead she glanced across the room to where on a table inlaid with ivory on which reposed some

21

priceless Sèvres porcelain was a basket containing lilies-of-the-valley.

Mrs. Vandevilt followed the direction of her daughter's eyes, and her lips tightened.

"Lilies-of-the-valley!" she said scathingly. "I suppose your admirer thought you were like a lily. Well, I want to know what he wrote to you."

There was an uncomfortable silence before Magnolia stammered in a frightened little voice:

"I . . . do not . . . know what you mean . . ."

"Stop trying to hoodwink me, Magnolia," Mrs. Vandevilt said sharply, "which you have never been able to do. I know the man who sent you this rubbish, and I want the note which came with it!"

Magnolia did not reply, and her mother saw that her face was very pale and her hands were trembling.

Mrs. Vandevilt moved a little closer.

"I have not beaten you, Magnolia, since you were fifteen, but if you go on lying I shall have no hesitation in giving you the biggest thrashing of your life!"

"Mama!"

It was a cry of sheer terror.

"You know I mean what I say," Mrs. Vandevilt said. "Give me the note!"

She held out her hand, and after a second's effort to stand firm before a parent who had always frightened her, Magnolia unbuttoned the front of her gown and drew the note from its place of concealment.

With shaking hands she gave it to her mother, who said:

"The man who wrote this will be dealt with, and in the future you will leave the house only in my company and will attend no dances or parties until we leave for England."

Magnolia stiffened and there was a pregnant silence until she questioned:

"Leave for . . . England? Are we going . . . abroad, Mama?"

"You are going to England to marry the Duke of Otterburn," Mrs. Vandevilt answered.

She intended to speak severely, but there was a note of triumph in her voice that was unmistakable, and she was quite unmoved by the fact that her daughter was looking at her with an expression of horror.

"B-but ... Mama ..." she said at length, as her mother said no more, "how can I ... marry the Duke of ... Otterburn? I have ... never met ... him."

"That is immaterial," Mrs. Vandevilt snapped. "Everything has been arranged by Lady Edith Burn, and you can consider yourself a very fortunate young woman. I am just waiting to see Mrs. Astor's face when the engagement is announced."

"But ... Mama ... I cannot ... I cannot ... it is ... impossible ... !" Magnolia began.

Her mother, as if she had nothing more to say, turned towards the door.

She had almost reached it when she looked back at the basket of lilies-of-the-valley on the table.

She walked towards it, picked it up, threw it on the ground, and deliberately stamped on the fragile blossoms.

Then she left the room without another glance at her daughter.

Magnolia gave a cry and put her hands over her face.

She felt as if in destroying her flowers her mother had destroyed something that had been born within her last night and seemed in retrospect like the first flowers of spring.

It had been quite an ordinary Ball until she had danced with him.

Her other partners were all so familiar from the years when she had met them first at her children's parties, then her teen-age dances, and finally the Ball that had been given for her on her eighteenth birthday.

As she had grown older she felt the boys were all exactly the same: either tongue-tied, or over-effusive with their remarks, such as: "Gee-whiz, you're a honey!"

As she had said once to her father:

"It sounds absurd, Papa, but I feel as if I am immeasurably older than the men with whom I have to dance, and when I sit next to them at the dinner-table, they literally have no conversation except about horses, and then they more often back them than ride them!"

Her father had laughed, but she thought there was a sad expression in his eyes as he said:

"It is quite unnecessary, my darling, for you to be clever as well as beautiful."

"I am glad you think I am both of those things," Magnolia said with a smile.

"Of course I do," her father answered, "and now I want to show you this painting I have just bought, which no one else in the house will appreciate as you will."

Magnolia had known that in an obscure manner he was referring to his constant frustration where her mother was concerned, since Mrs. Vandevilt despised her husband's interest in art and thought it was a waste of time.

She also thought the very extensive education he had insisted Magnolia should receive had cost money which would far better have been spent on jewels.

But while Mr. Vandevilt was a quiet, complaisant man in many respects who bowed to his wife's wishes and let her do just what she liked, where his daughter's education was concerned he had been adamant.

The Governesses and teachers who instructed Magnolia were chosen by him, and because Mrs. Vandevilt was not interested in anything that could not be seen and admired, she accepted his choice.

Magnolia was quick and intelligent and what she

learnt opened the windows of her mind to new vistas.

This was fortunate for the simple reason that no other girl in the whole of America was so confined, restricted, and, as she often thought herself, imprisoned.

But then, no other girl in America was quite as rich as Magnolia Vandevilt.

When her father and mother had married it had been a union not only of two extremely good-looking people but of two huge fortunes.

These had been accumulated by their pioneering ancestors who had come to the New World to make money and had had the intelligence to invest it in the land on which they stood.

Mr. Vandevilt's grandfather and great-grandfather had bought acres and acres of the swampy islands on which New York was now built, and Mrs. Vandevilt's father had invested in the first gold mines, then in the first oil strikes.

The big tragedy for the present-day Vandevilts was that they had only one child to whom to leave their vast fortune, but it was much more of a tragedy for Magnolia.

As soon as she was old enough to think for herself, she realised that she was "special."

She could not go out in her pram, or later walk in Central Park with her Nanny, without there being two body-guards in close attendance.

She got used to this, and it was only when she realised that no man could reach her mother's standard of what she considered to be a suitable husband for her that she began to be afraid.

Because she was romantic—a trait that had been much cultivated by her father—she had imagined that someday she would find love with the Prince of her dreams.

It was her father who gave her *Romeo and Juliet* to read, who told her the story of Dante and Beatrice, who made her cry with the tale of Heloise and Abelard, and who, looking back further still, sat on her bed when she was only five and told her the story of Cinderella.

As she grew older, Mr. Vandevilt found with an irrepressible delight that his daughter had the same feeling for paintings that he had.

He had started his collection when he was a very young man, on his first visit to Florence.

He had always found it difficult to explain to anyone but Magnolia what he had felt when he had stood entranced in the Uffizi Gallery, looking at the paintings by Botticelli.

His heart went out to them and he actually fell in love for the first time.

It was a love that mattered to him more than anything else in the whole of his life, and he was lucky in that his huge fortune enabled him to acquire paintings not only from Art-Dealers but from artists whose works had for him a magic that other collectors missed.

Hanging in private rooms in the huge brownstone house on Fifth Avenue were Sisleys, Monets, and a Renoir that he had bought for a few paltry francs when everyone else was laughing at the absurdity of the Impressionists.

"There is something about you, my darling," he said to Magnolia as she grew up, "which reminds me of Sisley's paintings."

She gave him an enchanting smile.

"Now you are really flattering me, Papa."

"I am stating a fact," Mr. Vandevilt said. "You have a grace, a fragility, and an impression of light that only Sisley could portray on canvass."

Her mother had a very different opinion.

"You are too tall, your neck is too long, and I can't think from where you get that absurd baby-face," she would say sharply. "Massage your nose to try to make it grow longer."

She gave an exclamation of annoyance and went on:

"Heaven knows, I wanted a daughter with classical features, and you would think all those pictures your father drools over would have produced one."

Her mother was thinking of all the paintings by Rubens, Rembrandt, and Van Dyke that hung in the huge Drawing-Room, the Hall, and the Picture-Gallery.

Mrs. Vandevilt's friends looked at them with envy, and the Press described them as being "part of the most important private collection in America."

When she was allowed to do so, Magnolia would sit quietly with her father in his small Study, which was very unostentatious, and look at the light on Sisley's trees, on a field of corn that seemed to shiver in the wind, praying that her father would always think her as lovely as the paintings that meant so much to him.

Yet she found as she grew up that it was difficult ever to be alone with her father.

Now her mother was concentrating on her as if she were one of those projects either social or charitable for which she was extolled almost daily in the National Press.

There were fittings for clothes until Magnolia said to her father:

"I wish I could run about naked, or have just one simple robe like those the Greeks used to wear."

Her father had smiled at her and she knew he understood how boring she found it.

"I tried to read during the fitting," Magnolia went on, "but Mama took the book away from me and told me no man would want a woman whose head was stuffed with a lot of dreary facts and figures."

Her father sighed but he did not say anything, and after a moment Magnolia asked:

"Why did you marry Mama?"

They had always talked very frankly to each

other ever since she had been a small child, and she asked him questions to which no one else would give her answers.

Her father did not reply at once, but Magnolia knew it was not because he was embarrassed by her question, but merely because he was looking back into the past so that he could answer her truthfully.

"Our parents brought us together because they thought the union between two such large fortunes would be a suitable one," Mr. Vandevilt explained at length. "And indeed your mother was very beautiful."

He smiled a little wryly before he went on:

"I knew very little about women in those days, since I had concentrated almost exclusively on paintings. But she looked to me very like one of the Madonnas portrayed by the early Italian Masters."

Magnolia did not speak and he said no more.

They were both aware that Mrs. Vandevilt, after nineteen years of fighting her way to the pinnacle of social fame, did not look in the least like a Madonna, but perhaps more like a Medusa with diamonds instead of snakes in her hair.

What had emerged soon after their marriage was the fact that Mrs. Vandevilt had a will of iron and a determination to have her own way whatever the opposition.

She browbeat those she employed, and her husband, finding it distasteful to be involved in arguments of any sort, retired into the background of her life.

He was content to enjoy his paintings and the very few congenial friends who shared the same interests that he had.

Therefore, it was impossible for him to interfere with Magnolia's early upbringing, even though he thought his wife's handling of her was too strict.

"I have to be both father and mother to my child," Mrs. Vandevilt would confide to her intimates.

"My husband does not take the slightest interest in her."

This was untrue, but Mr. Vandevilt had already accepted that it would be hopeless for him to assert his authority, which in most cases would only make matters worse.

It was therefore his wife who punished Magnolia when she was naughty, and as Mrs. Vandevilt had been whipped by her own father when she was a child, Magnolia received the same treatment.

She was usually lashed on the legs with a riding-whip, and because she had a pride that was unusual in so young a child, she forced herself not to scream nor even to cry until she was alone.

This inevitably made the punishment more severe, owing to Mrs. Vandevilt's determination to break her daughter's spirit.

She did not succeed, but because Magnolia was vulnerable and sensitive not only to physical punishment but to stormy rows and sharp voices, she was frightened of her mother.

Her one consolation was that she could escape as her father escaped, only in her case it was through books.

She read and read, and was beaten innumerable times for reading when she should be asleep, but that did not stop her.

She built herself a dream-world where things were very different from the reality of her own home.

Because she was very feminine, inevitably her world contained a Knight in shining armour, a Prince Charming who protected her and fought for her and to whom she eventually gave her heart.

Last night at the Ball, she thought she had found him.

The man who had come up to her and asked her to dance had been English, a nephew by marriage of one of the most important hostesses in New York, whose sister had married an English Lord. Their son, as announced in the Press, had just arrived in America on a trip round the world.

Tall and fair, with blue eyes, when Magnolia looked at him she felt he might have stepped straight out of one of the fairy-stories which her father had told her when she was small.

They danced together and he said:

"You are very beautiful and different from any other girl I have ever seen. In fact, you remind me of a lily-of-the-valley."

"Thank you," Magnolia said with a smile, "but actually my name is Magnolia!"

"That suits you too," he replied. "How did you get such an unusual name?"

Magnolia laughed.

"Apparently, when I was born, the Nurse said to my father: 'She is a funny little thing, but she has skin like a magnolia'!"

The man with whom she was dancing laughed. Then he said:

"I am sure your skin has not changed with the years, and I would like to touch it."

Magnolia looked at him in surprise, thinking it a very familiar thing to say. Certainly none of the gauche young Americans with whom she normally danced would have dared to make such a remark.

Then as her eyes met his blue ones, she had a strange feeling of excitement, and yet at the same time she felt shy.

"I have to see you again," he said insistently. "How can we manage it?"

Magnolia shook her head.

"It will be impossible unless you come with your aunt to call on Mama."

"You know I did not mean that," he said. "I want to see you alone."

"I am never allowed to see people alone."

"I will think of something," he replied. "Leave everything to me."

She felt his fingers tighten on hers, and with his other arm he seemed to draw her a little closer. Then the dance came to an end and he took her back to her mother.

There was no chance of her having another dance with him, as her programme was full, but their eyes met across the room and she knew that she wanted to see him again and felt despairingly that it was something which would never happen.

Now she knew with a kind of sick horror what her mother had been planning so arduously these last three weeks.

She had had a feeling that something strange was going on, when Lady Edith Burn was incessantly in the house and her mother was locked in close conversation with her so that Magnolia was left unexpectedly free to be with her father.

"Oh, Papa, I have missed you," she said the first day they could be together.

"And I have missed you, my dearest," he replied.

They smiled at each other, then he said eagerly:

"Look what I have to show you. It is a Boudin, one of the loveliest I have ever seen, and I have also bought another Sisley."

"How gorgeous!" Magnolia had exclaimed.

They sat together eulogising over the light in the trees and the sun-kissed beach that Boudin portrayed better than anyone else.

When they had finished talking about paintings, they had ranged over a whole field of philosophy, history, and of course literature.

"I have a new French novel for you to read," her father said, "but do not let your mother see it."

"No, of course not, and anyway Mama does not speak French," Magnolia answered.

"But she might have heard of Gustave Moreau, as everyone is talking about him," her father said drily.

"I will hide it away as I always do," Magnolia

31

told him, "and now, Papa, I have some very important questions to ask you about Buddhism which I feel only you can explain to me."

They talked away happily until Lady Edith had left, but she was back again the next day and the day after that.

Magnolia thought now that she should have realised that something of immense importance was taking place.

The Duke of Otterburn! Who was he?

She took her hands down from her face to look at the bruised and battered lilies-of-the-valley which her mother had left on the carpet.

They seemed to her to be a symbol of her own feelings, her own future life.

Then because she was frightened in a way she had never been frightened before, she knew she must find her father.

She ran down the stairs to his Study, and to her relief she found him, as she had hoped, studying some more paintings which one of the Art-Dealers who never missed an opportunity to interest such a rich client had left for his inspection.

At first he was not aware that she was there, then as he turned to see who was disturbing him, she threw her arms round him and hid her face against his shoulder.

He could feel her trembling, and after a moment he said in a quiet voice:

"I imagine your mother has told you."

"I cannot do . . . it, Papa! I cannot . . . marry anyone I have not . . . seen and do not . . . love."

It was the cry of a child, and as he held her close Mr. Vandevilt said:

"I was afraid you would be upset, my dearest."

"You . . . have to . . . save me, Papa. You know Mama will not . . . listen to . . . me if I say I will not . . . marry him."

Her father kissed her forehead. Then he said:

"Come and sit down, my dear. I want to talk to you."

She was surprised at his tone, expecting, because they had always been so close and he understood her as no one else had ever done, that he would promise to talk to her mother.

Instead, he drew her to a sofa and they sat down together.

"You have to save me, Papa!" Magnolia insisted. "I know you never ... oppose Mama and always let her ... have her ... own way ... but you understand, as she will ... never do ... that I am not interested in becoming a ... Duchess ... but in ... marrying a man I ... love."

She thought of the man with the blue eyes who had looked into hers last night, and added in a very low voice:

"I thought ... last night at the ... Ball I had met ... someone I could love ... if I was ... allowed to ... see him."

Her father sighed but did not speak, and Magnolia said:

"What can I do, Papa? If you do not ... help me, Mama will ... force me into doing ... something which I know is ... horrible and degrading! And anyway why should the Duke ... want me, when he has ... never ... seen me?"

Even as she said the words, she knew the answer.

She had not been particularly interested, but the conversations of friends at the luncheons and dinners which she had been allowed to attend since she was officially grown up had all centred on the social gossip of whose daughters would make the best marriages.

It had not been of the least interest to Magnolia, but she gathered that there had been tremendous excitement when Jennie Jerome, whose family every-

one knew, had married an Englishman called Lord
Randolph Churchill.

And even more so when Consuela Ienaga of 262
Fifth Avenue had become the Duchess of Manchester.

The ball of conversation had bounced backwards
and forwards across the table.

Magnolia would have been very stupid, which
she was not, if she had not been aware that the
mothers with daughters of the same age as herself
were all manoeuvring to get important and if possible
titled men to their parties.

One hostess was giving a Ball for an Italian
Prince who had just arrived in the country.

Another had invited—and she produced his name
as if he were an "ace"—an English Earl.

Several other ladies, who Magnolia thought
looked slightly green with envy, had no better trumps
in their hands than a somewhat dubious Count or a
Texan oil Magnate.

She had not paid very much attention at the time,
but now ominously it all came back to her.

She realised that if her mother could pull a Duke
like a rabbit out of a hat, she would definitely be the
winner of the contest.

"I will ... not do it, Papa!" she said fiercely. "I
will run away ... or rather ... you must ... take me
away. We can ... hide so that Mama ... cannot find
us."

She clasped her hands together as she spoke, only
to stiffen as he said very gravely:

"You know that would be impossible, my dearest,
and you have to marry one day."

"Yes, of course," Magnolia agreed, "but I want to
marry the man I ... choose ... and someone I ... love,
as in all the stories you told me when I was a little
girl."

There was a very sad expression in her father's
eyes as he said:

"That is something I would like too. But, Magnolia, you are intelligent enough to face facts. Where are you going to meet such a man?"

"I thought ... perhaps I had ... met him ... last night."

There was silence before her father said:

"I saw you dancing with the man you are thinking about."

"If you know him, please tell me about him, Papa," Magnolia said eagerly.

"I grant you he is an attractive young Englishman," her father answered. "I talked to him later in the evening, and I realised he had asked to be introduced to me so that he could meet you again."

"Oh ... Papa ... !"

The exclamation was very revealing and so was the excitement in Magnolia's eyes.

"There were, however, plenty of people to tell me why Mr. Eric Dinsdale was in America."

There was something in the way her father spoke which made Magnolia look at him enquiringly, and he went on:

"He is here, my darling, to find a rich wife!"

His reply made Magnolia feel as if her heart had suddenly fallen onto the ground and smashed into a thousand pieces.

Then her father went on:

"You have not, my dearest, met many young men, which I have always thought has been a mistake, so now it is going to be difficult for you to sift the grain from the chaff."

"And you ... think," Magnolia said in a voice that did not sound like her own, "that he was only ... interested in ... me because I am ... rich?"

"I am quite certain," her father replied, "he was interested in you because you are beautiful, which made it impossible for him to notice any other girl at the Ball. At the same time, he was thinking how very lucky it was that someone whom he fancied, and it was very easy for him to do so, was so heavily gilded!"

Magnolia tried to stifle a little cry and jumped to her feet.

"You make ... everything seem horrible and ... unclean!" she stormed. "How can I ever ... trust any ... man if all he ... thinks about is my ... money rather than ... me?"

Her voice broke on the last word and her father reached out to take her hand and pull her back beside him on the sofa.

He put his arm round her, and after a moment's instinctive resistance she laid her head against his shoulder as she had when she was a child.

"Now listen to me," he said quietly. "Everybody has some form of handicap in their lives."

He knew that Magnolia was attentive as he asked:

"Have you ever thought what it would be like to be born crippled or blind? Or if you had inherited some incurable disease through no fault of your own?"

Magnolia made a little murmur but did not interrupt, and her father continued:

"Money can be a blessing and a comfort. It can also be a handicap. Therefore, you have to adjust yourself to living with it, just as the blind have to train their senses to compensate for their loss of sight, and a deaf man has to lip-read."

"I can ... understand what you are ... saying, Papa. At the same time ... there must be a man ... somewhere in the world who would ... love me for ... myself."

Her father smiled.

"There will be a great many men who will love you, Magnolia, and doubtless, sooner or later, you will fall in love yourself. But in the world in which you live, for a girl to be free of the restrictions which confine her from the cradle to the grave, she has to be married!"

"But she only ... changes the jurisdiction of her father and mother for that of a husband," Magnolia answered.

Even as she spoke, she thought that her mother was certainly very free of any jurisdiction and that her friends, either male or female, were her choice, without any interference from the man she had married.

It then flashed through Magnolia's mind that the ladies at her mother's parties had also talked of the love-affairs taking place in New York.

Although they had chosen their words carefully in front of the girls, she had been sharp enough to realise the innuendo in much of what had been said.

She had been aware that the man and woman concerned were both already married, but she was not interested because she did not know that their "liaison," if that was what it was, was a clandestine one.

There was also, she thought, a great deal said about the infatuation of the English Prince of Wales for Lily Langtry.

She was an actress who had taken America by storm, but in some incomprehensible way she was also a lady and was accepted by a number of hostesses in New York, although Magnolia's mother was not one of them.

Aloud she said:

"Are you seriously suggesting, Papa ... that I should marry this ... Duke, as Mama says I am to do, without ... knowing him ... let alone ... loving him?"

"I think it is quite wrong that he will not come to New York to meet you," her father replied. "If it were in my power, Magnolia, I promise you I would prevent your mother from taking you to England, and your wedding would take place here, as it ought to do."

"You will let Mama do . . . this to me?" Magnolia cried. "How . . . could you, Papa?"

"I do not think that anything I said would make the slightest difference," her father answered frankly. "And in a way I think, my dear, it is your only solution and you have to accept it."

Magnolia raised her head from his shoulder.

"I do not know what you are . . . talking about, Papa. I do not . . . understand."

"Then let me explain," her father said, taking her hand in his. "You know without my telling you that you are one of the richest heiresses in America. Not only my fortune but also your mother's will come to you when we die, and also you were left a great deal of money in your grandmother's will. That, while you have been growing up, has increased astronomically."

"Yes, I know," Magnolia remarked.

"This means you are the target of every fortune-hunter in America, England, Europe, and, for all I know, Outer Mongolia!"

Because she could not help it, Magnolia felt a faint smile curve her lips, but she did not interrupt and he went on:

"In the circumstances, it is very unlikely that any decent man who had any pride would ask you to marry him."

Magnolia looked startled, and her father continued:

"That is the truth, and one you have to accept. Most men dislike a wife owning more money than they have. Englishmen particularly would run a mile rather than be accused of fortune-hunting."

"You mean," Magnolia said in a very small voice, "that . . . no one whom you would call 'decent' would . . . ever ask me to . . . marry him?"

"Shall we say that it is such an outside chance that it is not worth thinking about," her father replied. "Therefore, you have to face the alternative."

"What is that?"

"If you are going to sell yourself, for that is what it comes down to, you might as well accept your mother's proposition and aim for the highest!"

"The Duke!" Magnolia exclaimed scornfully.

"As a matter of fact," her father answered, "I know she was considering a Prince, if there is a reputable one still free in Europe, but an English Duke is almost the equivalent. Kings, she discovered, insist on mixing their Royal blood with that of other Royalty!"

Her father spoke in such a funny way that despite herself Magnolia gave a little laugh.

"You are making a joke of it, Papa," she said accusingly, "but it is not . . . funny for me."

"I know that, my dearest," her father replied, "and because I realised that this was what your mother was contemplating as soon as Lady Edith Burn arrived back in New York, I made some enquiries about the Duke of Otterburn."

"And what did you find out, Papa?"

"That he did not expect to inherit the title as he had an elder brother. That he has had a distinguished career in the Army, and was capable of supporting himself until he became unexpectedly the Duke of Otterburn with a mountain of debts."

"Which can be paid off with . . . my money," Magnolia said sharply.

"I do not suppose otherwise the Duke would demean himself to marry an American."

"Demean himself? What do you mean?"

"I mean," her father replied, "that the English aristocrats who give themselves great airs consider they are doing us a favour if we prop up their crumbling ancestral homes and modernise their out-of-date farms in return for our daughters being able to walk about with a moth-eaten coronet on their heads."

Now Magnolia laughed and it was a very pretty sound.

Then the smile slid from her lips and she said:

"But the . . . Duke would be my . . . husband. I . . . suppose you could not . . . give him the money to do . . . all the things you say need . . . doing and let me stay with . . . you?"

"It would, unfortunately, be a quite impractical solution, my dearest. Your mother is determined to be able to boast: 'My daughter is a Duchess!' "

"What you are . . . saying, Papa, is that if it is not this . . . Duke, then it will be . . . another?"

"Exactly!" her father agreed. "However, he sounds a slightly better bet than others your mother has been contemplating ever since you left the School-Room, so I can only say that—speaking about a man whom I have never met and who has not the decency to cross the Atlantic to meet you—you might do worse!"

"Oh . . . Papa!"

Again it was the cry of a child who feels that her sense of security is being taken away from her.

For the first time since she had come into the Study, Magnolia's eyes filled with tears.

She looked at her father and said brokenly:

"I thought you would . . . save me . . . I thought you would . . . stand up to . . . Mama . . . and think of some . . . wonderful way in which I could go on being with you . . . I do not want to marry some . . . horrible . . . beastly fortune-hunter who does not care if I am . . . black . . . white, or yellow . . . or have a . . . hare-lip . . . or a deformed body . . . so long as I am . . . r-rich!"

"That is not quite true," her father replied. "Lady Edith has undoubtedly told him how lovely you are."

Then as the tears ran down his daughter's face, Mr. Vandevilt pulled her against him and said harshly in a voice she barely recognised:

"Do not cry, my dearest. If you cannot bear it, I cannot either. Can you imagine what my life will be without you, and how much I shall miss you?"

40

Because of the pain in his voice, Magnolia burst into tears and sobbed unrestrainedly against him as she had done when she was a child.

"I-it ... is so ... hard ... Papa."

When he realised how much it upset her, Mr. Vandevilt forced himself to say in a completely different tone:

"I can cross the Atlantic now in nine days, and I promise you, if your husband will invite me, I will be staying with you a dozen times a year, and anyway I believe the Duke has some very good paintings."

Magnolia choked on her tears and said:

"If he had ... he would ... s-sell them."

"He probably is not entitled to," Mr. Vandevilt replied. "But, paintings or no paintings, I promise you, my dearest, I shall be a constant visitor to England, because I cannot lose you."

Magnolia raised her head.

She looked very lovely, despite the fact that her long dark eye-lashes were wet and there were tears running down her cheeks.

Looking at her, her father thought she was so beautiful that it was not only wrong but positively obscene that she should be married off in the social marriage-market to a man who was interested only in her Bank balance and not in her as a woman.

He knew only too well that what he had said to Magnolia was true.

Of the men who would contemplate taking anyone as rich as Magnolia as their wife, there were few, if any, whom he would welcome as a son-in-law.

The others were so disreputable that he could not bear to think of her being subjected to the humiliation that such a marriage would entail.

There was one young Italian Prince whose escapades since he had married an American heiress had been the talk of New York, and Mr. Vandevilt was glad that Magnolia had not heard of him.

It was reckoned that in seven years the Prince had spent over five million dollars of his wife's money.

He had spent it on gambling, on women of every class and nationality, and on yachts, houses, fireworks, dancers, musicians, and enough drink to fill an ocean.

In America and in Europe, the Prince's extravagances made him a celebrity, while his wife, from whom the money came, had faded into an insignificant ghost who was seldom recognised and usually forgotten.

"That shall not happen to Magnolia" Mr. Vandevilt had vowed.

At the same time, as he listened to other stories in the same vein, he had been afraid.

When his wife set her heart on anything, it was with a one-point concentration, and nothing and nobody could prevent her from obtaining what she desired.

Mr. Vandevilt, who had travelled a great deal in Europe, knew that an English gentleman did on the whole behave in a respectful manner towards his wife. He also had an inborn dislike of publicity and scandal and therefore in most cases would behave circumspectly.

What was more, where the aristocracy was concerned, they believed it was their duty to look after those who were dependent upon them. This embraced their old-age pensioners and impoverished relatives, their Alms-Houses and their Orphanages, and included in the same category were their wives.

It was not much of a choice, Mr. Vandevilt had thought bitterly, when he viewed Magnolia's future objectively and with the intelligence which he brought to everything in his life.

However, on the whole he favoured the British, and his daughter, whom he loved and who he thought was far too clever and sensitive for the sons of New

York socialites, might, as he had said to her, do worse than marry an Englishman.

Magnolia had risen now from the sofa to walk across the room to where the first Sisley her father had ever bought was hung in a place where the light from the window seemed to be reflected in the painting itself.

She stood looking at it, and now it made her feel as if she were reaching out towards something so beautiful and yet so intangible that she could not put a name to it.

However, the feeling was so unmistakably there that she knew it lifted her mind and a living force within her up into the light.

If only she could see it more clearly, she felt as if the whole secret of the Universe would be hers.

It was like a light her father had told her glowed in Greece, which had been the light of the gods.

The revelations had come to the Greeks with the light so that the splendour and the glory of what they had thought would spread to bring enlightenment to the world.

It was what she had always tried to find herself, the light which had made men think and in thinking become as gods.

Then, as if even the magic of Sisley could not prevent her from knowing that she was very human, tears once again misted her eyes and she ran back to her father to put her arms round him.

"Oh, Papa ... help me ... help me! How can I do ... something which I know is wrong ... and at the same time ... go on living?"

Chapter Three

"Lady Edith Burn, Your Grace!" a flunkey announced, and the Duke, who was reading the newspaper in a chair in his Study, rose to his feet.

His cousin came in, looking extremely elegant and as usual dressed in the latest fashion, but before she spoke he knew by the expression on her face that she was perturbed.

"I can hardly believe there could be such a chapter of disasters!" she exclaimed.

The Duke held out his hand.

"What else has gone wrong?" he enquired.

Lady Edith had journeyed to Southampton to meet the wedding-party, consisting of Mr. and Mrs. Vandevilt and Magnolia, because he had refused firmly and categorically to do so.

"How can you be so discourteous, Seldon?" his cousin had asked.

"I have so much to do here," the Duke replied, "and I have no intention of standing about, waiting on a Quay for a ship which is already delayed by several days."

"How could one imagine that there would be a gale in the Atlantic to upset all our arrangements?" Lady Edith groaned.

"Perhaps even the gods are on my side in delaying my marriage," the Duke remarked cynically.

"Really, Seldon!" Lady Edith snapped. "You are making things very difficult! What with you and Mrs. Vandevilt, I wish I had not started the whole thing in the first place."

"And so do I!" the Duke said in a tone of deep sincerity.

Lady Edith sighed in an exasperated fashion.

It had been hard enough to make the Duke agree that the only way to save the Castle, the Estates, and everyone dependent upon him was for him to marry Magnolia Vandevilt.

What Lady Edith had found far more difficult was to persuade Mrs. Vandevilt that the marriage should take place in England.

Mrs. Vandevilt had wanted a really fantastic wedding with typical American opulence to impress the world, and she did not think it could be the same if they went to England, where Magnolia's wedding would not have the same publicity or impact on the social scene.

Lady Edith had to be extremely persuasive to make her change her mind and accept the Duke's inflexible determination that he would not be made a "Peep-Show" for the Americans to gape at.

"I have heard," he had said to his cousin, "of the Carnivals the Americans make of their weddings."

He paused to make sure that Lady Edith was listening before he added:

"I have read of hundreds of doves being released over the heads of a happy couple, watched by a mob of thousands who grappled with one another to get into the Church and grab a flower or a ribbon as a souvenir, which resulted in the Police having to be summoned."

He brought his fist down hard on the table at which they were sitting, as he added:

45

"If you think I will go through that sort of thing, even to marry the daughter of Midas himself, then you are much mistaken."

If the Duke was determined, so was Mrs. Vandevilt, so it required hours of patience and a great deal of charm on Lady Edith's part before the Vandevilts had finally agreed to leave New York.

They had been expecting to dock in Southampton a week ago, but the ocean had been unprecedentedly tempestuous, and first there was an announcement of three days' delay, then of four.

Finally the ship had limped into harbour with damage to her superstructure, an astronomical amount of breakages, and a number of her passengers injured.

As she sat down on a chair and undid the sables she wore round her neck, Lady Edith related what had happened and added:

"One of the casualties was Mr. Vandevilt!"

"He was swept overboard?" the Duke enquired.

"No, of course not! It was not as bad as that!" Lady Edith replied. "But his leg was broken, and we had to make arrangements to take him to London on a stretcher, which was the reason I did not get here yesterday, as I intended to do."

"I wondered what had prevented you from doing so," the Duke remarked in a tone which told his cousin it had not worried him unduly.

"He is now installed at the Savoy," Lady Edith went on, "and Mrs. Vandevilt has taken over a whole floor. I managed to get his leg attended to by Sir Horace Deakin, who, as you may know, is one of the Queen's Doctors. He had provided two Nurses and has promised that Mr. Vandevilt will be on his feet within a month."

The Duke's eyes seemed to light up.

"Does that mean the wedding has to be postponed?"

"It does not!" Lady Edith replied. "Mrs. Vandevilt is determined the plans shall go ahead as they were made before they left."

She did not add, because she knew it would annoy the Duke, that the reason for this was that Mrs. Vandevilt had paid the fares of the reporters from some of the most important newspapers in New York.

They had travelled over in the same ship, and it would obviously be impossible for them to stay longer than was strictly necessary before returning home.

The Duke, who was looking forward to a quiet wedding because he had insisted on it being in England, must, Lady Edith had decided a long time ago, be kept in ignorance of his future mother-in-law's intention to ensure, by every means in her power and whatever it cost, that it hit the headlines.

In case the Duke should be curious, Lady Edith said hastily:

"Mrs. Vandevilt has no wish, Seldon dear, to upset your plans, and she will therefore arrive with Magnolia as arranged, to stay with the Farringtons, tomorrow afternoon."

It was Lady Edith with her usual tact who thought it might be uncomfortable if the Vandevilts stayed at the Castle before the wedding. Moreover, she thought the less the Duke saw of Mrs. Vandevilt, the better.

She had therefore arranged with Lord Farrington, who was a relative by marriage, to have the Vandevilts stay with him, and from his house it would be easy for them to drive to the Castle in under an hour.

The Duke had remarked cynically:

"I am sure that as William's house is much more comfortable than mine, Mrs. Vandevilt will be satisfied with the arrangements you have made for them."

Now Lady Edith said:

"I thought you would agree, Seldon, that in the

circumstances William Farrington should give Magnolia away. She is naturally upset that it cannot be her father."

"In that case, I am sure she would prefer to wait until he is well enough to perform such an important task."

"It is quite impossible to change everything round at the last moment," Lady Edith replied. "Besides, I expect your tenants and employees are looking forward to their party."

The only thing the Duke had agreed to with a good grace was that, as was traditional, there should be a party in a marquee for all those employed on the Estate, together with the tenant-farmers.

This meant that barrels of beer had been ordered and a large quantity of local cider, which was almost as intoxicating.

The Cooks at the Castle had been preparing the traditional fare, such as boar's head, great joints of roast beef, and hams which had been cured by ancient recipes passed down from mother to daughter.

The Duke was well aware that to put off the wedding now would entail a great number of difficulties.

No less than six hundred guests had already accepted the invitations that Lady Edith had sent out with the help of a secretary borrowed from Mr. Fossilwaithe's office.

Presents had been pouring in and the Picture-Gallery was full of them, so much so that Lady Edith had wondered whether there would be room for the large number which she was quite certain Mrs. Vandevilt would be bringing with her from America.

The Duke had merely looked in surprise at the presents already there.

"As I have never met half of these people, or at any rate have not seen most of them since I was a boy," he had remarked, "I cannot imagine why they should wish to spend so much money on me."

Lady Edith had laughed.

"You are being naïve, Seldon. You must be aware that not only is a Ducal wedding a unique excitement in the rather dull countryside, but the fact that you will have money to spend in the future in the same way that your father spent it in the past will not escape anyone's notice."

The Duke's eyes had darkened.

"If you imagine I am going to throw my wife's money about in the same profligate manner that my father threw his, you are very much mistaken!"

He spoke angrily, but Lady Edith only laughed again.

"Of course I am not suggesting anything of the sort," she said. "At the same time, I imagine the neighbours are feeling deprived of the parties, some of which were very raffish, that your father gave here whenever he was at home."

"There will be no parties," the Duke said categorically, "not until the debts are paid and the roofs on the houses of the farmers, the pensioners, and the employees have been repaired."

"Your wife might have something to say about that!" Lady Edith remarked.

She only meant to tease him out of his sombre mood, but she realised as soon as she had spoken that she had been tactless, as she saw his chin square and his lips tighten.

He was resenting more than ever that he had to be beholden to a rich wife, and an American at that!

Because Lady Edith was extremely astute where men were concerned, she deliberately was not too fulsome in her praise of Magnolia, nor did she eulogise about her beauty.

'He will find out for himself,' she thought, and hoped that in consequence the Duke would become curious.

Instead, as the weeks passed and letters and telegrams sped backwards and forwards across the

Atlantic with instructions, requests, and information, Lady Edith was aware that the Duke was withdrawing more and more into a reserve that was difficult to penetrate.

The announcement of his engagement in the newspapers only seemed to make him worse, and she knew he was deliberately isolating himself from those who wished to meet him, on the pretence of having too much to do.

But however difficult he might be, she was well aware, as he was, that no solution other than that of marriage had presented itself for the problems that his father had left him.

Now as the Duke brought her a glass of sherry she sipped it gratefully as she said:

"I do not mind telling you, Seldon, I feel quite exhausted from all I have been through, and you are very lucky you were not in my place."

"I apologise for not having said 'thank you' more graciously," the Duke said, with a charm that Lady Edith thought made him seem very attractive.

"I am disappointed that you will not meet Mr. Vandevilt before your marriage," she said. "He is such an intelligent and delightful man that I know you would get on well with him."

As she spoke, she thought that his presence would certainly have mitigated the effect that she was sure Mrs. Vandevilt would have on her future son-in-law.

Following the accident to her husband, she had arrived at Southampton in what Lady Edith had recognised was one of her worst moods, and the fact that she had been extremely sea-sick during the storm had not made things any better.

She first of all demanded a special train to convey to London her incapacitated husband, herself, Magnolia, their mountain of luggage, and their army of servants.

As such a thing was impossible at such short

notice, she had to be content with the whole of a First-Class coach, and even then, Lady Edith thought, it seemed somewhat overcrowded.

Used as she was to rich Americans, she had no idea that three people could require so much baggage for a nine-day sea voyage.

There was not only a Courier, secretaries, and assistant secretaries to organise everything, but two lady's-maids, one each for Mrs. Vandevilt and Magnolia, and two valets for her husband.

There were also, Lady Edith saw, four or more special guards who were always in attendance on the family, and a number of young men who she suspected were reporters and photographers.

When they reached the Savoy, Lady Edith found that the mountainous pile of luggage which had filled two vans contained not only a great number of presents but the luxuries that every American millionairess considered important to her comfort when she travelled.

Mrs. Vandevilt's own linen, some of her own silver, as well as rugs for her feet and an ermine cover for her bed, had all been transported across the Atlantic.

Lady Edith longed to tell the Duke how funny she thought it was, but then she decided he might not be amused and she had best keep such information to herself.

Instead she said:

"I am so sorry for Magnolia. She adores her father and is actually very upset not only by his accident but also that he cannot be present at the wedding."

Again the Duke's lips tightened but he said nothing, and Lady Edith went on:

"You will of course meet her tomorrow night at a family dinner-party that I have arranged before the wedding. We shall only be thirty, or rather twenty-nine now that Mr. Vandevilt cannot come."

"Fossilwaithe informed me," the Duke said, "that he had received a letter summoning him to London as soon as the Vandevilts arrive. I suppose now they will not have time to see him before they leave London to stay with the Farringtons."

"There is no need to worry about that," Lady Edith answered. "I saw Mr. Fossilwaithe at the Savoy. He had the papers ready to be signed, and he was quite resigned to waiting until either Mr. Vandevilt or his wife was willing to see him."

"I suppose," the Duke said after a moment's pause, "I should be glad that he is so business-like, but even now, Edith, I have an impulse to call the whole thing off."

Lady Edith gave a little cry.

"If you try to do such a thing I shall never speak to you again!" she said. "It has taken years off my life making all these arrangements, and if you upset them I think I shall kill you!"

"Perhaps death might be preferable to the tortures to which you have subjected me!" the Duke said.

He tried to speak lightly, but somehow, despite himself, there was a serious note in his voice.

Lady Edith sighed.

"Oh, Seldon, we cannot go through all this again —unless while I have been waiting at Southampton you have found a gold mine in the herb-garden, or the gravel on the drive has suddenly turned to diamonds! You need the Vandevilt millions as much as they need your coronet. It is a fair exchange."

"I am glad you think so," the Duke replied in an uncompromising voice.

"I am too tired to argue," Lady Edith said. "I am going upstairs to lie down, and I will see you at dinner. Who else has arrived?"

The Duke reeled off the names of some of the older members of the family who had come from various parts of England to be the advance guard for the rest of them.

They would therefore have the first look at the heiress whose millions of dollars would make a great difference to them all.

At the same time, the Duke knew already that they would none of them be in the least grateful to Magnolia as a person for the money she would pour into the family coffers.

Instead, they had come ready to criticise and if necessary to disparage his future wife because she was to them a foreigner.

They were, however, too diplomatic to say anything to which he could take exception.

He merely sensed their attitude, and instead of it making him annoyed because it was what he felt himself, he only felt more guilty than he had before.

"Am I a man or a mouse?" he asked himself.

It was a question which repeated itself over and over again as he wondered how he personally could find a solution to the financial problem rather than rely on an unknown woman whom he hated because she was marrying his title.

During one of their arguments the Duke had said to Lady Edith:

"How can you expect me to do anything but despise a woman who will marry me not as a man but simply because I am a Duke?"

"Do not be so ridiculous!" his cousin replied. "You know as well as I do that Magnolia herself has had no say in the matter, any more than an English girl would be allowed to refuse you if you offered her marriage."

She thought the Duke looked surprised, and she said crossly:

"I cannot think where you have been living all these years, Seldon. With your looks and your undoubted attractions, you must have known a few women in whatever benighted places in which you were fighting."

The Duke smiled.

There was no point in explaining to his cousin that the women he had met at Simla when he was on leave, or at any other station, meant nothing serious to him.

They were the attractive, sophisticated, flirtatious wives of men who were sweating away in the heat of the plains or on some special mission in another part of the country.

His *affaires de coeur* had therefore often been fiery and alluring, but definitely only interludes in a life of discipline and danger. Moreover, they had not taught him anything about the habits and minds of young girls.

Nor, as he thought about it, did he remember ever having even a conversation with one.

He told himself cynically that he would pay for the money he obtained from his marriage with years of undoubted boredom, if nothing else.

"God knows what one talks about to a girl of eighteen," he would murmur, especially at night when he had lain awake thinking of his future.

Instead of it being one of excitement and anticipation as it had always been before, now his future appeared dark and dreary.

He knew he would spend his days working to restore the Estates to a perfection which he had expected never to be able to do, and those he employed would look to him for leadership, just as his sepoys had in India.

Of one thing he was determined—if he enjoyed the good things of life, they should share them with him.

He was almost startled when, just before the Vandevilts had sailed for England, Lady Edith had said:

"Mrs. Vandevilt is anxious to know where you intend to take Magnolia for a honeymoon."

"A honeymoon?" the Duke had repeated blankly.

"You will have to have one," Lady Edith said, "and people will be astonished if you do not go abroad."

"I had not thought of it," the Duke said simply. "There seemed to be so much to do here."

"You could go to the South of France, where your father's Villa would certainly be a good place from which to start."

"His Villa?" the Duke questioned.

"Surely Mr. Fossilwaithe has told you that two years before he died your father bought a Villa near Nice at a small place called Beaulieu. It is, I believe, very attractive. He certainly spent a great deal of money enlarging it."

"I had no idea of this."

The Duke vaguely remembered that on the long list of expenses there had been an item for something in France, but he had not examined it very closely because of the amount of money owed in other directions.

On Lady Edith's insistence, he sent for Mr. Fossilwaithe, who told him to his surprise that not only had his father bought a Villa but there was also a yacht moored nearby in the harbour at Villefranche.

His father's yacht, which was kept fully manned, was an expensive item which had somehow been ignored amongst the other extravagances!

As soon as he learnt of these new possessions, the Duke had related his findings to Lady Edith, and added:

"I intend to sell both the Villa and the yacht."

Lady Edith had given a cry of protest.

"For Heaven's sake!" she exclaimed. "Not until after the honeymoon!"

"Why?"

"For the simple reason that the South of France is exactly where Mrs. Vandevilt would wish you to start your married life so that she can enjoy saying:

" 'My daughter, the Duchess, is spending her honeymoon in the South of France, where my son-in-law has a Villa, and of course there is a yacht which will carry them when they are bored to romantic places like the Greek Islands.' "

Lady Edith not only mimicked Mrs. Vandevilt's voice but also her American accent, and despite himself the Duke laughed.

He was just about to say that he had no intention of spending a honeymoon of that sort with a woman whom he had never seen and already despised.

Then he thought that he personally would enjoy being the owner of a yacht, if only for a short time.

Later, he thought, it would be easier to endure the silences that he expected would exist between himself and his wife at mealtimes, the dreariness of dinners in Restaurants, or, worse still, when they were alone in an empty Dining-Room.

"Of course," he said aloud, "Mrs. Vandevilt and her daughter must not be disappointed. Find out the size and importance of the Villa, and you had better ask Fossilwaithe the tonnage of the yacht, which I forgot to do."

As Lady Edith expected, Mrs. Vandevilt had written back quite enthusiastically about the suitability of such a honeymoon, and added that she was buying her daughter many new clothes, some with quite a nautical appearance, which she could wear on board the yacht.

Lady Edith, as she read the letter, could only think it was a good thing that the Duke would not read the gossip-columns in the American newspapers, which she was certain would grab at every juicy tit-bit which concerned the Vandevilt/Otterburn wedding.

When Lady Edith went upstairs, the Duke left the Castle by a garden-door and walked down towards the lake.

Whenever he found himself having to discuss his wedding, he always felt desperately in need of air, almost as if he were choking.

It had been a warm day, but now there was a sharpness in the air which was just what the Duke wanted.

He wanted to feel something cold and astringent as an antidote to the feeling that he was being suffocated by all the exotic and expensive things that money could buy.

Then he thought savagely that he positively liked the discomforts of the Castle—the plumbing that needed improving and the parts of it, although they were not seen, where the walls were crumbling and the ceilings were damp and stained.

He knew the gardens required a lot of money spent on them, and he told himself that as soon as they went back to their jungle-like wildness, the better.

Then he remembered that old Briggs, who had served his father and grandfather for over forty years, would be retiring in a month or two, and he was glad he would be able to give him a decent pension and a comfortable cottage in which to spend the remainder of his life.

"I am being damned ungrateful," he chided himself.

At the same time, it seemed humiliating and pretentious.

His cousin Edith had been right when she said he was idealistic about women. But his ideals had not concerned him until now because women had played a very small part in the life he had had in the Army.

Then he thought that when he married he would treat his wife with respect, which was in itself a kind

57

of chivalry. And he believed that every woman should be protected, cosseted, and directed by a man.

Of course, if he put it into plain English, that meant that they should be entirely dependent on him.

But an American who was extremely rich would be very different from an Englishwoman who had to ask her husband for "pin-money" and be effusively grateful for everything he spent on her.

'I suppose at Christmas and on birthdays I shall be buying my wife presents with her own money,' he thought bitterly. 'I will drink her health in the wine she has paid for and arrange some sort of treat which will be a quite impossible extravagance unless we open her purse to pay for it.'

He felt as if he had reached the point where he wanted to hit something.

It was no use telling himself that from the moment he married Magnolia Vandevilt her money became his, as the law decreed.

He knew he would always be conscious that if he remonstrated or disagreed with her on any subject, she would always be able to say:

"It is *my* money which is enabling you to live in your Castle, *my* money which is paying for the servants who run it and the horses you ride, and *my* money which provides the entertainment for your friends."

These were the same thoughts that had bedevilled him insistently day and night, and the Duke, knowing he must relieve his feelings one way or another, turned round and walked quickly back towards the stables.

He knew that only by riding both himself and his horse to the point of exhaustion would he be able to sleep tonight.

*   *   *

In the bedroom of the Savoy which overlooked the Embankment and the Thames, which had a fairy-like quality about it now that the lights were just beginning to gleam in the houses on the other side of the water, Magnolia, holding her father's hand tightly in hers, asked:

"How do you feel, Papa?"

"Not too bad," her father replied. "I think the Surgeon that Lady Edith brought here has made my leg much more comfortable, and he says it is not a very bad fracture."

"I am so glad, Papa. How could such a terrible thing have happened to you?"

"I must say I have always prided myself on my sea-legs," Mr. Vandevilt said, "and who could suspect in that gale that a spar, or whatever the thing was, would hit me and be able to do so much damage?"

He smiled before he said:

"Perhaps it is a punishment for thinking I was such an experienced traveller that I could even defy the weather!"

Magnolia's fingers tightened on his.

"Papa, I cannot be ... married without ... you there."

"I was afraid you would say that, my dearest," Mr. Vandevilt replied, "but there is no point in upsetting your mother, or indeed, as Lady Edith has pointed out, all the arrangements that have been made at the Castle."

There was a little pause. Then Magnolia said in a voice he could barely hear:

"I ... I cannot ... face the ... Duke without ... you."

Mr. Vandevilt put his free hand in a consoling manner over his daughter's.

"We have been through this before, my dearest," he said. "I promise you things will not be as bad as

59

you expect, and you have promised me you will try to do what is right."

"I ... will try ... Papa, but it is not ... going to be ... easy."

"I think you should look on this as a challenge," Mr. Vandevilt said, "something you must tackle, and win!"

Magnolia gave a deep sigh.

"I love you, Papa! If only we could have a few more years ... together."

She bent her head as she spoke and therefore did not see the sudden pain in her father's eyes.

Apart from his paintings, his daughter was the only thing that mattered in his life, the only thing he really loved. He knew that if she would miss him, he would feel as if he had lost a part of himself.

Yet there was nothing he could do but persuade her to marry the man her mother had chosen for her, and pray that she would not suffer in the same way as other women had suffered in arranged marriages.

Because he had been to France so often, he was aware that among his French friends their marriages were generally *mariages de convenance*, based on an advantage for both parties.

What was more, in a great number of cases they turned out to be extremely successful and produced, if not the perfect, idealistic love that Magnolia wanted, at least a companionable contentment which lasted for life in a Society where social and religious convention did not allow divorce.

Not that there was any question of Magnolia being able to obtain a divorce in England, as it was possible to in America.

There was no point in saying so, but divorce, Mr. Vandevilt knew, would, in the case of the Duke, have to be approved by Parliament, and a scandal was something he would never contemplate in any circumstances.

Because he wanted to comfort Magnolia and at the same time give her the courage which he knew she would need, he said:

"Listen to me, my dearest. When we have talked on subjects like Oriental religions and especially Buddhism, we have both agreed that what you give to life is what you get back."

Magnolia raised her head to look at him, and when he saw that she was listening he said:

"If you want love, you have to give love; if you hate, then you receive hatred. That is an unwritten law which exists the world over, in every nation, in every culture, in every creed."

"I know what you are trying to say to me, Papa," Magnolia replied. "You are asking me to love a faceless man who desires only my money. I am giving him what he wants. Surely there is no need to offer him any more?"

There was a little smile on Mr. Vandevilt's lips as he replied:

"That would be a very logical argument, my darling, if I did not know that you are deliberately trying to evade the point I am making. Let me put it very plainly—try to make your husband love you, then perhaps you will find it easy to love him in return."

He knew from the expression on Magnolia's face that it was something she thought would never happen and she shrank from the implications of it.

Because he was afraid to press her any further, he only said:

"Love is a strange thing. It comes sometimes when you least expect it, or it grows from a small, forgotten seed into something large and overwhelming. But remember this—"

He paused for a moment before he went on:

"Love is what we all want, what we all need in our lives; and love, when you do find it, is worth all the pain, the sacrifice, and the agony that you have suffered."

His voice was very deep and moving. Then as Magnolia did not answer he realised that she was crying.

Chapter Four

As the private train sped towards London, the Duke thought he had never spent a more unpleasant and uncomfortable day.

He had not expected to enjoy his wedding; at the same time, he had not anticipated that it would be an occasion which would make him continually grit his teeth with sheer fury.

It had all started the night before when a groom had driven over from Lord Farrington's house with a note to say that the Vandevilts' plans had been changed.

Mr. Vandevilt would after all be arriving with his wife and daughter in a private train, which it had been arranged would stop at the nearest halt to Lord Farrington's Estate.

The note also informed the Duke that dinner would have to be later than had been intended, since the party escorted by Lord Farrington could not arrive until nearly nine o'clock.

The Duke found this irritating, as it meant that other relatives who were staying in the neighbourhood could not be informed of the change of hour. They would therefore arrive at the Castle just before eight, and there would be a long wait before the American party appeared.

Lady Edith suspected that the reason for the change of plan was that Magnolia would not come without her father, but she did not say so.

However, she was relieved that the Duke would meet Mr. Vandevilt and find him as charming as she did, instead of being subjected exclusively to the overwhelming personality of his wife.

But even this plan went awry.

The strain of the journey caused Mr. Vandevilt so much pain that it was impossible, once he had arrived at Lord Farrington's house, for him to make the effort to drive for nearly an hour to the Castle and be present at a large dinner comprised of strangers.

Therefore, to Lady Edith's consternation and the Duke's annoyance, both Mr. Vandevilt and his daughter stayed away from the family dinner-party.

"It certainly is a case of Hamlet without the Prince," Lady Edith remarked wryly to one or two of the Burn relatives who had more sense of humour than the others.

But as soon as Mrs. Vandevilt walked into the Castle, she knew that, as she had expected, the Duke's hackles rose.

Owing to the upset and undoubtedly because she was slightly on the defensive, Mrs. Vandevilt was at her very worst.

The fact that she looked in her own way magnificent did not soften the impression she made on the Burn family, who, as the Duke had suspected, had come prepared to criticise the bride.

Wearing a gown that had obviously cost a fortune, the design of which had originated in Paris, Mrs. Vandevilt had made the mistake of wishing to appear impressive without realising that her appearance would seem to the conventional English ostentatious, if not outrageous.

The gown she wore would have been more suitable in a Ball-Room or on the stage of a Theatre, and she wore enormous diamonds which glittered in her hair, round her neck, and outlined the low-cut bodice of her gown.

Her wrists were weighed down with bracelets, the rings on her fingers were dazzling, and to the Duke she exemplified everything for which he had sold his title and—himself.

There was, however, nothing he could do but make a super-human effort to be pleasant to his future mother-in-law and try not to be aware that her sharp eyes were taking in every detail in the Castle which required money to be spent on it.

As far as his other guests were concerned, the evening passed off well, owing, the Duke thought afterwards, to the fact that while they were waiting for Lord Farrington's party to arrive, the amount of champagne they consumed was considerable.

When finally at what seemed a very late hour dinner was over and the gentlemen joined the ladies in the Drawing-Room, relatives who lived some distance from the Castle started to make their farewells.

"I shall be looking forward to meeting your future wife tomorrow, Seldon," they all said to the Duke in one way or another.

He thought there was a slight note of commiseration in their voices, which he instantly resented.

Lady Edith could have related how overwhelming Mrs. Vandevilt had been when the ladies had retired to the Drawing-Room while the gentlemen drank their port.

Instead of being quietly pleasant to the older women in the family, she had gone out of her way to impress them by boasting of her husband's wealth and possessions, of the unassailable social position the Vandevilts held in New York, and the fortune that Magnolia was bringing into their family.

She left them in no doubt as to who would provide the money to pay for the repairs to the Castle and to the Estate and to redeem the debts which had been incurred by the late Duke.

His prodigality was something of which not only his son but his relatives were deeply ashamed, and the fact that a stranger was confronting them, as it were, with the bills made it worse.

Only when the front door had closed behind Mrs. Vandevilt and she was carried away from the Castle in Lord Farrington's carriage did Lady Edith draw a deep sigh of relief.

However, she knew by the expression on the Duke's face what he was feeling, and she had no intention of discussing it with him.

"I am tired, and tomorrow will be another tiring day," she said. "I am going straight to bed . . . Good-night, Seldon."

"Good-night, Edith!"

He had walked away without another word, and she had known by his voice that the depression encompassing him was like a black cloud.

He had in fact sat for a long time in the Library before finally he went up to bed, and even then he thought it unlikely he would sleep.

He had actually fallen into a doze and his troubles had receded for the moment into an indecisive mist, when he was awakened by the sounds of voices, hammering, and the movements of people.

For a moment it flashed through his mind that burglars were attempting to steal the presents.

Then he was aware that no self-respecting burglar would create enough noise to draw attention to himself, and remembered vaguely that Lady Edith had said that the private train which had brought the Vandevilts down from London had also carried the presents, which would be arriving early in the morning at the Castle.

The Duke looked at the clock by his bed and saw that it was not yet five o'clock. Mrs. Vandevilt's employees, he thought, started work earlier than their English counterparts.

When finally he rose, finding it impossible to rest,

let alone sleep, with such a commotion going on, he found to his astonishment that a positive army of men was invading the Castle and a gang of workmen was erecting in the garden something that looked like a huge crown of flowers.

He thought it quite unnecessary that the Vandevilts should wish to add to the flowers that were there already, which, being natural to their surroundings, made a most attractive picture.

But he told himself it would be foolish to criticise or alter any arrangements of his future in-laws.

At the same time, he thought angrily that he should have been consulted.

The bower of flowers was being erected outside the rooms where the Reception was to take place and in the centre of the lawn where the guests would, if it was a fine day, walk and talk in the sunshine.

But as the day proceeded, this was just one of the innumerable irritations which occurred.

The Duke discovered, too late to countermand the order, that champagne, in fact innumerable cases of it, was being supplied to the employees and tenant-farmers in the Tithe barn, for whom he had already ordered beer and cider.

It was an expensive addition to the menu the Duke could not afford, and also he knew that as the majority of them were not used to drinking it, they would inevitably become quite unnecessarily drunk.

He was also astonished to find that inside the Castle, Mrs. Vandevilt had arranged for huge wreaths of flowers to be affixed to the staircase in the Hall.

Most of the Reception-Rooms were literally smothered in white blossoms in such profusion that they obscured the paintings and even the furniture itself.

When he dressed, he put on his uniform for what he thought would be the last time.

This added to his depression, for he had delayed sending in his formal resignation just in case his marriage fell through and he could continue to be a soldier.

Now the life he had organised was closed to him forever, and it did not make his future seem any brighter.

But it was when the Duke realised how many photographers and reporters there were, easing their way in his own words "into every nook and cranny of the Castle," that his anger finally spilt over.

"What the devil are all these newspaper-men doing here?" he demanded of Lady Edith, and her answer did nothing to soothe his feelings.

"I was afraid you would be annoyed, Seldon."

"Annoyed?" the Duke almost shouted. "Do you know, I found two of them in my bedroom a few minutes ago, photographing the bed, and they asked me if that was where I intended to sleep with my bride!"

"I am sorry, Seldon."

"Is that all you can say?" the Duke enquired. "They informed me that they had come from New York at the invitation of Mrs. Vandevilt. I told them what I thought of their behaviour and they wrote it down in their note-books!"

"I am afraid Mrs. Vandevilt wants the wedding to be very fully publicized," Lady Edith said meekly, "but I am sure that nothing of that sort will appear in an English newspaper."

The Duke glared at her as if he were bereft of words. Then he said:

"The whole thing makes me sick. I deliberately insisted on being married in England so that I could avoid this type of vulgarity, which I find degrading both to me and to the family."

"I agree with you," Lady Edith said, "and I can only say again how sorry I am. I had no idea, I promise you, that Mrs. Vandevilt would bring reporters over with her."

The Duke made an exclamation that was untranslatable and walked out of the room.

Lady Edith looked out the window at the workmen on the lawn, an anxious expression in her eyes.

There was every need for her to be anxious.

* * *

When the bride and groom had finished receiving the long line of guests which had filtered from the Hall, through the Drawing-Room, and out into the garden, it was to the Duke the climax of an intolerable afternoon.

Because it was such a lovely day and there seemed to be more guests than expected, Lady Edith had arranged at the last moment for the wedding-cake, or rather cakes, to be brought from the Dining-Room into the garden.

This in itself was another irritation to the Duke, for when he had seen the cake that Mrs. Vandevilt had brought with her from New York, it had been difficult for Lady Edith to restrain him from having it removed and thrown away.

The cooks at the Castle had worked day and night to produce the sort of cake which had always graced the family weddings.

With three tiers, it had been made from an old recipe and the icing had been skilfully applied to portray the family crest, which was a raised hand holding a sword.

The same crest, cleverly modelled in sugar, surmounted the top tier of the cake.

The Duke had warmly congratulated the Cooks when they had shown it to him and had said, to their delight, that he considered it such a work of art that it was almost a pity that it had to be demolished.

"They'll enjoy eatin' it all th' same, Master Seldon —I means Your Grace!" said the oldest of them, who had been at the Castle for over forty years.

The Duke had smiled and said that he was looking forward to eating a piece himself, and he knew that everybody concerned was delighted at his praise.

Later in the day, when proceeding into the garden to cut the cake in the traditional fashion with his sword, he saw not only the cake that had been baked at the Castle but also the other one, which, when he had been shown it earlier, he had considered such a vulgar monstrosity that his first intention had been to have it destroyed.

Instead, he was forced to cut both cakes and it was no consolation to find that the one from America was commanding the most attention from his guests.

This was because it consisted not of three tiers but of seven, and the bottom one was as large as a cart-wheel.

There was certainly nothing refined in its decoration, which consisted of lucky horse-shoes, tufts of white heather, and a profusion of silver bells. It was surmounted on top by two dolls, one dressed, it seemed to the Duke, entirely in diamonds, the other in a parody of his Regimental uniform.

It was when the cakes were cut and pieces of them were being distributed to the guests that a Toast-Master who the Duke had not previously realised was there and who had obviously been imported by Mrs. Vandevilt called for attention.

Speaking with a nasal American accent, he commanded everyone to drink the health of the bride and bridegroom.

Then, as they obediently raised their glasses, there was a sudden explosion which seemed to shake the windows of the Castle behind them. The bower of roses in the centre of the lawn opened and out of it shot a huge bird high into the air, from which fell ten thousand red roses.

The confusion caused by the noise and the exclamations of fear from some of the elderly turned into what the Duke thought was a murmur of contempt at an exhibition which obviously had been planned entirely for publicity.

He saw the excitement among the photographers with their cameras and the reporters with their notebooks, and he knew that whatever Lady Edith might say, this would undoubtedly be an item for the English papers as well as for the American.

Only years of self-control prevented the Duke from saying what he thought of so vulgar an innovation.

When finally he and his bride drove away from the Castle in an open carriage bombarded with flower-petals supplied by Mrs. Vandevilt, drawn by horses decorated with wreaths of roses, he felt he had passed through a maelstrom of horror and indignity which he would never forget.

However, the ordeal was not over, for the drive to the station took them through a small village which was part of the Estate, where they passed under an arch decorated with bunting, flowers, and flags.

The carriage was brought to a standstill while the Duke received an address from the oldest inhabitant, while Magnolia was presented with a bouquet from a small child who at the last moment was unwilling to relinquish it.

When they reached the station, the Duke saw apprehensively that there was a crowd outside it and what he thought were more decorations than were fitting.

"Let us hope this is the last Reception we have to endure," he remarked sharply.

He realised as he spoke that it was the first time he had addressed his bride since they had left the Castle.

He had in fact not looked at her, either when she joined him at the altar or when they walked together the short distance from the Church to the Castle.

The Church was so near that it would have been ridiculous to drive on a fine day, and the Duke, with

Magnolia on his arm, had set off briskly up the gravel path which had mysteriously been covered with a red carpet.

It was only when he found that his wife had difficulty in keeping up with him that he was aware that what he thought was her ridiculously long train was being carried by three small pages dressed in the white satin Court-dress of the time of Louis XIV.

The train was obviously far too heavy for them, and the mothers of two of the little boys were assisting them to keep it off the ground.

The Duke supposed that the pages, whose mothers he recognised as his relatives, had been provided by Lady Edith.

However, the train which impeded their progress was undoubtedly American, and he disliked it as he disliked everything else that had transformed the simple wedding-service he had envisaged into something very different.

For one thing—again he supposed it was on Mrs. Vandevilt's insistence—they had been married by a Bishop, assisted by four other Clergy-men.

As the Church was small, there were far too many Priests congregated round the altar, and similarly the choir-stalls were filled to overflowing with a choir that had been brought from London to augment the villagers whose usual duty it was to perform at weddings and funerals.

That they sang like angels did nothing to mitigate the Duke's feelings that despite all his efforts the wedding had become a "Peep-Show."

Enormous arrangements of lilies filled the Chancel and all the pews had bunches of flowers affixed to them, with long white ribbon bows trailing to the ground with a very theatrical effect.

They reached the station and the Duke thought he might have expected that the small platform, which was little more than a halt for the Castle, should be covered with a red carpet, with huge bowls of lilies set outside the entrance, and inevitably, framed in flowers, were the American photographers and a large posse of journalists.

They descended on the newly married couple like a swarm of bees.

The Duke was bombarded with questions, and he heard his wife attempting to answer what seemed to him to be extremely impertinent ones in a soft, rather frightened voice.

Fortunately, the private train which had brought the Vandevilts from London was waiting for them, and the Duke pushed Magnolia through the photographers and into the compartment, telling the attendant to keep everybody out.

The doors were shut, but the cameras were at the windows and so were the faces of their persecutors.

The Duke indicated the seats on the far side of the carriage.

"I suggest," he said, "that we sit over here and keep our backs towards them. There is little they can do then."

Magnolia obeyed him without replying. At last, to the Duke's relief, the train started and, amidst cheers and waving hands, moved slowly out of the station.

It was then that he said, as if the words burst through the control that he had exerted all day:

"I never in my life thought I would be subjected to such a disgusting display of vulgarity!"

He rose as he spoke and walked out of what was the Drawing-Room carriage of the train to find his way to another compartment where he could be alone.

It did not assuage his temper to discover that the train was larger than he had expected, and quite a number of the photographers and journalists were fellow-travellers.

73

Because he had no wish to involve himself with them, knowing that anything he said would be taken down and used in their newspapers, the Duke returned to the compartment he had just left.

He saw that his wife, who had been staring out the window, quickly opened a magazine when he appeared.

He therefore made no effort to sit in an arm-chair either near or opposite her, but sat down on the other side of the coach and picked up a newspaper.

They travelled for a little while in silence, then stewards came in to offer them food and drink.

The Duke now realised that he must behave in a civilised manner, whatever he might think of his wife and her mother's arrangements.

He had been able to have only a few words with Mr. Vandevilt, who had been brought to the Castle in Lord Farrington's carriage just before the wedding.

His quiet, cultured voice, without a trace of an accent, his handsome appearance, and the manner in which he greeted his future son-in-law told the Duke that here was a man he could like and respect.

He had always prided himself on being a good judge of character, and he knew the moment he met Mr. Vandevilt that he was very different in every way from his wife.

Unfortunately, there had been no time for conversation, and almost as soon as he arrived, Mr. Vandevilt had been taken from the Castle to the Church in a wheel-chair where he was to watch Lord Farrington bring his daughter up the aisle in his place.

Now as a steward arranged a table in front of Magnolia and placed upon it sandwiches, cakes, and biscuits, besides tea that she had obviously asked for, the Duke crossed the carriage to sit down opposite her.

"I suspect," he said in what he hoped was a

pleasant tone, "that you and I were the only people at the Reception who had nothing to eat or drink."

There was a little pause before Magnolia answered him, and because her head was bent it was difficult for the Duke to see her face.

He knew that when they were being married he had been afraid of seeing what she looked like.

Last night, after Mrs. Vandevilt had left, he had known that if his wife was like her mother it was impossible to contemplate the horror his married life would be.

Now, as if she forced herself to do so, Magnolia raised her head and he saw that she was in fact very different from what he had feared.

To begin with, she was very slight, and her face was thin and had somehow a fragile look about it, dominated by her eyes.

They were very large and he was not sure whether they were blue or grey, but one thing was very obvious: she was frightened.

The pupils were dilated and there was an expression on her face which told the Duke, although he could hardly believe it, that she was looking at him with an unmistakable expression of terror.

Then, having looked at him, her eyes flickered and her eye-lashes were dark against her pale cheeks as she said, although he could barely hear it:

"I ... I am afraid you must have ... been upset by the ... explosion of roses."

It struck the Duke before he answered her that her voice was also very different from what he had expected, being soft and musical, and like her father she had no accent.

"It was not something that should happen at a wedding in England," he said before he could stop himself.

Only after the words had been said did he realise that he had spoken sharply in the same way as he might have addressed a recalcitrant soldier or a servant he was reprimanding.

"I ... I am ... sorry."

Once again the words were faint, but he could hear them.

"I do not suppose it was your fault," he said, and thought even to himself it sounded somewhat patronising.

"M-Mama did not ... tell me what she had p-planned ... but I ... knew when it h-happened that it ... annoyed you."

The Duke felt that was an understatement, but nothing he could say now could undo what had been done. He was only too well aware what his relatives would say and the amusement it would cause amongst their neighbours.

Because he thought it would be a mistake to express any further his feelings in the matter, or about any of his mother-in-law's other arrangements at the wedding, which was now over, he picked up the glass of champagne which the steward had poured out for him without his really being aware of it, and drank it.

He noticed that his wife sipped some tea but ate nothing.

Because he still felt angry, he thought that food would choke him, but he deliberately ate a cucumber sandwich as if he felt that to do something ordinary and normal might help him to control the temper he felt rising within him like a tide that nothing could suppress or turn back.

After a moment he was calm enough to say:

"I expect you are tired, but the railway has made the journey to London far quicker than it was, so we should be at Otterburn House by about eight o'clock."

"That ... will be very ... nice."

Magnolia had once again dropped her head so that it was impossible for the Duke to see her face.

He decided she must be shy and supposed it

must be an ordeal for any woman to be married to a man she had never even seen until she walked up the aisle.

Yet, that was her choice, not his, and he hoped that she would become more conversational later on. If not, he was appalled by the future.

He tried to think of something to say to ease what was obviously a tension between them, but then he decided it was too difficult to talk above the noise of the train.

A steward appeared to ask if there was anything else they required, and, having refused another glass of champagne, the Duke, while the tea was being cleared from in front of Magnolia, moved to the other side of the carriage.

He picked up a newspaper and attempted to read it, but all the time he was conscious that he was married and there was nothing he could do about it, however disagreeable he might find it.

As they journeyed on it seemed to him that the wheels beneath him were laughing at his discomfort, but at the same time telling him that his financial difficulties were at an end, and however unpleasant he might find his wife, his other problems had disappeared.

As the daylight began to fade, the Duke found his head nodding and knew that his lack of sleep last night was beginning to take its toll of him.

He shut his eyes and awoke with a start as a steward said at his side:

"We're just coming into the station, Your Grace. The carriage'll be waiting."

With an effort the Duke remembered where he was.

"Thank you."

He glanced across the compartment and saw the back of his wife's head as she stared out the window.

She was sitting upright and he wondered what

she had thought about his inattention and his lack of effort to entertain her.

However, there was nothing he could do about it now, except to make amends by saying as the steward left them:

"You must forgive me for sleeping, but I was in fact awake most of last night."

"I ... understand," Magnolia answered. "I ... also found it ... difficult to ... sleep."

The Duke was saved from having to reply by the fact that the train drew up at the platform, and the Station-Master, resplendent in gold braid and top-hat, was waiting to receive them.

After receiving somewhat fulsome congratulations on their marriage, they were escorted to where the town carriage, drawn by extremely fine horses which had belonged to his father, was waiting at the main entrance.

There, a small child, who the Duke learnt was the Station-Master's daughter, presented Magnolia with another bouquet, and there were quite a number of officials to shake hands, who had also brought their wives to stare at the bride.

Finally they drove away, and now the Duke thought with a feeling of relief that there were only the servants at Otterburn House left to greet them, after which they could cease being offered any further expressions of good-will.

"We will have a meal as soon as you are ready," he remarked as they set off from the station. "I understand that your lady's-maid and my valet left with the luggage early this afternoon, so that everything should be in readiness for us."

Magnolia inclined her head but did not reply, and the Duke went on:

"Tomorrow we have to leave early to catch the boat-train to Dover."

As he spoke, he thought it sounded as if he were going to suggest that they both have a good night's sleep. Then he remembered it was his wedding-night.

The thought of this made him feel that he was in a trap that had been baited for him skilfully from the moment he had learnt of his father's debts, and which now snapped shut and there was no escape.

Just for a moment he recoiled from the whole implication of it.

Then he told himself that whatever else might be involved in this flamboyant and unpleasant wedding, he himself would behave like a gentleman and do what was expected of him.

It was a sentiment which he reiterated in his mind as he was changing for dinner, and which made him feel grateful for the champagne he was offered when he descended to the Drawing-Room just before the clock in the Hall struck nine.

The room was decorated with white flowers, and he hoped irrepressibly that he would never again see so many white flowers, until he was comfortably in his grave.

Then he told himself that if he had disliked his wedding, for his wife it had presumably been an enjoyable experience and the least he could do would be to avoid depressing her with his reactions.

As he thought of her, Magnolia came into the room.

She was wearing a very beautiful gown, although the Duke thought she was slightly overdressed for an evening alone with him.

He hoped that in a few years she would not look like her mother, and he thought that if she attempted to do so, he would have to do everything in his power to prevent it.

Now as she walked towards him he realised that she was much more slender than he had expected, and she also moved with a grace that he was sure was unusual in a young girl.

She might almost have been a ballerina, he

thought, and wondered if in America girls took ballet-
lessons as part of their education.

Without looking directly at her, he said:

"I expect you are tired and would like a glass of
champagne. It has been a very long day for both of
us."

"Thank . . . you."

He thought there was a tremor in her voice, as if
she was shy or frightened.

She accepted the glass he handed her.

Then as she took it he saw to his surprise that she
was trembling, and he thought that her fingers held
the glass very tightly, as if she was afraid she might
spill the contents or even drop it.

"Come and sit down," he suggested. "You must
have been standing for hours while we shook hands
with that endless stream of guests."

Magnolia sat as he had suggested.

As she sipped the champagne, he looked down at
her and realised for the first time that her hair was so
fair that it had little silver lights in it.

It was something he had never noticed in another
woman's hair, and he saw too that the skin on her
hands was very white and clear.

Before he had a chance to see her face, dinner
was announced, and as Magnolia rose and put down
her glass of champagne, he offered her his arm.

He had a feeling that she hesitated for a moment
before she laid her fingers very lightly on it.

Then as they moved towards the Dining-Room,
the Duke was quite certain that he was right and she
was afraid.

He thought it strange, then substituted the word
"shy" for "afraid."

Of course she was shy! Any girl finding herself
alone for the first time in her life with a man whom
she had never met before but whose name she now
bore would be shy!

The Dining-Room table was also decorated with

white flowers but they were not overwhelmingly prominent amongst the gold candelabra and goblets, which were very old. They were something which the Duke was certain his wife, as an American, would appreciate.

Then he remembered the conversation he had had with Mrs. Vandevilt at dinner last night, in which she had made it clear that whatever possessions he might have, she and her husband had more and better because they had ransacked the store-houses of Europe to furnish their own houses.

Lady Edith had described to the Duke in great detail Mr. Vandevilt's collection of paintings.

But Mrs. Vandevilt had not minced her words in describing the statuary, the giltwood furniture, and the tapestries, all of which she assured the Duke had a history twice as long as any possessed by the Otterburns.

Because it was in his mind, he said to Magnolia:

"I wonder, as your father collects paintings and your mother collects antiques, if you are a collector too?"

There was a pause before she replied:

"If I collect anything . . . it is books."

"Books?" the Duke questioned. "Do you mean first editions?"

"No, books to read."

Her answer surprised him, and he asked:

"What subjects do you enjoy, or do you prefer novels?"

He thought there was a faint smile on her lips as she replied:

"I like any books. They are the only way that I have been able to . . . escape."

"Escape? From what?"

"From the . . . life I have . . . lived."

The Duke was puzzled.

"I do not understand."

"Why should you? But I suppose it is ... ungrateful of me to think ... like that."

"Think like what?"

"That I have been in a ... prison."

"Did I hear you aright?" the Duke asked. "You tell me you were a prisoner. Do you mean at home or at School?"

Magnolia shook her head.

"I did not mean to become involved with explanations. When you asked me what I collected, I replied 'books' because in that way I can travel and explore the world."

"Are you telling me that is something you have not done otherwise?" the Duke asked.

"No, of course not."

"Why not?"

"Because ... I am who I ... am."

"I suppose I am being rather obtuse, but I still do not understand. I imagined that you could have everything you wanted."

He thought it was unnecessary to add, "with your money," but that was obvious unless she was really stupid.

"It is boring talking about ... myself," Magnolia said unexpectedly. "Will you tell me instead about your life in India? That is a place I would very much like to visit."

"It is a little late for that now," the Duke replied. "You should have gone out there as a young girl and enjoyed the Balls which take place in the hill-stations and the excitement of being one woman amongst a great number of men."

"I would never have been allowed to do that!" Magnolia replied. "What I would have liked to see in India would have been the Temples and the people. I knew when Papa and I studied Buddhism that here was a place I would really like to visit."

"You have studied Buddhism?"

"We also read a great deal about Hinduism. But

it was Buddhism which I found the more interesting and the more helpful."

"Helpful in what way?"

"In learning how to live."

Magnolia spoke quite simply and without pretension. Then she said with a little sigh:

"I want you to tell me what you found in India."

The Duke was aware that he had expected to tell her about the beauty of the Taj Mahal, the appearance of the Red Fort at Delhi, the crowds of pilgrims by the Ganges.

Instead he said:

"I am surprised that you are interested in Buddhism. I always felt that because it was so unemotional and perhaps in a way difficult to understand, it was much more a man's religion than a woman's."

He thought Magnolia smiled, but her face was turned away from him as she said:

"That is obviously a man's point of view about all religions, but women, I think, need the calmness and the inevitability which is very much a part of Buddhism."

The Duke was astonished.

He never in his life remembered talking to any woman about the religions of the East, and it was certainly something he had never expected to do with a young girl, and an American one at that!

"I know many of the Buddhists teachers and Priests feel . . ." he began.

Then he was describing to her the men he had met on his travels; men who he had sensed had hidden powers, men who brought solace and healing to all those with whom they came in contact.

He talked for quite a long time, because he realised that Magnolia was listening with rapt attention to everything he said.

When finally dinner was at an end and they rose to leave the Dining-Room, he was aware that once again she was frightened.

They walked back to the Drawing-Room and the Duke said, looking with slight surprise at the clock on the mantelpiece:

"I see it is growing late and I think that as your maid will be waiting up for you, you would be wise to retire. As I have already said, we have to leave early tomorrow morning."

"Yes ... that would be a ... good idea," Magnolia agreed.

They had only just entered the Drawing-Room, and now the Duke moved back into the Hall with Magnolia beside him.

She paused at the foot of the stairs, and he thought she was about to say something. Then without a word she put her hand on the bannister to walk up.

He expected her to look back but she did not do so, and when she reached the top he returned to the Drawing-Room.

He was aware that the evening had been very different from what he had expected, but whether it was better or worse he could not decide.

He only knew that for the moment he was not hating his wife as violently as he had done earlier in the day.

Then he told himself with a feeling of resignation that the night was not yet over.

It was his wedding-night, and he was a bride-groom.

He walked up the stairs to his own room, where his valet was waiting. As he undressed, because he thought to say nothing seemed unnatural, the Duke enquired:

"Is everything ready for the morning, Jarvis?"

He actually knew the answer before he asked the question.

"Yes, Your Grace, and the luggage'll go ahead. I've only to pack the things you'll use tonight."

"That is good," the Duke said. "We do not want a rush."

"No, Your Grace."

"Good-night, Jarvis."

"Good-night, Your Grace."

The valet left the room, and the Duke, wearing a long robe over his night-shirt, walked to the window.

He drew back the curtains and stood looking out at the trees in Hyde Park.

The shadows beneath seemed dark and mysterious, but the sky overhead was alight with stars, and the Duke had a longing to walk, as he would have done at the Castle, across the grass and to feel free and unrestrained.

Then he told himself that he had saved the Castle by sacrificing his freedom, which was something he had resented from the day he had learnt everything about the bargain he had made.

The meaning of all that had occurred seemed to surge over him, and he was drowning in the feelings of hatred and disgust that had coursed through him when he saw the huge wedding-cake and heard the explosion which had brought a shower of red roses falling onto the heads of the unsuspecting guests.

"Could anything have been more unsuitable at an English wedding in an English garden?" he asked himself.

As he had watched, he had found himself clenching his fingers together until his nails hurt the palms of his hands.

It was only with the greatest difficulty that he had prevented himself from telling Mrs. Vandevilt, as she stood with an expression of triumph on her face, what he thought of her and her ideas.

Now he thought that by refraining he had behaved with a gentlemanly restraint, and the final part of his duty was waiting for him. He would be expected to contribute his "pound of flesh" down to the very last ounce.

For a moment he felt a throbbing in his head, as

if he must revolt against what was expected of him and what he had contracted to do.

But there was no appeal.

It was as clear as if it had been written on the documents he had signed, which had been countersigned by Mr. and Mrs. Vandevilt.

The documents had given him the handling of such an immense sum of money that he wondered whether, if he did everything that was necessary for the Estates, the Castle, and all his other possessions, he would spend even a tenth of what his wife had brought him on their marriage.

His wife!

Although he had sat opposite her and talked to her, he still could not really visualise what she looked like.

It seemed, looking back, as if he had seen her face only vaguely through a mist when she had looked at him and he had known she was afraid.

After that, she had always managed somehow to keep her head bent or else turned away from him, and now he thought that her profile was another thing that was different from what he had expected.

The small, delicate nose, the softly pointed chin, the curved lips which he fancied trembled.

Why should she be afraid, and of what?

He had always understood that American girls were positive and independent, with strong ideas of their own, very different from the sheltered, gauche English variety who were not allowed out of the School-Room until they made their débuts.

Of course he must have been mistaken in thinking that Magnolia was afraid. Perhaps she was trembling because she felt ill. With her millions behind her, there was nothing to make her afraid, except the collapse of the American economy, which was very unlikely ever to happen.

His mind was far away and he had no idea how

long he had been standing looking out at the green leaves of the Park.

Then he braced his shoulders, almost as if he were a soldier going on parade, and walked to the communicating-door which opened from his bedroom into a small passage leading into Magnolia's bedroom.

With a sigh of resignation, the Duke opened the door, walked a few steps into the passage, and put his hand onto the door which led into her room.

He turned the handle gently, then more firmly. The door would not open.

It struck him that perhaps the servants had been foolish enough to leave it locked, as it had been in the past, when visitors had used these rooms during his father's lifetime.

The Duke therefore went back into his own room to open the door onto the main passage. To the right there was the outside door to Magnolia's room.

He turned the handle, thinking he must apologise for the inadequacy of his staff, but as he did so he found that door too would not open.

He tried it again until he was unmistakably aware that the door was locked.

This was something he had not expected, and now it struck him that perhaps Magnolia's fear was of him as a man.

For some seconds the Duke stood looking at the door, wondering what he should do. Then as if he could find no answer to his question, he walked not back into his own bedroom but slowly down the front stairs.

There was nobody on duty in the front Hall because the Duke had learnt from the Butler that it had been an arrangement during his father's time that when the last person in the house had retired, the footman on duty could also go to bed.

"I don't know if it's something Your Grace would

like to continue?" the Butler had asked a little anxiously.

"I find it an eminently sensible idea," the Duke had replied. "I see no point in keeping the footmen up all night. There are night-watchmen?"

"Yes, of course, Your Grace. They go round the house every hour."

"You may make what arrangements you think best," the Duke had said with a smile.

The house was very quiet and he walked not to the Drawing-Room but to the Library, which also opened out of the Hall.

The lights had been extinguished, but by the light from candles in the sconces in the Hall he could see his way to the desk.

He lit the candelabrum which stood on it, the three candles enabling him to see his way to the grog-tray in the corner of the room.

He was in need of a drink, hoping it would help him to think what he should say to his wife in the morning.

"Surely," he asked himself, "she does not intend to keep me at arm's length and start off our married life in what would obviously be an abnormal and unusual manner?"

With the glass in his hand, the Duke drew back one of the curtains over the windows and opened the casement as if he was in need of air.

Now he was looking not at Hyde Park but onto the garden at the back of the house.

It was not very large but it contained several fine trees, and the gardeners who tended it had ensured that it was regularly ablaze with flowers, although they were impossible to see at this time of night.

The starlight seemed to give the trees a mystery which the Duke thought was echoed at the moment in his own life.

How could he have imagined, how could he have thought for one moment, that his wife, who was so eager for his title, would lock her door against him, and not one door but two?

He thought with a faintly wry smile that it was the first time any woman in whom he was interested had locked her door.

That was why it had surprised him.

Always before, bedroom doors, if not wide open, were very easy to manipulate, after which there had been somebody warm, eager, and passionate waiting for his arms, a face turned up to his, and lips hungry for his kisses.

"Now what am I to do?" the Duke asked himself.

As the question repeated itself he was suddenly aware of a sound behind him.

He had left the door open, and by turning round he could see part of the Hall and the staircase, and now he was aware that there was someone on the stairs.

For a moment, whoever it was was only a shadow, then as the shadow moved, the Duke knew that his wife was moving slowly and on tip-toe down the stairs, so softly that if he had not been particularly alert and keen of hearing he would not have heard her.

Still moving very slowly and surreptitiously, she reached the Hall.

Because she was now out of sight, the Duke turned from the window to walk nearer to the door to see what she was doing.

If she had come in search of him, she was certainly behaving as if she did not wish to be seen or heard.

Then, still in the room, he realised that she was not looking for him but was in fact standing at the front door, trying to open it.

Chapter Five

Slowly, because he was not quite certain what he should do about it, the Duke moved quietly into the Hall.

Only when using all her strength and both hands Magnolia was still unable to move the bolt at the top of the door, did he say:

"Perhaps I can help you."

If he had fired a pistol she could not have seemed more startled. She appeared almost to jump into the air before she turned round to stare at him, her eyes seeming to fill her whole face with terror at his appearance.

The Duke saw that she was wearing a dark gown and over it a long cloak trimmed and lined with ermine.

She had a small, comparatively plain bonnet on her head, and beneath it her hair with its strange streaks of silver looked very unusual and, if he had thought about it, very lovely.

As she was obviously stricken into silence, he asked:

"May I, as your husband, know where you are going?"

There was a long pause before, in a voice that

trembled so much that it sounded as if it were strangled in her throat, Magnolia managed to murmur:

"A-away!"

"That is obvious," the Duke replied, "and I imagine someone is waiting for you outside."

"N-no . . . !"

"You really mean there is no one?"

"No . . . of course . . . not . . ."

"Am I to understand," he asked, deliberately
keeping his voice very quiet and calm, "that you are
going out into the street alone? Where to?"

Again there was a pause, before she said, almost
as if she was reluctant to answer him:

"I . . . I do not . . . know."

The Duke looked at her as if he felt she could not
be telling the truth.

Her eyes in the light from the candles in the
sconces revealed only that she was frightened to the
point of immobility, and he realised that she had not
moved since first he had spoken to her.

He looked down at her feet and saw there was a
leather box that she must have placed on the floor
before she tried to move the bolt on the door.

It was a very expensive-looking box, and he suspected it held her jewels.

Again quietly, so as not to frighten her more than
she was already, he said:

"Suppose we sit down and you explain to me
what is happening and why you feel you have to leave
me."

She made a convulsive little movement, and he
thought she was going to refuse.

Then, as if she was too helpless to do anything
but obey him, she moved a trifle and the Duke walked
forward to pick up the jewel-case.

Carrying it, he walked back into the room where
he had been when she came down the stairs, and was
aware as he did so that she was following him.

91

He set the jewel-case down on the desk, and as she stood indecisively in the doorway he said in quite an ordinary, casual tone:

"This room seems rather cold. I think I should light the fire."

As he spoke, he took a spill from the place where they were kept on the mantelpiece, lit one from the candles on his desk, and applied it to the fire.

As the flames burnt the white paper against which the wood and coal were laid, he rose again to his feet to see that Magnolia was still standing by the doorway.

"Come and sit down," he said invitingly.

As she obeyed him, he lit four more candles, two on each side of the mantelshelf.

She sat down in an arm-chair and the Duke first crossed the room to shut the door, which she had left open. Then he turned to sit opposite her on the other side of the hearth-rug.

The flames from the fire illuminated her face and he saw that she was very pale as she stared at the fire, her fingers clasped tightly in her lap.

The Duke knew that this was to stop them from trembling.

There was silence while he wondered what he should say to her and how he could persuade her to tell him the truth.

Then at last, when he realised that she was waiting for him to speak, he said:

"You have just told me that you have no idea where you are going. If that is true, how could you possibly manage alone in a country in which you are a stranger?"

"I . . . I thought I could h-hide somewhere where . . . no one could . . . find me."

"I suppose by 'no one' you mean me."

"And . . . Mama."

He hardly heard the words but they were spoken.

"Now that you are a married woman, your mother is no longer responsible for you," the Duke said. "But I am, and you must be aware what a commotion there would be if the day after our marriage you vanished."

"I . . . thought you would be . . . glad."

Magnolia was not looking at him as she spoke, but was still staring at the fire.

He thought there was for a moment a faint flush on her cheeks as she said the words.

"I should not be glad," the Duke said quietly, "but extremely perturbed, worried, and upset."

He felt that she did not believe him, and he went on:

"Surely you must be aware of the danger you might encounter?"

As he spoke, he wondered how he could explain to her that if, as he suspected, the leather case contained jewels, both that and her expensive fur-lined cloak would doubtless be stolen from her before she reached the end of Park Lane.

If she was not attacked by thieves, then undoubtedly it would be by the women who were always lurking about the streets at this time of the night.

"I . . . I want to . . . go away!"

The words, spoken a little louder and more positively than she had spoken until now, seemed to burst from her lips.

"But why?" the Duke asked.

"Because I do not . . . want to be your . . . wife . . . and you . . . hate me!"

The Duke was surprised, and now as he did not answer Magnolia turned her head to look at him. Once again he saw the terror in her eyes as she said:

"I knew it in the . . . Church, in the garden, and in the train. It was almost as if you were . . . saying it out loud."

This was indisputable, and for the moment the

Duke was astonished into silence, and as he felt for words, Magnolia went on hurriedly:

"Let me go...please...let me go away...and find somewhere where I can...live quietly...you can...keep my money...all of it...but as you do not want me...I cannot...stay with you...let me go!"

Her voice was very insistent but at the same time pathetic, and the Duke said:

"You must be intelligent enough to realise that it is not as easy as that. If I have upset you today, then I can only apologise."

"I thought Mama's...arrangement would annoy you," Magnolia said, "but neither Papa nor I had any...idea of what she had...planned."

"I was annoyed," the Duke admitted, "because I thought, as we were being married in England, that it would be a quiet, private ceremony for ourselves, our relatives, and our friends."

"I...know," Magnolia said with what sounded like a sob in her voice, "but Mama would have... found that very...dull because there would have been...nothing for the Press to...write about, and she wanted everybody to know I had married a... Duke."

There was something in the way she said the last word which made the Duke ask inquisitively:

"And you did not wish to marry one?"

"No...of course not!" Magnolia replied. "I had no wish to marry anybody...except..."

She paused, and after a moment the Duke said:

"Except who?"

He thought she was not going to answer him, but now she looked away from him again, and after a moment she said:

"Somebody who...loved me...and as no one can...ever do that...I had no wish to be...married."

"I do not understand," the Duke said.

Magnolia made a little gesture with one hand, then because it was obvious that her fingers were still trembling she clasped them once again in her lap.

"Please explain what you mean."

He spoke coaxingly, as he would have done to a child, and as he did so he thought that there was something very child-like about Magnolia.

She seemed in fact very immature as she sat upright on the edge of the chair, and he could see the delicacy of her profile silhouetted against the marble mantelshelf.

"After I left ... School," she murmured, "I realised that Mama was ... planning to ... marry me to somebody very ... important ... and Papa explained that no one of whom he would ... approve would wish to ... marry me because I am so ... rich."

Her voice deepened on the word. Then with an effort she went on:

"He ... convinced me that if I did not ... marry you, there would always be ... somebody else who might ... in fact be ... worse."

After she had spoken there was silence for a moment. Then the Duke said:

"I had not thought of that, but I think I know what your father meant. At the same time ..."

He was about to say: "There must be a man somewhere in the world who would marry you for yourself."

Then he thought that because of her great wealth, Mr. Vandevilt had been right in thinking that the average man, like himself, unless in exceptional circumstances, would have no wish for a wife who was so outrageously rich.

As if she knew what he was thinking, Magnolia said:

"Now that you understand, please ... let me go. I will ... find somewhere ... where I shall be safe ... and if no one knows where I am ... I can make a ... life of my own."

He did not answer, and she went on:

"I thought if I was near ... places where there were ... books, like a ... Library or a Museum, I would have ... plenty to occupy ... me."

Now she was looking at him appealingly as she begged:

"Let me go ... please ... please ... let me go!"

The Duke thought that never in his whole life had he been confronted with quite such a difficult problem. He knew he must handle it with the utmost tact and diplomacy.

After a moment he asked:

"You have thought of how you would keep your-self?"

"Yes ... of course," Magnolia replied. "I am not ... stupid. I have a little money with me ... not very much, but my jewels are worth a great deal."

"You intend to sell them?"

"Yes. I know I may not ... get what they are really worth, but certainly ... enough to ... live on."

"What I think you do not understand," the Duke said, "is that a woman living alone would be open to a great deal of misunderstanding and insults."

He saw Magnolia look at him in surprise. Then she said:

"Not if I do not ... speak to anybody ... and live very ... quietly."

"It is not that," the Duke explained. "I am afraid you will find that no Hotel would accept you unaccompanied, especially without proper luggage, and it is unlikely the Landlord of a house or rooms would let them to a young woman with no credentials."

He saw that this was something which Magnolia had not understood or considered, and after a moment she asked:

"Why should they ... think there is ... anything wrong? After all, even in England ... women are more ... emancipated now than they have ... been in the past."

"There are women like that," the Duke conceded, "but they do not look like you, nor are they so young."

"Then . . . what am I to . . . do?"

Again it was a cry that came from her heart, and the Duke answered:

"Suppose you try staying with me?"

Instantly the fear was back in her eyes, and he said quickly:

"We can make our own arrangements as to how to live and how we behave towards each other."

He knew she did not understand what he was saying, and he went on:

"We only met today for the first time, which is most unfortunate. We should have had at least a week to get to know each other before we were married."

He saw that she was listening and considered:

"Suppose we avail ourselves not only of that week but a number of other weeks and try to see if we are suited to each other. Meantime, we can be just— friends."

"You . . . mean," Magnolia said after a moment, "that I . . . would not be . . . your wife?"

There was no doubt what she meant by the word, and the tremble in her voice was very revealing.

"I suggest," the Duke said, "that from the very beginning we behave as if we are not married but are strangers who have been brought together by circumstance, or fate, if you like."

He thought she shuddered, but she did not speak, and he went on:

"We will discover whether or not we have anything in common and if there is any chance of our friendship developing into something deeper."

"You mean . . . I might . . . fall in love with . . . you?" Magnolia enquired.

"It is what I hope you may do in the future."

"I thought . . . you . . . wanted me only for my . . . money . . . not because you wanted . . . love."

"I understood," the Duke retaliated, "that you wanted me only for my title!"

"It was Mama who wanted ... that," Magnolia commented. "She would have preferred a Prince, but there was not one available."

She spoke scathingly, and the Duke said with a faint smile:

"I thought myself it was rather a bad exchange, but as I was desperate I accepted it."

"You were ... desperate for ... my ... money?"

"I expect you have been told that my father left such enormous debts that it meant closing the Castle, and all our pensioners, besides many of the older members of the family who are dependent on me, would starve."

Because even to speak of it upset him, there was a sharpness in his voice which made Magnolia cry:

"So although you ... hated me you had to ... marry me!"

"You appeared to have the answer to my problem. But I was hating not you but the fact that I had to marry anyone under pressure. I too wished to fall in love."

Magnolia's eyes widened and he knew this was something which had never occurred to her before.

"You wanted to ... marry somebody who would ... love you for ... yourself?"

"Of course!" the Duke replied. "If you had no wish for a husband who wanted you only for your money, I certainly did not want a wife who is not interested in me as a man but merely because I am a Duke."

"There ... must have been ... other ways to obtain ... the money," Magnolia murmured after a moment.

"I have only been a soldier and have no other trade," the Duke answered. "And as you have said that to me, I shall say to you: 'Surely you have met men who would love you for yourself?'"

He thought that an expression of pain flashed across Magnolia's face. Then she said:

"No ... no ... there was ... no one."

"So, as your father said, I was the best of what was undoubtedly a bad bunch!" the Duke exclaimed. "It is a humiliating thought, even if it is the truth!"

There was a note of sarcasm in his tone which made Magnolia look up at him nervously. Then she said:

"You must be ... aware that it would be ... best for you to let me go somewhere so that I shall not ... irritate and annoy you ... and you can spend my money without ... h-hating me."

"I hope, if that happened," the Duke said, "I would have the decency and sense of propriety not to touch your money, for I would not have earned it."

"That is a very stupid ... attitude."

"Stupid or not, it is the honourable way to behave. So if you leave me I shall be as poor as I was this morning before we were married."

"But I want you to have my money. Besides, legally it is yours already."

"I am not concerned with the law but with what I feel personally," the Duke said. "We entered into a business arrangement, you and I. Unless you honour your part of the bargain, I cannot honour mine."

Magnolia bent forward, her lips parted as if she would argue with him. Then she made a helpless little gesture with her hands.

"What am I to ... do?" she asked. "Please ... what am I to ... do?"

"I think what we can both do," the Duke said, "is to talk this over sensibly. As it is getting warm in here, I suggest you take off your cloak and your bonnet and let me give you a glass of wine."

"No, thank you, I do not want wine."

"Then perhaps some lemonade?" the Duke suggested.

He rose from where he had been sitting and went

to the grog-tray, where, as he expected, there was a small jug of home-made lemonade which he remembered as a child had always been included amongst the other more potent drinks.

He poured out a glass and as he took it to Magnolia he saw that she had unfastened her cloak and let it fall on the chair behind her, and was at the moment lifting her bonnet from her head.

Her hair was swept back from her forehead and arranged very simply in a knot at the back.

He was sure she must have arranged it herself after her maid had gone to bed and she had dressed again, so that she could escape from the house when everybody was asleep.

The Duke handed her the lemonade and as she took it he walked back to the grog-tray to pour himself a brandy and soda.

He thought he needed something strong to help him cope with a situation which he had never in his wildest dreams imagined would occur on his wedding-night.

As he sat down again in the chair opposite Magnolia, he realised that when he had handed her the glass of lemonade she had shuddered and had been afraid of him.

He had never imagined that he would evoke fear in any woman, although quite a number of men had shuddered when he was angry or had remonstrated with them.

The Duke sipped his brandy before he said:

"You know, Magnolia, that if the newspapers which your mother has alerted in this country, as well as in America, to an awareness of our marriage heard you were missing or had disappeared, the whole country would be out looking for you! It would be impossible for you to hide anywhere where you would not have people hunting you as if you were a fox."

Magnolia gave a little cry.

"You are . . . frightening . . . me!"

"I am only telling you what is the truth," the Duke said. "And I think on the whole you must admit it would be easier and much safer for you to be with me than alone in a very strange world of which you know nothing."

"I will...stay if you...promise..." Magnolia began.

"There is no need for me to promise," the Duke interrupted, "when I have already given you my word. You must have heard that the word of an English gentleman is something that can be trusted, at least as far as I am concerned."

"And...we can just...get to know each other ...as you say...and you will not...touch me?"

Once again the last word was almost inaudible, and by the way she spoke the Duke knew exactly what she was saying.

"I promise that I will not touch you unless you ask me to do so," he said, "and I think, Magnolia, that we must both be sensible about the extraordinary and unusual circumstances in which we have been married."

He spoke more slowly as he went on:

"The first step is for us to forget the reason why we have been drawn together and accept that since for the moment it is impossible for us to separate, we have to make the best of it."

"Does that...mean I shall have to...come away with...you tomorrow?"

"That is what has been planned," the Duke said, "but we can stay in England if you prefer."

He tried to sound casual. Then she said:

"But all the ...arrangements have been...made for us to go...and I would like to see the South of France."

"It is something I should enjoy myself."

"You have never been there?"

"We called at Villefranche for two days in a ship which was carrying troops to Egypt."

101

"Then it will be . . . interesting for you as well as for . . . me."

"Very interesting," the Duke agreed. "And I am looking forward to seeing the yacht which my father bought, and which I did not even know I possessed until a few weeks ago."

"I should like that too," Magnolia said simply. "And I am a good sailor. Neither Papa nor I felt in the least sick during the storm in the Atlantic, while Mama and almost everybody else were very ill."

"Then we shall certainly make use of the yacht."

Magnolia put her glass down on the table beside her before she said:

"Perhaps I should go to . . . bed, and . . . you too must be . . . tired."

"Although I slept in the train," the Duke said with a smile, "I admit to feeling somewhat exhausted."

He picked up the jewel-case, but when Magnolia would have risen to her feet she hesitated and asked:

"You are . . . quite . . . quite sure you are doing the . . . right thing? Suppose when you . . . get to know me you hate me even more than you do now?"

"If that happens, which I am convinced is an impossibility," the Duke said, "then I think we must be frank with each other and discuss the future very carefully."

He paused to say with a smile which many women had found extremely attractive:

"I assure you I no longer hate you. But if you continue to hate me, then there are a number of possibilities concerning what we can do about it."

"What are they?" Magnolia asked curiously.

"I own several houses in different parts of the country where, if you wish to make a life for yourself on your own, you could be very comfortable," the Duke replied. "Of course, you can always afford to buy any house you want for yourself in London, or in the country, or anywhere else you please."

He spoke in a business-like manner, and even as

he did so he thought it would be impossible for anyone so fragile, so young, and so helpless to cope on her own.

He had a sudden feeling that whether he liked it or not, he must protect and look after Magnolia. It was a question of protecting her not only from other people but also from herself.

"I do not ... have to make ... any decisions at the ... moment, do I?" Magnolia enquired.

"If you remember, we were discussing what would happen if we hated each other so violently that it would be impossible for us to stay together," the Duke replied.

"Yes ... of course," Magnolia agreed, "and because I am so tired I am afraid I am being rather stupid."

"I think actually you are very sensible and intelligent," the Duke said, "and when you think it over, you will be as glad as I am that you are not stepping out the front door alone. You are much safer here."

Magnolia picked up her ermine-lined cloak and put it over her arm. Then she looked up at the Duke, and because he was so much taller than she was, she had to tip back her head to do so.

Her eyes were enormous in her face as she said hesitatingly:

"I think ... perhaps I ought to ... thank you for being so much ... kinder and more ... understanding than I ... thought you ... would be."

"If you intend to thank me," the Duke replied, "I should apologise for frightening you in the first place."

"I ... understand why you were so ... angry," Magnolia said, "and it is a ... pity that the big wedding-cake and the ... bird filled with roses were not ... lost during the ... storm!"

She looked up at him anxiously as she spoke, and the Duke found himself smiling quite naturally before he answered:

"I agree, that would have been a merciful release. I certainly found them both extremely obnoxious!"

Magnolia suddenly gave a little laugh.

"I have only just thought of it," she said, "but when the bird flew out of the roses, I saw one of the waiters dive under the tablecloth."

"I can understand his feelings."

Now the Duke too found it possible to laugh at the commotion that Mrs. Vandevilt's idea had caused.

"I will go to bed . . . now," Magnolia said quickly, as if she was afraid that once again he might be angry.

"As I intend to do the same thing," the Duke replied, "I will carry your jewel-case for you. May I suggest tht you put it in a safe place until tomorrow morning?"

"You are not afraid of my being burgled?"

"No, of course not," the Duke said, "but very valuable jewellery can be a temptation even to the most honest of men."

As he spoke, he thought that money, in whatever form it was, was a temptation in one way or another; temptation to a sneak-thief, and a temptation even to somebody like himself.

Then he realised that Magnolia had reached the door, and he turned back to blow out the candles on the mantelpiece, then those on the desk.

When he left the room it was to find that she was already halfway up the stairs, and only when she reached the door of her own bedroom did she wait for him to catch up with her.

As he did so, she held out her hand for the jewel-case.

"Shall I take it?" she asked. "Or will . . . you keep it . . . safe?"

He had the feeling that she was telling him that when he left her she would not try to run away again.

"I will do whatever you want, Magnolia. But rest,

and try to sleep. We have a long journey in front of us tomorrow and I feel you will find there are a great many things to interest you and to talk about."

There was a smile on her lips and he thought he saw a light in her eyes, which were no longer frightened as she said:

"You will tell me about India?"

"Of course, and if we are to visit the Greek Islands as your mother suggested we should, we should both polish up our mythology."

Magnolia gave a little cry.

"Do you mean we might go to Greece? It is somewhere that has always interested me."

"We can go anywhere you like," the Duke replied.

As he spoke, it flashed through his mind that the sentence should continue: "because you are paying," and he was angry that the idea should be there when he had not invited it.

But while he said nothing, he was sure his thoughts had communicated themselves to Magnolia, for he thought the light had gone from her eyes as she said:

"It is not . . . as you well know, for me . . . to make such . . . decisions, but . . . you."

As she spoke she did not look at him but opened the door of her bedroom.

Then without another word, without even glancing in his direction, she left him and he found himself standing outside a closed door with her jewel-case in his hands.

*　　*　　*

The sun was shining, it was extremely hot, and the garden of the Villa was a riot of colour.

Magnolia stood outside the long windows on the terrace and thought the view over the blue sea was indescribably beautiful.

In fact, she wondered how she could ever explain

in the letters she was writing to her father the beauty they had found when they had stepped out of the train at Nice into what seemed for the moment to be an enchanted land.

The journey from England had been comfortable in a way that was new to the Duke, although he was aware that it was something to which Magnolia had been accustomed all her life.

The Courier had made all the arrangements and travelled with them to see to the luggage and the servants.

The only contretemps was on the first morning, when before Magnolia had come down to breakfast the Duke was told that the luggage, his valet, and Magnolia's lady's-maid had already left with the Courier for the station.

"Three guards have gone with them, Your Grace," the Butler said. "The fourth is waiting to accompany Your Grace to the station when you're ready to leave."

"Guards?" the Duke questioned.

"The Body-guards, Your Grace. They came here yesterday in the special train and stayed the night."

"Are you telling me," the Duke enquired, "that it has been arranged for Body-guards to accompany Her Grace and myself on our honeymoon?"

"That was the orders given, I understand, Your Grace, by Mrs. Vandevilt."

"Well, they can be cancelled!" the Duke said sharply. "I have no intention of proceeding on my honeymoon with four Body-guards. This is England, not America! And we shall be as safe in France as we are here."

The Butler looked uncomfortable and the Duke said quickly:

"It is not your fault, of course, Dawkins, but tell the Body-guard who is left here in the house that I do not require his services and I will send the others back when we reach Victoria Station."

"Very good, Your Grace."

When Magnolia appeared, the Duke did not tell her of his decision, but she saw the three men waiting for them at Victoria.

Before they proceeded to the train, escorted by the Station-Master, the Duke dismissed the three guards and left them standing indecisively, and at the same time looking sulky, before he joined her.

Only when they were alone in the private coach which was to carry them to Dover did Magnolia ask:

"Did you refuse to . . . allow the Body-guards to . . . come with us?"

"Of course!" the Duke answered. "You may need Body-guards in New York, Magnolia, but I assure you in this country and in France I myself can protect my own wife."

"They must have been surprised that you did not need them."

"I am not concerned with their feelings but with mine and yours," the Duke said. "It is absolutely ridiculous to move about as if we were Royalty, expecting anarchists to throw bombs at us."

"We might be kidnapped and held for ransom."

"That is extremely unlikely," the Duke said firmly.

He thought Magnolia might argue with him, but instead she smiled.

"You are making me . . . feel that I have escaped from my . . . prison."

"So that was what you meant when you said you only felt free when you read!" the Duke exclaimed.

Magnolia nodded.

"I have never been anywhere without being guarded. There were always two men with us when my Nurse took me out in my pram in Central Park, and armed guards all around the house when we stayed in the country."

She gave a little sigh.

"The girls at School used to laugh at me because a guard would wait in the Hall to escort me home, however many Nannies or Governesses I had with me!"

"All I can say is that I am sorry for you."

"When I thought about it, I was sorry for myself," Magnolia answered. "I often used to envy the children who ran about the streets bare-footed because I thought they had more fun than I did."

"I suppose it is inevitable that we should imagine that other people are more fortunate than ourselves," the Duke said. "Personally, until now, I have enjoyed almost every minute of my life."

He did not realise exactly what he had said until he heard Magnolia repeat almost under her breath:

"Until . . . now?"

"I did not mean it like that," he said quickly. "I was referring to the moment when I had to leave the Regiment and come home to all the troubles and difficulties of being a Duke."

"Which . . . included . . . me!"

"I have a feeling," he said with a twinkle in his eye, "that you are asking for compliments."

"No . . . no, of course not!" Magnolia said in a voice of horror. "I was actually . . . thinking I am . . . sorry for . . . you."

"There is no need for you to do that, because if I want to, I am quite capable of feeling sorry for myself," the Duke said. "What I suggest we both do, Magnolia, is to try to enjoy ourselves."

He looked at Magnolia as he spoke, and added:

"We are travelling very much *de luxe*, which is something that as a soldier, and a poor one at that, I have never been able to do before."

Magnolia gave a little laugh.

"Tell me about it," she begged.

"I will tell you what it is like to travel in a Troop-ship," the Duke answered.

He proceeded to describe the discomforts of an overcrowded Troop-ship where the majority of the soldiers who had never been at sea before were extremely sick.

He described the difficulties in keeping the horses in the hold from panicking and how when they reached the Red Sea the sun was unbearable and it was sometimes difficult to get decent water to drink.

He had already found out that Magnolia was a good listener, and all the way across France she plied him with questions about his travels, the countries he had visited, and the different people he had met and studied.

He was surprised at the intelligence of her questions, and he found that he enjoyed the novelty of being a teacher.

At the same time, he was aware that she was still frightened of him as a man.

If he touched her inadvertently, or took her arm to help her down the stairs, he would feel her give a little shudder at the physical contact.

He told himself somewhat wryly that it was extremely good for his ego, but at the same time it was somewhat insulting.

Not a conceited man, the Duke would have been very stupid, which he was not, if he had not been aware that women found him extremely attractive and that almost any woman to whom he made himself pleasant would regard him with a glint in her eye which was more flattering than anything she said.

While Magnolia obviously found that what he had to tell her was interesting and informative, there was no doubt that she shrank from him as a man and even more so as a husband.

What is more, she was always on her guard in case he presumed on what appeared, on the surface, to be a quite pleasant but distant relationship.

When he went to bed at night in the comfortable bedroom in the private sleeping-car, which the Duke was aware cost an astronomical sum to have attached to the main Southbound Express, he found himself thinking of Magnolia.

It was in a very different way from how he had

thought before, when she had been just a faceless American with whom he was making a business contract.

Now, as he grew to know her better, he realised how absurdly sensitive and vulnerable she was, and that while she was extremely intelligent and well read, she was as innocent as a new-born baby about the world outside the cloistered and guarded life she had lived as a great heiress.

When he thought of what might have happened to her if she had done as she intended and run away into the streets alone and unaccompanied, the Duke was appalled.

Because she was so innocent, she would undoubtedly have found herself either being robbed and left senseless by the roadside, or, worse still, inveigled into some unsavoury brothel from which there would be no escape.

The Duke had no idea that American heiresses were guarded and isolated from reality to the point where they lived not in the real world but in a "Cloud Cuckoo Land" that left them completely helpless as people.

It struck him that if she had married a different type of man from himself—perhaps some European Prince who was interested only in her money—she might have been shocked and intimidated to the point where she would have found it impossible to go on living.

Then he told himself that he was exaggerating, but the thought was there and it made him in consequence speak very quietly and gently to Magnolia and do nothing to make her more fearful of him as a man than she was already.

Then he found himself asking the question to which there was no reply:

"How can I be sure that in the future I shall not frighten her?"

Chapter Six

The sea was smooth, it was early in the morning, and there was a mist over the horizon which the sun was just beginning to disperse when the Duke came up on deck.

He was not surprised to see that Magnolia was already there.

He had realised ever since they had set out in the yacht that she seemed to have an energy which he had not noticed before, and each new day was an excitement she would not miss.

She was certainly unrestrained in a way that she had never experienced in the past, and it amused him to see her reaction to being free from a constraint which had encompassed her ever since she had been born.

To begin with, when he had said they were boarding the yacht for an unknown destination, Magnolia's lady's-maid flatly refused to go with them.

"Not for all the tea in China, Your Grace, would I go through what I suffered crossing the Atlantic!" she said firmly.

When she realised the woman was adamant, Magnolia had gone in search of the Duke.

She was looking worried, and before she could speak he asked:

111

"What has upset you?"

"I am not exactly ... upset," she replied, "but my maid refuses to come with me on the yacht."

The Duke smiled.

"So the earth-shaking problem is whether you engage another lady's-maid or look after yourself."

He saw from the surprise in Magnolia's face that this was something she had never thought of doing.

"If you are in difficulties," he said, "I assure you that Jarvis, my valet, will be able to help you, if necessary, and I am quite prepared to lend a hand."

"Are you saying that I can come with you in the yacht without a maid?"

"Of course," the Duke answered. "We shall not be going anywhere very smart, I hope that nobody will wish to entertain us, and if you do not look as if you have stepped out of a band-box, there will be only the fish and me to criticise!"

There was silence for a moment. Then Magnolia said:

"I know you are ... laughing at me ... and think it ... ridiculous, but I have never been ... allowed to look after ... myself before."

"Then that will be a new experience for you," the Duke said.

When they had gone aboard without the somewhat austere American lady's-maid who stayed sulking and disagreeable at the Villa, he was sure, although he said nothing, that Magnolia enjoyed being on her own.

He could hear her moving about in her cabin very early, and she was usually upon deck long before he appeared.

She had arranged her hair in the way she had done on the night of their wedding when she had tried to run away, and because it was so simple he thought that it became her better than any elaborate coiffure could possibly have done.

As the Army had given him a sharp eye for any disorder, he noticed that sometimes Magnolia's gown was wrongly buttoned at the back and her sash was not always as well tied as it could have been, but he said nothing.

After two days' sailing he was quite prepared to admit that her face lighting up with excitement and her eyes shining compensated for any disarray in her clothes.

Knowing his father's extravagance, the Duke was really not surprised to find that the Steam Yacht *Werewolf* contained every possible improvement, gadget, and luxury that could be found in any yacht of the same size anywhere in the world.

It was elaborately decorated, and, as he might have expected, the main cabins all contained very comfortable brass bedsteads large enough for two.

He had thought of giving Magnolia the Master Cabin, which his father had occupied, but she preferred the one next to it, which was far more feminine and decorated in pink, which made her exclaim that it looked "like a rose."

As she said it spontaneously, she looked at the Duke from under her eye-lashes a little apprehensively.

He knew she was remembering the ten thousand roses which had fallen from the air on their wedding-day and was wondering if even to mention the flowers would make him as angry as he had been then.

But he merely remarked:

"I said you could choose whichever cabin you prefer, and one which reminds you of a flower is certainly a suitable background for you."

It was a compliment, but he knew that she was wondering if he meant it. Then after a little pause she said:

"Then, please, I would like this one."

The *Werewolf* included in its crew an excellent

Chinese Chef, and as they moved along the French coast towards Italy, the Duke felt almost guilty of enjoying such comfort.

The Captain and the crew were delighted to see him, for they had found it boring and slightly demoralising to spend their time waiting in harbour for an owner who never appeared.

He learnt that his father had held two large and very gay parties aboard the *Werewolf* the previous year, and the captain had in fact been apprehensive as to whether they would now be dismissed and the yacht sold.

The Duke did not enlighten him to the fact that this had been his intention before he married, and until now he had not actually been certain whether a yacht was necessary.

But Magnolia's delight in it, and the pleasure she obviously gained from the thought of seeing the Greek Islands and perhaps going on to Constantinople, made the Duke feel that, as their marriage stood at the moment, the yacht might play an important part in their search for happiness.

He had already admitted to himself that that was what he wanted, and it would be ridiculous to go on hating Magnolia's wealth instead of accepting it, if not with pleasure, at least with gratitude.

What surprised him after their first week of marriage was that she was even more intelligent and certainly better educated than he had at first realised.

He knew, without Lady Edith having said so, that no English girl could have conversed with him on subjects that would have been unusual even if he had been talking to a man of his own age.

Magnolia had told the truth when she had said she collected books and read them avidly.

Not surprisingly, there was no Library on board the yacht, for the Duke knew that his father had studied not books but the human species and especially the feminine branch of it.

He had therefore taken the precaution of going to the largest Library in Nice before they left, to buy almost every book that he thought might interest Magnolia in one way or another.

Her delight was all the thanks he needed.

"Did you really get all these for me?" she asked.

"I thought we might both read them if we ran out of conversation," the Duke replied.

She gave a little laugh.

"I think what you are really saying is when you get tired of answering my questions you will give me a book to keep me quiet!"

"I had not thought of it that way," he said with a smile, "but it is certainly an idea!"

She looked down at the book that she had picked up from the stacks of others on the floor and asked a little hesitatingly:

"You do not ... really mind my being so ... inquisitive?"

"I am delighted to tell you everything I know," the Duke replied. "The only thing is, I am rather afraid that I shall disappoint you by not knowing the answers or giving you a wrong one."

"It is very exciting for me," Magnolia said seriously, "to find somebody who has done so many things ... personally."

She hesitated, as if she was feeling for the right words, then went on:

"Papa has travelled all over the world, but he really only looks at paintings, not people or places, so everything you tell me and everything you have done is quite different from anything I have heard before."

"I think what you have to face," the Duke said, "is that you must live your own life and not get it in a second-hand manner from anyone else, whether your father or me."

She looked at him in a startled fashion as if this was a revolutionary idea.

"You have started already," he went on. "You are here, you are married, and you have left behind everything that has been familiar for eighteen years of your life."

"When you say it like that, it sounds rather frightening," Magnolia replied. "But I like being here and I am looking forward to what we shall see tomorrow, the day after that, and the day after that."

"That is exactly the right attitude," the Duke approved, "and it is in fact living."

He knew she had thought over what he had said to her, because when they were having dinner that evening in the pretty Saloon decorated in sea-blue which was the colour of the sea in the sunshine, Magnolia said:

"What do you feel when you are in danger?"

The Duke thought for a moment.

"If you are speaking of a battle or when one is faced with an enemy, I suppose it is excitement, mixed with fear."

"Fear!" Magnolia exclaimed. "I thought that men were never afraid."

"Anyone, if he is honest, is afraid of being wounded or killed," the Duke replied. "But a soldier is trained to control himself to the point where he does not show fear, and in most cases this makes the feeling less acute than it would otherwise be."

Magnolia considered this for a moment, then she said:

"So discipline teaches self-control."

"That is what it should do."

Then, as if the Duke knew what she was thinking, he smiled and said:

"It is of course very regrettable when one's feelings break through the control which discipline imposes so that they become revealed to other people."

He knew they were both thinking of how his feelings at the time of their wedding had not been controlled as they should have been, and after a moment he said with a twinkle in his eye:

"At least I did not hide under the table-cloth!"

Magnolia gave a little laugh that seemed to echo round the Saloon.

"That would have been very undignified. No, you stood straight and unshrinking, as a soldier should. At the same time, there were sparks coming out of your eyes and, I suspect, your heart."

"You are making me feel ashamed," the Duke complained.

"I am actually being unfair," she said quickly. "I do not think ... anyone else would have been ... aware of your ... feelings."

"Nevertheless, I shall reprimand myself," the Duke said, "and on another occasion of that sort keep well away from you."

Magnolia chuckled before she said:

"You are not suggesting we might have to be married again?"

"God forbid!" the Duke said half-seriously. "At the same time, your mother might wish to celebrate the anniversary of our wedding, or perhaps ..."

He broke off his words quickly, realising that he had been about to say, "a christening."

It flashed through his mind that as things were at the moment, there was no chance of the bells being pealed according to the Burn tradition when an heir was born to the reigning Duke or to his eldest son.

And there would certainly not be the fireworks and a party for the workers and the tenants which always took place when the heir came of age.

As if it suddenly struck him that despite the easy way they had talked and become friendly these last few days, the marriage was still a sham, the Duke put down the glass he had been holding, put his hand over Magnolia's, and said in a very different tone:

"I want to have a serious talk with you, Magnolia."

She read his thoughts as she had done before and with a little cry she snatched away her hand and answered:

"No ... no ... we have ... nothing to talk about ... nothing ... I want to go up on deck ..."

Before he could stop her, she had jumped up from the table, and snatching the wrap which matched her gown, which was lying on a chair, she slipped out of the Saloon before he could even rise.

Hearing her footsteps running towards the companionway, he did not attempt to follow her. Instead, his lips tightened and he told himself he had been a fool to be impatient.

But because she had talked so easily and unaffectedly ever since they had been at sea, he had almost forgotten her initial fear of him.

He had thought, perhaps optimistically, that she had begun to like him, but now he knew he was back to the beginning again, trying to make her trust him, trying to make her believe that he was a friend and not an enemy.

He knew the answers, and yet he found the situation extremely frustrating and at the same time worrying.

How could they go on playing games?

He could understand that at first she shrank from him in a natural reaction to a hasty marriage. But how could he ever make her accept him in his rightful position as her husband and—lover?

The last word as it came into his mind seemed almost to hit him between the eyes.

He knew that if he was honest, he already desired Magnolia as a woman.

He would in fact have been blind and deaf if he had not been beguiled by her beauty and had not found extremely fascinating the soft, rather breathless way she spoke.

It was certainly different from the way in which any other woman he knew had talked, and she seemed to make any subject, even the most erudite, feminine or perhaps the right word was "enchanted," because of the music in her voice.

He liked the way she moved, her grace, and the pride with which she carried her small head on a long, swan-like neck.

'She is lovely!' the Duke thought. 'And, dammit, she is my wife!'

Then he berated himself for being not only impatient but perhaps too easily aroused by their surroundings, the warmth of the weather, and above all the fact that he was alone on what was supposed to be his honeymoon with a very desirable woman.

"God knows, I would be inhuman if I did not desire her!" he excused himself.

At the same time, he was aware that he had acted far too hastily in the task he had set himself of wooing a woman as he had never had to do before.

Always in the past his conquests had been very easy ones. In fact, he had often thought that it was the women who were the victors, not himself, which as a very masculine man he intended to be.

But with Magnolia it was going to be very different, and already he had been stupid enough to frighten her away and make things perhaps even more difficult than they had been before.

The Duke suddenly realised that this was a campaign in which he was totally inexperienced and which would require tactics that he had never employed before.

He had worked out a plan for an operation which he had the uncomfortable feeling might take a very long time and which indeed he could not even be certain of winning.

Supposing that, instead of making her like him, if not love him, he merely increased her hatred to the point where when they returned to England she would leave him as she had tried to do that first night?

He thought of the embarrassment and the difficulties this would entail. He saw also how bleak his own life would be, and found himself wondering frantically what he could do about it.

If there was one thing the Duke had always disliked, it was married men who philandered with other women.

He had always thought it not only cheating but also unsportsmanlike, since a woman did not have the same opportunities for illicit enjoyment that were open to a man.

He had always felt slightly disgusted when he had heard a man say:

"My wife? Oh, she is quite safe in the country!"

He knew men who were always on the look-out for every bit of fun they could find, and he was determined that he would not be like them and that once he was married, clandestine love would play no part in his life.

But even as he thought of it he knew that Lady Edith would laugh at this as being another of his out-of-date ideals.

Nevertheless, the feeling was there. At the same time, he was practical enough to realise that marriage to a wife who would have nothing to do with him would make his own life very difficult, frustrated, and lonely.

A man needed a woman, and as he was no longer fighting a dangerous enemy on the North-West Frontier, he knew that was what he now required.

What was more, now that he was married, he wanted a family to fill the Castle with the noise of children, and to know that the Nurseries in which he had been brought up were being used again.

Then in a few years there would be a son he would teach to ride and shoot, and daughters who would grow up as lovely as their ancestors.

He had never thought of it before, but now he knew that Magnolia's strange, fragile, rather ethereal beauty would add a new lustre to the beauty of the Burn women and the handsome features of the men.

But—only if she became his wife in reality as well as in name.

Then his feelings rose like a flood-tide.

He wanted her! He wanted to hold her close against him, to feel her quiver not with fear but with excitement. He wanted to take the pins from her hair and let it fall over her white shoulders.

Then he wanted to kiss her, to hold her soft, innocent, untouched lips captive with his.

The Duke pushed his glass away from him as if the intensity of his feelings had no need of a stimulant.

Then as he decided that he would join Magnolia and try to erase from her mind the fear he had evoked in her, he heard her footsteps passing the door.

He knew she was retiring to her own cabin and he would not see her again that night.

✿　✿　✿

The following day the Duke was aware that there was a barrier between them which had not been there since they had left Villefranche.

He therefore schooled himself to talk amusingly and lightly of many things, and to make no reference to what he had said at dinner the night before.

By the end of the day he thought the trust was back in her eyes and she had forgotten that she had been frightened.

But he could not be sure.

Knowing now what he felt about her, he had the idea that with every turn of her head, every movement of her hands, with every glint of sunshine on her hair, she seemed lovelier than she had been before.

It was a feeling that persisted and grew as the days passed and they reached the foot of Italy and started across the Ionian Sea.

It was then, when it was almost too hot to do

anything in the afternoons but rest under the awning that had been erected over the deck, that the Duke admitted to himself that he was madly in love.

It was something he had not expected, and yet he realised it as he started each day with a feeling of excitement because he would see Magnolia.

He would pass lonely nights tossing restlessly because he was alone, and she was only a wall away in the next cabin.

And he admitted that it was love that was making him feel differently about his wife than he had ever felt about any other woman.

It was love that made the pulse in his temples throb and his lips ache because he longed to kiss her, but it was also love that made him feel that she was not only desirable as a woman but that she filled his mind to the exclusion of everything else.

It was impossible to think of anything but her. He not only wanted to touch her and hold her against him, he wanted to hear her joyous, almost child-like, musical laughter and the softness of her voice when they talked together.

Her English was almost classical in its purity, and she had a vocabulary far greater, the Duke thought, than any other woman he had ever known.

He loved her little flashes of humour and the way she would sometimes tease him, then look at him apprehensively in case he had misunderstood and been offended by what she had said.

"I love her! Dammit—I love her!" he said to the stars, and it was an agony that was inexpressible to stand looking at them alone when he wanted Magnolia with him.

They had been married for nearly three weeks when they passed through the Strait of Messina and began to steam towards Greece.

"Which island shall we visit first?" Magnolia had asked after they had left Messina, where the Captain insisted they should call in because of some small repair he wished done to the yacht.

She had enjoyed seeing a little of Sicily but the Duke had been aware that she was more excited at the thought of the Greek Islands.

They had already talked of the gods and goddesses who were particularly connected with each island, and had tried to cap each other's quotations from Lord Byron, until the Duke was obliged to admit that Magnolia's knowledge of his poems was greater than his own.

"I suppose the first island we shall encounter," he replied in answer to her question, "will be Corfu."

"Kérkyra," Magnolia corrected.

"Are you suggesting," he asked, "that we should speak Greek? In which case I feel I shall be at a distinct disadvantage."

"You have learnt it?"

"A very long time ago."

"Then you must try to remember what you know," she said firmly, "and anyway, I want to understand what the Greeks say to us. One of my Governesses taught me a smattering of modern Greek."

While they were talking, a steward came to tell the Duke that the Captain wished to speak to him.

"What is it?" the Duke enquired when he had joined the Captain on the bridge.

"If you would not mind, Your Grace," the Captain replied, "I would like to put into a harbour on the mainland before we proceed any farther."

"What is wrong?"

"The new fitting which we picked up at Messina is not as well adjusted as I should like. It is only a question of two or three hours' work, but I would rather not proceed until it is working as perfectly as possible."

"Of course, I understand," the Duke agreed.

"What I would like to suggest, Your Grace, is that

we anchor in one of the small bays along the coast. The men can start work at dawn and that should enable us to move on to Corfu by midday."

"That sounds excellent!" the Duke agreed.

He went back to tell Magnolia and she exclaimed delightedly:

"That means we can set foot in Albania, if only for a few minutes, and that can be another country I have visited."

"Are you counting them up?"

"But of course! I have to catch up with you, and I have already counted no less than fifteen countries you have mentioned visiting, while so far I have only been to four, or is it five?"

"You must certainly add Albania to your list," the Duke replied, "but it is not very prepossessing, although there are impressive mountains and the flowers should be attractive at this time of the year."

"You are not to spoil it for me before I even get there!" Magnolia chided, and they both laughed.

Next morning the yacht lay at anchor, and as usual the Duke heard Magnolia rising very early and thought it was something he should do himself.

He found her on deck, and arranged that as she wished to go ashore as quickly as possible, they should have an early breakfast.

The air was cool and fresh and the sun had not a great deal of warmth in it when they were rowed ashore.

Magnolia jumped from the boat onto the sand.

"Albania!" she exclaimed triumphantly. "Now it is definitely on my list!"

"Thank goodness for that!" the Duke said. "Now we need go no farther!"

"I have every intention of exploring the top of the cliff."

The Duke realised that the sailors who had rowed them from the yacht were waiting for his instructions.

"Come back for us in an hour and a half," he ordered.

"Aye, aye, Your Grace!"

He turned and followed his wife, who was already climbing up a path which led from the bay.

There was a twisting, stony sheep-track to the top of the cliffs, then an undulating panorama to the south, while to the north the mountains rose sharply.

Trees covered the lower slopes while the barren peaks were silhouetted against the blue of the sky.

It was very beautiful and Magnolia exclaimed in delight at the many species of flowers that were profuse in the thick grass.

They followed a path that wound away northwards and were soon in the thick of the trees.

The Duke hoped that Magnolia would see some of the wild animals that he knew were to be found in the Albanian mountains, but although there were plenty of hares and occasionally small deer, there was no sign of the chamois or even the mountain-goats that were characteristic of the country.

However, she was very happy with what she was seeing. Then suddenly she stopped and said:

"How stupid of me! I never thought of it until now, but we should have brought a camera with us."

"I did not think of it either," the Duke said. "I believe there is a new one on the market which is quite easy to use, and it would certainly provide us with delightful souvenirs of our honeymoon."

"I particularly want to show Papa where we have been," Magnolia said. "That is why it was stupid of me not to think of it before."

"I am sure we can purchase a camera when we reach Athens," the Duke consoled her.

"Can we do that?"

She looked up at him eagerly.

"We can certainly try."

"Think what the view would be like at the top of these mountains!"

"You are not suggesting, I hope, that we should climb them with or without a camera?" the Duke said quickly.

"I want to climb a little higher," Magnolia answered. "Then we can look down at that magnificent view."

"Very well," the Duke agreed, "but I would not want you to tire yourself."

"I am not tired," Magnolia replied, "and we have taken very little exercise these past weeks except for a walk around the deck."

"That is true," he admitted, "and when we reach the Greek Islands I intend to swim every day."

She gave a little cry.

"May I do that with you?"

"Can you swim?"

"I always swam in the pool we had at one of our houses, so I am not likely to drown, if that is what you mean."

"I am surprised."

Then he thought it was not really surprising. It was the sort of thing he would expect an American girl to be able to do, while English ladies would be too modest to appear in a bathing-dress, even privately.

"Please let me swim when we reach Greece," Magnolia said pleadingly.

"I shall look forward to your doing so," the Duke replied.

She smiled at him so delightedly that he had to control an impulse to put his arms round her and say he would let her do anything she wanted while she looked as happy as she did at that moment.

He forced himself instead to make some commonplace remark about a bird that flew out of the bushes as they approached.

When at last they rested for a little while under

the trees and looked back at the view, he found it was
well over an hour since they had left the yacht, and
suggested that they should go back.

"The Captain will be worrying what has happened to us."

"It is so lovely and peaceful," Magnolia said. "I
think perhaps I would like to build a house here.
Then we could escape from everybody and everything."

"It is certainly an idea," the Duke agreed, "but
perhaps you would become bored after a while."

She looked at him speculatively for a moment.
Then she answered:

"Not if you will go on telling me of the things you
have done and the places you have been."

"By that time we might be down to the things I
want to do," the Duke answered.

"And what are those?" Magnolia asked.

He was about to reply when suddenly from the
trees behind there was a sound, and he turned his
head to see, to his astonishment, that a number of
rough-looking men were approaching.

They had long hair and moustachios and carried
long, old-fashioned muskets.

Instinctively the Duke rose to his feet and Magnolia rose too, and as the men came nearer she put out
her hand and held on to his arm.

The Duke knew she must be frightened, for he
saw that their visitors had stuffed into their wide belts
swords and knives that he had always connected in
his mind with bandits.

Moreover, he knew that Albanians were usually
fighting amongst one another or attacking their neighbours and these need not necessarily be outlaws.

Before he could move, the Duke found that the
men, and there were about a dozen of them, had
already encircled them.

He was just wondering if he and Magnolia could
try to run away through the trees when one man,

older, taller, and obviously with more authority than the rest, said in almost incomprehensible English:

"You—own—big ship?"

He pointed with his finger in the direction of the yacht and the Duke nodded his head.

"Yes."

A smile emerged from under the man's long moustachios and he said:

"Good! You come—with us!"

"Why?" the Duke asked. "We are just returning to my yacht."

"You—come with—us!" the man repeated.

There was no doubt now that he meant what he said, and the men with him moved nearer to the Duke, one of them putting a hand on his back to push him forward.

Magnolia gave a little cry, slipped her hand into the Duke's, and held on to his arm with the other.

"What do you want? Where are you taking us?" she asked.

"I do not know," the Duke answered, "but unfortunately I am afraid we have to do what they say."

As he spoke, he felt that he knew what the men intended, and he had the uncomfortable feeling they were being kidnapped for ransom.

It was then, to his surprise, that Magnolia, still holding tightly to his hand, spoke to them in Greek.

"What do you want? Where are you taking us?" she enquired in a clear voice.

The men stood still for a moment to listen to what she said. Then the leader who had spoken before replied in a half-Greek, half-Albanian that was even more difficult to follow than was his English.

To the Duke it was completely incomprehensible, but after he had spoken and once again they were moving forward along the path as it wound between the trees, away from the direction of the yacht, Magnolia said:

"I think, although it is difficult to understand, that we are his prisoners and he is going to shut us up while he applies to somebody ... I cannot understand who."

"Ask him how much money he wants to set us free," the Duke said sharply.

Magnolia did as he told her, and now they did not stop walking, but the leader moving ahead of them merely shook his head and made it quite obvious, although he took a long time in saying so, that he was replying "No!"

"It is not money they want," Magnolia said when he had finished speaking.

"Then what do they want?"

Again Magnolia put the question, and this time the answer was even longer than the one before.

"I think, although he is almost incomprehensible," Magnolia told the Duke, "that he has taken us as hostages because two of their 'brothers'—I think he means their 'band'—are to be hanged in Athens."

"Athens!" the Duke exclaimed. "Do you mean to say that we are going to be kept prisoner until we can be exchanged for two criminals?"

"I am sure that is what he means."

"Tell him ..." the Duke began, then stopped.

He wondered frantically what they could say to threaten that if they were not released immediately there would be dire consequences.

Too late the Duke realised he had been extremely foolish in going ashore in a strange country without making certain that he and Magnolia were properly protected.

Now he remembered hearing how the bandits of Albania were extremely powerful, and although they appeared romantic when written about in magazines and newspapers, the Duke was aware that they could be ferocious and cruel when it suited them.

If they were the Pallikares they were famous, and

he remembered reading that Otto I experienced a great deal of trouble with them when he was King of Greece.

These might be the same, or they might be a very different gang, but whatever they were called, the Duke was quite certain that being their prisoner would be very uncomfortable if not dangerous.

Had he been alone, he thought he might have found some opportunity of fighting or outwitting them and making his escape, but with Magnolia there was nothing he could do but obey their commands.

They walked on for about half-an-hour until the trees cleared and they saw what appeared to be the remains of a ruined village.

It was built on the very edge of the mountain which towered above it, and the Duke saw that the reason why it had been abandoned was that there had been a landslide which must have destroyed at least half of the village and left the rest of the houses in a precarious condition.

No self-respecting person could have braved there a winter of torrential rains, floods, and, doubtless, avalanches.

They were escorted over rubble and stones which hurt Magnolia's feet until the bandits came to a stop in front of a tall building which appeared to be only half-demolished, with one side still remaining.

The heavy door was opened and as the Duke hesitated he was pushed inside, and with Magnolia still clinging to his arm they were propelled through another door into what appeared to be a long, high cell without windows.

It was then that the Chief bandit made a long speech. While he spoke he looked at Magnolia, knowing that she was more likely to understand him than the Duke.

Once or twice she checked him to ask a question in her very halting Greek, and impatiently he proceeded with what he wanted to say until finally as he finished he said to the Duke in English:

"You stay—if brothers not released—you die!"

Then he left them, shutting the door behind him, which they realised, because of the noise it made, was of iron, and a few minutes later they heard the outer door being closed.

Then there was silence.

Magnolia was looking at the locked door with frightened eyes and the Duke said quietly and calmly:

"Tell me what he said."

"He said, I think," she answered in a strangled voice, "that the two men ... who have been ... taken to Athens for trial ... are to be ... hanged for their ... crimes ... but these men will exchange us for them ... if the authorities ... agree ... if they will not ... we ... d-die ... as they ... will die!"

Her voice trembled so much that she could hardly say the last words and the Duke said:

"It is obvious that it will take some time for them to get to Athens and make the authorities understand that they are holding us prisoner, so what we have to try to do, Magnolia, is to escape."

"H-how ... how can ... we do ... that?" Magnolia asked.

She looked round her desperately as she spoke, and the Duke realised it was a good question.

"I imagine we are in what was the old prison in the village," he said.

It was certainly an unprepossessing one. The walls of the cell in which they found themselves had been scrawled all over by the prisoners who were the last to use it, and where the plaster had crumbled away there was only the bare bricks.

He looked up at the ceiling, which did not look as if it would keep out the rain, and far out of reach there was a very small barred window.

In one wall there was an opening, and as the Duke moved towards it he saw that it had once been either a kitchen or a washing-place for the prisoners.

But the washing-bowls or any other equipment it had contained were now gone, and there was only a rusty tap projecting from a wall and a drain on the floor that was blocked by moss and fungus.

This room had no light, and he moved back into the cell to note that there were two hard benches against the walls, which might have been used for beds, but there were no mattresses or furniture of any sort.

While he moved round, Magnolia had been watching him, and now she asked:

"H-how can we ... stay here? Please ... find a way ... out!"

If the Duke had not been so worried, he might almost have been pleased that she had turned to him to save her.

The only trouble was, he had not the slightest idea how he could do so.

He sat down on one of the benches somewhat gingerly, wondering if it would support him, and found it was securely made, being one continuous plank of plain wood, firmly nailed to three legs protruding from the wall.

It was so firm that it had survived the devastation of the village when a great many other things, including the houses themselves, had crumbled.

He put out his hand towards Magnolia.

"Come and sit down while I think," he said. "It has been a long walk and I know that soon the Captain of the yacht will be worrying as to why we have not returned."

"But ... how can he ... find us?" she asked.

The Duke thought it would not be impossible, except that if the Captain and the crew tried to rescue them, the bandits might shoot at them, and they had the advantage of knowing the country.

He sat thinking for some time. Then he said:

"You saw how this place was built when we approached it. I imagine that as there is a sheer drop on one side, they will not guard us as carefully there as they would have done if they thought it was possible that we could escape. That is why somehow we have to find a way of doing so."

"How? How?" Magnolia asked.

"That is what I have to discover," the Duke replied quietly. "I suggest you sit as comfortably as you can and put your feet up. We may have another uncomfortable walk during the night."

As he spoke, he knew that it was not going to be easy. In fact it would be very difficult, especially as he had to protect Magnolia from the men who would undoubtedly handle them very roughly if they thought there was any chance of their getting away.

Then he thought that if he had managed to escape from some difficult situations on the North-West Frontier, it should not be impossible to escape from a few Albanian bandits who he could not believe were experienced in holding prisoners to ransom in this isolated part of the country.

Magnolia watched him wide-eyed as he sat thinking and looking up at the small window at the very top of the cell, until finally, rising to his feet, he walked into the dark, low-ceilinged washing-place.

From where she was sitting she could see him bending down to look apparently at the floor, then touching the walls beneath the rusty tap.

When he came back to her, he was smiling.

"What . . . have you found?" she asked.

"I may be mistaken," he replied, "and I may be raising your hopes in vain, but the wall next door seems not nearly as thick as those in here. In fact, because it has been continually kept wet by the tap, I imagine it should be easy to push through."

Magnolia gave a little exclamation as he went on:

"At the same time, we have to be very, very careful that we are not seen doing it, in case our jailors are warned and tie us up."

Magnolia gave a cry of fear and put out her hands towards him.

"Please ... do not let them do ... that! I should be ... frightened ... very ... frightened if it happened ... to you."

"When they return, which I imagine they will, we must try to look resigned to our fate. And, Magnolia, let me say how sorry I am."

"About what?"

"About being conceited enough to think I could look after you without guards."

She stared up at him for a moment as if she thought he was not serious. Then she answered:

"You do realise that they are not the least interested in me or my money? It is you who are important to them, because you own what they call a 'big ship.' When I offered them millions of dollars or pounds if they would let us go, they said they did not want money."

She gave a little laugh.

"Mama would be horrified! It is the first time our dollars have been quite useless and unable to buy what we want!"

Magnolia sounded so amused that the Duke laughed too.

"It is certainly a salutary lesson," he agreed, "from which we must draw the obvious conclusions."

"And what are they?"

"That we have to rely on ourselves and our brains," he replied. "That means that you and I, Magnolia, have got to do something together."

She laughed as if she thought it funny.

Then her eyes met the Duke's, and it was difficult for either of them to look away.

Chapter Seven

Magnolia stood with her ear to the door, listening.

All she could hear was the Duke in the small wash-room striking at the wall with both his feet.

She knew that he was lying on his back to do it, and, having taken off his coat to blunt the noise, he was driving both his feet with all his strength at the damp wall.

He had explained to her simply what he intended to do, and she was well aware that if they were overheard, there would be no future chance of their escaping, since they would probably be tied up to prevent them from trying again.

As she listened she prayed, and the intensity of her prayers somehow made her feel as if she had an extra acuteness of hearing as well as of thinking.

Although the Duke was calm and quiet, she knew perceptively that he was really very anxious, and it made the fear that kept rising within her threaten at times to overwhelm her.

Because she wanted to be brave, and because she wanted him to think she was controlled, until darkness fell she hid her fear successfully.

Now she was aware that they must either effect

their escape or remain prisoners, perhaps to be killed after the criminals in Athens were hanged.

There was suddenly a rumbling noise which made her start, and she knew that the Duke must have succeeded in demolishing part of the wall and what she had heard were stones rolling down the side of the mountain.

Magnolia held her breath.

If the bandits had heard it too, then they would come storming into the prison.

They had brought them coarse brown bread, cheese, and a bottle of local wine about two hours ago, but the men who came into the cell did not include the Head-man and when she tried to talk to them there was no answer.

Instead they looked at her curiously in what she thought was an unpleasant manner which made her shrink towards the Duke.

They said something obviously impertinent or rude to her, which fortunately she did not understand, then they went away, slamming and locking the door behind them.

Now Magnolia waited, but the bandits made no move, and after a few minutes she realised that the Duke was near her.

She moved towards him, groping with her hands in the darkness, until she touched him.

"Now listen to me ..." he said in a deep, serious voice.

❋ ❋ ❋

Afterwards Magnolia could never bear to think of the awful moment when, following the Duke's instructions, she had crawled through the hole in the wash-room wall to find that there was a sheer drop of thousands of feet directly below her.

"Do not look down!" the Duke commanded. "Stand up slowly, facing the wall of the prison, and hold on to it with both your hands."

He told her how to move very, very slowly along the ledge, from which one slip would mean instant death.

He had instructed her before she left the cell to remove her shoes to give her feet a better chance of holding on to the rocks.

It seemed to take hours, although it was actually only four or five minutes, before following him step by step she had rounded the wall of their prison.

While the ledge along which they moved was now a little wider, there was still that frightening precipice below it.

"Keep moving!" the Duke ordered in a whisper. "Do not look down. Press yourself as closely as you can against the wall. You have not far to go now."

Because he was so authoritative she obeyed him automatically, while at the same time her heart was beating frantically with fear and her lips were dry.

When the ledge came to an end, the Duke ordered her to stand still while he dropped down several feet.

Then, although he had told her not to look, Magnolia could see in the moonlight that there was a chasm to cross, caused by a landslide, before they could reach what seemed security amongst the trees on the other side.

She felt the Duke lift her gently from the ledge down beside him. Then he said in a voice that she could barely hear:

"I am going to carry you over my shoulder. It will be uncomfortable, but it is the safest way, so trust me."

She wanted to answer, but somehow it was impossible and she was afraid he would know that her teeth were chattering.

Without waiting, he picked her up, put her over his shoulder in a fireman's lift, and set off across the chasm, feeling his way to find each foothold and gripping the rocks with one hand.

Only once during that perilous journey did Magnolia open her eyes, and when she saw what lay beneath her she had to stifle the scream of terror that rose in her throat.

Then, when she thought the Duke must fall and they would both die, he was scrambling up on the other side, pulling himself and her to safety by the shrubs that overlooked the chasm, and when she dared look again they were in the shadows of the trees.

He put her down gently on the ground. Then, when she was unable to do anything but rest her head against his shoulder and gasp for breath, he said:

"We have to get out of here quickly! It may make the blood go to your head, but I am going to carry you in the same way until we reach ground where it will not be painful for you to walk without shoes."

She did not answer because it was impossible to find words, and once again he put her over his shoulder, and, holding her tightly with his left arm, he started to run.

She had not expected that he would move so swiftly or that he would be so strong that her weight made little difference to his progress.

She was bumped about, but the discomfort was unimportant beside the knowledge that they were free of their prison and, if they were lucky, would be back in the security of the yacht before their captors discovered what had happened.

On and on the Duke ran, sometimes stumbling, sometimes slipping on the loose stones, but always holding her securely until unexpectedly he stopped and put her down.

"What ... is the ... matter?"

She could barely speak and the blood coming into her head made her feel dizzy. But she was terrified that there was a new danger and an unexpected one.

"Are you all right?" the Duke asked. "The way I am carrying you must be agonisingly uncomfortable."

"I am . . . all right," Magnolia said breathlessly, "please . . . please . . . let us . . . go on, in case . . . they come after us."

Instinctively the Duke looked over his shoulder into the darkness behind them, and now in the moonlight they could see the roof of their prison above the trees.

It seemed a long way away, but there was still some distance between them and the yacht.

"Please . . . let us hurry," Magnolia begged. "I can . . . run now."

"The ground is too stony," the Duke replied.

He picked her up in his arms but now he held her against his chest.

Magnolia wanted to protest that she would be all right, but the closeness of him and the fact that her cheek was against his thin shirt so that she could feel the warmth of his body gave her a strange feeling that she had never known before.

With his arms tightly round her, he started running again, and she knew that she was safe and close to him. Although she could not understand it, her fear had gone and she was happy.

So happy that she instinctively put her left arm up round his neck to make it easier for him to carry her.

As if he thought she was afraid, he said, and there was a note of triumph in his voice:

"Do not worry. We have won, they will not catch up with us now."

Even as he spoke there were men's voices shouting far away in the distance behind them, and as if he knew he had boasted too soon, the Duke accelerated the speed at which he was running and Magnolia clung to him in sudden terror.

They could not lose now, at the last moment!

They could not be recaptured after that perilous, terrifying escape along the side of the prison!

She thought in a panic that the men's voices were growing louder, then there was the sound of a shot followed by several others that echoed in the silence of the night.

She heard the Duke give an exclamation, then looked to see ahead of them the light of two lanterns. As they drew near, she saw that they were carried by two of the crew from the yacht.

The Duke reached them and as he did so an English voice said:

"We've been awful worried about Your Grace. We thought perhaps you'd had an accident."

"Worse than that," the Duke answered, "but get us back to the yacht as quickly as possible. There is no time to be lost."

One sailor hurried with his lantern ahead of them down the twisting path from the cliffs to the beach, the other following behind.

A boat was waiting in the sandy bay and the Duke deposited Magnolia in it before he helped the sailors push it out into the water.

The lights from the yacht were the most welcome sight that Magnolia had ever seen, but as the sailors began to row towards it there was a sudden shout from the top of the cliffs!

Looking back, Magnolia with an exclamation of sheer terror saw the bandits silhouetted against the starlit sky.

"Move quickly!" the Duke ordered. "They may shoot at us!"

Even as he spoke there was the sound of an explosion from a pistol fired in their direction. It went wide, and the next minute, on the Duke's orders, they rounded the yacht and were out of sight.

A rope-ladder was let down from the deck and Magnolia was helped up it.

She stood indecisively, shivering with fright until the Duke joined her. Then he picked her up in his arms, saying as he did so:

"Put to sea immediately, Captain Briggs! Are there any weapons aboard?"

"There are several sporting-guns, Your Grace."

"Get them!" the Duke ordered.

He carried Magnolia into the Saloon and set her down on the nearest sofa.

When he would have left her, she put out her hands to hold on to him, crying:

"No ... no ... do not ... leave me! They may ..."

The words she would have spoken were lost, for the Duke had already gone from the Saloon and she heard his voice asking again for a gun.

Then she thought with a sudden terror that the bandits might shoot him before the yacht could get under way and out of range.

With the lights blazing from the port-holes and the lanterns lit on deck, the Duke would be an easy target, and if he was killed ...

The mere thought of it made Magnolia cry out. Then there was the sudden sound of shots from the shore and the noise of them being returned from the yacht.

"He will be killed ... I know he will be ... killed!" she murmured beneath her breath, and fainted ....

* * *

It seemed a long time later before Magnolia was fully conscious, and then all that mattered was that there was no longer the sound of shots but only the steady throb of the engines.

They were moving—moving away from the bandits, and the Duke was safe and unharmed, because Jarvis had told her so.

It was Jarvis who had found her unconscious and

141

who, as she realised later, had carried her down to her cabin, revived her with brandy, and helped her undress and get into bed.

She had been too scared about the Duke, too bemused, and too exhausted from what she had been through to feel that he was anything but an attentive Nanny, and she was in his charge.

Only when she heard the Duke's voice outside in the passage did she ask anxiously:

"His Grace is . . . all right?"

"Perfectly all right, Your Grace. I'll just see to him. I expect he wants to clean himself up. Then I'll tell him Your Grace'd like to see him."

The valet did not wait for her answer but left.

Lying back against the pillows, Magnolia thought the sound of the Duke's voice in the next cabin was the most comforting thing she had ever heard.

He was alive and safe, and now she knew that she need no longer be afraid, and they could relax and rest after all they had been through.

"He is safe!"

The words came to her lips as she felt once again that he was holding her against him, and she could feel his heart beating as he ran with her to safety.

She had liked the strength of his arms and the feeling of security he gave her even though she had been afraid, and she knew it was something she did not want to lose.

Then as she heard the Duke laugh next door, she knew she loved him!

It was so astonishing and so unexpected that as the feeling crept over her, for a moment she stiffened, thinking it must be untrue.

Then she realised it was what she had felt in New York when the Englishman had danced with her and she had wanted to see him again, but it was now multiplied and intensified until it invaded her whole body from the tips of her toes to the top of her head.

"I . . . love . . . him!" she said to herself, and felt it could not be true and she must be dreaming.

How could it have happened? How could she love a man she had hated and despised?

But her brain told her that her love was really very understandable.

The Duke was not only the most handsome and attractive man she had ever seen in her life, he was also the kindest, the most gentle, and the most protective.

She was intelligent enough to realise that no other man, not even her father, would have been clever enough to make her walk without screaming with fear along a ledge only a few inches wide, from which one slip meant certain death.

Because the Duke had made her trust him and because as she now realised she had loved him, she had never envisaged that he would not succeed in what he had undertaken.

"He is . . . wonderful! Magnificent!" she told herself, and felt her heart beating frantically in a very different way from how it had beaten when they were escaping.

The door of her cabin opened, but when she looked up eagerly she saw that it was not the Duke but Jarvis.

"His Grace's compliments, Your Grace, but the Chef should have some nourishing soup ready by now, and His Grace asks if he can drink it in here with Your Grace."

"Yes . . . of course!" Magnolia said eagerly.

Jarvis disappeared and returned a few minutes later with a tray on which was a tureen of soup and cups into which to ladle it, besides a bottle of champagne in an ice-bucket.

He arranged them on a table by the bed, and Magnolia knew that while she was not hungry, because the Duke had made her eat some of the food the robbers had brought them to keep up her strength,

143

she would linger over the soup so that he would stay with her longer.

"His Grace's been having a bath," Jarvis said conversationally, then he went from the cabin.

When the door next opened the Duke came in.

His hands, as well as the clothes he was wearing when they had escaped had been, Magnolia knew, like her own, dirty and stained from both the cell and the rocks.

Now he was wearing a long robe of dark blue satin, there was a silk handkerchief tied at his neck like a stock, which made him look, she thought, somewhat raffish, and his hair, which he must have washed, was still a little wet.

Because she was so pleased to see him, Magnolia did not think of her own appearance.

She did not realise that in the pink-draped bed, with her fair hair hanging over her shoulders, she looked very lovely and insubstantial, while her eyes seemed to fill her whole face.

"You are feeling all right now?" the Duke asked in his deep voice as he came nearer to the bed.

"Yes . . . thank you."

"Jarvis told me that you fainted."

"It was . . . stupid of me, but I was so . . . afraid they might . . . shoot you."

There was a little silence. Then the Duke asked:

"You were thinking of me?"

"Yes . . . and I was sure they would want to . . . kill you for being so . . . clever as to . . . escape from them."

"Well, they failed!" the Duke said in a tone of satisfaction. "And we definitely wounded if not killed two of them."

As he spoke he ladled the soup into a cup and held it out to her. Then he filled a cup for himself.

She drank the soup because he had given it to her, but she realised she was not really hungry and

144

after a few sips she set it down on the table by the bed.

As the Duke drank his soup she realised that his eyes were on her and it made her feel shy.

At the same time, because he was there and because he was safe, she could only feel an inexplicable gladness that seemed to light the whole cabin as if it were filled with sunshine.

The Duke finished his soup. Then he said:

"How could I have imagined—how could I have dreamt—that we should be involved in such a terrible situation? But because we have survived, and I think with honours, we should drink a toast to ourselves."

As he spoke, Jarvis came into the cabin and removed the tureen and the cups, leaving only the champagne.

The Duke filled two glasses, handed one to Magnolia, and lifted his glass.

His eyes met hers, then he said very softly:

"To the bravest woman I have ever known!"

Magnolia felt the blood rising in her cheeks, but she replied:

"To the ... bravest man ... who ... rescued us!"

Her eyes flickered and her eye-lashes were dark against her cheeks as she took a sip of the champagne.

Then with a little leap of her heart she realised that the Duke had sat down on the bed and was facing her.

"I want to tell you," he said, "how wonderful you were. I did not think any woman in such frightening circumstances would not scream or cry, or at least protest and complain."

Because of the way he spoke and because of the note in his voice, which she had never heard before, Magnolia not only felt shy, she felt tears come into her eyes.

It was so marvellous that he should think of her like that when it was he who made their escape possible, he who had carried her to safety. If he had not been so strong, they could easily have been recaptured and would now be in a very different position.

"It was . . . you who were . . . wonderful!" she said impulsively.

The Duke put down his glass.

"It is difficult to find the right words to tell you what I am feeling," he said, "and I am desperately afraid, Magnolia, of frightening you."

"I do not . . . think after . . . today," she answered a little breathlessly, "I shall . . . ever be frightened of . . . anything . . . if you are there."

"I hope that is true," the Duke said, "but I was not thinking of your fear of bandits, but of me!"

He saw the flush that made her look lovelier than she was already, and he knew too that at his words she gave a little tremor, but it was not one of fear.

Then he said very softly:

"If you were not an heiress and were not married already, I would ask you, if necessary on my bended knee, if you would be my wife!"

As he spoke, he felt almost as if like a gambler he was throwing everything he possessed on a green-baize table and praying that the right card would turn up.

After what seemed to him a very long pause, Magnolia answered:

"If you . . . were not a . . . Duke and did not have a very . . . possessive wife . . . I would say . . . 'Yes!' "

The Duke drew in his breath.

"Is my wife possessive?"

"Very . . . very possessive! She will . . . never let you . . . go."

The Duke moved nearer.

"My darling, my sweet!" he said. "Do you mean what you are saying to me?"

146

Magnolia could not answer him, and after a moment he said in a different tone:

"For God's sake, Magnolia, do not play with me! I want you so desperately that I cannot think clearly. But I could not bear that you should turn away from me in fright. I will do anything you want, but I beg you to try to trust me."

Magnolia looked up at him and now his face was near to hers.

"I do... trust you..." she whispered. "And... and... I... love you!"

The Duke made an inarticulate sound as his hands clasped hers.

"Do you mean that?" he asked. "Do you really mean it? Oh, my darling, when I was running with you to safety I had a strange feeling that I was also running towards our happiness."

"I thought that... too. I could feel your heart... beating... and I wanted you to hold me... closer and still... closer."

"That is what I will do now."

He put his arms round her, then slowly, very slowly, as if he was still afraid to frighten her, his lips found hers.

As he kissed her he knew, just as he had expected, that her mouth was soft, sweet, and innocent, and gave him an ecstasy he had never known before in his whole life.

To Magnolia it was everything she had wanted and longed for and which she had thought she would never find.

It was the love she had been told would always be out of her reach, a love that had nothing to do with her money but only with herself.

As he kissed her she felt that she gave the Duke her whole heart and soul, and she was sure that was what he gave her.

He was so close and she felt as if she had ceased

to be herself but was part of him, and he was part of her.

As his lips became more demanding, she felt as if the Duke carried her away to the very topmost peak of the mountains, where the world was left behind them and there were only the stars, the sky, and themselves.

She wanted to press herself closer and still closer to him, and when he finally raised his head, she said in a voice that seemed to lilt with happiness:

"I ... love you ... I love ... you!"

"And I love you, my darling," the Duke said. "I love you because you are the most enchanting person I have ever met, and I think that we were meant to belong to each other since the beginning of time."

"That is ... what I want to ... believe," Magnolia said, "and it would not ... matter who we ... were or what we ... possessed ... would it?"

The Duke knew how important the question was.

"I would love you as I do now," he averred, "if you had been born in the gutter and possessed nothing but your adorable, fascinating lips."

He kissed her again until she felt as if he carried her even higher, from the peaks of the mountains up into the very stars themselves, and they were enveloped in a light which she believed was the light of the gods.

"I ... love you!" she said again, when she could speak, "and I wish you were not ... a Duke ... then we could live in some small cabin somewhere in the mountains ... where I could look after you ... and show you that nothing is of the least ... importance to me except ... you, who are so ... clever and so ... brave."

"Do you really think I am brave?" the Duke asked.

He looked down at her and she could see the love in his eyes as he added:

"You are the most beautiful person I have ever

148

seen, besides being the most intelligent and the bravest. But now you must be something else as well."

"What is . . . that?"

"The most loving! I want your love, Magnolia. I want it desperately! And I cannot contemplate my life without you."

"It is . . . yours . . . all yours," she said with a note of passion in her voice. "I want to . . . belong to you . . . to be with you . . . always . . . safe . . . as I was when you carried me over that . . . terrible chasm!"

"I will protect you in the future very much better than I have so far," the Duke promised firmly.

"Perhaps it was a . . . good thing that it . . . happened, because it made me realise how much I . . . love you. When I thought the bandits might shoot you . . . I felt that if you . . . died . . . my whole world would . . . come to an end."

"My precious, my sweet!" the Duke exclaimed. "It was foolish and careless of me not to realise that in wild, primitive places like that, there are always bandits of some sort,wanting to use people for their own ends."

"I am not . . . afraid of them if you are . . . with me."

"I will never let you be afraid of anything again," the Duke said. "And never of me."

"I shall . . . be . . . afraid only if you are . . . angry with . . . me."

"How could I be angry with anyone so sweet and perfect!"

"There . . . might be . . . another ten thousand red roses . . . to upset you."

The Duke laughed.

"If there are, I will make you pay for them with ten thousand kisses!"

"I would like . . . that."

Magnolia put her arms round his neck to pull him closer to her as she spoke, but instead of kissing her lips, as she expected, he kissed the softness of her neck, and he felt her quiver with a new sensation which she had never felt before.

He kissed her until the breath was coming quickly from between her lips, her eye-lids felt heavy, and she stirred beneath the bed-clothes.

She did not understand what she was feeling, but she wanted him to go on kissing her in an exciting, strange way that was different, so very different from what she had imagined anyone could feel.

"I love you, Magnolia!" the Duke said, and his voice was deep and hoarse. "And I want you, my darling, I want you as my wife! But I will do nothing you would not wish me to do."

"I ... I want to be ... close to you," Magnolia whispered breathlessly. "Much ... much ... closer ... please ... darling ... wonderful Seldon ... make me your wife ... your ... real wife."

The Duke made a sound of triumph. Then he turned out the lights except one, and pulling off his blue robe he slipped into bed beside her.

He took her in his arms.

"It is rather late to say this now, my adorable one," he said, "but I did promise I would not touch you until you asked me to do so."

Magnolia gave a laugh of sheer happiness which swept away her shyness. Then, moving nearer to the Duke than she was already, she whispered:

"Touch me, please ... please touch me ... only, Seldon ..."

"Only what?"

"You make me feel ... so strange ... so excited."

"That is what I want you to feel," the Duke said, "and if I excite you, my beautiful little wife, you excite me to madness."

His voice was deep with passion but he checked himself to add:

"But I will be very gentle. You must not let me frighten or shock you."

As he spoke, he pulled away her nightgown from her shoulders and his hand was touching her breast.

"I love... you!" Magnolia cried. "I love you and everything you do... will be perfect and... also... Divine."

"I love you! I adore you! I worship you!" the Duke cried.

Then their hearts were beating against each other's and his kiss was that of a fighter, a conqueror who had fought against tremendous odds and was the victor.

Yet he was very gentle as she surrendered herself to the insistence of his mouth, his hands, and his body.

Then love carried them on the waves of ecstasy into the starlit sky, and they knew that nothing mattered except that as a man and woman they were one now and through all eternity.

ABOUT THE AUTHOR

BARBARA CARTLAND, the world's most famous romantic novelist, who is also an historian, playwright, lecturer, political speaker and television personality, has now written over 200 books.

She has also had many historical works published and has written four autobiographies as well as the biographies of her mother and that of her brother Ronald Cartland, who was the first Member of Parliament to be killed in the last war. This book has a preface by Sir Winston Churchill.

Barbara Cartland has sold 100 million books over the world, more than half of these in the U.S.A. She broke the world record in 1975 by writing twenty books, and her own record in 1976 with twenty-one. In addition, her album of love songs has just been published, sung with the Royal Philharmonic Orchestra.

In private life, Barbara Cartland, who is a Dame of the Order of St. John of Jerusalem, has fought for better conditions and salaries for Midwives and Nurses. As President of the Royal College of Midwives (Hertfordshire Branch), she has been invested with the first Badge of Office ever given in Great Britain which was subscribed to by the Midwives themselves. She has also championed the cause for old people and founded the first Romany Gypsy Camp in the world.

Barbara Cartland is deeply interested in Vitamin Therapy and is President of the British National Association for Health.

Depth of Field

Depth of Field

A Granville Island Mystery

Michael Blair

A Castle Street Mystery

THE DUNDURN GROUP
TORONTO

Editor: Shannon Whibbs
Design: Erin Mallory
Printer: Webcom

Library and Archives Canada Cataloguing in Publication

Blair, Michael, 1946-
      Depth of field : a Granville Island mystery / by Michael Blair.

(A Castle Street mystery)
ISBN 978-1-55002-855-3

      I. Title. II. Series: Castle Street mystery

PS8553.L3354D46 2009   C813'.6   C2008-906215-9

1   2   3   4   5   13   12   11   10   09

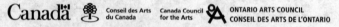

We acknowledge the support of **The Canada Council for the Arts** and the **Ontario Arts Council** for our publishing program. We also acknowledge the financial support of the Government of Canada through the Book Publishing Industry Development Program and **The Association for the Export of Canadian Books**, and the Government of Ontario through the **Ontario Book Publishers Tax Credit** program, and the **Ontario Media Development Corporation**.

Care has been taken to trace the ownership of copyright material used in this book. The author and the publisher welcome any information enabling them to rectify any references or credits in subsequent editions.

J. Kirk Howard, President

Printed and bound in Canada.
Printed on recycled paper.
www.dundurn.com

Dundurn Press	Gazelle Book Services Limited	Dundurn Press
3 Church Street, Suite 500	White Cross Mills	2250 Military Road
Toronto, Ontario, Canada	High Town, Lancaster, England	Tonawanda, NY
M5E 1M2	LA1 4XS	U.S.A. 14150

For Pamela …

Author's Note

Many of the locations in this book — Granville Island, Sea Village, Bridges Restaurant, and various marinas — are real, although not necessarily as portrayed. All events and characters, however, are entirely fictional and any resemblance to actual events or people, living or dead or undecided, is purely coincidental.

chapter one

It was Tuesday, a little past nine in the morning. The fog outside my third floor office window was so thick you could scoop it up with a shovel and cart it away in a wheelbarrow. Unusual for Vancouver in June — virtually unheard of, in fact — but given the winter we'd just been through, nothing would have surprised me weather-wise. The environmentalists blamed it on global warming. The conspiracy theorists blamed it on scalar weaponry run amok. I just groused.

I was alone in the studio, feet up — definitely not unheard of — coffee cup nestled in my lap, wondering where the hell everyone was, when I heard the elevator rattle to a stop and the door bang open. I dropped my feet to the floor, startling Bodger, who'd been cat-napping on the sagging leather sofa against the opposite wall, tattered ears twitching as he dreamed of fat, complacent mice — or the cat treats I kept in my desk drawer, which were a lot easier to catch.

"Well, it's about bloody time," I said, as I went into the outer office.

"Pardon me?"

"Oops," I said, looking at a shapely blonde. "Sorry. I was expecting my associates."

"That's quite all right," she said.

The top of her head was level with the tip of my nose. She had sharp, emerald-green eyes, nice cheekbones, and a wide, generous mouth painted the colour of cherry Jell-O. I guessed she was thirty-five, give or take.

"Can I help you?" I asked hopefully.

"I'm looking for Thomas McCall," she said, surveying the chaos. We were relocating on the weekend and the studio looked as though a giant child had thrown his toys about in a fit of temper.

"You've found him," I replied. "What can I do for you?"

"I'd like to hire you," she said. Her voice was light and slightly scratchy, as if her throat were lined with fine sandpaper. A smoker, I thought, although she didn't smell of tobacco. In fact, her scent was faintly reminiscent of marshmallow, simultaneously sweet and musky and powdery.

"I'd like to be hired," I said. "Never mind all this. We're in the throes of moving to a new location. Come into my office. Would you like some coffee?"

"No, thank you," she said.

"Don't sit there," I said, as she looked down at the sofa and Bodger looked up at her. "You'll get cat hair on your skirt."

She was wearing a three-quarter-length black leather coat, narrow at the waist, flared at the hip, and an above-the-knee black skirt. Her patent leather lace-up boots, also black, had long, pointy toes and three-inch stiletto heels. I placed a straight-backed chair in front of my desk, held it for her as she sat down. She crossed her legs with a whisper of nylon. She had very nice knees.

"You're sure you wouldn't like a cup of coffee?" I asked again, as she unfastened her coat, revealing, I couldn't help but notice, a very impressive superstructure.

"I'm sure, thank you," she said.

I went around my desk and sat down. "So, how can I help you, Miss …?"

"Waverley," she said in her scratchy voice. "Anna Waverley. And it's missus. Or at least it will be until my divorce becomes final."

"Miz, then," I said.

She smiled. She had a very nice smile, revealing near-perfect teeth, except for one slightly crooked upper incisor, to go with the nice knees and impressive superstructure. Her complexion was clear and smooth, no telltale crow's feet around her eyes and mouth. I revised her age downwards half a decade, and wondered why she wore her hair and dressed in a style that made her look older.

"In any event," she said. "I got the house in Point Grey, the condo in Whistler, and the boat, which I'd like to sell. I don't see any reason why I should pay a broker's commission, so I thought I'd sell it privately, which is why I came you. I need photographs to send to prospective buyers. I tried to do it myself with my little digital camera, but I didn't like the way they turned out."

"Okay. That —"

"Except it has to be done right way. This evening, if at all possible. I've already lined up a potential buyer I'd like to email the photos to, but he's leaving for Hawaii first thing in the morning."

"That shouldn't be a problem," I said. We'd recently purchased an almost-new Nikon digital SLR that was compatible with all our older Nikon gear, lenses and flashes and such. "What's the name of the boat?" I asked. "And where is it?"

"It's called *Wonderlust* — with an 'O' — and it's at the Broker's Bay Marina at the west end of Granville Island."

"I know the marina," I said, adding, "I live on Granville Island."

"Oh, do you?" she said. "How convenient. Will you be doing it yourself, then?"

"Yes, probably," I said. No sacrifice was too great.

"Would eight o'clock be all right?" Ms. Waverley said. "I could meet you there."

"That sounds fine," I said.

"I really appreciate you doing this on such short notice, Mr. McCall." She opened her purse and took out a plain white business envelope, from which she removed a pair of keys with a paper tag and a wad of fifty-dollar bills. "I wasn't sure how much you would charge. I hope you don't mind cash."

"Not at all," I said. "But it isn't necessary to pay in advance. We'll invoice you." I took our standard work order form out of my desk drawer.

"If you don't mind," Ms. Waverley said, "I'd prefer to pay in cash. It leaves less of a paper trail." She smiled her very nice smile. "You know how it is with divorce."

"I do," I said. I slid the work order form back into the desk drawer.

After we'd agreed on an amount, to which she insisted on adding another fifty — "For the inconvenience," she said — she returned the balance to the envelope, tucked it into her purse, and stood. "I'll see you this evening at eight, then," she said, holding out her hand.

I stood and took her hand. It was warm and strong, and ever so slightly work-roughened, perhaps by a hobby; I couldn't imagine her doing manual labour. "Where can I reach you if I, um, need to reach you?"

"My cellphone number is on the key tag." She indicated the keys on the desk. "In case I'm running late, you can let yourself aboard."

I walked her out into the studio. She jumped a little as the stairwell door opened and Bobbi Brooks, my business partner, came into the studio. Bobbi's eyebrows went up as Ms. Waverley went into the elevator.

"I'll see you at eight," Ms. Waverley said. The elevator door rattled shut on her.

"Who was that?" Bobbi asked, as she followed me into the office.

"A new client," I said.

"How lucky for you," she said.

"Indeed," I said.

"Her hair wasn't real, though." She sat down on the sofa next to Bodger, who grunted softly as she picked him up and cuddled him in her lap. "Or her boobs, probably," she added.

"Could've fooled me," I said.

"Not exactly a challenge. What did she want?" Bodger rumbled contentedly as Bobbi stroked his ears and I explained the job. When I was done, she said, "Not a problem. I've got nothing on till later this evening."

"Um," I said. "I thought I'd handle it."

She sighed. "Aren't you supposed to be meeting what's-his-name about his catalogue shoot?"

"What's-his-name" was the ex-Honourable Walter P. Moffat, former Member of Parliament for Vancouver Centre, the riding that encompassed downtown Vancouver and Granville Island. Wally the One-Term Wonder, as the media had dubbed him after he'd been roundly trounced in the most recent exercise in democratic futility, was a pal of Mary-Alice, my sister and our new junior partner, and her husband, Dr. David Paul. Moffat had contacted us through Mary-Alice about producing a catalogue of his art collection, which he evidently intended to send on tour to raise money for his wife's charitable foundation, something to do with children. However, first thing that morning a man named Woody Getz, who'd said he was Mr. Moffat's manager, had called to say that something had come up and Mr. Moffat couldn't make it.

"How lucky for you," Bobbi said again, when I told her.

"Yes, indeed." She smiled. "Here, deposit this some-place safe," I said, and handed her the cash Ms. Waverley had given me.

Cradling Bodger, she lifted her backside off the sofa and straight-armed the money into a front pocket of her jeans. Safe enough, I supposed. I certainly wouldn't have tried to take it away from her. While Bobbi wasn't what you'd call strapping — strapping implied, to me at least, a certain amount of, well, upper-body development and Bobbi was, truth be told, almost as flat as a boy — years of schlepping heavy photographic equipment around had made her as strong as many a man her size, stronger than some. Moreover, she had recently begun to study some form of martial art.

"Moffat hasn't changed his mind about the cata-logue, has he?" she asked worriedly.

"I don't know," I said. "I hope not." Neither of us had any idea what type of art Mr. Moffat collected — it could be dryer lint and chewing gum collages for all we cared — but business was a bit slow and we needed the work. "His manager just said he couldn't make it to-night, nothing about rescheduling."

The phone on my desk warbled. I pressed the speakerphone button. "Tom McCall," I said, just to be reassuring.

"Tell me it isn't so," my sister Mary-Alice said.

"Okay," I said. "It isn't so."

I could hear car horns in the background. She was calling on her cellphone, likely stuck in traffic on the Lions Gate Bridge. She normally didn't come in until af-ter the worst of the morning rush hour was over, and usually left before the worst began. The unseasonable fog had thrown rush hour off schedule, I supposed, with-out much sympathy.

"You don't know what I'm talking about, do you?" Mary-Alice said, in her best schoolmarm voice.

"That's right." I assumed she was referring to the cancellation of the appointment with the ex-Honourable Walter P. Moffat. "But whatever it is, it isn't my fault."

An exasperated sigh hissed from the phone speaker. "I just got off the phone with Jeanie Stone." Jeanie Stone was vice president of the British Columbia Association of Female Forestry Workers, the BCAFFW, for short.

"Oh-oh," Bobbi said under her breath.

"Tell me you didn't let her talk you into doing a nude calendar," Mary-Alice said.

"Okay. I didn't let her talk me into doing a nude calendar."

"Well, she seems to think she did," Mary-Alice said.

"Actually," I said, "she didn't have to." Bobbi groaned. I glared at her across the desk. "Anyway, they won't be nude," I said. "Not really. It's just pin-up girl stuff. With axes and chainsaws and logging machinery covering the important bits."

There was a momentary and very pregnant silence, followed by, "Oh, for god's sake, Tom."

"Look, Mary-Alice. I know it's lame, but —"

"Lame? It's bloody crippled. Ever since those damned women in England started it, it's been done to death by everyone from senior ladies' knitting circles to female hockey players."

"Relax, Mary-Alice," I said. "It's for a good cause, remember."

All proceeds from sales of the calendar were going to the Stanley Park restoration fund; on December 15, 2006, the one-thousand-acre, densely forested park had been savaged by a freak windstorm that had destroyed as many as ten thousand trees, leaving gaping wounds that would take decades to heal.

"Anyway," I added, "Jeanie's the client, isn't she? If

she and the other members of her association want to do a pin-up calendar, who are we to argue?" Before Mary-Alice could reply, the phone bleeped, indicating another call. "Hang on, M-A." I pressed the flash button before Mary-Alice could object. "Tom McCall," I said.

"Tom," another female voice said. "It's Jeanie Stone."

"Hi, Jeanie," I said.

"Tom, you guys want this job or not?" She was also calling on a cellphone, maybe from the middle of the woods, if the poor quality of the connection was any indication.

"Oh-oh," Bobbi said again, even more under her breath.

"Yes, Jeanie," I said. "We want the job."

"Then maybe you could get your sister off my case."

"She's just thinking about what's best for your organization's image, Jeanie," I said.

"What *she* thinks is best," Jeanie said. "Look, I get that she doesn't like our idea for the calendar, and maybe she's right that it isn't all that original, but it's our damned calendar, Tom. If we wanna do it in our skivvies, we'll bloody well do it in our skivvies. Or stark effing naked, for that matter. You guys aren't the only photographers in town, you know."

"I know, Jeanie, but —"

"Tom, I gotta go," Jeanie interrupted. "I'll come by the studio about seven, seven-thirty this evening. We'll work it out over a beer or two." The line went dead.

"Don't worry about it," Bobbi said. "She won't fire us. She likes you."

"She does?"

"God knows why." She pointed a finger at the phone. "Mary-Alice."

I pressed the flash button to switch back to Mary-Alice's call. "M-A? You still there?"

"Where the hell else would I be? The traffic hasn't moved a goddamned inch since you put me on hold. This fucking fog. Whoever heard of fog in June?" I heard the bleat of her little Beamer's horn. Mary-Alice wasn't the most impatient person on the lower mainland, but she was a close third. "Who were you talking to? Jeanie, right? God, *men*," she added disgustedly. "You just want to see her naked, don't you?" She then became the second person inside of a minute to hang up on me without letting me get a word in.

My fancy ergonomic chair wobbled and creaked as I slumped back with a sigh. The chair had been a parting gift from my co-workers at the *Vancouver Sun* when I'd left almost ten years before to start my own business, and it was showing its age. I knew how it felt, if I may be permitted to anthropomorphize.

"Do you want to see Jeanie naked?" Bobbi asked.

"What? No, of course not."

"Why not? She's very attractive. For a lumberjack."

"She's not a lumberjack."

"Lumberjill, then."

"She's a 'forestry worker.' She drives some kind of big machine that bites trees off at the roots." Bobbi was right, though: Jeanie was attractive, very much so, in a fierce and brawny kind of way, and I thought she'd make a very interesting study in black and white, clothed or not. I just didn't want to arm-wrestle her.

"If you want, I'll talk to her," Bobbi said. "So you can go shoot Ms. Phoney Boobs's boat."

I shook my head. "I'd better do it," I said. "Mary-Alice has really got Jeanie's feathers in an uproar. Would you mind doing the Waverley job?"

"Sure," she said with a shrug. "No problem."

"Thanks. All right, let's get to work. We've still got a lot of packing to do before the movers come on Saturday."

After nine years in the Davie Street studio we were moving to a storefront studio on Granville Island in False Creek, the narrow inlet that separates most of Vancouver from the West End and the downtown core. I lived in Sea Village, a small community of floating homes moored two deep along the quay between the Granville Island Hotel and the Emily Carr Institute of Art and Design. Granville Island was the former industrial heart of Vancouver, converted in the early seventies by the federal government to a trendy arts, recreation, shopping, and tourist area. It was still managed, with surprising competence, by the feds through the Canada Mortgage and Housing Corporation. The move was Mary-Alice's idea. I wasn't quite sure yet that I liked it.

I stood up. Bobbi didn't move. I sat down again. "What's the matter?" I asked. "Need I remind you that you thought relocating to Granville Island was a good idea?"

"That's not it," she said.

"So what's bothering you?"

"It's Greg."

Oh-oh, I thought. Greg was Detective Sergeant Gregory Matthias of the Vancouver PD Major Case Squad, Homicide Division. Bobbi and he had been seeing each other since they'd met the previous fall, during his investigation into the death of the man whose body I'd found on the roof deck of my house the morning after my fortieth birthday party. Had it become serious between them, I wondered, while I wasn't looking?

"What about him?" I asked cautiously. I tried to keep things between Bobbi and me strictly professional, generally with only moderate success, when I was successful at all.

"I think we've broken up," she said.

"What do you mean, you *think* you've broken up? Don't you know?"

"No." She shook her head, rather too vigorously, I thought. Her long, brown ponytail swished, like a horse swatting at flies.

The situation wasn't one with which I was familiar. Typically, when I broke up with someone, it was made abundantly clear, in no uncertain terms, that the party in question never wanted to see me again, ever. Linda, my former spouse, had hired lawyers to make her point. So far, to the best of my knowledge, none had hired a hit man. So far ...

"It was tough enough growing up with a cop," Bobbi said. Her father had retired a few months earlier from the Richmond RCMP detachment. "I thought dating one would be easier, but ..." She shrugged.

I looked at her. Her eyes were dry and slightly bloodshot, and the corners of her mouth drooped. When she put her heart into it, she had a megawatt smile, but I'd seen far too little of it lately. Now I knew why. "Does Greg know?" I asked.

"I think so," she said. "I'm not sure. We're having a late dinner to work it out."

"I'm really sorry, Bobbi," I said. "If there's anything I can do to, you know, well, help ..."

She stared at me in mock horror, as if my offer of aid in matters of the heart was akin to Willy Picton offering to cook barbecue. Then she smiled, releasing a couple of kilowatts. "It's no big deal, Tom. Win some, lose some. Thanks for caring, though."

"You're welcome," I said, thinking that maybe it was a bigger deal than she let on.

We got to work. Half an hour later, Mary-Alice arrived.

Mary-Alice was younger than me by slightly less than two years, but had always treated me as though I were her slightly slow younger brother. She had become a partner in January, buying fifteen percent and taking over the marketing and administrative aspects of the business, leaving Bobbi and me free to concentrate on the photographic and creative end of things. I was still the majority shareholder — Bobbi owned twenty-five percent — and remained more or less in charge, but I had gone along with Mary-Alice's proposal to relocate to Granville Island. Digital photography was putting a lot of traditional commercial photographers out of business, or at least forcing them to adapt. The new digs, which along with a studio space and a small darkroom, included a gallery and retail area, would allow us to tap the consumer and tourist trade, while still maintaining our commercial business. Bobbi was dead keen, as was D. Wayne Fowler, our lab guy, who was equally at home with traditional and digital photography, not to mention the computers, and was a fair hand with a camera himself. As I said, I wasn't sure ...

Especially considering the amount of junk we had accumulated over the years. A good deal of it went down the freight elevator and straight into the rented Dumpster or recycling bins, and we'd actually managed to get a few bucks for the old Wing-Lynch film and transparency processor, as well as for some of the redundant darkroom equipment, which had already been carted away by the buyers, but there was nevertheless a daunting amount of photographic and office equipment, furniture, file and storage cabinets, and miscellaneous bits and pieces to pack up before Saturday. By two o'clock, despite the best efforts of the four of us, we seemed hardly to have made a dent, so we took a break.

"Whose bright idea was this, anyway?" Mary-Alice wondered aloud as she collapsed onto the sofa in my office and raked webs of dust out of her pale blonde hair.

"YOURS!" Bobbi, Wayne, and I shouted in unison.

"Why the hell didn't you try to talk me out of it?"

"We did," I said. Wayne handed out cans of Coke.

"You should've tried harder," Mary-Alice said, nodding thanks. "You could have at least told me how much rubbish you had hidden away."

"I didn't realize myself how much there was," I said.

"I hope everything f-fits in the n-new place," Wayne said.

We put in another couple of hours, then ordered pizza, courtesy of Ms. Anna Waverley. Mary-Alice had given me a hard time about accepting a cash client, but I told her we did a fair amount of cash business and, yes, we declared it. I wasn't sure she believed me. Any more than she believed me when I told her I would try my best to talk Jeanie Stone out of doing a pin-up calendar. Mary-Alice subscribed to the philosophy that the customer — or the boss — was never right.

Bobbi hung around the studio with me for a while after Mary-Alice and Wayne left. The place looked as though a herd of hyperactive rhinos had stampeded through it — and back again. Bodger wouldn't come out from under the sofa, even for Bobbi.

"You still think this was a good idea?" I asked her.

"I'll miss this place," she said. "But, yeah, I think the move is a good thing. We were getting in a rut."

"I liked my rut," I said. "It was familiar, comfortable. It took me a long time to break it in." Truth be told, though, I had been feeling a vague sense of discontent of late, as if things weren't turning out quite the way I'd expected them to when I'd started the business. Nothing I could put my finger on, just a nebulous feeling that a change was in order — just not this one.

"What's the news from Hilly?" Bobbi asked.

"I got a postcard yesterday," I said. Hilly — short for Hillary — was my soon-to-turn fifteen-year-old daughter. She'd been in Australia since the fall, with her mother and her stepfather Jack, the Fat Food King of Southern Ontario. She liked it Down Under well enough, but was eager to get back home to Toronto and her friends. "She says hi."

"Say hi back."

"Will do," I said.

After a short silence, she said, "How's Reeny doing?"

"All right," I replied. "I guess."

"She's still in France, then?"

"Germany," I said.

Irene "Reeny" Lindsey was an actress I'd been seeing since the previous September. Except that I hadn't been seeing much of her in recent months. Reeny was the co-star of *Star Crossed*, a syndicated sword-and-sex sci-fi series in which she played Virgin, a time-travelling bounty hunter who'd come to present-day Earth with her companion and senior bounty hunter, Star, to track down evil shape-shifting alien outlaws and bring them to justice, generally shedding most of their clothing along the way. It was almost painfully cheesy, but it had earned Reeny and her co-star Richenda "Ricky" Rice a huge cult following, not to mention quite a few dollars. The third season was being shot in Germany.

"Uh, look at the time," I said. "You'd better saddle up."

"Right," Bobbi said.

I helped her lug her gear down to the van, although she didn't really need my help, then went back upstairs, got a Granville Island Lager out of the film fridge, another thing digital photography had made more or less obsolete, and put my feet up to await the arrival of Jeanie Stone. I hoped she wouldn't be too put off by the mess — and that she brought more beer.

chapter two

I was dreaming of Reeny when the telephone rang. In that weird way of dreams, the ringing was integrated into my dream, interrupting our lovemaking on the roof deck of my house, which became *Pendragon*, the old sailboat Reeny had lived on until it had burned to the waterline the year before. Linda, my former spouse, said, "Aren't you going to answer it?" as she sat naked on the ironing board in the kitchen of our first apartment, clipping her toenails. "No," I replied, bailing the water from the bilge of my house with a cowboy hat. The ringing continued, so I tumbled out of bed and stumbled down the hall into my home office to answer it.

"H'lo," I mumbled.

"Tom? It's Greg Matthias."

"Greg?" I peered at the clock radio on the bookcase under the window. It read 1:53 a.m. "What's wrong?"

"It's Bobbi," he said. "She's in Vancouver General emergency."

A jolt of adrenalin seared away the cobwebs. "What

happened? Is she all right?"

"She was found floating just offshore under the Burrard Street Bridge," he said. "We're not sure what happened, but it looks like she was attacked. She hasn't regained consciousness."

The Burrard Street Bridge spanned False Creek about a quarter kilometre west of Granville Island, a little more than a stone's throw from the marina where she'd gone to photograph Anna Waverley's boat.

"I'll be there in twenty minutes," I said.

Twenty-three minutes later I was standing with Greg Matthias beside Bobbi's bed in the emergency ward of the Vancouver General Hospital. She lay on her side, a tube down her throat, connected to an oxygen feed, and an IV in her arm, connected to an IV pump and a bag of clear fluid. Her face was a mass of raw, red abrasions, purpling bruises, and deep lacerations, some of which were closed with butterfly bandages, some with stitches. There was a strip of tape across the bridge of her nose and dried blood at the rims of her nostrils. Her eyes were swollen shut and beginning to blacken, and her left eyebrow was shaved partly away so a cut could be stitched. I could see the ends of black threads protruding like tiny worms from between her cruelly distended and discoloured lips and dried blood caked the corners of her mouth. A big gauze bandage bulged behind her right ear. A bundle of coloured wires snaked from the loose neck of her hospital gown, attached to electrodes glued to her chest. More electrodes were affixed to her head. A sensor was clipped to the tip of the first finger of her left hand. All were linked to machines that beeped softly and displayed her vital signs on colourful LCD screens that looked more like video games than medical monitors. I wanted to take her hand, but the knuckles of both hands were like raw hamburger and two fingers of her right hand were splinted.

"It was touch and go for a while," Matthias said. "She's stable now."

My gut was twisted in knots and my eyes burned. "When do they think she'll wake up?"

"They say it could be minutes, hours, or days. She's taken a terrible beating, Tom. There's no indication of major internal trauma, but they're worried about intra-cranial swelling. And there's no way of knowing how long she was in the water or how long her brain may have been deprived of oxygen. She's fortunate that it was an off-duty paramedic who found her. He was able to give her CPR right away and undoubtedly saved her life."

"Excuse me, gentlemen," a woman said behind us. Matthias and I turned to see a tiny Asian nurse who looked like a teenager but whose no-nonsense manner left no doubt about who was in charge. "Would you go back to the waiting room, please? The doctor would like to examine the patient. We'll let you know if there's any change."

"Have you called her father?" I asked, as we walked to the waiting room. Matthias was out of uniform, in jeans rather than his usual suit and tie.

"I tried," he said. "There was no answer. We asked the Richmond RCMP to send a car around to his home, but I haven't heard if they've found him."

There were two uniformed VPD cops in the waiting area. "When can we talk to her?" one of them asked Matthias.

"Obviously not till she wakes up," he replied.

"How long should we wait?"

"Why don't you go back out? Someone will let you know if there's a change."

The cops left. We were alone in the waiting area then, except for the triage nurse behind his Plexiglas window. I doubted it would be quiet for long. Matthias asked me if I wanted to risk a cup of coffee from a machine against the wall.

"Why not?" I said. "We're close to medical attention." He paid.

"Pardon me for sounding like a cop," Matthias said when we were seated with our coffee, "but was Bobbi working last night?"

I told him about Ms. Waverley and her boat. He made notes while I talked, then asked me to describe Ms. Waverley, which I did.

"Do you know if Bobbi met her at the marina?" he asked.

"No, I don't. She left the studio a little past seven and I haven't spoken to her since."

As I sipped the coffee, I remembered Bobbi telling me that she and Matthias were supposed to have had a late dinner to discuss their relationship. The coffee tasted awful, weak and bitter, but it was hot and I needed the caffeine. Obviously, Matthias and Bobbi hadn't met, so I didn't bring it up. I took another sip of coffee instead. It hadn't improved.

"Do you have an address for her?" Matthias said.

"Eh?"

"Anna Waverley. Do you have an address for her?"

I shook my head. "Only that she lives in Point Grey," I said. He made another note. "She paid cash up front," I told him. "I was supposed to do the job, but I had to meet with one of our other clients, so Bobbi took it."

"It's not your fault," Matthias said.

"Nevertheless, I feel responsible."

"I understand," he said. He looked as though he was having trouble framing his next question. I beat him to the punch.

"The client's name is Jeanie Stone. I'll have to get back to you with her contact information. She left a few minutes past nine. I got home around ten, watched a little

TV, and went to bed at eleven-thirty. Not much of an alibi, is it?"

"I've heard better," he said, smiling thinly. "Where did you meet with her?"

"At the studio," I said. I took a breath and asked, "Was she raped?"

Matthias shook his head. "It doesn't appear so."

"From the look of her hands, she must've put up a hell of a fight," I said. "Whoever attacked her wouldn't have escaped unscathed. That'll help you find the bastard, won't it? And convict him when you do?"

"Perhaps," Matthias said, in a voice like glass. "We ran an assault kit and took scrapings from under her fingernails, but the doctor who examined her thinks her hands were stomped on."

Anger rose in my throat. I swallowed it and drank some more of the cooling coffee, but it just made me more nauseous. There was a water fountain by the coffee machine. I got up, drank some water, then dumped the coffee into the drain and refilled the cup with water.

"Sorry," I said when I'd returned to my seat, not sure what I was apologizing for.

"It's me who should apologize," Matthias said, running his hand through his hair, which was the colour of wet sand. "I forget sometimes that not all my friends are cops."

I found it strangely reassuring that Greg Matthias thought of me as a friend, even though I didn't know him all that well. It made me feel as though my world was a slightly safer place somehow, until I remembered why I was sitting in the emergency waiting room of the hospital.

We turned at the sound of a commotion by the entrance to the ER. The two uniformed cops were confronting a heavyset, middle-aged man who was waving his arms and shouting, trying to push his way past them.

It was Norman Brooks. He'd put on weight since the last time I'd seen him.

"That's Bobbi's father," I said to Matthias.

"Yeah," Matthias said. "Christ, is he drunk?" He got up and went to the entrance. I followed. "It's all right," Matthias said to the uniformed cops. "I'll handle this."

"Who the fuck are you?" Norman Brooks demanded.

"Greg Matthias. I'm a detective sergeant with the Vancouver police. I'm also a friend of Bobbi's."

Brooks glared at me. His chin was stubbly and eyes were bloody and a match would have ignited the alcohol on his breath. Did he drive to the hospital in that condition? I wondered, with a feeling of horror.

"McCall," he barked. "Where's my daughter? What the hell's going on?"

Bobbi's father and I had never got on. The very first time we'd met, he'd evidently taken an instant dislike to me. I had no idea why; I'd always treated him with deference and respect, but to no apparent avail.

"Mr. Brooks," Matthias said, taking the older man by the arm, leading him toward the chairs. "Try to calm down, please. Would you like some coffee?"

"Take your hand off me," Norman Brooks said, trying unsuccessfully to wrench his arm from Matthias's grasp. "I want to see my daughter, goddamn it."

"Then settle down," Matthias said sternly. "Okay?" Brooks glared at him, face flushed. Matthias gave his arm a squeeze that made him wince. "*Okay?*"

"Yeah, okay," Brooks said.

"Because if you don't settle down, I'll have these officers arrest you for being drunk and disorderly and you'll spend the night in jail. Understand?"

"Yeah, yeah. I understand. Now let me see my daughter."

"Wait here," Matthias said to me, then led Brooks through the automatic doors into the examination area.

While I waited, the waiting room began to fill up. A man and a woman came arm-in-arm into the ER. They were in their fifties, I guessed, well-dressed and both more than a little inebriated. The knees of the man's light grey trousers were torn and bloody. They spent a few minutes talking with the triage nurse, then took seats in the waiting area. The woman asked the man if he wanted a cup of coffee. He said, "Yes." I wanted to tell him not to bother.

A few minutes later a scruffy-looking man came in, wearing filthy jeans, a ratty leather jacket, and a toque that looked as though it had been used to wash floors pulled down over his ears. He cradled his left hand, which was wrapped in a grease-blackened rag that dripped blood on the floor as he spoke with the triage nurse. He too was consigned to a seat in the waiting area.

A woman came in with her son, who looked about eight, and threw up twice while his mother shouted at the triage nurse. They were admitted immediately.

Matthias and Bobbi's father came back into the waiting room. Norman Brooks looked as though he wanted to kill someone. I couldn't blame him. Except that evidently the someone he wanted to kill was me. He lurched at me, lifted me out of my chair by the lapels of my jacket, and shoved me hard against the wall.

"You son of a bitch," he snarled into my face, breath sour, spittle flying. "This is your fault."

Matthias pulled him off me. Although he was shorter than Brooks, and not as heavy, he didn't have any trouble handling the bigger man. "Mr. Brooks," he said, marching him to a chair and pushing him down into it, while the middle-aged couple and the scruffy man watched cautiously. "I don't care if you used to be a cop. I will have you arrested if you don't pull yourself together. Mr. McCall had nothing to do with your daughter's attack. If you lay a hand on him again, I will make damned sure he presses charges against you for assault. Do you understand me, sir?"

"It's all right, Greg," I said. "He's upset. So would I be if it was my daughter lying in there."

"No, it's not all right. He's not doing anyone any good acting like a drunken bully. Bobbi or himself."

Brooks sneered. "I s'pose you think I should be grateful for your sympathy, eh, McCall? Well, I'm not. It's your goddamned fault she's in there."

"How is it my fault, sir? I didn't attack her."

He jerked his chin at Matthias. "He said she was working. You should've been with her."

"She's gone on dozens of jobs on her own," I said.

"Yeah, but it's just this one that counts, isn't it?" He waved me away. "Get out of here. Go. You're not needed here."

Anger boiled up in me. I wanted to hit him. "If anyone's not needed here, it's you," I said, teeth clenched so hard my jaw ached, fists knotted at my sides. "When was the last time you saw her? When was the last time you even spoke to her? She told me the other day she hasn't seen you in months and that the last time she did see you, you were drunk and feeling sorry for yourself."

Suddenly, he was on his feet, in my face again, before Matthias could stop him. "She's still my daughter," he shouted as I backed away from him. "There's fuck all you can do about that, you pissant faggot punk. Get out of here. You, too," he added to Matthias. "Neither of you has any right to be here."

I opened my mouth to tell him that I had just as much right to be here as he did, maybe more, but Matthias put his hand on my arm.

"Tom, there's nothing to be gained by arguing with him. Let's go. I know the staff here. They'll call me if there's any change in her condition."

Brooks smirked as Matthias led me toward the exit.

"Does he know you and Bobbi are seeing each other?" I asked, still seething, as we left the hospital.

"No, I don't think he does. Although I doubt right now it would make much difference to him."

"He must've been a hell of a cop," I said.

"Don't judge a man till you've walked in his shoes, Tom. As you said, what if it was your daughter in there?"

My anger evaporated.

"What's the problem between you and him, anyway?" Matthias asked.

"I don't know what his problem is," I said. "Mine seems to be him."

We rounded the corner onto Oak Street. His personal car, a Saab 950 Turbo, was parked in a restricted zone. I couldn't remember where I'd parked my Jeep Liberty, which I'd bought to replace my venerable old Land Rover. It was a few minutes after three. Sunrise was still two hours away.

"Do you want me to help you find your car?"

"No, it can't be far away. I'll just walk around till I find it."

"You're sure? I don't mind."

"Thanks, yeah, I'm okay. You'll call me when you hear something?"

"Of course. The RAS — Robbery and Assault Squad — investigators will likely want to talk to you."

"I'll be available," I said.

We shook hands. He got into his car and I went looking for mine. It didn't take me long to find it. Or the parking ticket under the wiper blade.

chapter three

I drove home, undressed, and got into bed. I was exhausted, but I couldn't sleep. My eyes kept sliding open and it was too great an effort to keep them closed. I got out of bed, went downstairs, and out of desperation made a cup of camomile tea from the box Reeny had left behind. After the first sip, I poured the vile stuff down the drain. I trudged upstairs and climbed back into bed, to lie staring into the dark for another hour, unable to erase the image of Bobbi, battered and bruised, surrounded by muttering machines, with tubes down her throat, needles inserted into her veins, and electrodes glued to her head and chest. I didn't know what frightened me more: that she might die, that she might never wake up, or that when she did wake up she wouldn't be Bobbi anymore.

I finally gave up trying to sleep, got out of bed, showered, dressed, and at ten past six was standing on the quay by the main entrance to Broker's Bay Marina. The sun was rising over the coastal mountains. The fog of the previous day had moved out and the cool morning air was so clean and clear it had an almost surreal quality, like cut crystal. Gulls wheeled and shrieked, squabbling over the carcass of a big fish in the water by Fisherman's Wharf. Above and behind me, thirty metres over Anderson Street and the entrance to Granville Island, morning traffic hummed and rumbled on the Granville Street Bridge, the deeper notes resonating in my chest cavity.

It hadn't been difficult to locate the *Wonderlust*. She was a fifty-foot-plus motor yacht, easily the largest pleasure boat in the marina, occupying the full length of the T at the end of the fourth and longest of the marina's eight floating docks, almost directly opposite Fisherman's Wharf. Although she was a bit dowdy and her chrome was dull and her hull grungy from neglect, she was a sturdy, well-equipped boat that would sleep eight without crowding. Although I was no expert, I guessed she would easily fetch a quarter of a million or more if she was cleaned up. It struck me as odd that Ms. Waverley had wanted photographs of the boat before she was shipshape. A few dollars invested in sprucing her up would have added considerably to the price.

The marina entrance was gated, but the gate was propped open, despite the sign that read "Do Not Prop Door" in large white lettering. I walked down the ramp and out to the end of the floating dock to where the *Wonderlust* was moored. I climbed the short, portable gangway onto the afterdeck, and knocked on the hatch to the main cabin. A few seconds later, I knocked again, harder. Then harder still. The hatch rattled in the frame. If Ms. Waverley was aboard, she was a very sound sleeper indeed. I tried the handle; the hatch was locked.

From the afterdeck of the *Wonderlust*, through a thick forest of masts and spars and booms, I could see the area under the Kitsilano end of the Burrard Street Bridge where Greg Matthias had told me Bobbi had been pulled from the water. The shoreline of Broker's Bay, from the western tip of Granville Island — technically not an island at all, but a mushroom-shaped peninsula joined to the Kitsilano mainland by a thick stem of land — around to the little park known as Cultural Harmony Grove just east of the Burrard Street Bridge, looked like one continuous marina. It was really three marinas: the Broker's Bay Marina, the False Creek Harbour Authority, and the Burrard Bridge Civic Marina. The latter extended a hundred metres beyond the bridge and had moorings directly beneath the span. I didn't know precisely where Bobbi had been found by the off-duty paramedic in his kayak, but I guessed it must have been somewhere near the docks under the bridge.

I returned to the quay.

Bobbi was supposed to have met Ms. Waverley on the *Wonderlust* at eight. Matthias had said she'd been found just past eleven. Where had she been between eight and eleven o'clock? What had she been doing under the bridge? Had she been fleeing from her attacker or attackers? Or had she been attacked somewhere else and dumped into False Creek under the bridge? At some point while I had lain abed and sleepless after returning from the hospital, it had occurred to me that I hadn't asked Matthias if the police had found the van. Had someone assaulted and dumped Bobbi in order to steal the van and the photo equipment? That didn't explain how Bobbi had ended up in the water under the bridge. She'd have parked the van in the nearby lot between the boat works and Bridges restaurant and pub. It wasn't there; I'd looked.

I was still standing on the quay at a few minutes to seven, wondering if I really wanted to walk around the bay to where Bobbi had been found, when a man in a red squall jacket and a Seattle Mariners baseball cap arrived to open the marina office. He wasn't alone. With him were two uniformed cops. The cops worked out of the Granville Island Community Police Office and I knew them both. Constable Mabel Firth was a friend, a strapping dirty blonde in her forties whose husband Bill also worked for the city. Mabel's partner, a former professional football player named Baz Tucker, was younger and bigger and blonder. Neither appeared pleased to see me.

"What're you doing here, Tom?" Mabel asked. Before I could reply, she said, "Go home. Let us do our job."

"I won't get in the way," I said.

"Since when?" she said.

"I just want to talk to Anna Waverley, the woman who owns that boat." I pointed toward the *Wonderlust*. "Bobbi was supposed to meet her last night, to take some photographs of the boat. Maybe she saw who attacked her."

"Have you spoken to her?"

"No. She's not aboard."

"Leave it to the RAS investigators, Tom. They'll be here in a minute. Go on home now," she said sternly, as if speaking to her ten-year-old. When it was obvious I wasn't going to leave, she said, "I understand how you feel, Tom. Bobbi's my friend, too. Look at it from our point of view. You could be a suspect yourself. I know," she added quickly, holding up her hand to cut off my response, "it's ridiculous, but tell that to the suits. As far as they know, you and Bobbi could've had a falling-out over business. It happens all the time. Or maybe you were more than just business partners and had a lover's quarrel. See how it can get complicated?"

"Heads up," Baz Tucker said quietly as two men came along the quay, dressed almost identically in suits so plain they were like uniforms.

"Which one of you is Firth?" the older of the two men asked. He was in his mid-fifties, with watery blue eyes and a pale, acne-scarred complexion. His partner was in his thirties, with a smooth, olive complexion, and full, almost voluptuous lips that I imagined many women would envy. There was nothing even remotely feminine about his piercing, dark eyes.

"I am," Mabel said.

"I'm Kovacs. He's Henshaw. Who's this guy?"

"Tom McCall," Mabel said. "The victim's partner."

"As in husband? Boyfriend?"

"Her business partner."

"Okay," Kovacs said. "But he still shouldn't be here."

"I told him that."

He turned to me. "We'll come find you when we need to talk with you."

"I'll save you the trouble," I said.

He turned his head slightly, squinted one pale blue eye and peered at me with the other. "Are we gonna have a problem with you?"

"A problem? With me? Heck, no." Mabel looked as though she wished she were home in bed.

He scowled and shrugged and said to Mabel and Tucker, "We can take it from here." He and his partner went into the marina office.

Mabel turned to me. "Go home."

"I'll just hang around out here till they're finished talking to the marina operator."

She heaved a sigh of resignation, then she and Baz left. A few minutes later, the detectives came out of the marina office.

"You still here?" Kovacs said.

"So it would appear," I replied, which earned me another scowl.

"Tell me about the woman who hired you to take pictures of her boat. What'd she look like?" I assumed Greg Matthias had passed on the information I'd given him.

"She had medium-length blonde hair," I said, "but her eyebrows were dark, almost black. She had an oval face with big green eyes and even features. Good teeth, except for a slightly crooked left upper incisor. She wore a little too much makeup perhaps, but she was quite attractive. In her early thirties. Say five-six in her bare feet. Well built, but Bobbi didn't think it was all natural. She may have been joking, though."

"That's a very detailed description," he said. "Mostly we get crap. You got a good eye. I suppose that comes with being a photographer."

"I suppose so," I said.

He consulted his notebook. "And she told you her name was Anna Waverley and that she got the boat as part of her divorce settlement."

"That's what she told me."

"Who's Bobby?"

"My partner, the victim. Bobbi — with an 'i' — Brooks."

"Right. Bobbi. Short for Roberta. Does she usually work alone?"

"Not always, but we both do from time to time, especially when we're busy. Depends on the job. I would have taken this one, but something came up with another client."

"Did Anna Waverley give you a billing address?"

"No. She paid cash. Something to do with her divorce. She told me she lived in Point Grey, or rather that she got the house in Point Grey in her divorce settlement, but I assumed she was staying on the boat. She isn't aboard now, though. She told me she had a possible buyer who was leaving for Hawaii today, which is why she needed the photographs last night."

"All right, thanks."

He nodded to his partner, then they both walked down the ramp onto the floating docks. I guessed the younger detective hadn't lived in Vancouver long, or else he hadn't spent much time on the water; he walked with the exaggerated care of a drunk as the linked sections of the floating docks rolled beneath his feet. As they climbed aboard the *Wonderlust*, I went into the marina office. The man with the Seattle Mariners baseball cap was behind the counter.

"I know you," he said. "You live in Sea Village, right? It was your house that almost sank a few years back, wasn't it?"

"It was," I confirmed.

"Bernie Simpson, the salvage guy who patched her up, he's my uncle."

Living on Granville Island was like living in a small town or a large goldfish bowl. Everybody knew everybody else's business. The residents of Sea Village were the only permanent residents, except for a few who lived (semi-illegally) on boats in the marinas. We tended to stand out and were frequently the subject of local gossip, not all of which was undeserved. A few years before, a small deadhead — not a Grateful Dead fan, but a water-saturated log that floats below the surface, usually more or less vertically — had drifted under my house. When the tide had gone out, the log had cracked the ferroconcrete hull and my house had begun to sink. The barman at Bridges had probably known about it before I had.

"Name's Witt DeWalt," the Mariners fan said, sticking out his hand. "What can I do for you?"

I introduced myself and said, "Did the police tell you that a woman was assaulted near here last night?"

"Yeah. They did." He shook his head slowly. "Terrible."

"The woman who was assaulted is one of my closest friends and my business partner. We're commercial photographers. We were hired to take photos of Ms. Waverley's boat. Bobbi, my partner, she was supposed to meet Ms. Waverley here at eight last night. You didn't happen to see anything, did you?"

"Sorry. I got off at six. But you sure you got the right boat? The police asked about the *Wonderlust*."

"That's right."

"Well, like I told them, there must be some kind of mistake, then. The Waverleys don't own that boat. It's owned by some company that's just a number. They've been trying to sell it for months, except they haven't been taking care of it. The Waverleys have a sailboat." He waved in the general direction of the docks. "Thirty-eight-foot Sabre called *Free Spirit*. They don't use it much, either, but take better care of it."

"Anna Waverley," I said. "Is she blonde, about thirty, with green eyes and, um, a full figure?"

Witt DeWalt shook his head. "Not even close. She's at least forty, maybe a bit more. Slim on top, a bit huskier down below. What you might call a low centre of gravity, but not fat or anything. A runner. I don't remember what colour her eyes are, but her hair's a dark red. Auburn, I guess you'd call it. About this long." He held his hand level, just below his earlobe, and sliced it back and forth. "Good-looking woman. Handsome, you might say. Always friendly, too, although she doesn't smile much."

"Do the Waverleys come around here often?"

"They haven't kept the Sabre here long, just since the winter before last. But, like I said, they haven't used it much. I don't think it's been out in months. Mrs. Waverley comes by in the evenings couple of times a week. Just to check her out, I guess."

"Where does she live?"

He looked uncertain. "Point Grey," he said. "But, look, I'm sure Mrs. Waverley didn't have anything to do with your friend getting hurt."

"You're probably right," I said. "Mr. Waverley, what does he do?"

"No idea. Whatever it is, though, he must do all right to have a house in Point Grey and that boat."

"What's he like?"

"Only seen him a couple of times. Seems friendly enough. About sixty, sixty-five, a little on the chunky side, but not obese or anything. Lotsa hair. Might even be his. Both times I seen him he was wearing a suit that looked like it cost as much as my car. He drives a big Mercedes."

"I appreciate your help," I said.

"No problem," he said.

I hesitated, then said, "Can you give me the Waverleys' address? I promise no one will know where I got it."

He shook his head. "Look, man, I'm sorry about your friend and all, but it would be my ass — not to mention my job — if my boss ever found out I gave out the addresses of the people who keep boats here."

"Just this one," I said.

"Sorry. No can do. There must be some other way you can get it. Maybe they're in the book."

"You gave it to the police."

"Sure, but that's different, isn't it?"

I didn't press him. When I went outside, the two detectives were climbing the ramp from the docks. The younger detective looked relieved to be on solid ground again.

"Look," Kovacs said to me. "I appreciate that the victim is your friend, and that you're a pal of Constable Firth and Greg Matthias, but neither one of them will be a help to you if you interfere with our investigation. Am I making myself clear?"

"Yes, you are," I said. "I have no intention of interfering with your investigation, but I don't think you can do a damned thing to stop me from talking to people."

"Don't count on it."

"Can I ask you a question?"

"You can ask," he said. "No guarantee I'll answer."

"Bobbi was driving our van. A white '94 Dodge Ram. She also had a few thousand dollars' worth of photo equipment with her. I don't give a damn about the van or the equipment — it's all insured — but if either turns up it'll provide you with a lead, won't it? Have you found the van?"

Kovacs shook his head. "I haven't heard," he said. "Give me the plate number."

I gave him the van's license number, which he wrote in his notebook. "I'll have to look in my files to give you any information about the equipment. Can I fax it to you?"

Kovacs wrote something on the back of a card. "That's the case number," he said, handing me the card. "Write it on each page of the fax. Are we done?"

"Just one more thing, if you don't mind."

"Why should I mind?"

I told him what Witt DeWalt had told me, that Anna Waverley didn't own the *Wonderlust*, and that the woman who'd hired us probably hadn't been Anna Waverley.

Kovacs nodded. "Yeah, so what's your question?"

"If the people who own that boat didn't hire us, who did? And why?"

"Yeah," Kovacs said again. "Good question. The woman who called herself Anna Waverley, she touch anything while she was in your office?"

"Now that you mention it, no, I don't think she did."

"She paid you in cash. What about the money?"

"We used a couple of twenties to pay for pizza last night. The rest Bobbi may have still had on her."

"So fingerprints are out. How much money are we talking about?"

"Not a lot. Two hundred and fifty."

"We'll put out a description of the woman, but if it

was a set-up, chances are she altered her appearance. Did she seem upset or disconcerted at all that your partner was going to meet her here, not you?"

"As far as she knew, I was going to meet her, not Bobbi."

"We'll canvass the area to see if anyone saw your partner here last evening," Kovacs said. "Do you have any idea why anyone would want to set you or her up like this?"

"You mean you think it was just a ploy to get Bobbi or me, or perhaps both of us, here to beat us up?" Or worse …

"It's a possibility," Kovacs said. "Sergeant Matthias told me you've had your share of excitement in the last couple of years. Trouble tends to follow you around, he says. Usually wearing a skirt. Figuratively speaking, of course. It's been a while since I've seen a woman in a skirt."

"Maybe you hang out with the wrong crowd."

"No doubt about it," he agreed. "So have either you or Bobbi pissed anyone off lately?" He said it as though he'd be surprised I hadn't.

"No one who would hurt her like that." As far as I knew, Vince Ryan was still in the wind, and since I'd thrown a wrench into his resort development deal in Whistler a few years earlier, he might think he had reason enough to beat the crap out of me and throw me into False Creek to drown. He was certainly crazy enough. As crazy as he was, though, he had nothing against Bobbi. Chris Hastings, Reeny Lindsey's old boyfriend, was also out there somewhere, but he had even less reason to hurt Bobbi.

"What about ex-boyfriends?" Kovacs asked. "She break anyone's heart lately? Or their balls?"

"Well, there was a guy she was living with three or four years ago," I said. "An artist named Tony Chan. He tapped her credits cards out to the tune of about twenty thousand dollars, and she sued him. The van she was driving last night used to be his. He might hold a grudge, but the last we heard, he was doing okay."

He made a note. "That's it? No one else?"

Besides Greg Matthias? I wondered. "Not that I can think of."

"Well, if you do think of anyone else, you'll let me know?"

"Of course."

"And," he added emphatically, "don't go poking your nose where it doesn't belong."

"Certainly not," I said. From his expression, it was obvious he didn't believe me.

chapter four

It was after nine by the time I staggered off the elevator into the studio, eyes grainy, feeling as though I hadn't slept in a month. My exhaustion must have been plain to see, because even Mary-Alice noticed it.

"You look terrible," she said. "What were you up to last night?"

"And a good morning to you, too, Mary-Alice."

"Did Jeanie Stone give you a bad time? Please tell me you managed to talk her into keeping her clothes on for the calendar."

"Most of them," I said.

She regarded me with a mixture of exasperation and disappointment. "Poor Tom. Any judgment you possess goes straight out the window at the thought of photographing women without their clothes on, doesn't it?"

"Oh, fuck off, Mary-Alice," I said wearily.

She stared at me, eyes wide. "My, aren't we Mr. Grumpy Pants this morning."

"Sorry, Mary-Alice," I said. "I've had a tough night."

"Is there something wrong? Did something happen? Oh, god, it's not Hilly, is it?"

"No. Hilly's fine. Where's Wayne?"

"He's in the back," she replied. "Why?"

"There's something I need to tell you both."

"What?" I looked at her and waited. I didn't want to have to go through it twice. "I'll go get him," she said, finally getting the hint.

While Mary-Alice was fetching Wayne, I looked up the number of the Vancouver General Hospital. Wayne and Mary-Alice came into the office as I was dialling. I hung up before the call went through. There was no point in beating around the bush.

"Bobbi was attacked last night," I said. "She's in the hospital."

Wayne's face went white.

"Oh my god," Mary-Alice said. "What happened?"

"She was beaten up and dumped into False Creek under the Burrard Street Bridge."

"Is she g-g-going to b-be all r-r-right?" Wayne said, his stammer worsened by the stress.

"God, was she raped?" Mary-Alice asked.

"No, she wasn't raped. But she was still unconscious when I left the hospital at three this morning. I'm going to call now."

I pressed the redial button on the phone while Wayne and Mary-Alice watched. Wayne was almost wringing his hands with worry. When he'd first started working for us, he'd developed a terrible crush on Bobbi and was rendered almost incoherent in her presence. He was mostly over it, but from time to time I suspected that it had grown into something deeper and stronger, albeit unrequited. With a sudden cold clench of dread, I wondered if his frustration had finally got the better of him. I immediately rejected the idea as absurd; Wayne couldn't have done that to Bobbi. The police didn't know him as well as I did, though. I hoped he had a better alibi that I did.

I finally got past the hospital's automated phone system to a human being, who told me that Roberta Brooks had been admitted, and transferred me to the appropriate nursing station, where I had to navigate yet another set of menus to get an actual nurse. I lied then, telling the nurse that I was Bobbi's brother, otherwise she wouldn't have given me the time of day. Miss Brooks was still in a coma, the nurse said, but otherwise stable. Scans indicated there were no overt signs of brain damage, but in such cases it wasn't unusual for the patient to remain in a coma for a few days while the system healed itself.

"Your father's with her now," she said. "Do you want to talk to him?"

"Um, no, it's all right," I said.

"I was hoping you could persuade him to go home."

"Not much chance of that," I said. "We don't get along. It might be a good idea not to mention that I called. It would just upset him."

"We wouldn't want that, would we?" she said, sounding as though she'd seen through my ruse. She hung up.

"Is she going to b-be all right?" Wayne asked.

I repeated what the nurse had told me. It didn't seem to reassure him. He naturally wanted to go to the hospital immediately. "There's nothing you can do," I said. "She won't even know you're there."

"They say that p-people in comas are aware of what g-goes on around them," Wayne said.

"Maybe that's true," I said. "I don't know."

I wanted to be with her, too, so that someone she knew, besides her father, would be there when she woke up. Was it fair to tell Wayne not to go? Probably not. Definitely not, given how he felt about her. Let him get it out of his system, I thought. He'd be next to useless until he did. Besides, what could it hurt? There was something he wanted to get off his chest before he left, though.

"She shouldn't have been alone," he said, an edge of angry disapproval in his voice.

"In retrospect, you're probably right," I said. "But what do you think she'd have said if you'd said that to her?"

"Uh, she'd have t-told me to stick it in my eye."

"I'm not sure she'd have picked that particular part of your anatomy," I said. "But she wouldn't have appreciated any suggestion that she isn't capable of looking after herself."

"Especially since she started taking those stupid karate lessons," Mary-Alice said.

"She was studying k-kung fu," Wayne said.

"Kung fu, feng shui," Mary-Alice said dismissively. "Whatever, maybe it made her overconfident and she tried to fight rather than just let them take the goddamned truck and camera equipment."

"I'm not sure robbery was the motive behind the attack," I said. They both looked at me. "The woman who hired us to photograph the *Wonderlust* wasn't the owner of the boat. The real owner is some numbered corporation. Anna Waverley likely wasn't her real name, either. The real Anna Waverley is older. She and her husband own a sailboat at the same marina, though."

"Waverley," Mary-Alice said. "There's something familiar about that name. I've heard it before."

"Like here, yesterday?" I suggested.

She shook her head. "No. I'm sure I've heard it somewhere else. I can't put my finger on it." She shrugged. "Maybe her husband is one of David's patients."

"Why w-would someone hire us to t-take photographs of a b-boat they don't own?" Wayne asked.

"I haven't any idea. The police think it may have been a set-up to lure me or Bobbi — or maybe both of us — into a trap."

"You can be a jerk sometimes, Tom," my sister said. "But who would want to hurt you that much, or — better yet — Bobbi?"

"Another good question I don't have an answer for," I said.

In the end, Wayne went to see Bobbi, but was back within an hour. Bobbi was in the ICU, he reported, and only immediate family members were allowed to visit. She was still in a coma, but according to the nurse he talked to, she was stable, out of any immediate danger, and would probably be released from the ICU in a day or two.

"Was her father with her?" I asked.

"I d-don't think so."

If he wasn't there, maybe later I could try passing myself off as her brother again.

We got back to work. At a few minutes past 1:30, Greg Matthias emerged from the elevator into the studio, sandy eyebrows rising at the mess. A semi-official visit, he said, explaining that they were treating Bobbi's case as attempted murder, given the circumstances. Due to his association with Bobbi and me, he wasn't the primary investigator, but his rank and seniority afforded him certain privileges. After he told me that there hadn't been any change in Bobbi's condition, I told him what I'd learned about Anna and Samuel Waverley from the marina operator that morning, and about my subsequent conversation with Detective Kovacs.

"Jim Kovacs is a good guy," Matthias said. "And a good cop. But he doesn't take kindly to civilians getting in the way of his investigations. None of us do, really."

"I'll be careful," I said.

Matthias smiled thinly. "Kovacs and Henshaw interviewed the real Anna Waverley at her home in Point Grey this morning. The description you got from the marina operator is accurate as far at it goes. Kovacs de-

scribed her to me as quite attractive, but cool and somewhat patronizing. 'A redheaded ice queen' is how he put
it. Her husband, Samuel, is a fine art and antiques dealer.
He has a gallery in Gastown. However, according Mrs.
Waverley, he's away on a buying trip in Europe with his
assistant, a woman named Doris Greenwood, and isn't
due back for a week. Kovacs got the impression she
wasn't overjoyed that her husband was travelling around
Europe with another woman, but that she wasn't too upset by it, either. I don't suppose it will come as any surprise to you that she denies hiring you to take pictures of
the *Wonderlust*. She's never heard of you and has no idea
why anyone would impersonate her to sell it, especially
as she doesn't own it."

"Does she know who does own it?"

"She confirms what you learned from the marina operator, that it's owned by a numbered corporation and
that they've been trying to sell it for some time. In the
meantime, they rent it out for parties, business meetings,
and such. She and her husband have been on it a couple
of times, she says, but she has no idea who the real owner
is. Kovacs isn't sure he believes her," he added.

"How reliable are his instincts?" I asked.

"After a while in this game, you get so you can read
people. If he thinks she's lying about something, she
likely is."

"Where was she last night?"

"When she was asked to account for her where-
abouts, Kovacs said she was mildly offended, but she
answered. She told him she runs from Jericho Beach to
Granville Island and back a couple of times a week, usually stopping to check on the sailboat she and her husband keep in the same marina, before returning along the
same route. Last evening she got to the marina around
nine, a little later than usual, spent half an hour or so on
her boat, then headed back. She didn't talk to anyone

and couldn't say if anyone saw her or would remember her if they did."

"If she runs along the shoreline path," I said, "she'd have gone right by the place where Bobbi was found."

"Kovacs says that when he pointed that out she was quite upset that she might have gone right past someone in the water without noticing. But the path is more than fifty metres back from the water at that point. Unless she detoured along the path through Cultural Harmony Grove east of the bridge, she couldn't possibly have seen anything. Besides, the off-duty paramedic found Bobbi just before eleven and neither he or the doctors think she was in the water for more than twenty minutes to half an hour."

"It doesn't take half an hour to drown, does it?"

"No. Just a couple of minutes. The paramedic found her near shore by the docks under the bridge. Maybe whoever attacked her didn't want to get his feet wet and dumped her in the shallows hoping the tide would take her out. High tide was at eleven-fifteen or so. Or maybe she just fell and lay unconscious as the tide came in. Either way, if the paramedic hadn't found her, she'd have certainly drowned."

"How did he find her?"

"He was kayaking."

"At eleven o'clock at night?"

"He works odd shifts."

"Is there any sign of the van?" I asked.

He shook his head. "Not yet. You should probably make an official report so you can start the insurance process."

"I faxed a copy of the registration and the serial numbers of the cameras and a list of the other equipment she had with her to Kovacs this morning." Along with the van, our "new" Nikon digital SLR and Bobbi's older Canon 35 mm SLR were also missing, as well as tripods, a couple of slave strobe flash units and stands, plus miscellaneous lenses, light meters, battery packs and chargers, cables, and whatever else Bobbi hauled around with her. "I'll call the insurance company this afternoon and see what else I need."

Matthias stood. "I'll need to talk to Wayne Fowler and your sister."

"They're in the back, packing files," I said, standing as well.

"Are you going to see Bobbi later?" he asked, as we went out into the studio.

"If I can," I said. "I don't feel like going another round with her father, though."

"Can't say as I blame you. I'm going to try to drop by around six. Why don't you meet me there? Safety in numbers."

"All right, I will," I said.

We went into the back room. The rotating "light lock" door to the darkroom had been removed and stood forlornly in its frame against a wall, yet another victim of the Digital Age; we hadn't been able to find anyone who wanted it and there wasn't space for it at the new studio. Wayne and Mary-Alice were in the darkroom, filling a couple of cartons with plastic jugs, bottles, and cans of old chemicals to be hauled to the hazardous waste recycling depot.

"I'll leave you to it," I said to Matthias.

We shook hands and I returned to my office to continue cleaning out my desk. A few minutes later, Mary-Alice came into my office.

"Greg seems to be handling it well," she said. "Wayne's a basket case, though."

"He'll be fine," I said.

"How about you?"

"What about me?"

"Come on, Tom. I'm not a complete idiot, no matter what you think. I know how you feel about Bobbi."

"I'm not sure you do," I said.

"You're in love with her."

"Oh, for Pete's sake, Mary-Alice. Bobbi is my friend and, yes, I probably love her. Maybe not quite as much as I love Hilly, and maybe not even as much as I love you. But I am not in love with her. Not in the sense you mean. Romantically."

"Bullshit. Do you expect me to believe that you and Bobbi have worked together for almost ten years without sleeping together even once?"

"I can't help what you believe, Mary-Alice."

"What's that supposed to mean?"

"Just what it sounds like," I said.

The year before, Mary-Alice had been convinced that her husband David had been having an affair with his nurse/receptionist, and two years before that, that our father, a retired engineer, had been having an affair with Maggie Urquhart, my Sea Village neighbour. The latter suspicion had proved, at least so far as I was concerned, to be unfounded; I had no opinion about the former. Mary-Alice's faith in her own infallibility was as unshakeable as the Pope's. Of course, just because Mary-Alice, or the Pope for that matter, believed something to be true didn't necessarily make it not true, although in this case, she was dead wrong.

I ushered her to the door of the office and out into the studio. "We've still got a lot to do by Saturday," I said, but I could tell from her expression that the subject was only temporarily closed.

chapter five

I left the studio at a little past three, hoping to catch a short nap, a shower, and a bite to eat before meeting Greg Matthias at the hospital at six. There were a number of things I wouldn't miss about the Davie Street studio: the creaky, unreliable freight elevator; the leaky windows; Dingy Bill, the incontinent homeless man who occasionally camped out in the stairwell; and clients' complaints that they could never find parking. One of the things I would miss, however, was the twice-daily commute to and from work. The half-kilometre morning walk from my house to the Aquabus dock by the Public Market, the short ferry ride across False Creek, and the slightly longer hike from the ferry dock at the foot of Hornby Street to the studio gave me time to switch mental gears and prepare myself for the daily grind. The return trip at the end of the day helped me relax and recharge my depleted psychic batteries. And it was about the only exercise I got. The new studio space was at most a five-minute walk from home, hardly time at all to change modes, recharge batteries, or burn off a pint of Granville Island Lager.

Disembarking from the tubby little Aquabus ferry at the dock by the public market, I climbed the steps to the quay and trudged toward home along Johnston Street, past the Ocean cement plant, one of the last vestiges of Granville Island's industrial past, and the Emily Carr Institute of Art and Design, where a pair of students were wrapping another in clear plastic packing tape while a fourth video recorded the process. I might have paused to watch, just to see if I could figure out what the hell they were doing, and why, but I was so tired that all I could focus on was the siren song of the sofa in my living room. As I angled across the parking lot toward the ramp down to the Sea Village docks, I saw Loth sitting on the end of the raised pad of the old freight crane in the middle of the lot, drinking something from a brown paper bag. Unfortunately, Loth also saw me.

Loth — I didn't know if it was his first name or his last — had been loitering about Granville Island since the New Year. He was a huge old man, seventy if he was a day, two or three inches shy of seven feet tall and weighing in at three hundred pounds or more. He was immensely strong. I'd seen him lift the rear end of a Ford Focus clear off the ground, for reasons known only to him. There was a rumour making the rounds that he was an ex-con, recently released from the Kent Institution, the federal maximum-security prison in Agassiz, the Corn Capital of B.C., where he'd been serving time for manslaughter. I'd never put much stock in it.

"You, mister man," Loth called out as he dropped his paper bag with a glassy thud onto the pavement and heaved himself off the crane pad. He loomed toward me, his stout wood cane bowing under his massive weight. "Any work you got?"

"What?" I asked.

"Work. You got work?"

"For you, you mean?" I said, backing away from him.

He kept coming and I kept backing away. He was huge. And he had a body odour that would peel paint, an overpowering mix of dried sweat, urine, and what smelled like rotting meat. I imagined that the only reason he wasn't surrounded by flies was that any fly that got too close would instantly drop dead from the toxic stink.

"O' course for me. Who else you see, yeah?" He waved his cane. "I paint good. Carpenter, too."

"Sorry," I said. "No." He accepted it with a shrug.

"I hear about yer fran, yeah?" he said.

"My what?"

"Yer fran," he repeated. "Mouthy cunt with no tits. Someone beat her up good, yeah." He laughed and the alcohol fumes on his breath made my eyes water. "Mebbe now she learn to keep her mouth shut, 'cept when she sucks on men's dicks, yeah."

He howled with laughter and, leaning on his cane, shambled off across the lot toward the Granville Island Hotel to entertain the guests there. My heart was thudding and I realized I was holding my breath. *What part of fight or flight was that?* I wondered.

I picked up the bottle and paper bag he'd discarded and headed toward the ramp down to Sea Village and the safety of home. Home was a small, two-storey cedar-plank cottage, painted forest green and built on a reinforced concrete hull. The roof was flat, a deck surrounded by a cedar railing, the access shed sticking up in one corner like an afterthought. It had three bedrooms, one and a half baths, a practical kitchen, and a small sunken living room containing the aforementioned sofa.

As I started down the ramp, someone called, "Mr. McCall, oh, Mr. McCall." I turned to see a man striding toward me along the quayside, briefcase dangling from one hand, BlackBerry clutched in the other. His name was Blake Darling and he claimed to be a real estate broker. He was as slick and slippery as he looked in his natty yellow jacket. Ignoring him, I started down the ramp again.

"Wait, sir, please," he called. "Just a moment of your time."

"I have nothing more to say to you, Mr. Darling," I said. "Nothing has changed. I wasn't interested in selling yesterday, I'm not interested today, and I won't be interested tomorrow. Neither are any of my neighbours. Give it up. You're only wasting your time, and your client's money."

"I never waste either," he said. His voice was high-pitched and grated on the ear like feedback from a cheap guitar amp. "Time is money, as they say. Feel free to ask any of my clients if they've gotten their money's worth. My list of satisfied clients is quite long."

"You're becoming a nuisance," I said. "Some of my neighbours are talking about applying for a restraining order against you."

"They'd just be wasting their time," he said.

"Look, why can't you get it through your head that none of us is interested in selling our shares in Sea Village?" Which was the only way to acquire a house moorage, as there was no room to expand along the quayside.

"My client is a very determined man, Mr. McCall. He usually gets what he wants." He chortled and smiled, as if at some secret joke. "He didn't get to where he is today by taking no for an answer. Neither did I."

"Well, I hope he — and you — can handle the disappointment," I said. "But even if someone was willing to sell, your client, whoever he is, would likely never be approved by the board, of which we are all members. To paraphrase Groucho Marx, Mr. Darling, anyone who'd hire someone like you to represent him isn't the kind of neighbour we want."

"There's no need to be rude about it."

"Nothing else seems to have worked."

"You haven't heard the latest offer."

"I don't want to. It doesn't matter. Go away."

"It's a very good offer," he said.

"Whatever it is," I said, knowing it was pointless to try to get the last word, "it won't be good enough."

"How will you know until you hear it?"

"Good day, Mr. Darling." I turned and walked down the ramp to the floating docks.

"I won't give up, Mr. McCall," he called out to my back.

I wondered if Loth was available for part-time security work.

"You think this Loth character might be the one who attacked Bobbi?" Greg Matthias said quietly. We were in Bobbi's room. She was out of intensive care, but still in a coma and hooked up to an IV pump and monitors. She was in a semiprivate, but the other bed was unoccupied.

"Detective Kovacs asked me if we'd pissed anyone off lately," I said. It wasn't until my encounter with Loth that afternoon that I'd remembered Bobbi tearing a strip off him at the Public Market a few weeks before; he'd been making fun of a wheelchair-bound little person named Francis Peever, who taught at the Emily Carr Institute. "Loth looked like he was ready to kill her before Mabel and Baz arrived to break things up. And he strikes me as the kind who might hold a grudge."

"Does he strike you as the kind who would send a woman made up like Marilyn Monroe to lure you to the marina in order to beat the living daylights out of you?"

"Well, no, when you put it that way," I conceded.

He scratched a note in his book. "We'll check him out."

On the bed Bobbi whimpered and stirred, setting off a flurry of bleeps from the machines, then lay still and quiet again. Presently, the machines settled down again, too.

"The doctors say that's a good sign," Matthias said.

"I hope they're right."

I'd been thinking about what Mary-Alice had said. I was reasonably certain I wasn't in love with Bobbi, but I was also reasonably certain that I couldn't be absolutely certain I wasn't. Naturally, because Bobbi was a very attractive woman, in a wholesome girl-next-door kind of way, I'd entertained the possibility of a romantic relationship, but I'd never considered it very seriously for very long. In point of fact, I suspected that if I suggested it, in all likelihood Bobbi would laugh, which would tend to dampen my enthusiasm.

There was no doubt in my mind, however, that I would be equally willing to throw myself in front of a bus to save her as I would to save my daughter Hilly, Mary-Alice, or even my former spouse, Linda. (I hoped it would never be necessary, particularly in Linda's case; she'd just think I was trying to weasel out of paying child support.) As I looked down at Bobbi lying in that hospital bed, battered and bruised and comatose, I also knew for a certainty that if whatever or whoever was in charge of the particular dimension of reality in which we lived offered me the opportunity to change places with her, I'd do it in a nanosecond. From the expression on Greg Matthias's face, I suspected he would, too.

I just didn't want to marry her.

Or have Norman Brooks for a father-in-law.

"What are you doing here?" he demanded as he came into Bobbi's room. "I thought I told you not to come around last night."

"You didn't, as a matter of fact," I said. "You told me to leave. Not the same thing at all."

"Well, I'm telling you now. Get out and don't come back."

"Are you drunk?"

"Get him out of here," he barked to Matthias.

"I think Bobbi would want him here," Matthias said.

"I don't give a fuck what you think," Brooks snapped back. "I don't want him here."

"Then I guess you don't care what Bobbi thinks, either," I said.

Brooks's face clouded with rage. Matthias took my arm. I shook his hand off.

"What the hell is your problem?" I demanded.

"You are," Brooks snarled. "I don't like you …"

"I get that," I said. "But why? What did I ever do to you?"

"You're a punk. You and the kind of people you associate with. You damn near got my daughter killed."

"That's not —" I was going to say he wasn't being fair, that it wasn't my fault that Bobbi had been hurt, that it could have just as easily been me lying in that hospital bed, but Matthias gripped my arm again.

"Let's go," he said, giving my arm a brief squeeze for emphasis. There was no shaking him off this time.

Outside Bobbi's room I said, "I'm getting damned sick of that guy."

"Look, let's go have a beer," Matthias said. "How about that place near where you live? Bridges. I haven't had anything to eat since breakfast. I hear they do good burgers."

So we got in our respective vehicles and drove to Granville Island. Bridges was busy, but we were able to find a seat on the terrace overlooking the marina. From where we sat we could see the *Wonderlust*. We could also see the point under the Burrard Street Bridge where

Bobbi had been found. Neither of us spoke, except to the waitress, until she had taken our order. Then Matthias asked:

"What's Norman Brooks got against you?"

"I wish I knew," I said. "He obviously blames me for what happened to Bobbi. I suppose that's understandable. In some way I guess I am, but — shit, you don't think he thinks I did it, do you?"

"I don't know. It's possible. You don't have the best alibi I've ever heard. You and Bobbi are getting along all right?"

"Sure."

He cocked an eyebrow. "But …"

"No but," I said. "We're getting along fine. At least, I think we are. Why? Has she said anything to you?"

"No, but she might have said something to her father."

"They don't talk much," I said.

"Well, whatever it is, it's clear he doesn't have much use for you — or your friends," he added with a wry smile.

Our beers arrived, and his hamburger, a fat half-pound charcoal-grilled patty in a crusty Kaiser, with onions, tomato, and mushrooms. He tucked in.

"Good," he said after a few bites. He ate a few more mouthfuls, drank some beer, wiped mustard off his chin, then said, "Let's change the subject. How's your daughter? Hilly, right? Is she back from Australia yet?"

"She's not due back till the fall," I said.

"She's what, sixteen?"

"She'll be fifteen in August."

"You must miss her."

"I do," I said. "She usually spends a good part of the summer with me. This is the first summer in nine years she hasn't been with me." I sipped my beer.

"How's Reeny doing?" he asked, after washing down a mouthful of burger.

"Fine. She's still in Europe."

"But you two are, um, still together, aren't you?"

"To be honest," I said. "I don't really know. We like each other — a lot, I think — and we get along, but the last time we spoke on the phone we both agreed there was something missing. I'm not sure what, though." Maybe love, I added to myself.

Matthias nodded. "That's essentially how it is between Bobbi and me," he said. He gestured toward my almost finished beer. "Want another?"

I shook my head. "Thanks, but I think I'll call it a night." I started to take out my wallet.

"My treat," he said.

I thanked him and left him there with the remains of his burger and his beer.

As I left the pub I saw Eddy Porter sitting on a bench, looking woebegone as he stared out at the boat traffic on False Creek.

"Why so glum, Eddy?" I asked. I should've known better.

"Apophis is coming," he said.

"Who?"

"Not who. What. Apophis is a near-Earth asteroid. It's going to hit the Earth in 2036."

"Oh," I said. "We still have plenty of time to stock up on bottled water and freeze-dried food, then."

"Won't do any good," he said. "It was an asteroid like Apophis that killed off the dinosaurs sixty-five million years ago. Apophis'll do the same to us."

"Well, in that case, I'll immigrate to the moon." And Hilly. Reeny, too, if she wanted to come. We'd live in a dome and raise hydroponic veggies.

He shook his head. "It's going to hit the moon, too."

"Mars, then. Or is it going to hit Mars as well?"

"No. Mars is okay," Eddy said.

"That's good to know," I said. He nodded.

Eddy Porter was employed at the Granville Island boat works, where he'd probably inhaled too much fibreglass solvent. A few years earlier he'd been abducted by aliens who, he said, had inserted an implant in his head, which was no doubt how they kept him apprised of upcoming celestial events. He was harmless. In fact, I often wondered if he was one of the saner people I knew.

"Um, how's Bobbi doing?" he asked.

"She's doing okay," I said. "Thanks for asking."

"Good thing Arty Smelski happened along in his kayak when he did, ain't it?"

"Is that the name of the paramedic who found her?" I said. "No one told me. I'd like to buy him a beer."

"Arty'd let you."

"Where would I find him?"

"Dunno where he lives," Eddy said. "But he's got an old fishing boat in the Harbour Authority marina he's fixing up to someday retire on. Likely you'll find him there most days."

The Granville Island boat works was on the other side of the parking lot next to Bridges, facing Broker's Bay, where the *Wonderlust* was berthed. The police had probably interviewed Eddy and his co-workers — or maybe not; it was early days yet — and it was unlikely that I'd learn anything they hadn't, but it wouldn't hurt to ask if he'd been in the area the night before and if he'd seen anything.

"Tuesday evening is when my abductee support group meets," he said, shaking his head.

Don't ask, I sternly enjoined myself, lest my curiosity about what went on at an alien abductee support group meeting got the better of me. Eddy seemed disappointed. There was nothing, I knew from experience, he enjoyed more than talking about his off-world adventures. He'd even showed me an X-ray once, purportedly of his very own head, and pointed out the tiny smudgy speck that was, he said, his alien implant.

"I'll ask around," he said.

"I'd appreciate it," I said. And left him there, looking woebegone and staring out at the boat traffic on False Creek, waiting for Apophis.

"She was right there," Art Smelski said, pointing to a spot on the rocky shoreline by the civic marina docks beneath the Burrard Street Bridge. Late evening traffic rumbled high overhead and the gloom deepened as the sun went down over Vanier Park. "It looked like maybe she'd crawled out of the water a bit," he added, "then passed out. The tide was starting to fall, so it's a good thing I came along when I did or she'd have been swept all the way out into Burrard Inlet." He gestured toward the dark expanse of water beyond the civic marina. "I got her out of the water, called 911, then started CPR."

"You carry a cellphone in your kayak?" I said.

"Sure do. It's waterproof."

The shoreline sloped steeply down from where we stood at the edge of the path that looped through the small park called Cultural Harmony Grove, virtually treeless except for a handful of saplings. At that time of night, despite the lights from the surrounding marinas, Smelski wouldn't have seen Bobbi at all if he hadn't been on the water in his kayak.

"Do you always go kayaking at eleven at night?" I asked.

"Not always. Depends on which shift I'm working. Helps me relax. Most o' the time," he added with a shrug.

"Did you see anyone else nearby? On the path, maybe."

"Nope. Can't see the path from down there. And I was kinda busy."

"Sure, I understand. You saw nothing out of the ordinary at all?"

"Nope. Just your friend in the water."

"What about on the boats?"

"Nope. It's fairly quiet that time of night. Sorry."

"That's okay," I said.

"Your friend, is she going to be okay?"

"I think so," I said.

"That's good, because she was in pretty bad shape. Whoever ..." He stopped.

"Whoever what?" I asked, my voice hollow.

"My job," he said awkwardly. "I mean, I see a lot of what people do to other people. Whoever beat up your friend, well, it was nasty. She's lucky to be alive."

"It's thanks to you she is, Mr. Smelski," I said. I offered him my hand. He took it. "You saved her life," I said, voice cracking.

"Maybe so," he said self-consciously. "But, well, I guess it's what I do. And call me Art. Mr. Smelski is what my kids' friends call me."

"Okay, Art, the next time you're in Bridges, tell Kenny Li, the manager, who you are. Drinks and dinner for you and your wife are on me."

"That isn't necessary," he said. "But thanks. I appreciate it. So'll my wife."

As we walked along the footpath back to the False Creek Harbour Authority where I'd found him working on his partly converted fishing boat, I asked him if he knew anything about the *Wonderlust*. He didn't recognize the name, he told me, but when I described the boat to him, he said he knew it to see it.

"Do you know who owns it?" I asked.

"Nope," he replied. "Whoever it is, they sure don't take very good care of it, though. Older boat like that needs a lot of TLC." He shrugged as he stopped at the top of the ramp to the long dock on which his boat was moored with dozens of other fishing boats. "You know the definition of a boat."

"Yeah," I said. "A hole in the water you fill with money."

"Glad to hear your friend is doing okay," he said.

I thanked him again and trudged homeward to my very own hole in the water. I was no sooner through the door than exhaustion hit me like a load of bricks. I staggered upstairs, I gave my teeth a perfunctory scrub, dropped my clothes onto the floor, and fell into bed. I was unconscious before my head hit the pillow.

chapter six

Thursday morning, rather than taking the ferry across False Creek, I drove to work. Parking the Liberty in the loading bay behind the building, where we normally parked the van, I took the rickety freight elevator up to the studio on the third floor. Garibaldi Air Services had recently acquired a new Bell 412 passenger helicopter for the Vancouver to Whistler run, just in time for the 2010 Winter Olympics, and wanted a series of interior, exterior, and in-flight photographs for a promotional brochure and website. It was a two-person job — well, two and a half, really, if you counted Wes Comacho, whose helicopter I'd chartered for the morning to take the aerial shots. I'd thought about cancelling, but we couldn't afford to lose the work. Normally, if Bobbi was busy, I would have taken Wayne along, but he was so afraid of flying that he broke into a sweat and stammered uncontrollably at the very thought of going up in a helicopter. Mary-Alice had volunteered, but aerial photography could be tricky and I was afraid that despite her good intentions her lack of experience would be more hindrance than help, especially since I would have to use the Hasselblad and the Nikon 35 millimetre film cameras. I had managed to borrow a decent "prosumer" digital camera from Meg and Peg Castle, the twin sisters who ran an escort service and soft-core porn website out of their offices on the second floor — I hadn't asked what they used it for — but I wasn't sure it was up to the job.

At ten, as I was about to lug my gear down to the Liberty, someone knocked on the door to the stairwell. I unlocked it, and when I opened it there was a waspish, sharp-featured man standing on the landing.

"You Tom McCall?" he asked.

He was dressed in a dark suit and maroon tie, with a raincoat slung over his arm, even though the weather was fair. He had dark, liquid eyes and his thick, slicked-back black hair had an oily sheen. His voice had a nasal quality that made me think of Joel Cairo, Peter Lorre's character from *The Maltese Falcon*. The climb to the third floor seemed not to have winded him at all.

"Yes, I am," I said. "But if this is about a job you'll have to speak to one of my associates. They're not in yet and I'll be late for an appointment if I don't leave now. You'll have to come back, I'm afraid."

"This won't take long," he said as he stepped into the studio. His cologne was sharp and salty and he wore too much of it.

"I hope not," I said. "I really am in a hurry."

"I want to know who hired you to take pictures of that boat," he said.

"The *Wonderlust*?" I said.

"Of course the *Wonderlust*," he said impatiently.

"I'd like to know who hired me, too," I said. "Who are you? Are you with the police?"

"Never mind who I am. Who hired you to take pictures of that boat?"

"Your guess is as good as mine," I said.

"You're telling me you don't know who hired you?" he said skeptically.

"That's precisely what I'm telling you. Now, if you'll excuse me …"

"I don't believe you," he said.

"That's certainly your prerogative," I said. "But why would I lie?"

"For the same reason most people lie," he said. I waited for him to continue, thinking that perhaps he was about to impart some deep philosophical truth, but he just smiled thinly and said, "Let's try a different approach."

"Fine by me. But not now. Do you have a card? I —"

"Someone hired you to take pictures of that boat. Why?"

Who was this guy? I wondered. I didn't figure him for a cop; a cop wouldn't have refused to identify himself. If I'd had to guess, I'd have said he was a lawyer. Representing whom? Again, if I'd had to guess, I would have said that he represented the nameless corporation that owned the *Wonderlust*, perhaps concerned about liability issues. "Who are you?" I asked again. "What's your name?"

"You don't need to know that," he said.

"Fine," I said. "Don't tell me. I'll just have to call you 'Mr. Cairo,' then."

He blinked. "Pardon me?"

"Never mind," I said. "I've got to go. I'm late for an appointment." I pulled open the door to the stairwell.

"I don't care if you're late for your own funeral," he said. "I want to know who hired you to take pictures of that boat."

"I told you," I said. "I don't know who she was."

"It was a woman that hired you?" he said sharply. "What did she tell you her name was?"

I didn't know the real Anna Waverley from Sheena, Queen of the Jungle, but the chances were good that she too was an innocent bystander, like Bobbi and me, so I was reluctant to tell this man her name. "She gave a false name," I said.

"What'd she look like?"

"Good day, Mr. Cairo," I said, urging him out the door.

"Just hold on," he said. "I'm not going anywhere till you answer my questions."

"No, you hold on," I said. "If you don't leave right now, I'm going to call the police. I'm sure they'd be only too happy to answer your questions. They might have a few of their own, too."

He stared at me for a long moment, dark eyes hardening, before finally shrugging slightly and stepping through the door onto the landing.

"We'll talk again," he said and began to descend the stairs.

I closed the door and locked it and took the freight elevator down to the loading dock.

I got back to the studio at 2:30. I gave Wayne a dozen rolls of exposed film to send to the outside lab we used from time to time. I also gave him Meg and Peg's digital, with which I'd shot a couple dozen frames, some of which might even be usable. With Mary-Alice hovering over his shoulder, asking questions and making him nervous, he downloaded them to his computer, then burned them to a couple of CDs, one of which he gave to me to check on my computer before erasing them from the card in Meg and Peg's camera. I was just finishing when Mary-Alice came into my office and dropped onto the sofa with a weary sigh.

"Tell Wayne he can return the camera to Meg and Peg," I said to her.

"Okay," she said. I looked at her. She looked back. "What?"

"Is everything all right?" I asked.

"You want a list?"

"I mean, with you. Are you all right?"

"Sure. Why?"

"You look tired." She was neat as a pin, nary a hair out of place, clothes clean and carefully co-ordinated and accessorized, but despite her makeup, her complexion seemed dry and pale and there were dark smudges under her eyes.

"I haven't been sleeping very well lately."

"Oh?" I said warily. Call me insensitive, but my sister prided herself on the control she exercised over her life. If something was getting sufficiently under her skin to keep her up at night, I wasn't sure I really wanted to know what it was.

Her eyes narrowed. "What's that supposed to mean?"

"Nothing," I said. "I'll be glad when things get back to normal, too."

She made a derisive gagging sound, got up, and left the office. I wondered if somehow I'd stumbled into a David Lynch movie.

When I got home that evening, I turned on my computer and looked up Waverley in the Internet telephone directory for Vancouver. There weren't many. There weren't any S. or Sam or Samuel Waverleys in Point Grey or elsewhere. It wouldn't be hard to find Samuel Waverley's gallery in Gastown, but I couldn't see myself walking in off the street and asking for the owner's home address. I was going to have to find some other way to get Anna Waverley's address. Why I felt I needed it, I wasn't sure.

After fixing something to eat, and eating it, I flaked out for a while on the sofa and tried to read. I came to at eight o'clock. Although it was late, I decided to go to the hospital, anyway. There was a good chance I'd run into Bobbi's father, but there was also a chance he'd gone home or to a bar somewhere. As I drove past the Broker's Bay Marina on my way off Granville Island, however, a parking space opened up, so, acting on impulse, I parked and walked out to the quay overlooking the moorings. The *Wonderlust* wasn't in her slip. I went into the marina office. A middle-aged woman was behind the counter, leafing through a magazine. She looked up at me and smiled.

"Where's the *Wonderlust*?" I asked.

"The *Wonderlust*? Police towed her away this afternoon. Said she was a crime scene."

"A crime scene?"

"Yeah. A woman was raped on her the other day. Almost killed."

My guts clenched, even though I knew that Bobbi hadn't been raped. As I looked out over the marina, I had a sudden inspiration. I wouldn't have recognized a Sabre 386 if one rammed into my house, but I remembered Witt DeWalt, the Mariners fan, telling me that the Waverleys owned a sailboat called *Free Spirit*. I turned back to the woman behind the counter.

"Almost forgot," I said. "I was supposed to deliver some photographs to Mrs. Waverley. I was told she was staying on her boat. Which one is the *Free Spirit*?"

"I dunno who told you that," the woman said. "She hardly ever stays on that boat. She and her husband live in Point Grey."

"Yes, I know," I said. "Um, look. I have to deliver the photos tonight. They're very important. I left the address at home, though, because I thought she was supposed to be on the boat. I don't suppose you could give it to me, could you? I'd really appreciate it. Mrs. Waverley will, too."

"Sure, why not?" the woman said helpfully.

Three minutes later I was heading up Granville toward 12th, Anna Waverley's Point Grey address in my shirt pocket. Now that I had it, I still wasn't quite sure what I was going to do with it. I didn't think Mrs. Waverley was very likely to speak to me if I just walked up and knocked on her door and told her that someone posing as her may have been responsible for my friend getting half beaten to death.

As I circled the block around the Vancouver General Hospital, looking for parking, I spotted what I thought was Greg Matthias's Saab. I wanted to ask him some questions about the investigation. And if Bobbi's father was visiting, Matthias might be able to keep me from doing something stupid or that I'd regret, not necessarily the same thing. Fortunately, Brooks wasn't there. Matthias was, though.

"How's she doing?" I asked him as I stood beside Bobbi's bed. I gently touched the back of her hand with the tips of my fingers, hoping she'd wake up. She didn't.

"No change," Matthias said. "For better or worse. The doctors say it's just a waiting game, but that they have every reason to be hopeful."

"How long have you been here?" I pulled a straight chair next to the bed and sat down.

"Not long," Matthias said. "Your sister and Wayne Fowler were here for a while about an hour ago."

"And Bobbi's father?"

"Haven't seen him."

"I stopped at the marina on my way here. The *Wonderlust* is gone. The woman in the office told me the police towed it away because it was a crime scene. Is that where Bobbi was attacked? On the boat?"

"The crime scene people found blood traces and

evidence of a struggle," Matthias replied. "Someone tried to clean it up, but didn't do a very thorough job of it. Maybe they watch forensic shows on television and thought it wouldn't do any good. We won't know for sure if she was attacked on the boat until the test results are back. As for how she got from the boat to the bridge, the *Wonderlust*'s Zodiac is missing. Her attacker may have transported her from the *Wonderlust* using the Zodiac. The footpath between Granville Island and the bridge is well lit and fairly busy, even late at night. If she were dumped from shore, her attacker would have had to transport her by foot half a kilometre or more along the seawall and the promenade overlooking the False Creek Harbour Authority. Someone would have seen something. Likewise, if she ran and he caught up with her under the bridge, she'd have screamed for help and someone would have heard. Unfortunately, the scene under the bridge was too badly contaminated by paramedics and curiosity seekers to be of any help. We're canvassing, but so far haven't turned anything up."

"If he moved her by Zodiac," I said, "why dump her in the shallows in the middle of the civic marina?"

"I dunno," Matthias said. "Maybe she came to, struggled with her attacker, fell overboard, and tried to swim ashore. We're just going to have to wait until she wakes up." He paused, looking at Bobbi, then started to add something else.

"Don't say it," I interjected quickly, before he could speak.

He nodded and said nothing.

"Did you check out Loth?" I asked.

"Kovacs and Henshaw talked to him, but I don't think anything came of it. I'd have heard."

"What about Anna Waverley? Could she be involved?"

"She could be, of course. She admits to being at the Broker's Bay Marina at approximately nine o'clock that evening, although no one seems to have seen her. And how likely is it that the woman who came to your studio pulled Anna Waverley's name out of a hat? Other than that, though, so far there's nothing to connect her to Bobbi or you or the boat."

"Except that she admitted to being on it once or twice."

"Except that."

"Maybe the woman who came to the studio was trying to set Mrs. Waverley up for something. She and her husband are pretty well heeled, aren't they?"

"Comparatively, I suppose," Matthias said. "I'm sure Kovacs is considering that angle."

We sat in silence for a few minutes, watching Bobbi sleep, listening to the soft whir and murmur of the IV pump and the medical monitors.

"How are you getting on?" Matthias asked eventually.

"Trying to keep busy," I said. I remembered my visitor, and told Matthias about him. "He wouldn't tell me his name, but he wanted to know who hired us to photograph the boat."

"Could he have been the owner's lawyer, trying to head off a personal injury suit?"

"That's what I thought at the time," I said. "He was too blunt and to-the-point for a lawyer, though, leastways the ones I've known. But he could be employed by the boat's owner in some capacity, I suppose."

"Give me his description again," Matthias said.

I did, then we sat for a while longer without speaking. A nurse came in, smiled at us, then checked Bobbi's IV, catheter bag, and the readings on the medical monitors. She smiled at us again as she left. It was nine-thirty, but visiting hours were flexible. It didn't hurt, either, that Matthias was a cop, and familiar to a number of the nursing staff.

"I spent some time here last year," he explained when I commented on it. "My partner was recovering from an injury."

I'd met his partner only once the year before, but I remembered her well, a strikingly handsome woman named Isabel Worth. "She was shot?"

"No," he said with a dry smile. "She broke her arm when she fell off the Stanley Park seawall while trying to apprehend a suspect."

"Are you still partners?"

"I should've said former partner," he replied. "She retired six months ago on partial pension and moved to Pemberton to raise horses and run a mountain trail guide business with her uncle. I've got a couple of years to go before I pull the plug, then I'm going to join her." He looked at Bobbi for a second or two, then back at me. "What you said about you and Reeny Lindsey, that you liked each other well enough but that there was something missing? Same with me and Bobbi. Well, Isabel and I discovered after she retired and moved to Pemberton that whatever the thing is that's missing between you and Reeny or me and Bobbi isn't missing between me and Isabel."

As we left Bobbi's room and walked to the elevator, I said, "Last night, on the local news, there was a story about Bobbi's attack. It reported that she was still in a coma. Do you think there's any chance that whoever did this might try to finish the job? I mean, when she wakes up, she's probably going to be able to identify him."

"That kind of thing only happens in the movies," Matthias said. "Besides, this place has good security. All the staff wear picture IDs and after ten-thirty you can't get in without clearance from the ward."

"Are visitors screened during the day?"

"No," he said, "but it's pretty busy during the day. You'd have to be crazy to expect to get away with harming a patient without getting caught."

"Crazy is just what I'm afraid of," I said.

"Security is aware of Bobbi's situation and will be keeping an eye on her. Look, Bobbi isn't the first assault victim who's been here for a while. We haven't lost one yet."

I was comforted, but not much.

chapter seven

The strangely unseasonable weather had moved in again. Fog haloed the street lamps, the lights of the cars and shops, the bulbs strung along the frame of the freight crane in the parking lot, hanging like a shroud over False Creek and cool on my face as I walked from my car toward the ramp down to Sea Village. It had been only two days since Bobbi's attack and I told myself it was unreasonable to expect the police to have made much headway in the case, but I was discouraged nonetheless. Nor was I encouraged by the rate of Bobbi's progress. I blamed it on being raised on television, where the bright young detective catches the bad guys or the brilliant but irascible doctor pulls his patient back from the brink of death just in time for the final commercial break. Real life didn't work like that, I had to remind myself. In real life, the bad guys often got away. In real life, likely as not the doctor working on your kid's case had graduated at the bottom of his class, drank too much, and was in the middle of a messy divorce. Who needed real life?

A man was sitting on the bench under the lamppost by the top of the ramp, wreathed in fog and cigarette smoke. He stood as I approached, a little unsteady on his feet, dropped the cigarette, and ground it out under his toe. It was Norman Brooks. Swell, I thought. Reality, as someone once said, bit. After which, I supposed, it sucked.

"Were you at the hospital?" Brooks asked gruffly, breath stinking of alcohol.

"Yes."

"How is she?"

"The same. Haven't you visited her today?"

He lowered his head. "They kicked me out."

"I'm sorry to hear that," I said.

"Yeah," he replied. "I bet."

"Maybe you should try visiting her sober," I said.

He stiffened. "Fuck you," he growled.

"Good night, Mr. Brooks," I said, and started down the ramp.

He grabbed my right arm in a vice-like grip. "Don't you walk away from me. I want to talk to you."

I twisted free. He'd hit a nerve, literally, and my right hand tingled painfully. "Go home," I said, rubbing my arm. "Get sober. Then maybe we'll talk."

"Jesus, you're an asshole. I don't know why my daughter thinks you're so great to work for. I think you're a pussy."

"You're mixing your meta-orifices," I said.

He growled deep in his throat. "I know my daughter was assaulted on that boat, but I figure it was really you they were after. You pissed somebody off."

"Wouldn't be the first time," I agreed glibly.

"Was it this Waverley guy? You fucking his old lady or something? I heard she's not too fussy. Or maybe you put nude pictures of her on the Internet. I checked you out. You like taking dirty pictures. Like of those lezzy twin sisters who run that porn website downstairs from your studio."

"First," I said, "I don't know Mr. or Mrs. Waverley, carnally or otherwise, so I've no idea when or how I might have pissed either of them off. Second, as for taking nude photographs, it's a dirty business, but someone has to do it. And third, Bobbi and I both work on Meg and Peg Castle's annual calendar. They're nice people, by the way, both married with kids." I wondered if he knew that when Bobbi was in university she'd earned extra money by posing nude for life study classes. If not, it wasn't my place to tell him. "And four, even if Mr. Waverley wanted to beat the crap out of me for some reason, why take it out on Bobbi?"

"So it was one of your drug-smuggling pals looking to settle a score."

"What are you talking about?" I said. "I don't know any drug smugglers." Well, maybe I did. Sort of …

"Don't give me that wide-eyed innocent crap," Brooks said. "I told you, I checked you out. I've still got connections. Christopher Hastings and his girlfriend were smuggling dope to the States in that old boat of his, till someone set fire to it. Hell, for all I know, it was you that did it. Now she's your girlfriend and she's graduated from dope smuggling to making cheap porn."

"Now that you're retired from the Mounties," I said, "I hope you aren't planning to set up shop as a private detective."

"Eh? Why?"

"Because you're a lousy investigator. Maybe Chris Hastings was smuggling dope in his boat. I wouldn't know. I didn't know him that well. I certainly wouldn't call him a friend. As for Reeny, she doesn't make cheap porn, she makes science fiction, and while it may be cheesy, it's far from cheap."

He shook himself, a little like a dog shaking off water.

"Tell me about the broad who hired you."

"No, I don't think I will. Besides, other than a physical description, which likely doesn't mean much, there's nothing to tell. Now, if you'll pardon me, it's late and I've got a busy day tomorrow."

"I'm not done with you yet."

"But I'm done with you," I said. "You're no longer a police officer, Mr. Brooks. Look, I know you're upset about Bobbi. So am I. But blundering drunkenly about making a nuisance of yourself isn't going to help her. Go home. Sober up. Then maybe they'll let you in to see your daughter."

"I don't believe you about the Waverley woman. I think you do know her and that she or her old man is involved in Bobbi getting hurt. I'm gonna find out how. And if I find out it was you they were really after, that she just got in the way, I'll pound the living shit out of you myself. Don't think I won't."

He turned, a little too quickly, losing his balance and almost falling. He braced himself on the railing at the top of the ramp, regained his balance, and walked away with exaggerated precision. I hoped he wasn't driving, but as I watched, he dug keys out of his pocket and fumbled at the door of a big GMC four-by-four parked in one of the spaces reserved for the staff of the Emily Carr Institute.

"Shit," I muttered and trotted over to him. "You're in no condition to drive," I said. "Why don't you take a cab home? I'll put your truck in one of the Sea Village spaces so it won't get towed."

He got the door open and climbed into the truck. "I got here, didn't I?"

"Probably blind luck," I said. "Look, it won't do anybody any good if you have an accident and end up in jail for killing someone with this monster. Give me the keys."

"Piss off," he growled. He was having trouble getting the key into the ignition.

He lived in Richmond somewhere, I recalled, out past Vancouver International Airport, a thirty-dollar cab ride at least. Maybe he didn't have the cash. I had forty or fifty dollars in my wallet. Would his pride allow him to accept the offer of a loan? If it had been anyone else, I might have volunteered to drive him home, or even offered my sofa for the night, but I didn't want to spend any more time with him than I had to, particularly in a confined space.

While I dithered, he managed to insert the key into the ignition and start the engine.

"Mr. Brooks," I said, over the noisy clatter of the diesel engine. "At least come inside and have a cup of coffee or two before you drive home."

I couldn't believe what I was saying. I was almost thankful when he yanked the shift lever into reverse and backed out of the parking space, forcing me to jump aside or get knocked down by the open door. The door swung shut as he jammed the transmission into drive with a lurch and accelerated out of the parking lot.

Well, I'd tried, I told myself.

It was almost 10:30 when I let myself into my house. It was so quiet that I could hear every creak and groan and murmur as the house shifted gently on the tide. The message light on the phone in the kitchen was flashing. Without any great enthusiasm, I pressed the button that speed-dialled my voice mail, entered my password, and was told I had three new messages. They were all hang-ups. Curious, I pressed the button that displayed the Caller IDs of the most recent calls. All three IDs were blocked, which suggested that they had been placed by the same caller.

I got a Granville Island Lager out of the fridge and took it up to the roof deck. Tendrils of fog writhed around the lights on the metal skeleton of the freight crane. I slumped into a deck chair, put my feet up on the railing, contemplatively sipped my beer, and thought about Reeny Lindsey. More specifically, I wondered what the future might hold for us, if anything at all.

For the most part, and for a variety of what I considered very valid reasons, such as not having to pick up my socks, make the bed, or put away my breakfast dishes, except that I usually did, pick up my socks, anyway, I liked living alone. For the most part. Also for the most part, except for slightly more than a handful of years of marriage and the occasional live-in girlfriend or equally temporary boarder, I had lived alone for a good chunk of my adult life. I generally liked my own company. We usually got along. Usually. Every now and again, however, I wondered if I wanted to spend the rest of my life with just myself to talk to. I wasn't *that* interesting, after all. Besides which, it was lonely sometimes. Okay, more than just sometimes.

All things considered, Reeny was perfect. She was smart, funny, and attractive, and we were good together in every important way, and some not so important ones. Her job required her to travel, so she wasn't always underfoot, although truth be told, I wouldn't have objected to her being underfoot a little more often. The problem was, when I thought about her and me, I didn't think *forever*. Not that I ever had with any other woman, not even my ex-wife. But it seemed to me that if a relationship was to last, both parties had to believe deep in their hearts that it was forever, whether it ultimately proved to be or not.

I wasn't ready to give up on Reeny. Maybe our relationship just needed a little tweaking. On the other hand, I thought, perhaps it wouldn't be a bad idea to have an alternate strategy, a contingency plan for my old age. Finding another person with whom one would want to grow old — and, more important, who felt the same way — isn't quite as easy as opening a registered retirement savings plan or buying mutual funds. It requires much more careful planning, as well as considerable research, market analysis, and expensive albeit not entirely unpleasant consumer testing. The risk of losing one's investment is significantly greater, too; there's no such thing as a guaranteed investment certificate for relationships. Unfortunately, it's an arena in which professional help is sorely lacking — I don't believe in astrology, singles' bars, or online dating services, although …

I awakened with a start, almost spilling what was left of my beer. The phone was ringing. I hurried downstairs — or below, if you insist — to my home office to answer it. It was after eleven, but I thought it might be Reeny calling from Germany, where it was only five or six in the morning. I almost crippled myself in the process, but I made it to the phone before the call was transferred to voice mail.

"H'lo?"

Nothing.

"Hello?"

Still nothing. Not even heavy breathing.

"*Hello!*"

Finally, a hollow click and the dial tone. I swore and put down the handset, none too gently.

The phone in my home office didn't have a call display screen, but I was certain that if I went downstairs and checked the Caller ID on the phone in the kitchen, it would show that the ID had been blocked. I did it, anyway, and my suspicion was confirmed. I thought about calling Greg Matthias and getting him to have the VPD technical support division "dump my LUDs," as they say on TV — my telephone local usage details — and trace the call's origin. It seemed a bit extreme, though. Anyway, it was probably just an overzealous telemarketer, or the world's most annoying real estate broker, Blake Darling.

I nearly jumped out of my shoes when the phone rang again. I peered at the LCD screen. No name, just a local cellphone number. I picked up the handset.

"Hello?" I said warily.

"Tom?" a woman said.

"Yes. Who's this?"

"It's Jeanie."

"Jeanie?"

"Jeanie Stone. Is something wrong?"

"No. Nothing's wrong, Jeanie. Sorry, I'm a bit jumpy, I guess."

"Tom, I just heard about Bobbi," Jeanie said. "Is she going to be all right?"

"I dunno, Jeanie. She's still unconscious."

"I know it's late, and a school night 'n' all, but if you feel like grabbing a beer or two, I'm just five minutes away from Granville Island."

I was waiting for her under the portico of the Granville Island Hotel when she emerged from the fog.

"Sorry," she said. "Took me longer than I thought. Geez, what's with this weather? It's like driving through marshmallow topping."

"You're not on your way back to Squamish, are you?" I asked, as we went into the hotel. She lived in Squamish, at the head of Howe Sound, about halfway to Whistler. Although Squamish billed itself as the Outdoor Recreation Capital of Canada, the forest industry was still the town's largest employer.

"I just drove down," she said.

We went into the Dockside Restaurant, where we were given a seat by the window, overlooking the fog-shrouded Pelican Bay Marina. The high-rises and office towers on the far side of False Creek were pearly ghosts, the heart of the city just a diffused glow through an ephemeral mist, like an incredibly fine pointillist painting.

"Pretty," Jeanie said.

"It is," I agreed. "But I wish the CIA would stop messing about with the weather control machines they stole from the Russians."

"Pardon me?"

"Don't tell me you've never heard of the scalar potential interferometer electromagnetic weather machines the Russians built back in the fifties."

"Uh, no, I haven't," she said. "And here I thought global warming was to blame for the weird weather."

I shook my head. "That's what they want us to believe, but global warming doesn't explain the popularity of reality TV or Jim Carrey movies. At this very moment we are very likely being scanned by the U.S. government's scalar beams and our unique personal frequencies recorded in their supercomputers for later programming. Can't you feel it?"

"Now that you mention it," she said, dissolving into a fit of giggles. With some difficulty, she composed herself. "You had me worried for a second."

"Sorry," I said. "I have a neighbour, a sweet old guy, but barking mad. Lectures me on the dangers of scalar-beam weapons every chance he gets."

The waitress came to take our order, two pints of Granville Island Lager.

"About Bobbi," Jeanie said after the waitress left. "If we have to put off the calendar shoot, I'll understand. I want you to know that."

"Thanks," I said. "Wayne and I should be able to handle it. If that's all right with you, I mean."

"Of course," Jeanie said, but I sensed a little hesitancy in her voice.

"Mary-Alice can come along as chaperone," I added.

"What? Oh." She smiled. "Well, all right, if you think you and Wayne need protection …"

Our beers arrived in tall frosted glasses. "Cheers," I

said. We touched glasses and drank.

Beer always tastes better when shared with an attractive woman. Everything does. And Jeanie was extremely attractive, dark and compact and muscular, with a brilliant smile and an infectious laugh. I'd been a little concerned about mixing business with pleasure when I'd accepted her invitation, worried that she might have designs on my virtue, such as it was. I wasn't afraid that she'd make a pass at me, just what I might do if she did. Besides being more than ten years younger than me, I didn't need that kind of complication in my life right then.

I needn't have worried.

"Relax, Tom, for heaven's sake," she said. "Maybe when the calendar's done I'll let you take me to some place nice, ply me with fine wine, and take your best shot. Assuming you're not spoken for. Are you?"

I wasn't sure how to answer that.

"In the meantime," she said, "you seemed like you could use someone to talk to and I'm a good listener. I'll even talk shop, if you want."

"That won't be necessary," I said.

"Would it be all right if I visited Bobbi?"

"Of course," I said.

Her eyes were an odd shade of blue, like the flower of the chicory plant, and looked almost as though they were lit from behind by LED Christmas lights. They were in startling contrast to her dark complexion and coal-black hair. Although she undoubtedly spent a lot of time outdoors, the skin of her face and neck was smooth and fine-grained. She didn't appear to be wearing much makeup. Her hands were small, blunt, and strong — shaking hands with her had been a humbling experience. Her fingernails, though short, were painted a bright Chinese red.

"How did you hear about Bobbi?" I asked.

"Your sister told me," she said.

"You and Mary-Alice are still on speaking terms, then."

"Sure." She smiled suddenly, releasing almost as much wattage as Bobbi did. "Say, it turns out we have a mutual acquaintance."

"Who's that?"

"Walter Moffat."

"Not sure I'd call him an acquaintance exactly. He is — or was — a potential client. I've never met him. Mary-Alice knows him, through his wife, I think. How do you know him?"

"I guess I can't really claim to know him, either," she said. "I only met him once. He wangled himself an invitation to speak at our annual general meeting last month. He's running in my riding in the next federal election. I'm not sure what he was hoping to accomplish. We're not a big organization. Or likely to endorse a candidate who seems to know as much about the forest industry as I know about, um, scalar-beam weapons. When I talked to him afterwards he seemed to have a hard time believing I was a logger."

He's not alone, I thought.

"He was quite charming," she went on, "and very good-looking, but he was, well, artificial, like he was just mouthing words written by someone else. No great surprise, I suppose. Many politicians are just sock puppets, aren't they? Now, Mr. Moffat's campaign manager, Woody Getz, he's another thing altogether. A real piece of work."

"How so?"

"Imagine a used-car salesman with a two-thousand-dollar suit and a bad comb-over."

"I know the type," I said, thinking of Blake Darling.

"It's weird," she said, with a mischievous chuckle.

"What is?"

"A lot of women would call Walter Moffat drop-dead gorgeous," she said. "He's not my type, but he had quite a few of our members all girlish and gooey-eyed. 'Creaming in her jeans' is how one of them put it."

If all female forestry workers were even remotely like Jeanie Stone, I found it hard to imagine them getting all "girlish and gooey-eyed" over anyone, never mind the cruder allusion. What was Jeanie's type? I wondered, as she went on.

"He probably could have had any one of half a dozen women for the night, just for the asking," she said. "One of our out-of-town members even claims she slipped him a note with her hotel room number on it. But he was a complete gentleman, polite and just attentive enough to make you feel like he cared, but not that he wanted to get into your pants. Woody Getz, on the other hand, practically drooled on the floor the whole evening. Despite being downright homely, he hit on just about every women who came within range. He even hit on me, for Pete's sake."

Don't say it, McCall, I told myself, but I wasn't listening. "And why not?" I said. "He might be a piece of work, as you say, but at least he exhibited a remarkable amount of good taste."

"Um, thanks," she said, squirming uncomfortably.

I was an idiot. I didn't want her to think I was hitting on her. Not only because I was more or less "spoken for," but I didn't want to be placed in the same category as a used-car salesman with a bad comb-over. We chatted for a while longer — I tried not to say anything else too stupid — until we'd finished our beers. Jeanie asked if I wanted another. Although I was tempted, if only to prolong the pleasure of her company, I said, "It's getting late, and we've got a lot to do to get ready for the movers on Saturday. I think I'd better call it a night. Sorry."

"Don't be," she said, signalling the waitress. "I should get some sleep, too. I'm meeting with my thesis advisor tomorrow."

"Thesis advisor?" I said stupidly.

"I'm doing a masters in geology at UBC. My thesis is called 'Movement on the Cascadia Subduction Zone and Liquefaction: Risk Assessment in the Metro Vancouver Region.' Catchy, eh?"

"Very. If it means what I think it means, it makes me glad I live in a floating home."

"As long as you're home when the Big One hits," she said with a smile.

chapter eight

Friday began as just another perfect day in paradise. The early morning rain was warm and soft and sweet, scrubbing the air until it smelled like new wine, and washing the dust off the huge blue-and-white ready-mix trucks that rumbled in and out of the Ocean cement plant as I skipped along the glistening cobbles to the Aquabus dock by the Public Market. I may be overstating the case slightly, the skipping-along-the-cobbles-part, anyway, but I felt pretty darned good that morning. Better than I had in a long while. Whether it was a "hangover" from my late-night beer with Jeanie Stone or the result of having unconsciously arrived at some conclusion about the future of my relationship with Reeny, of which I was still consciously unaware, it had been just what the doctor ordered.

When I got to the studio, Mary-Alice and Wayne were already there. The movers were due in less than twenty-four hours and there was still a lot to be done. We got down to it. About half an hour later Mary-Alice threw an empty film canister at me.

"Will you please stop that," she said.

"Stop what?"

"That bloody humming."

It looked impossible, but between us, we managed to get everything done. It took all day, and by four o'clock we were dirty, grumpy, and tired. Well, Wayne and I were dirty, grumpy, and tired. Mary-Alice was just grumpy and tired. Somehow, even though she had worked just as hard as Wayne and I, she had managed to stay immaculately clean despite rooting through years of accumulated dust and grime. After Wayne and I cleaned up as best we could, I took us all downstairs to Zapata's, the Mexican restaurant on the ground floor, for a much-deserved beer or three and a plate of nachos. The beer and nachos improved our moods, but by five-thirty we'd run out of conversation and were almost falling asleep in our chairs. I paid the tab, leaving a fat tip for Ping, the waitress. I then exchanged hugs and kisses with Rosie, the owner and chef, promising to deliver her best wishes to Bobbi, then followed Mary-Alice outside.

"See you at seven," Mary-Alice said as I walked her to her car.

"Pardon me?"

"Our cocktail party," she said. "For the Children In Peril Network. You promised you'd come."

I groaned, recalling that in a moment of weakness I had accepted an invitation to attend a party Mary-Alice and her husband David were throwing in honour of Elise Bridgwater Moffat. She was head of the Josiah E. Bridgwater Foundation, Mary-Alice had explained, whose main preoccupation was the Children In Peril Network. She was also wife of the ex-Honourable Walter P. Moffat, erstwhile Member of Parliament for Vancouver Centre and would-be MP for West Vancouver — Sunshine Coast — Sea-to-Sky Country, the official name (I kid you not) of the riding that included the town of Squamish.

"I really don't think I'm up to it, Mary-Alice," I said. "I'm beat. And I want to drop by the hospital and see how Bobbi's doing."

"You don't have to stay all evening," Mary-Alice countered. "Besides, it'll give you a chance to schmooze with Walter Moffat. He may have changed his mind about the exhibition catalogue, but he's still in a position to send more work our way."

"Isn't schmoozing why we took you on as a partner, Mary-Alice?"

"Believe me, I'll being doing my share. I'm going to be busy with other duties, though. There'll be some interesting people there. Who knows, you might even enjoy yourself."

"I doubt it."

"It will do you good to get out, Tom, take your mind off things. You've been moping around for weeks, ever since — well, for weeks."

Ever since what? I wondered. "Who else is going to be there?" I asked.

"Well," she said, a cunning glint in her eye. "Jeanie Stone, for one."

"Oh."

"You'll come?"

"Yes, I'll be there," I said.

Mary-Alice and her husband, Dr. David Paul, lived in West Vancouver on the north shore of Burrard Inlet, in a big glass-and-redwood house that clung precariously to the rocky slopes above Marine Drive, propped on cantilevers that didn't look sufficient to support it at the best of times, let alone when it contained at least seventy-five guests and a dozen or so caterers. The view of Burrard Inlet from the living room was spectacular, though, and

David's taste in single malt whisky wasn't bad, either. I was enjoying both, while keeping an eye out for Jeanie Stone, when David came up to me.

"Glad you could make it, Tom," he said in his deep, wet voice. "Are they taking care of you all right?" I presumed by "they" he meant the caterers.

"They're being very generous with your Laphroaig," I told him.

"I was very sorry to hear about Bobbi," he said. "I'm certain she'll be fine. Are the police making any progress?"

"Not so's you'd notice," I replied.

"Terrible thing," he said. "Who's her attending physician?"

"I'm not sure. I've talked to a number of doctors."

"No matter. I'm sure she's in good hands."

David was in his mid-sixties, a year or two younger than my father. An inch over six feet, he had a short salt-and-pepper beard and thick, dark-grey hair that made him look very professorial and distinguished. He was, in fact, both, teaching at UBC and lecturing all over the world on things proctological. He could be a bit pompous at times. My father, never one to mince words, called him "that arse doctor." But he was a decent enough guy.

"Have you met our guests of honour?" he asked, voice rattling with phlegm. I resisted the urge to clear my throat.

"Not yet," I said.

"Well, let's rectify that oversight, shall we?"

"That's not really necessary," I said.

"As it happens," he said, as he guided me across the room, "I'm under orders." I didn't have to guess whose. "And who knows?" he went on. "You might even find Walter Moffat interesting. Walter certainly does. He styles himself as a real Horatio Alger boy-made-good type, a true self-made man." David snorted, which sounded like someone inhaling a raw oyster. "Who was it who said self-made men tend to worship their own creators?"

"Conrad Black?"

David laughed and gave me a laudatory clap on the shoulder. "He'd know, wouldn't he? Walter Moffat thinks just as highly of himself."

Across the room a small crowd of mostly middle-aged women had gathered around a tall, broad-shouldered man with immaculately coifed dark hair, highlighted with just enough silver to give him an air of maturity without making him look old. Jeanie Stone had been right: Walter Moffat was indeed a handsome man, although personally I wouldn't have described him as "drop-dead gorgeous." Nevertheless, he was favoured with just the kind of sincere good looks that television — and television viewers — loved. In his expensive haircut, perfectly tailored suit, and understated tie, he exuded warmth and trustworthiness. You might not have to worry about your daughters around him, but you'd be well advised to keep your eye on your mother.

I wondered what sort of art he collected. I asked David, "Have you seen his art collection?"

"No. Neither has Mary-Alice. We have it on good authority, however, that it is one of the finest collections of its type in the country." He smiled, leaving little doubt as to the source of the authority. "Walter can be something of a bore on the subject, so perhaps you would be wise not to bring it up." He shook his head and smiled ruefully. "Although, of course, that's the point, isn't it? Oh, well. Nothing for it, I suppose."

"Mm," I agreed.

He leaned close and rumbled wetly into my ear. "Oh, and, Tom, be careful of your language. Neither Walter nor his wife care for profanity. She's become quite religious since she found God."

"That's typically what happens," I said. "I'll try to limit myself to scatological or anatomical references."

He grinned. "You know, I think they're both faintly embarrassed by my speciality."

"What was she before she found God?" I asked.

"Something of a wild child, I understand," he said. "Sex, drugs, and rock 'n' roll, although in Elise's case it was a jazz musician, I think. There are rumours of a — well, never mind, it's just gossip. She settled down after her father died and saddled her with the foundation. Running it suited her. It was she who refocused it on the plight of children in the Third World. Walter is also deeply committed to its cause."

David used his bulk to shoulder through the knot of women surrounding Moffat and a slim, severe-looking woman of about forty-five. Walter Moffat's head seemed unusually large in proportion to his body. So, evidently, had been Albert Einstein's. In Einstein's case, the extra size had been necessary to accommodate his larger-than-average brain, which some believed contributed to his genius. I wondered if Walter Moffat was a genius. I didn't think so. Geniuses did not, in my opinion, go into politics. Politics was a game that attracted only the stupider of the species. The proof, if any was required, could be found in any newspaper or on any television news program, or observed directly during question period.

"Excuse me, ladies," David said. The matronly throng melted away. "Walter, Elise. There's someone I'd like you to meet. Tom McCall, Walter and Elise Moffat."

"Pleased to meet you, Mr. McCall," Walter Moffat said as he gripped my hand. He had a deep, smoothly resonant voice. Up close, he was still a handsome man, but his age, which I knew to be fifty-five, was beginning to show, particularly in his face, which was starting to sag here and there, under the eyes and his jowls. A quick visit to a plastic surgeon would take care of the dewlap, I thought. It also looked as though he was wearing makeup. You never knew when a news camera might show up.

"Mr. McCall," Elise Moffat said as she placed her hand in mine. Her voice was as tentative as her grip. Her eyes were a deep, rich brown and quite lovely despite the complete lack of makeup. I realized as I looked into her eyes that she was a very attractive woman who tried hard to make herself look dowdy. Her complexion was pale but flawless, and her fine, shoulder-length hair was the colour of wild honey. She wore it straight, parted in the middle, and secured at the nape of her long neck. She was dressed plainly but well, in a long wool skirt and matching jacket over a white blouse, demurely buttoned to her throat. The suit didn't completely disguise what appeared to be a fine figure. She wore a silver brooch of a crucified Christ upon her lapel, a beatific grimace on the tiny face.

"Tom's my brother-in-law," David said.

"Yes, of course," Walter Moffat said, feigning interest as only a politician can. "The photographer."

"That's right," David said.

"Mary-Alice is a charming woman," Moffat said. "You must be very proud of her, Mr. McCall."

"Indeed I am," I said. "She married very well."

David laughed, a little hollowly, I thought, but Walter Moffat's smile was as weak as my attempt at humour. Mrs. Moffat didn't appear to get the joke. She looked as though she wasn't there at all.

"Do you live in Vancouver, sir?" Moffat asked.

"I'm one of your former constituents," I said. "Except that I didn't vote for you. Either time."

He laughed easily. "No?" he said. "Well, I lost by more than one vote, didn't I?"

"Perhaps you'll do better next time," I said.

"Thank you," he said, with a glint in his eye.

He took his wife's arm. Did she flinch slightly? Perhaps he'd caught her off guard. She impressed me as a very guarded and nervous woman. "It's been a pleasure making your acquaintance, Mr. McCall," Moffat said.

I'd been dismissed, and would have gratefully retreated, but David wasn't done. "Walter," he said, "Tom was just asking me about your collection."

"Oh? Are you interested in art, Mr. McCall?"

"Um, well, not really, it's just that, um, well ..." I could see he was losing patience. "I was looking forward to the opportunity of working with you on the photography for your exhibition catalogue," I blurted.

"Ah, yes, that," he said, glancing quickly at his wife, whose expression perceptively hardened. "I'm very sorry," Moffat went on. "But we have decided not to go ahead with the exhibition. It was all very last-minute, I'm afraid. Please accept my sincerest apologies for any inconvenience it may have caused you. If something else comes up that you can be of assistance with, I won't hesitate to contact you."

"Thank you," I mumbled.

"Now, if you will excuse us, we should circulate. David." He took his wife's arm.

Before he could drag her away, Elise Moffat extended her hand to me again, and said, "Mary-Alice told me of your associate's assault, Mr. McCall. I'm very sorry. I shall pray for her full and speedy recovery."

"Yes, yes, a terrible thing," Walter Moffat added quickly. "She will be in both our prayers."

"Thank you," I said again, with more sincerity. Prayer wasn't something I personally put any faith in, but what could it hurt?

"Walter," David said. "Last week, when you were telling me about the latest additions to your collection, you mentioned that you knew Samuel Waverley, did you not?"

"I may have," Moffat replied. "I don't recall. I'm acquainted with him, of course. I've purchased several pieces from him over the years. Why do you ask?"

"It's a coincidence, I'm sure," David said. He looked at me. "Perhaps Tom should explain."

"Explain what?" Walter Moffat wanted to know, eyes narrowing suspiciously.

"On Tuesday a woman calling herself Anna Waverley hired us to take photographs of a motor yacht called the *Wonderlust*, which she claimed to have received as part of her divorce settlement. I had to meet with another client, so Bobbi, my partner, kept the appointment. She was attacked later that night. The attack evidently took place on the boat."

Mrs. Moffat's pale complexion grew even paler, except for highlights of colour on her cheekbones. Her lips moved as she uttered what I assumed was a silent prayer.

"I'm certain that neither Mr. Waverley nor his wife had anything to do with your partner's attack," Moffat said. "Besides, if I'm not mistaken, he is out of the country. And while the Waverleys do own a boat, I believe it's a sailboat."

"I'm sure Tom didn't mean to imply that the Waverleys were in any way involved," David said.

"No, of course not," I said. "The woman who hired us wasn't Mrs. Waverley and the boat belongs to some numbered corporation. As David said, it's purely coincidental that you know them."

"Correct me if I'm wrong, David," Moffat said, in a tone of voice that made it clear he didn't expect David to challenge him. "Haven't you also purchased works from Samuel Waverley's gallery?"

"You're not wrong," David said. "I bought a watercolour from him last year, and that bronze just last month." He gestured toward a niche that contained a small, dark sculpture of a young ballerina. "I visited

Samuel Waverley's gallery on your recommendation. Although I don't know the Waverleys personally, I have met them both at various charitable events. He's, well, a bit cold, I thought, but she's very charming. Quite lovely, really. Quiet, though, and … sorry," David said, with an apologetic smile. "I'm prattling."

Walter Moffat nodded, as though he agreed, but Elise Moffat's smile, while distant, was not without sympathy.

"And you've no idea who the woman was who hired you?" Moffat said to me. "No, of course you don't. It was a foolish question. I am rattled. We are not accustomed to such violence hitting so close to home."

It was then that a man slid into position partly between David and me and the Moffats. He reminded me of my daughter's pet ferrets, Beatrix and Harry, except that he was nowhere near as cute or cuddly. His suit looked expensive and his dark, thinning hair was combed over his skull from above his left ear and lacquered into place. Jeanie Stone's description fit him to a tee.

"Is everything all right here, Walter?" the man asked, eyes darting suspiciously between David and me.

"Yes, yes, of course, Woody," Moffat intoned reassuringly. "Everything is fine."

"Woody Getz," the man said, thrusting his hand toward me. "Walter's campaign manager. And you are …?"

"Pleased to meet you," I said, reluctantly taking his hand. It was cold and damp and limp. I let go quickly.

"My brother-in-law," David said. "Tom McCall."

"Oh, right. We spoke on the telephone the other day," Getz said.

Moffat took his wife's arm. She leaned against him.

"David," he said, "I think it's time Mrs. Moffat and I said good night. Mr. McCall, I hope that your partner makes a full and speedy recovery."

"Thank you," I said.

David reiterated Moffat's best wishes for Bobbi, said good night, then led the Moffats away in search of Mary-Alice, leaving me alone with Woody Getz. He smiled at me. I felt like a fish stranded on the beach and Getz was a hungry weasel.

"So you're Mary-Alice's brother?" he said.

"I am," I admitted.

"You live on Granville Island, don't you?"

"Not exactly," I said.

"Eh?"

"I live in a floating home in Sea Village."

"But isn't …? Ah, I get it. Very good. I should've said 'at' not 'on,' eh? Arh arh." He didn't quite nudge me with his elbow. "I've been thinking about maybe buying a place there myself."

"Is that right?" I said. "Well, good luck."

"We have a mutual acquaintance, you and I," he said.

"Who's that?" I asked. Did he mean Jeanie Stone? I hoped not. Perhaps he was referring to Blake Darling, the real estate broker, recalling Darling's little chortle as he'd told me that his mysterious client "usually gets what he wants."

"Kenny Shapiro," Getz said.

"Who?"

"Kenny Shapiro. The director. I used to be in the industry. Kenny's an old friend."

"I'm sorry, I don' t …"

Then I remembered. Kenny Shapiro had directed the second season of *Star Crossed*, Reeny Lindsey's syndicated sword-and-sex sci-fi series. They'd shot part of an episode at Sea Village the previous fall.

"You mean Mr. See-em-sweat," I said.

"Eh?"

"Never mind." Reeny had dubbed Kenny Shapiro 'Mr. See-em-sweat' because he had frequently overheated the sets to satisfy his penchant for authenticity. No spray-on sweat for Kenny. He wanted to see the real thing. His predilection for the real thing did not extend too far, though. Reeny had come close to quitting the series when he'd tried to persuade her to get breast implants.

I excused myself and went looking for Mary-Alice. There was still no sign of Jeanie Stone. "She was on the guest list that Walter's manager provided," Mary-Alice claimed, but I was certain she'd fibbed to lure me into her charitable web. I hated it that I could be so easily manipulated. I left soon after, which necessitated manoeuvring my car past a sleek Jaguar coupe, a couple of Mercedes sedans, and a hulking Cadillac Escalade that made my little Jeep Liberty feel downright puny. It was after ten, too late to go to the hospital, I decided, so I drove straight home.

chapter nine

The movers arrived at the Davie Street studio promptly at eight o'clock Saturday morning, three hulking ster-
oidal men in their twenties and a tall, wiry black woman
in her thirties, who appeared to be the boss. In under two
hours, notwithstanding our good-intentioned help, they
moved everything it had taken us all week to pack down
the freight elevator and into their truck. Although the elevator complained loudly and frequently, fortune smiled
upon us and it didn't break down. The drive to the new
location took less than thirty minutes and by noon, the
truck was empty. I thanked the woman and her crew,
handed her the envelope containing the prearranged
tip, then they all piled into the cab and the truck rumbled away, leaving us with our office furniture and filing
cabinets, crates and cartons and equipment cases, not to
mention the film fridge and Bodger's cat carrier, stacked
in the middle of the floor of the new studio space.

Prior to the rehabilitation of Granville Island in
the seventies, the building into which we were moving

had once been a chain and wire-rope manufacturer. It had been renovated to house artisans' workshops, artists' studios, and small galleries and shops. Originally, the building had had a concrete floor and a thirty-foot ceiling, with high, tall windows letting in plenty of light. Our new space still had a concrete floor, but it had been freshly painted a cheerful battleship grey. The front two-thirds of the space still had a twenty-foot ceiling and floor-to-ceiling windows. The back third, however, had been vertically subdivided, with office, washroom, and kitchen facilities upstairs, which is where we stashed a very unhappy Bodger's cat carrier while we unpacked and tried to get organized.

At four o'clock Constable Mabel Firth poked her head through the front door. She was dressed in jeans and a tweedy jacket, and her dark blonde hair was loose. Although she was stationed on Granville Island and her husband Bill worked for the City of Vancouver, they lived in Burnaby, not far from the Chevron tank farm just east of the Second Narrows Bridge, so I didn't often see her in mufti and almost didn't recognize her. At first I thought she was off duty, then I noticed she was armed. There's something about a big, attractive woman carrying a Glock …

"I guess you haven't come to help us get this place sorted out," I said.

"'Fraid not," she said. "We're re-interviewing all the witnesses in Bobbi's assault case, in case we missed something the first time."

"Have you been promoted to detective?"

"No, but a girl can always dream." She took a spiral-bound notebook out of her inside jacket pocket. "Have you got a minute to go over your meeting with the faux Anna Waverley again?"

"Sure," I said. We went outside and sat on a bench in the sun. "Faux?"

"Cute, eh? When I used it this morning, Jim Kovacs almost choked on his coffee. So …?"

I told her about the meeting, in as much detail as I could remember, but without embellishing or speculating to fill in the gaps in my memory.

"And when she left," Mabel said, when I'd finished, "she was under the impression that you were going to meet her at eight on the boat?"

"Yes." She made a mark in her notebook. "Am I to infer," I said, "from the fact that you're re-interviewing everybody, that you aren't making much progress?"

"I'd say that was a safe inference," Mabel agreed. "We canvassed residents of the condos with a view of the seawall and the path between the Broker's Bay Marina and the Burrard Street Bridge. No one saw anything. Baz and I talked to dozens of people on the seawall and the promenade, asking them if they were in the area between eight and eleven Tuesday evening and, if so, did they see anything. Nothing. Our best lead was Anna Waverley, but while she can't prove she was home alone after nine-thirty, there is the problem of motive. She doesn't seem to have one. We can't find any connection between you or Bobbi and the Waverleys." She raised her eyebrows. "Is there one?"

"Actually …"

"What?"

"There might be a kind of indirect connection. My brother-in-law bought some art from Samuel Waverley's gallery. He's also met them socially at charity events."

"What's your brother-in-law's name again?" I told her, plus Mary-Alice's home phone number. "Anything else?" she asked.

"Does the name Walter P. Moffat mean anything to you?"

"Sure. I know who he is. Wally-the-One-Term-Wonder. I wasn't one of his constituents. I wouldn't have voted for him even if I was. Why?"

"I found out last night that he buys art from Waverley, too."

"So do a lot of people, apparently, including the chief constable and the mayor. What's your connection to Moffat, besides being a former constituent?"

"I was supposed to meet him Tuesday evening to discuss photography for an exhibition catalogue, but his manager cancelled the appointment earlier in the day."

"La-di-da," Mabel said. "Keeping pretty highfalutin company these days, aren't we?"

"He's more impressive on TV than in person."

"That's not saying much. What about Bobbi? Could she have known Anna Waverley or her husband?"

"It's possible. Bobbi and I are close enough, I guess, but there are still some aspects of her private life she keeps private. But I didn't get the impression that the name meant anything to her. Have you spoken to her father?"

"Oh, yeah," Mabel replied sourly. "He's convinced it's your fault, that someone was out to get you, and Bobbi got in the way. What about that? You've had more than your share of trouble in the four years I've known you. Vincent Ryan was a nasty piece of work. Any man who would hire a psycho to rape and murder his own wife wouldn't be above this sort of thing."

"Ryan didn't like to get his own hands dirty," I said.

"He tried to kill your former girlfriend, Carla Bergman, didn't he? And he did shoot that guy on the boat."

"I don't know if he was trying to kill Carla or not. As for Frank Poole, I'm not sure Ryan really meant to kill him. He may have been just trying to protect Carla. He wasn't exactly firing on all cylinders at the time. Besides, if it was Ryan, or thugs hired by Ryan, why the charade of hiring me? They could have grabbed me on my way to or from work any time they wanted. And why, when Bobbi showed up instead, assault her? The same goes for anyone else who might have it in for me for real or imagined reasons."

"But if you can think of anyone ...?"

"I'll let you know, of course."

Mabel stood up. She was a big, powerful woman, whose every movement was so effortless it seemed to belie the existence of gravity. "We're pretty much dead in the water. Sorry. Poor choice of words. There's not much we can do till Bobbi wakes up. Then maybe she'll be able to tell us what went down on that boat. Assuming she remembers. I'm told that retrograde amnesia isn't uncommon in cases involving head injury. In the meantime, we're focusing our investigation on the faux Anna Waverley, whoever she is. But I'm afraid we haven't got much to go on there, either."

We shook hands and she left. I went back inside.

Mary-Alice, Wayne, and I had, in the course of the day, managed to get everything positioned more or less where it belonged, but the place still looked a shambles. We knocked off at five. Mary-Alice and Wayne went off together in Mary-Alice's little white BMW while I locked up and walked home, where I showered, had something to eat, then drove to the hospital. I was grateful that neither Greg Matthias nor Norman Brooks was there. I sat with Bobbi until seven, talking to her about the move, telling her that she'd better get the hell better soon and do her share of the work, since she was so keen on the idea in the first place. The tube had been removed from her throat, but she was still catheterized and had an IV in her arm, electrodes taped to her chest, and an oxygen feed under her nose. As I talked to her, she muttered and twitched occasionally, setting off a flurry of bleeps from the monitors, and from time to time her eyelids fluttered, but she did not wake up. I wanted to shake her, but I didn't, of course.

I left the hospital at seven and drove toward home. I didn't go home, however. Instead, I turned west on 4th Avenue and drove toward Point Grey and the vast green of the University of British Columbia Endowment Lands. At seven-thirty I was parked on Belmont above Spanish Bank and Locarno Beach Park, a few metres up the street from a sprawling ranch-style house — the home of Samuel and Anna Waverley.

It wasn't the biggest house on the block, not by a long shot, but it was big enough. Appropriately, it had a vaguely Spanish look, stone and stained wood and glass, with a terra cotta tile roof and deep eaves. A nice house, I thought, that I might be able to afford in my wildest dreams, but not otherwise. It was surrounded by mature trees on a good-sized lot, modestly landscaped with rock gardens and a water feature, but uncharacteristically devoid of topiary, which was abundant on the adjacent properties. The house next door to the Waverleys' had a small cedar clipped into the shape of a poodle with puffball legs, chest, and tail. The things people will do to innocent trees and animals …

There was no car in the Waverleys' wide cobbled drive in front of the attached three-car garage, but as I sat wondering what I was going to do, a dark green Volvo Cross Country went past me and turned into the driveway without signalling. Brake lights flashing, it stopped in front of the garage, driving lights bright on the stained-wood doors. A woman got out, leaving the door open and the engine running, and aimed something at the garage. A remote door opener, I presumed. When nothing happened, she leaned into the car, turned off the engine, then swung the door shut. The car horn bleated and the lights flashed as she walked away from it toward the front door of the house. She was wearing an athletic top, shorts, and high-tech runners. Her upper body was slim, almost petite, while her hips and rump were nicely rounded, legs elegantly tapered. Despite what Witt DeWalt had said, I thought her centre of gravity was fine just where it was.

Now what? I wondered. I couldn't sit there long. It was a fairly exclusive neighbourhood. Sooner or later, most likely sooner, someone would get worried and call the police. Maybe they wouldn't wait until they were worried. So I started the Liberty, put it in gear, and drove into the wide driveway, parking beside Anna Waverley's Volvo. The boxy Liberty and the sleek Volvo looked good together, I thought, as I walked to the front door. Maybe they would mate.

There was a little box with button and a speaker grill by the front door. I pressed the button. A far-off chime sounded, like church bells. A moment later a woman's voice crackled from the speaker.

"Yes?"

"Mrs. Waverley?" I said. "Mrs. Anna Waverley?"

"Yes, I'm Anna Waverley. Who are you?"

"Mrs. Waverley, my name's Tom McCall. I'd like to speak with you, if you don't mind."

"You don't have to shout into the speaker, Mr. McCall. I can hear you just fine if you talk normally. And if you stand back a bit, I'll be able to see you." I stepped back. "Look up, Mr. McCall. Look way up." I looked up and saw a glowing red dot beneath the lens of a small video camera. "What would you like to talk about?"

"We could start with old children's television programs," I said. "I used to watch *The Friendly Giant*, too." Silence. "Mrs. Waverley?"

"I'm still here. I'm waiting for you to get to the point. You've got thirty seconds. Then I call the police."

"Do you know who I am?"

"Yes, I know who you are. You're that photographer whose assistant was attacked and thrown into False Creek. I feel just awful about that, Mr. McCall. I really do. But if you're looking for some kind of compensation, it hasn't anything to do with me or my husband, despite the fact that the woman who hired you evidently used my name."

"It's not about money," I said. "It's about my friend lying in the hospital in a coma. I'd just like to talk to you for a few minutes, to see if there's anything you might be able to tell me that will help me figure out who attacked her."

"I've already told the police everything I know," she said. "Which is nothing."

Her voice had an odd stereophonic quality, as if it were coming from two places at once. I realized that she must be standing on the other side of the door and that I could hear her voice through the mail slot as well as the intercom speaker. I moved closer to the door. "Mrs. Waverley," I said, speaking up slightly, but keeping my voice calm and even and as reassuring as I could. "Someone who said her name was Anna Waverley hired my partner and me to take photographs of that boat. The police have evidence that my partner was attacked on the boat, before she was thrown into False Creek under the Burrard Street Bridge to drown. I'm sure that neither you nor your husband are involved in any way, but I would nevertheless appreciate it if you could spare me a few minutes of your time. I'm just trying to understand why Bobbi was attacked. The police aren't getting anywhere. I —"

A chain rattled and a bolt clicked and the door opened.

Anna Waverley was a handful of inches shorter than me, with wavy reddish-brown hair worn short, rectangular hazel eyes, and a long, straight nose. Her most arresting feature was her mouth. It was wide and slightly crooked, and her lips, which were full and almost too straight, had a bruised quality, like overripe plums. It was not, I thought for some reason, a mouth that smiled often. Matthias had told me she was forty-five, but she could have looked much younger, if she'd tried a little.

"I don't know what I can tell you, Mr. McCall, but come in." She stepped back, holding the door open. "Please excuse the way I'm dressed," she added as I went into the house. "I just got back from a run." She closed the door. "This way, please."

From the outside the house had looked spacious, but inside it seemed dark and cramped. It wasn't that the rooms were small — they weren't — but the front hall and the living room contained enough heavy, ornate furniture for three houses. Likewise, the dining room. Anna Waverley read my expression.

"I'm afraid my husband regards this house more as a warehouse than a home," she said. "Come through this way. We'll be more comfortable in the day room. Would you care for a glass of wine? Or something stronger?"

"Wine is fine," I said.

She excused herself and left the room.

The day room wasn't quite as big as the living room, but contained less furniture. What it did contain was eclectic and casual and comfortable. There was a big, blond wood entertainment unit containing a medium-sized flat-screen TV, a DVD player, and mismatched but high-quality stereo components. One wall of the room was mostly glass. Sliding doors opened onto a patio surrounded by semitropical plants in big terra cotta planters and beds of live bamboo and overshadowed by a towering magnolia. An ornate Victorian dining table by the windows looked as though it had seen better days, the finish scarred and cracked. One end of the table was piled high with magazines and newspapers and books. At the other end of the table, a white Apple laptop sat atop a four-inch stack of volumes from an old set of the *Encyclopædia Britannica*, raising the screen to a more comfortable height to use with the external keyboard and mouse. The computer's power adaptor was plugged into a heavy-duty orange extension cord that snaked across the flagstone floor to an outlet by the entertainment unit.

Mrs. Waverley returned carrying a tray loaded with a bottle of red wine, a bottle of white wine in a sweating beaten-silver cooler, and two tall wineglasses. She set the tray on a massive Spanish-style coffee table. In the short time she'd been out of the room, she'd also managed to brush out her hair, apply a little makeup, and change into jeans, a black turtleneck sweater, and sturdy Rockport walking shoes.

"I wasn't sure if you wanted white or red," she said, sitting on a heavy, worn leather sofa.

"I'll have whatever you're having," I said.

"White, then," she said, lifting the bottle from the silver cooler. "Please, sit down, Mr. McCall. I don't know what I can tell you that I haven't already told the police. I feel just terrible about what happened to your friend. You said she is still in a coma. The police told me she's expected to make a full recovery, though." She deftly levered the cork out of the bottle.

"That's what the doctors tell me." I sat in an equally worn burgundy leather tufted armchair, facing her across the coffee table.

"Well, I certainly hope it's true." She handed me a glass of wine. It had a rich, slightly fruity aroma. I imagined that that one bottle cost more than what I usually spent on three bottles. She raised her glass. "Here's to your friend's full and speedy recovery," she said. We drank. The wine was very good. I upped my estimate of its cost.

"I understand you were at the marina at around nine that night."

"That's right," Mrs. Waverley replied. "Three evenings a week I park my car at Jericho Beach Park near the Royal Vancouver Yacht Club and run to Granville Island and back. Don't look so impressed. It's a total of only a little more than ten kilometres. Ten years ago I used to run more than a hundred kilometres a week. Slowing down in my old age, I suppose."

"It's all I can do to run to answer the phone," I said.

"I'm sure that's not true," she responded.

It wasn't true, or at least not quite, but I was hoping to make her smile. I wanted to see what a smile looked like on that wide, sensuous mouth. I was disappointed when she remained straight-faced. I was going to have to try harder.

"Do you normally run at that time of day?" I asked. "After dark, I mean?"

She shook her head. "No, in the summer usually I run between six and seven, but I was, well, running late that day." She didn't even smile at her own joke. "More wine?" she asked, holding out the bottle.

"No, thank you," I said. My glass was still almost full. Hers was almost empty. She refilled it.

"Your friend — Bobbi?"

"That's right," I said.

"I saw her photograph in the newspaper. She's very attractive. Are you and she lovers?"

I was taken aback by the bluntness of the question. "No," I sputtered. "Just friends. Good friends, though. We've worked together for almost ten years."

"Is it interesting work?"

"It can be," I said.

"Have you exhibited?"

"My photographs? Not hardly. No one's interested in photographs of shopping malls or bridges and helicopters. I did win an award once, though, for a photograph I took when I was working for the *Vancouver Sun* of a man rescuing a huge potted cannabis plant from a burning house." Did her ripe, bruised mouth twitch slightly?

I couldn't be sure because she lifted her wineglass and drank.

She lowered the glass. "Ralph Steiner's photographs of everyday objects are quite beautiful," she said. "Although I think I prefer Aaron Siskind's abstract work. I am also a big admirer of Diane Arbus, although some critics feel her work is too intrusive. Of course, you don't want to simply repeat what's already been done, do you? However, there are many contemporary photographers whose vision of the common, the ordinary, the everyday, often says more about the values of our society than the rare or the beautiful or the fantastic. Do you work with digital, Mr. McCall? Although many people in the arts disapprove, technology has always been at the forefront of art, don't you think? Visual artists are always exploring ways of using technology to push the envelope, whether they be painters, sculptors, photographers, or performance artists."

"I don't really consider myself an artist," I said. "I suppose you could say that I used to be a news photographer, but nowadays I'm just a common, ordinary, everyday commercial photographer. I take pictures of whatever people are willing to pay me to take pictures of. Their kids, their dogs, their airplanes or construction sites, their chairpersons of the board." Not to mention half-naked lady loggers and almost totally naked escort service providers and their girls. As I'd told Bobbi's father, someone had to do it.

"Do you miss being a news photographer?" Mrs. Waverley asked.

"The pay was better," I replied. "But only marginally. More regular, though."

Mrs. Waverley held out the bottle. I held out my glass, although it was only half empty. She topped it up, then poured more wine into her glass. The bottle was nearly empty.

"Are you married, Mr. McCall?"

"I was," I answered, then added quickly, "Mrs. Waverley, the woman who hired us to photograph that boat, do you have any idea who she might be?"

She shook her head. "No, I don't. How would I? It wasn't even our boat. Not that that's relevant, is it? I'm sorry, I'm rambling, aren't I? I've had too much wine on an empty stomach, perhaps. I should eat something."

I stood up, prepared to take my leave, albeit regretfully, mission unaccomplished.

"No, please," she said. "You don't have to go. Unless you have another appointment, of course, if there's some other place you need to be."

"No, there's no place I need to be. But I don't want to be an imposition."

"You're not imposing. Not at all. I enjoy your company. But perhaps we could talk in the kitchen while I make something to eat."

"As long as I'm not imposing," I said.

"You're not," she said and started to pick up the tray.

"Let me," I said, and bent quickly to pick up the tray. A little too quickly. We thumped heads, hard.

She sat down on the sofa, eyes momentarily glazed. *Way to go, McCall.*

"I'm so sorry," I said, ears ringing. "Are you all right?"

"Yes," she said, rubbing her forehead at the hairline. She stood. "Let's try that again, shall we?" She gestured toward the tray. "If you would …"

I picked up the tray and followed her into the kitchen without further incident.

chapter ten

"Do you believe in parallel universes, Mr. McCall?"

"I'm not sure I know what you mean," I said.

She'd made a salad of leafy lettuce, spinach, blue cheese, and pine nuts, but ate very little of it, opening the other bottle of wine instead. We sat at a small, round, glass-topped table in her big, immaculate kitchen. I watched her as she spoke. She sat with her heels on the edge of her chair and her arms folded around her knees. She unwrapped only long enough to reach for her glass of wine, or to nibble on a leaf of lettuce, a crumb of cheese, or a pine nut.

"I read a very strange novel a few years ago," she said, "about a man who created parallel universes every time he made a choice between two or more courses of action. Every time he chose, say, between having the apple pie or the blueberry crumble for dessert, or whether to drive to work or take the bus, the universe split into two separate universes. Alternate timelines, the author called them. In one timeline, the protagonist drove to work, had a car accident, and became a paraplegic, but in the other, he took the bus on which he met the woman he would eventually marry. He was able to move between the different timelines at will, and discovered others who could do the same."

"Handy," I said. "Like being able to take back chess moves."

"It's the only science-fiction novel I've ever read. I don't remember the author's name, or even if it was very good. For some reason, I didn't finish it, so I don't know how it turned out, but I often feel as though I exist in two different universes at the same time, this me in this universe, getting blotto with a perfect stranger, and another me in another universe in which perhaps I'm also getting blotto, but all by myself because I didn't let you into my house. I think I prefer this timeline," she added, and almost smiled.

"Schrödinger's cat," I said.

"Pardon me?"

"Schrödinger's cat. It was a 'thought experiment' in quantum mechanics by a physicist named Erwin Schrödinger. I read about it in *The Complete Idiot's Guide to Physics*. It had something to do with the probability that an atom of uranium or some other radioactive substance would decay within an hour, trigger a Geiger counter, and release a gas that would kill a cat in a sealed container. In one quantum reality, the atom decays and the cat dies. In the other, the atom doesn't decay, and the cat lives. According to quantum theory, the cat's two possible states — alive and dead — are mixed or entangled together until we look into the box to see what happened, at which point the cat's realities separate and it will be either dead or alive."

"How awful."

"Tough on Dr. Schrödinger's cat, anyway," I said. "Fortunately for Felix, it was only a thought experiment.

No real cat involved."

"Do you believe it's possible that with each choice we make," she said, "we create a separate parallel universe for each alternative?"

"I suppose it's possible," I said.

"But unlikely?"

"The probability is not good," I said, and she almost smiled again, but once again hid behind her wineglass.

She refilled her glass from the bottle on the table between us. There was an almost visible aura of sadness about Anna Waverley, an emotional entanglement field in which I was trapped along with her. It was distorting my reality — *she* was distorting my reality — and while my reality was far from perfect, I liked it the way it was. Besides, like it or not, it was the only one I had, and I was stuck with it. I wondered what was so terrible about Mrs. Waverley's reality that she wished for another. Or was I misreading her? Maybe she was just plain nuts.

"How long were you married, Mr. McCall?" she asked.

She changed topics like a stone skipping across the water. "Six years," I said. "It ended ten years ago."

"Do you have any children?"

"A daughter. She'll be fifteen in August."

"My husband never wanted children," Anna Waverley said. "I did, but Sam had had a vasectomy even before I married him. We've been married almost twenty-five years. If we'd had children, they'd be grown now. I could even be a grandmother."

In an effort to get the conversation back on track, I said, "Is it possible that Bobbi's attack, or the woman who hired us, is somehow connected to your husband or his business?"

"What? No, the idea is ludicrous. If you knew my husband, you'd know just how ludicrous. My husband is an extremely boring man. He was boring when I married him twenty-five years ago and he's even more boring now. And his business is equally dull. Do you like this kitchen, Mr. McCall?"

I looked around. The kitchen of Sam and Anna Waverley's house was as big, if not bigger, than my living room. It was equipped as well as the kitchens in many small hotels. And it was spotlessly clean, like a model kitchen in an Ikea showroom.

"It's very nice," I said. "Very clean."

"It should be. It's rarely used. My husband doesn't like home-cooked meals. We eat in restaurants most of the time. Or order in. That's when we eat together at all, which isn't often. Sam lives for his work." She drank more wine, then topped up her glass.

"Mrs. Waverley, when you were at the marina the other night, did you notice anything unusual?"

"No, I did not."

"No strangers hanging around, especially near the *Wonderlust*?"

She shook her head. "No." She picked up the wine bottle and gestured toward my glass. There was still a bit of white left in it.

I shook my head. "I should be going," I said.

"How did you meet your wife?" she asked, as though she hadn't heard me. Perhaps I only imagined I'd spoken aloud.

"I met her in a club," I said. "I was doing photography for a lifestyles piece on working students and she was working her way through university as a bartender."

"She's younger than you are, then?"

"Just by a couple of years," I replied.

"My husband is quite a few years older than I," she said. I found her grammatical precision slightly pretentious, until I realized that she was more than a little drunk. "I was twenty-one when I married him. Sam was forty-two. I had graduated with a degree in art history and got a job in his gallery. There was another woman working for him then. Andrea. She was about thirty, plain, and it seemed to me that she hated me on sight. A month later she was gone, and less that a month after that Sam and I began having an affair. I was so damned utterly naive it embarrasses me to think about it even now. Andrea resented me because she'd been having an affair with him, too, and I was the usurper. She wasn't the first of his assistants with whom he'd had an affair, of course, nor was I the last. His current assistant is Doris. A lovely woman, really. A little plain, perhaps, as have been most of Sam's assistants, but very sweet. I don't know what she sees in him."

Once upon a summer afternoon a few years before, I'd happened across a couple in Stanley Park. They'd been sitting in each others' laps under a tree, mouths greedily fastened, her legs wrapped around his waist and her wide peasant skirt spread across their hips, as they'd rocked and writhed with ever-increasing urgency. I felt as I had then, a reluctant voyeur. I wanted to stop listening to Anna Waverley, as I'd wanted to stop watching the lovers in the park, but I couldn't. Although it was painful hearing her bare her soul to someone she had known for less than an hour, I felt a strange sense of duty to keep listening, to be there for her, to be her sounding board. Her passive therapist. Or her confessor.

"When you were married, Mr. McCall, were you ever unfaithful to your wife?"

"I was tempted once or twice," I admitted. "But I was never actually physically unfaithful." *In this timeline*, I added to myself.

"In the Bible the thought is often as sinful as the deed," Mrs. Waverley said.

"Then, biblically speaking," I said, "I'm doomed to burn in hell."

"Are you a believer?"

"Fortunately not."

"Nor I," she said. "Thoughts are easier to keep secret than deeds. My husband never tried to hide his affairs, perhaps because he does not consider himself to be unfaithful to me. In his mind, adultery is not a sin, any more than having red hair is a sin. As the scorpion said to the fox, it's simply in his nature. To give him credit, he was faithful for the first three years of our marriage, but it is unrealistic, is it not, to expect a scorpion to change its nature just because you wish it? And to be fair, he gave me a choice. He would grant me a divorce, if I wished, as long as the settlement was fair and reasonable, or I could take lovers myself, as long as I promised to be discreet. And careful, of course. Not about disease, although we were just beginning to hear about AIDS then, but about pregnancy. If he did not want children of his own, he certainly didn't want some other man's bastard around."

If thoughts were sins, it was fortunate for me that I didn't believe in hellfire and damnation, because I was doing some very serious sinning at that moment. Not only was Anna Waverley an exceptionally attractive woman, she was also fragile and vulnerable and so very lonely, which tended to bring out the ride-to-the-rescue romantic in me. Unfortunately, the romantic in me also wanted to take Anna Waverley to bed. Badly. I didn't for a moment believe there was a chance in hell of that ever happening, but it was, I thought reluctantly, finally time to take my leave, before I dug myself in any deeper.

"… long while before I took a lover," she was saying. "*Take* isn't the right word, though. I wasn't looking for a lover. I wasn't sure I even wanted one. It just seemed to happen. I've had five lovers since then, Mr. McCall, and, with few exceptions, each was less satisfying than the last. Would you believe me if I told you that I still love my husband? No, of course you wouldn't. Why would you? But I do. And, in his way, I suppose, he loves me as much as he's ever loved anyone. I've had five lovers, when all I've ever really wanted was a real marriage. To Sam. Instead, I'm trapped in this sham of a marriage and having affairs I don't really want with lovers I don't really like." Tears glittered in her eyes. She gestured toward the almost-empty wine bottle on the table in front of her. "And drink myself into a stupor every night so I can sleep."

Run away with me, I wanted to say. *I'll sell my business and my house. You can dump your lover and divorce your husband. We'll take his sailboat, fill it with good wine, and sail the South Pacific until we find a small, deserted island where we'll build a little tree house, lie naked on the beach, drink fermented coconut milk when we run out of wine, and live happily ever after without a care in the world.*

That was sure to make her smile. So what the hell, I thought, and said it. And it worked. After a fashion. It was a very sad smile, though, but a smile nonetheless. It near to broke my heart.

"That's the nicest thing anyone's said to me in a very long time," she said. "Would that it were possible."

"In some parallel universe we'll do it," I said.

"God," she said, gusting alcohol fumes. "You must think I'm a crazy woman. Maybe I am. You come here to talk about your dear friend's attack and find yourself trapped with a madwoman who gets blotto and blathers on endlessly about her pathetic excuse for a life as though you were her shrink or her priest. You poor man. If I weren't so goddamned drunk that I'd probably fall asleep the moment I became horizontal, I'd drag you into the bedroom and make it up to you."

"Maybe next time," I said.

And she laughed.

Her laughter was still ringing in my head an hour later as I got into my car and drove toward home. She'd made tea and she'd talked for a while longer, although I remembered very little of what she'd said, except in the most abstract of ways. When I'd left, I'd thanked her for seeing me, she'd apologized again for subjecting me to her foolishness, and we'd shaken hands. I'd wanted to tell her that I'd like to see her again, but she'd have likely smiled sadly and said, "Perhaps in another timeline," so I'd just let go of her hand and left. I knew, though, that I'd be calling on her again, probably within a matter of days, with whatever lame excuse was necessary to justify it, to ask if she'd have dinner with me, or go deep-sea fishing, or let me weed her garden. I didn't know if my feelings were based on infatuation, lust, compassion, empathy, or simple curiosity, but one thing I knew for certain was that in a very short span of time Anna Waverley had entangled me in her reality. She mattered to me, or her happiness did, and I would do whatever I could short of a felony to help her be happy again. Reeny would understand, I told myself.

It was after eleven when I got home. I brushed and flossed and fell into bed, and for the second night in a row slept like a baby until my bedroom filled with pearly light. I lay in bed for a while, watching dawn brighten in the bedroom window, then slipped comfortably asleep again, waking next a few minutes past seven, whereupon I got out of bed, showered, and went downstairs. I felt wonderful, even better than I had the day before, after my night out with Jeanie Stone. It was a today-is-the-first-day-of-the-rest-of-your-life kind of wonderful. An anything-is-possible, world-is-my-oyster kind of wonderful. In fact, it felt so good to be alive that I knew, deep down inside, where thoughts dwell before you become conscious of them, that something bad was bound to happen.

It was simple thermodynamics.

chapter eleven

I'd magnanimously given Wayne and Mary-Alice Sunday morning off and I was on my own, taking a break after assembling a steel shelving unit, dabbing my barked knuckles with a wad of toilet paper, when Skip Osterman ambled into the new studio. He was carrying two large takeout coffees from the Blue Parrot espresso bar in the Public Market. Skip and his wife Connie operated a deep-sea fishing and charter company out of the Broker's Bay Marina. Skip was always at loose ends on Sunday mornings when Connie was at church. Otherwise, they were inseparable.

"How's Bobbi doin'?" he asked as we prised the lids from the coffee containers.

I'd called the hospital for an update before coming to the studio. "The doctor thinks she'll be waking up any time now," I said.

"That's good to hear. The cops have any idea who done it?"

"If they do, they're not telling me."

"My money's on Loth," he said, blowing on his coffee. He took a cautious sip, sucking it in with a lot of air. "After Bobbi tore him a new one at the public market last month, he was goin' around cursin' and swearin' about how he was goin' to get even with her some way or another. Maybe he did." He took another noisy slurp of coffee. "Man, there's gotta be something we can do about that guy. Bad enough smelling the way he does, but grabbin' his crotch and makin' dirty remarks to women. Constable Mabel says there ain't much they can do. Whenever they talk to him 'cause someone's complained, he goes on about bein' a poor sick old man who ain't never hurt no one. But Christ on a crutch, the other day he's on the quay and Con is at the wheel on the flyin' bridge as we're comin' in from a charter, two couples from a Calgary church group on the deck, and he yells out at her that she can sit on his face any time, even if she does smell of fish. Con ignored him, but I don't care if he's a sick old man, I'll take a goddamn shark pike to him next time he talks dirty to her." He scowled and gulped his coffee.

Between them, Skip and Connie knew just about everyone who kept a boat anywhere near Granville Island, so I asked him if he knew the *Wonderlust*, in particular who the real owners might be.

"I know the boat," Skip said, "but I got no idea who's behind the company that owns it. Whoever it is, they've let it get badly run down. I thought about maybe makin' an offer on it, y'know, but Witt DeWalt told me not to bother, that everyone who's made an offer that's less than the asking price, and that's everyone who's made one, has got blown off. Con figures it's a tax dodge. They're happy to sit on it, cover the docking fees by renting it out for parties, in the meantime write it off as a loss until someone comes along dumb enough to pay the asking price."

"Do you know Sam or Anna Waverley?"

"Seen 'em around. Her more 'n' him. But that's it. They have a thirty-eight-foot Sabre they hardly ever use. Good-lookin' woman, I'll say that, but Con's talked to her a couple of times and says she's not a very happy one. Never seen her smile. I heard she had a run-in herself with Loth a while back. April, I think." He shrugged. "Name me a woman that hasn't."

"What happened?"

"I got it second-hand from Witt DeWalt. Loth was standing at the top of the ramp when Ms. Waverley came along the dock from her boat, dressed for running, and wouldn't move out of the way when she tried to get past him. When she asked him to let her by, he laughed and called her a whore and said he'd let her by if she — well, you know. She had to squeeze past between him and the railing and Witt figures Loth groped her or pinched her, because she yelped and jumped into the air and called him a filthy pig. He acted like he didn't know what she was talkin' about and launched into his usual routine about bein' a poor sick old man who never hurt nobody. Witt asked her if she wanted to call the cops, but she just said, 'What good would it do?' Witt said she was pretty upset, though."

Skip finished his coffee and looked around for some place to dispose of the cup. I took it from him and tossed it into an overflowing waste bin.

"I'll let you get back to work," he said, standing.

"Gee, thanks," I replied.

"Don't mention it. Y'know, I don't care if there is something wrong in his head, one o' these days maybe somebody's gonna pay that old man a visit where he lives and put the fear into him."

"Where does he live?" I asked.

"On some old fishing boat in the Harbour Authority marina. According to what I heard, he claims he's doin' work on it in exchange for living there, converting it into a yacht, would you believe, but no one I know has ever seen him doin' any work."

Art Smelski, the off-duty paramedic who'd fished Bobbi out of False Creek, was refurbishing an old fishing boat he kept in the False Creek Harbour Authority marina. It was a common enough pastime, I supposed. Given the sorry state of the commercial fishing industry, you could pick up old fishing boats for a song. Nevertheless, I asked Skip if it was Art Smelski's boat Loth was supposed to be renovating.

"No," Skip said. "The boat Loth lives on belongs to a fella name of Marshall Duckworth. Some kind o' hotshot lawyer that works for an organization that gets people who've been wrongly convicted out of prison — whether they're innocent or not," he added. "Con knows him and his wife from her church." He looked at his watch, a big waterproof chronometer with a rotating bezel and more dials and knurled knobs than my father's old shortwave radio. "Speakin' of which, they should be lettin' out about now. Gotta go."

A few minutes after Skip left, Constable Mabel Firth and her partner walked in, both in street clothes, but armed, with their badges in plain view. They looked less bulky and imposing in plain clothes — when in uniform they wore Kevlar vests — but they both wore serious, business-like expressions, so I knew immediately it was not a social call.

"We came by to give you a heads-up," Mabel said. "Detective Kovacs is mightily annoyed with you. Can't say I blame him. What the heck were you doing at Anna Waverley's house last night, anyway?"

"Having a very nice time, thank you," I replied, which caused Mabel to scowl darkly and Baz Tucker to shake his head in dismay at my irreverent attitude. "I wanted to talk to her about what happened to Bobbi," I added.

"That much we figured out for ourselves," Mabel said.

"How do you know I was there, by the way? Who are you watching? Her or me?"

"Her. Until we track down the woman who hired you, or the fellow who paid you a visit at your studio, she's our only lead. A slim one, I'll admit, but dollars to jelly doughnuts it wasn't a coincidence that the woman who hired you used her name."

"She's not a suspect, is she?" I said.

She shook her head. "A potential material witness at least. She says she was at the marina that night around nine, maybe she saw something. She claims she didn't, but Kovacs has a suspicious nature. He figures there's a reasonable probability that she knows who attacked Bobbi, maybe even witnessed the attack, but for some reason isn't talking. He figures it's likely because she's afraid that whoever hurt Bobbi will come after her. What was your take on her? Could she be afraid of someone?"

"I didn't get that impression," I said.

"What sort of impression did you get?" Mabel asked.

"Of an intelligent, very lonely and very unhappy woman," I said.

"Do you think she's telling the truth about being at the marina that night?"

"What do you mean? Why would she lie about being there?"

"The thing is," Mabel said, "no one remembers seeing her. It's a busy area, even at that time of day. Our canvass hasn't turned up anyone who saw her along her usual running route that night, either."

"You're thinking maybe she wasn't there?" I said.

"It's a possibility we have to consider."

"I don't get it. Why say she was if she wasn't?"

"Search me," Mabel said. "On the other hand, maybe she was there, but didn't want to be seen, so she said she was there just in case she was spotted."

I shook my head. Someone, maybe Greg Matthias or Mabel, had once told me that the first rule of police work was to keep it simple, that the most obvious explanation for something was usually the right one. "No one saw Bobbi, either, right?"

"Yeah," Mabel said. "Look, Tom, I know you. You're inclined to always think the best of people, and that's not necessarily a bad thing, but how has it worked out for you?"

"It hasn't always been good for my insurance rates," I agreed.

"Cops, particularly detectives, but street cops, too, have a tendency to be more realistic, pessimistic, even."

"No," I said, with mock incredulity.

"You said Anna Waverley was intelligent …"

"Yes," I said.

"While your average crook isn't all that bright, some are brighter than others. The smartest ones stick as close to the truth as possible, even if it means admitting to something that might be construed as circumstantially incriminating. A robbery suspect admitting to being in the vicinity of a robbery, for instance. They know it's not half as damaging as getting caught in an outright lie."

"So what you're saying is that Anna Waverley admitted to being at the marina because she's afraid to be caught in a lie if you do find someone who saw her there?"

"She also admits to having been at a party on the *Wonderlust* at least once, which would account for her fingerprints, if they're found. Kovacs doesn't believe she's responsible for Bobbi's beating, but he's sure she knows more than she's saying."

"What do you think?"

"I don't have an opinion," Mabel replied diplomatically. "I've never met her. I should know better than to encourage you, but what do you think? Could she have been involved?"

"I don't know," I said. "She told me she doesn't know anything about it."

"And you're inclined to believe her?"

"More than just inclined," I said. "I do believe her …"

"But …"

"I've been wrong before …"

"But …" Mabel prompted again, a little more firmly.

"Well …" I said.

"For Pete's sake, Tom," Mabel said. "What?"

"I think she might meet with her lover on the *Wonderlust*," I said, with a twinge of something that felt like guilt.

Mabel's eyebrows went up. Baz grunted softly. Neither of them was half as surprised as I was, though. I didn't like the direction my thoughts were taking me. It felt as though I was being disloyal to her, which was just plain silly; I hardly knew her. Nevertheless, I liked her and didn't want to believe that she'd had anything to do with Bobbi's attack.

"You think that maybe Bobbi interrupted them and lover-boy beat the crap out of her and dumped her in False Creek," Baz said, more than a hint of skepticism in his voice.

"Something like that, I guess."

"How do you know she even has a lover?" Mabel said.

"She told me her marriage was a sham and that she was having affairs she didn't want with lovers she didn't like. She's had five lovers since she got married, she said, so there's a good chance she has one now."

"You work fast, don't you?" Mabel said. "You knock on the woman's door and the next thing you know she's telling you all about her marriage and her lovers. Kovacs isn't going to like this. He isn't exactly

Mr. Charm, but he's a good interviewer. All he got out of her in an hour was her running schedule. Why did she spill her guts to you?"

"Well, she did drink almost two full bottles of wine in under three hours," I said.

Mabel groaned. "Please tell me you didn't sleep with her."

"I didn't sleep with her."

She breathed a sigh. "Sorry," she said.

"It's all right. Forget it."

"You liked her, though."

"Yes," I said. "Quite a lot. But I also feel, well, sorry for her. As I said, she's a very unhappy lady."

"Kovacs says she's very attractive. Your track record with attractive women is not great, Tom. Your track record with very attractive women is even worse."

"Thanks. It's good to have friends who will tell you exactly like it is. Keeps you humble."

"You're welcome."

"But maybe you're right," I said. "Maybe she was playing me. I don't like to think so, but ..." I shrugged. When I'd left her house the night before, I'd been certain that she hadn't had anything to do with Bobbi's assault. Likewise, the following morning. However, it was as if she'd cast some kind of spell on me, but it had finally worn off and I could think clearly again. I still didn't want to believe she'd lied to me, and maybe she hadn't, strictly speaking, but I couldn't shake the feeling that she'd played me like the proverbial fiddle.

"I don't suppose she told you her lover's name or anything that might help us identify him."

"No."

Mabel jotted something in her notebook. "Was she able to shed any light on who may have impersonated her?"

"No."

"Or why someone would pose as her to hire you to take photographs of the *Wonderlust*?"

"No …"

"But …?" Mabel said, drawing the word out to indicate her impatience.

"I asked her if she thought it might have had something to do with her husband or his business. She thought the idea was ridiculous, that her husband is a very dull man in a very dull business. Then she asked me if I liked her kitchen."

"Like she was trying to change the subject?"

"I didn't think so at the time, but, yeah, I think that's exactly what she was doing. She's very good at it."

"Okay, so you do think she might know more than she's telling?" Mabel suggested.

"I don't know," I said, then added, "Yes, I think she does."

"You seem disappointed."

"I guess I am." I thought about it for a moment, then said, "Look, what if she did meet her lover at the marina? She's there often enough. Maybe it's a regular thing."

"Are you suggesting that faux Anna Waverley hired you to interrupt real Anna's little tryst?"

"To hear you say it, it does sound farfetched," I said. "If faux Anna just wanted someone to interrupt real Anna and her lover, why not just have a pizza delivered?"

"Or call the cops and report a domestic disturbance," Baz said.

"Besides," I said, "wouldn't she be more likely to meet her lover on her own boat? Why on the *Wonderlust*?"

"I might be able to answer that one," Mabel said. "Many women don't like to make love with another man in the same bed they share with their husbands — or that their lovers share with their wives." I wondered if she was speaking from experience.

"Okay," I said. "But that still doesn't explain why

someone posed as her to hire me to photograph it." I thought about it for a moment, then said, "What if …?"

"What if what?" Mabel asked.

I thought about it some more, then said, "What if Bobbi's attack had nothing to do with the real Anna Waverley? What if it we were hired to do a legitimate job, but for, well, ultimately nefarious purposes? What if the faux Anna really wanted photographs of the *Wonderlust* and someone saw Bobbi go aboard, followed her, and assaulted her? Maybe someone who wanted to steal the photographic gear or hijack the van."

"Okay," Mabel said. "But it doesn't explain faux Anna's 'ultimately nefarious purposes,' as you put it. Why did she want photos of the boat?"

"I dunno. Maybe she's a nautical designer and the *Wonderlust* has a particularly innovative or unique design she wants to steal." Mabel made a face and Baz Tucker sniffed. I tried again. "Maybe she was planning to steal the boat, but didn't want to be seen hanging around the marina casing the job, so she hired us to do it for her with photos."

Mabel shook her head, but said, "All right, let's say you're right, in theory, anyway. Why pose as Anna Waverley?"

"Maybe she called herself Anna Waverley in case we checked in at the marina office for permission to go onto the docks. Normally, the gate is supposed to be locked. Boat owners can get touchy about unauthorized people wandering around on the docks." I was struggling; it was starting to get too complicated.

Mabel scribbled in her notebook while Baz Tucker looked over her shoulder. She looked at him. He shrugged. She looked at me.

"Not bad," she said. "I'm not sure Kovacs will buy it, though, even at a discount. He's convinced you're holding out on him, that Bobbi was attacked by someone out to get you and/or her and that you probably know who. Your visit to Anna Waverley's house didn't help. He's going to turn over a load of rocks to see if you've had any prior contact with her. Have you?"

"No. I never laid eyes on her before last night."

"What about her husband?"

"Him, either."

"Okay. I'll run it past him, see what he thinks. He's going to want to talk to you about Anna Waverley. Don't expect him to be happy about you sticking your nose in his case."

Mabel and Baz left and I went back to work. I tried to ignore the nagging sense of guilt at telling Mabel and Baz about my conversation with Anna Waverley, but as much as I liked her — or thought I liked her — it wasn't beyond the realm of possibility that she may have been manipulating me. As Mabel had pointed out, manipulating me wasn't a terribly difficult task for an even moderately attractive woman, let alone one as lovely and apparently vulnerable as Anna Waverley. I didn't like the idea that I could be that easily played, and it made me a little angry, although I wasn't sure who I was angry with, Anna Waverley or myself. Nevertheless, I felt as though I'd betrayed her and I did not feel good about myself for it.

Mary-Alice arrived, and shortly thereafter, D. Wayne Fowler, bearing lunch: fish and chips for himself, a veggie wrap for Mary-Alice, and a bacon cheeseburger for me. After lunch, we set up the portrait studio, the digital studio camera, and started work on the darkroom. At four o'clock the phone rang.

chapter twelve

"Tom," Greg Matthias said when I answered. "I'm at the hospital. I —"

"Is she awake?"

"No, not yet." He paused for a couple of beats, then just as I was about to ask him what was up, said, "This afternoon someone posing as a florist delivery man tried to get into her room."

My guts clenched.

"She's okay," he added hastily. "The nurses wouldn't let him in. They have orders not to let anyone in to see her but attending physicians, nurses, cops, or immediate family, unless they've been specifically cleared. From the description, it sounds like it might be the same guy who came to see you at your studio the other day."

"So much for this sort of thing happening only on television."

"It usually doesn't," he said, an edge on his voice. "Nor is he likely to try again. But just to be on the safe side we're moving her to another room, under a different name."

"Not Jane Doe, I hope."

"Give us some credit," he said, the edge sharpening. "I'm going to tell you the name, but I'm going to ask you not to reveal it to anyone else. Not even your sister or Wayne Fowler. Okay?"

"Okay." Wayne wouldn't like it, but he'd understand.

"The name is Edward Winston. I can't tell you the room number because I don't know it yet, but if you ask for Edward Winston at the information desk in the main lobby, that'll tell them you're cleared to see her."

"Got it," I said.

"And we'll also have a couple of plainclothes officers in the room with her."

After Matthias hung up, we called it a day. I went home, showered, then drove to the hospital. At the information desk in the main lobby, I asked the woman behind the counter for Edward Winston's room number. She consulted her computer screen, asked me to repeat the name, which I did, then gave me the floor and the ward number, but not the room number, telling me that I would have to ask for the room number at the nursing station. As I thanked her and turned toward the elevators, she picked up her phone and dialled, no doubt calling ahead to warn them that someone was on his way up. If anyone was expecting me when I got off the elevator, it didn't show, but when I asked for Edward Winston's room number at the nursing station, the nurse behind the desk asked me for my name and consulted a screen before telling me the room number.

As Matthias had said, there were two plainclothes cops in the room, Mabel Firth and Baz Tucker. They were sitting on the empty bed, playing cards on the rolling table.

"We'll wait outside if you like," Mabel said, standing up.

"No," I said. "Sit. Stay."

"Woof," Mabel said, as she sat down again.

Bobbi was on her side, still connected to the monitors, oxygen, IV, and catheter, a clear bag of vivid yellow liquid hanging on the side of the bed. She appeared to be sleeping and I'd unconsciously lowered my voice so as not to wake her, but she muttered and moaned, twitching and rolling onto her back.

"She's been very restless," Mabel said. "The docs say that's a good sign."

I put my hand on Bobbi's shoulder, shook her gently. "Bobbi. Wake up. It's time to go to school." Bobbi muttered querulously, rolling her head from side to side.

Mabel chuckled. "That's exactly what one of the doctors did."

Then Bobbi's eyes opened.

"Hey," I said. "She's awake." I leaned over her. "Bobbi. Hi."

But she didn't answer, just stared at me for a second, no recognition in her eyes. Then her eyes closed.

"She's been doing that, too," Mabel said. "The doctor says it's nothing to worry about."

Easy for them to say, I thought.

Baz Tucker put away the cards and stood up. "I'm for coffee. Either of you want any?"

"No, thanks," I said. Mabel shook her head. He left the room.

"He's mad at me," Mabel said. "He doesn't like hospitals."

"Who does?"

"I'm okay with them. I worked as an orderly for a while before joining the cops. But they give Baz the jitters."

"But why's he mad at you?"

"He blames me for landing us here. He's not interested in becoming a detective."

"Wouldn't it mean a bump in pay?"

"Yeah. Nothing great, but every little bit helps. Baz doesn't need the money. He made a packet when he was playing ball and invested it well. And he likes being a street cop. He says it's a lot like football, long periods of intense boredom punctuated by short intervals of violent activity. Baz likes the rush, but me, I like the periods of intense boredom. In the meantime, being seconded to major crimes is good experience for when I get my detective shield."

"When will that be?"

"Soon, I hope. I aced the exams, if I do say so myself."

"Congratulations."

"Thanks. Now it's just a matter of waiting for an opening."

I remembered what Greg Matthias had said about retiring to Pemberton to raise horses with his former partner. Someone would have to move up to take his place, perhaps creating an opening for Mabel. I would miss her when she became a "suit."

Bobbi mumbled and stirred in the bed and the monitors responded with a brief skirl of bleeps. The machines settled down.

"She'll be okay, Tom," Mabel said. "She'll come out of this."

"I hope so," I said.

Then Bobbi loudly passed wind.

"Oh, dear," Mabel said. "Let's not tell her about that when she wakes up."

It was after nine when I got back to Granville Island. I hadn't eaten dinner, so I stopped by Bridges for a pint and a bowl of chowder so hearty you could eat it with a fork. I ate at the bar. I wasn't in the mood for company and didn't look up from my food when someone legged onto the stool next to mine.

"That must be damn good soup," Norman Brooks said.

Phil the barman dropped a coaster in front of him. "What can I get you?"

"I'll have a pint of whatever he's drinking," Brooks said. "Bring him another one, too."

"Thanks, I'm okay," I said. Phil nodded and drew Brooks a pint.

"I know you and me haven't exactly got off on the right foot," Bobbi's father said. "But you could at least let me buy you a beer."

Phil placed Brooks's beer on the coaster, then moved down the bar to serve another customer.

"At the risk of appearing ungracious," I said, "why would I want to do that?"

"I dunno. Just to be friendly, maybe?" He downed half his pint in three or four big gulps.

"I'm not interested in being friendly," I said. "Or having a drink with you, for that matter. Why don't you find somewhere else to sit and leave me to enjoy my chowder in peace?"

"I want to talk to you."

"I don't want to talk to you. The last time we talked, you accused me of being a pornographer and a drug dealer."

"Jesus," he said. "You really are as big a prick as everyone around here seems to think you are."

"Size isn't everything, but I'm pleased I haven't disappointed."

"Goddamn it, McCall. My daughter's lyin' in the hospital in a coma and all you can do is make wise-ass remarks. She's supposed to be your friend."

"Sorry," I said, genuinely chastened.

"Yeah, sure you are," Brooks growled into his beer.

"She's doing better, by the way," I said. "She even

opened her eyes for a second while I was there. The doctors expect her to come out of the coma any time now."

"Bastards still won't let me in to see her," he grumbled.

"You're welcome," I said. Had the police given him the Edward Winston password? I wondered. I didn't want to ask, in case they hadn't; I didn't want to have to explain why a password was necessary to get into see her. As it happened, he knew.

"Tell me about the guy that tried to get into her room earlier today," he said.

"All I know is that the police think it might be the same person who came to my studio the other day asking questions about the woman who hired us to photograph the boat."

"This person have a name?"

A couple of wise-ass remarks occurred to me, but it was obvious Brooks wasn't in the mood. I simply said, "No."

"Not good enough," he said. "You lied to me about knowing the Waverley woman. Why should I believe you don't know the guy that tried to get into Bobbi's room?"

"I wasn't lying about Anna Waverley," I said. "I didn't know her. I still don't, not really."

"I know you went to see her last night," he said. "What did she tell you?"

"Nothing."

"Goddamn it, McCall. You gonna tell me what the fuck's goin' on or do I have to squeeze it out of you?"

I sighed. "It's late," I said. "I've had a long day," I added. "And I'm really not in the mood for this."

Brooks slid off his stool and loomed over me. "Fuck you and the horse you rode in on, McCall. Don't you get all high and mighty with me, you son of a bitch. You'll —"

"Sir," Phil said.

Brooks's head snapped around. "What?" he barked.

"Please leave the gentleman to enjoy his supper, sir, if you don't mind."

"I do mind, sonny. So why don't you just fuck off and mind your own goddamn business."

The manager, Kenny Li, came over. "Ev'ning, Tom," he said. "What seems to be the problem?"

"No problem," Brooks said. "I just want to have a quiet drink and a chat with my friend here."

Phil said, "This gentleman" — meaning me — "would like to enjoy his supper in peace."

Kenny turned to Norman Brooks. "Sir, let Phil top up your pint, on the house, and we'll find you another place to sit."

"Put a hand on me, sonny-boy," Brooks growled menacingly, "I'll break it off."

Kenny looked affronted. "Sir, I wouldn't dream of putting my hands on you. But I will have to ask you to leave if you don't calm down and show more respect for our other patrons' privacy."

Although I had eaten less than half my chowder, and taken only a few sips of my beer, my appetite had abandoned me. Climbing off my stool, I dropped money onto the bar.

"I think I'll be going," I said, and headed for the exit.

When I got outside, someone was leaning against the Liberty. It was Loth. He did not move when I pressed the remote and the locks thunked and the lights flashed, diffused by the gathering fog.

Screw it, I thought. I wasn't in the mood to deal with Loth, either, so I pressed the remote again, locking the car, and kept on walking. I'd go back and get it later, before the three-hour limit was up.

"You, mister man," Loth called out, heaving himself away from the side of the car, which rocked on its suspension. "What I ever done to you that you gotta go and tell the cops I hurt yer fran?" He lumbered after me, cane tocking on the cobbles. "Hey, you. Stop. I'm talkin' a you."

I turned toward him and he stopped in his tracks, radiating anger and righteous indignation. His body odour was breathtaking. It was a wonder it didn't rot the clothes off his back. Maybe it did; his shirt looked new.

"I didn't tell the police you hurt her," I said. "I just told them about your little altercation at the market last month."

He glared at me. "Alter what? Fuck's that?"

"Altercation. Confrontation. Argument. Difference of opinion. Look it up in your thesaurus."

He took a couple of steps toward me, an ambulatory mountain of noisome flesh.

The street was dark and quiet, the haloed street lights casting indistinct shadows in the fog. The few people about scrupulously ignored us, hurried on their way. I thought seriously about running away, too.

"You t'ink I'm stupid, eh? Maybe I dunno fancy words like you, but I ain't stupid. Why the cops talk to me, eh? 'Cause you told 'em I's the one that hurt her."

"Okay, fine. You didn't hurt her."

He took a couple more steps toward me and I backed away. "I ain't never hurt no one," he said menacingly, brandishing his stout cane.

A figure emerged from the shadows. It was Norman Brooks. I was almost relieved to see him.

"Jesus, McCall," he said. "This guy a friend of yours? You really gotta start hanging out with a better class of people." He waved his hand in front of his face. "Christ, you smell like a three-week-old corpse. When was the last time you took a bath? The day they let you out of the joint?"

Loth waved his cane at Brooks, repeating his familiar refrain. "I ain't never hurt no one. I'm just a poor, sick ol' man. My lawyer, he says I was *imprisoned falsely*. He *exonerated* me."

"I'll be sure to pass that on to the families of the women you raped and murdered in Coquitlam."

"*I ain't never raped no womens,*" Loth roared like an indignant lion.

With surprising speed, Brooks reached out and yanked the cane out of Loth's hands.

"Was it this stinking piece of filth that hurt my daughter?"

"No," I said, no idea if it was true or not, just hoping to defuse the situation before it got out of hand.

"Gimme my stick," Loth said.

"You don't need this thing any more than I do." He held it in both hands, as if he were going to snap it across his knee.

"I need my stick. I got art'ritis real bad in my hip."

"Mr. Brooks," I said. "Don't do anything stupid."

"Fuck you," he said, but he tossed the cane at Loth. It rebounded off Loth's broad gut and clattered onto the cobbles. Loth got stiffly down onto one knee and picked it up. He used it to help himself stand.

"I ain't hurt yer fran," he said to me.

"Do you know who did hurt her?" I asked him.

He shook his great head.

"Bullshit," Brooks said. "You know who did it, don't you, you sac of shit?"

"I ain't know nothing," Loth said, still shaking his head.

"Goddamn it," Brooks shouted, and for a second I thought he was going to attack Loth.

"You ain't listen, anyway," Loth said. "You t'ink I done it."

"All right, you didn't do it," Brooks said. "But you know who did. Tell me."

"Or you do what?" Loth challenged. He waved his

cane. "You ain't gonna hurt no poor, cripple ol' man." He turned toward me. "Tell him, mister man. I don' know who hurt yer fran. Them mens maybe."

"What men?" I asked.

"The mens that go with the whores," he said. "All them womens is whores, suck on men's dicks for money, spread their ass cheeks. Tell him. Tell him."

"Jesus," Brooks said. "What's he talking about? What whores? Is he crazy?"

"Whores," Loth said again, and lumbered away, cane tocking on the cobbles, muttering and swearing to himself.

Brooks looked at me. "A fat lot of help you were. He knows who attacked my daughter."

"I don't know," I said. "Maybe he does know something and maybe he doesn't. I'm not sure what you expected me to do, though."

"More than you did, that's for sure," he groused.

I looked at him. "Screw you and the horse you rode in on," I said, then left him there and walked back to my car.

Just another quiet Sunday evening on Granville Island.

When I got home, the message light on the phone was blinking. I accessed my voice mail. Reeny's voice was tinny and distant as the message played back.

"Tom? Damn, I'd really hoped to talk to you in person, not do it like this. Shit. Look, I guess there's no easy way to tell you, except straight out, before you see it in some tabloid. I know you don't read them, but — I met someone, Tom. He's a really great guy. You'll like him. Anyway, we got engaged last night. And, well, I don't suppose there's anything much left to say except

I'm sorry things didn't work out. You're a great guy, too. Take care. I'll call you when we get back to Canada. Maybe we can get together for a drink or something. Bye."

As I erased the message and hung up the phone, I remembered what Bobbi had told me about not being sure that she and Greg had broken up. I had no doubt whatsoever that Reeny and I just had. I wondered why it didn't hurt more.

chapter thirteen

I was at the studio early Monday morning. Things were starting to come together, but there was still a lot to do. It was another grey, drizzly day. Whether it was global warming, scalar beams, or normal meteorological unpredictability, the summer wasn't shaping up to be one of the better ones on record, although celestially speaking it was still spring. The streets of Granville Island were almost deserted, locals staying home and dry and the tourists huddling in their hotel rooms and B&Bs complaining about the Pacific Northwest weather. I sat with my coffee in a director's chair, feet on a table and gazing out the front window at the little quadrangle called Railspur Park, not thinking about Reeny's call by trying to decide what I would tackle first, unpacking the dozen or so boxes of files and photo archives or finish painting the upstairs office. The darkroom I was leaving for Wayne. Mary-Alice and I had a meeting after lunch with an architectural firm that wanted a photo spread of its new offices, but otherwise we had left the week open to get the new studio up and running. When Mary-Alice arrived, she found me trying to make up my mind whether to give Reeny a call or send her a congratulatory card to let her know that I harboured no ill feelings and wished her well.

"Hard at it, I see," Mary-Alice said.

"Yes, indeed," I replied.

"Don't strain yourself."

"I'll be careful."

She poured herself a cup of coffee and pulled over another chair.

I stood up. "Enough woolgathering. Time to get to work."

She scowled and sipped her coffee.

Wayne came in, followed by a gangly girl of thirteen or so who looked enough like him to be his sister. He introduced her as his niece Alison. She elbowed him in the ribs. "Oof. Sorry. Ali. No school today and my sister has to go out of town, so I said I'd keep an eye on her."

"I'm a photographer, too," Ali said. She unzipped her waist pack and took out a little Canon digital. I felt a brief stab of envy at the idea of photography for fun.

"But can you paint?" I said.

"Sure, I guess."

"You're hired," I said.

"The pay's lousy," Mary-Alice warned her.

When we broke at noon, Ali had paint in her hair and on her face, but she had managed to get more on the office walls than on herself. After cleaning her up, I put a sign on the door that we'd gone to the Public Market for lunch and would be back at one. The weather had improved so we ate outside on the quay. When we got back to the studio, the message light on the phone was blinking. The message was from the police. When I called back, I learned that they'd located the van. Or at least what was left of it. It had been ditched in Surrey, stripped of everything removable, and then some, and set alight. No sign of the camera equipment.

I called the insurance company and gave them the good news. Later, leaving Wayne and Ali to look after the studio, Mary-Alice and I went to our appointment with the architectural firm. We took her car. The meeting went well, and we came away with a nice contract, plus the promise of more work in the future, if things worked out. On the way back to the studio, Mary-Alice asked me how much the insurance company would reimburse us for the van.

"Not much. It was getting pretty old. Certainly not enough to buy a new one. The cameras and the other equipment were covered for replacement value."

"I don't think we can afford to replace the van," she said.

"Forget it. The Jeep will do for now."

"That's your personal vehicle."

"So?"

"Keep track of the mileage. The company will reimburse you for its use."

"Fine. Whatever." Then I remembered that she'd reset the Beamer's trip meter when we'd set out after lunch. "You're charging your mileage now?"

"Of course," she said. "Thirty-five cents a kilometre." I had no idea if that was the going rate or not, but it didn't strike me as excessive. "Do you have a problem with that?" she said.

"What? No, of course not. It's only fair."

"But you have a problem, don't you?"

"What makes you say that?"

"Come on, Tom. You're my older brother. I've known you all my life. I can tell when you're not happy about something."

I almost laughed, but my instinct for self-preservation kicked in. If Mary-Alice could sense there was something troubling me, it must have been tattooed on my forehead in bright green letters. Although she was right that something was bothering me, she was wrong about what.

"Is it me?" she asked. "Is it the way I've reorganized the company? I thought we'd settled all that." She took her eyes off the road for a second to glance at me. "Haven't we?"

If her idea of settling it had been me acceding to her wishes, agreeing with her plans, then it certainly had been settled. "No, it's not that," I said. "You've done a great job with the reorganization and I think the new studio is going to work out fine."

"But ... ?"

I didn't want to talk about Reeny's call, so I said, "I just need time to adjust."

Her eyes narrowed. "Adjust to what?" she asked, somewhat defensively, I thought.

It was a good question. When I'd started the business after leaving the *Vancouver Sun*, it had been just me I'd had to worry about. As long as I had enough work to cover child support payments, rent on the studio and my house, plus food, clothing, and car repairs, with a little left over for a decent bottle of Scotch now and again, I was happy. And if things got tight, which they had from time to time, especially during the first couple of years, I could always make do with cheaper Scotch. Not much had changed when Bobbi had come on board as my assistant, or even when she'd bought in as a partner a few years later, we worked that well together. But things were different now. The company was no longer just me and Bobbi and Bodger scraping by and having a good time doing it, despite the ups and downs. It was Granville Photographic Services, Inc. We had a logo. We had a corporate seal. We had a chairman of the board (me), and a president (Bobbi), and a secretary-treasurer (guess who). We had inventory control. And we charged mileage when we used our personal vehicles on company business. It wasn't as much fun anymore.

"Growing up," I said. "Responsibility."

Marry-Alice grunted. "We all have to grow up some-time, Tom," she said. "You're not Peter Pan."

"No," I said, wondering where Tinkerbell was when I needed her; I could have used a dose of pixie dust about then. Mary-Alice, too.

I didn't recognize the cop outside Bobbi's room when I got to the hospital at six that evening. He demanded my name and wouldn't let me past until he'd checked it against his list. When he finally let me into Bobbi's room, Greg Matthias was already there, sitting beside Bobbi's bed, reading aloud from a trade paperback with an old hand-tinted photo of a cowboy on the cover, *The Englishman's Boy* by Guy Vanderhaeghe, one of Bobbi's favourite authors. He closed the book and stood as I approached the bed.

"How is she?" I asked. She didn't look any different, although her bruises were yellowing and the lacerations were healing nicely.

"She seems closer to the surface," he said. "As if she'll wake up any time."

Her eyes fluttered.

"She hears us," I said.

"I think so."

"Hey, Bobbi. Enough of this already. No more slacking off. It's time to wake up."

Matthias grinned and Bobbi's eyes fluttered again and she muttered querulously. Then her eyes opened and she looked straight at me.

"Hi," I said, half expecting her to close her eyes again,

as she'd done the day before. She didn't, though. She continued to stare at me, but she didn't speak. There wasn't any recognition in her eyes. Just confusion. "Hi," I said again.

She blinked and in that instant came back from wherever she'd been.

"Tom?" she said, voice a raspy croak.

"Hey, Bobbi," I said, throat tight, eyes burning. "Welcome back."

"Where have I …?" She licked her dry, cracked lips. "Can I have a drink of water?"

Matthias handed me a cup with a bent drinking straw. "Just a sip," he said.

Her eyes swivelled toward him, but her lips closed around the tip of the straw. She sipped and swallowed, sipped and swallowed, then released the straw.

"Hello, Greg," she said, voice a bit less raspy.

"Hello, Bobbi. How do you feel?"

She looked at me, as if uncertain how to answer the question.

"I'll get a doctor," Greg said and went to the door.

"I know this is going to sound stupid," Bobbi said, "but where am I?" She looked around. "It looks like a hospital room."

"It is," I said. "You're in the Vancouver General."

"What happened? Did I have an accident?" She tried to sit up, sending the monitors into panic mode. She fell back. "Christ, I feel like shit." She reached up to touch her face. "My face feels funny when I talk."

"You're pretty banged up," I said.

"Am I — am I going to be okay?"

"Sure, you're going to be just fine."

"Then why are you crying?"

I rubbed my nose. "Allergies."

Matthias came back into the room with a nurse. She glanced at the machines beside the bed as she took Bobbi's hand and said, "How do you feel, dear?"

"Like I've been hit by a truck," Bobbi said. She looked at me. "Was I?"

"No," I said.

Another woman came into the room, an attractive Indian doctor I'd seen around, about forty, with the most amazing eyes, huge and inky black. Her photo ID badge identified her as Dr. I.R. Sandra. She shooed Matthias and me out of the room.

"She doesn't remember what happened," I said in the hall.

"It could take some time."

The door opened and Dr. Sandra came out. "You can go back in now," she said. "She's going to be fine. We'll leave the monitors on for the time being. Don't let her drink too much water. Just little sips. And don't be surprised if she goes back to sleep. Normal sleep. She'll likely wake up starving."

Matthias and I went back in. The nurse was adjusting the bed, propping Bobbi up a bit. She looked better already, more colour in her face, life in her eyes.

"Hi," she said as the nurse left. "Maybe one of you guys will tell me what the hell happened. I asked the nurse, but all she said was that I got hurt. Did I have an accident? Shit, did I crash the van?"

"No," Greg said. "You didn't have an accident."

"What, then?" Her voice took on an edge of panic. "Why can't I remember?"

"Don't worry about it," Greg said. "You will. What's the last thing you do remember?"

Her face screwed up in an almost comical expression of concentration. "I — we were in the studio, the office. I — we —" She closed her eyes and rolled her head slowly back and forth on the pillow. "I'm tired," she said in a little-girl voice, squirming down in the bed. She pulled the covers up under her chin, closed her eyes, and went to sleep.

Greg and I sat beside the bed and talked softly about nothing in particular, waiting for her to wake up again. Dr. Sandra came into the room, looked at the machines monitoring Bobbi. She cranked down the bed and told us Bobbi might sleep for a while, maybe we should go home. We thanked her and she left.

"How is the new studio coming along?" Greg asked.

"Fine," I said. "Still a lot to do, though. Do you want to get some coffee?"

"Sure," he said.

We went in search of coffee, found a reasonable facsimile in the coffee shop on the main floor, and took it back up to the room, bringing one for the cop on the door. Bobbi was still asleep, on her side with her hands under her cheek and her knees drawn up. Greg and I resumed our seats and drank our coffee.

"Should you call Kovacs?" I asked him.

"He'll know soon enough."

"What about her father?"

"The hospital will notify him."

I told him about my encounter with Loth and Norman Brooks the night before.

"I'll suggest that Kovacs interview Loth again," Matthias said. "You never know, maybe he does know something useful."

"I thought for a minute Brooks was going to try to beat it out of him," I said. "Loth may be old and arthritic, but I don't think he'd have any trouble handling Brooks. He was more than a little drunk," I added, lowering my voice.

"Norman Brooks is your classic loose cannon," Matthias said quietly. "His drinking cost him his job. He's lucky it didn't cost him his pension. He needs to get into a program."

I looked over at Bobbi. Her eyes were open and she was watching us.

"Hi," I said, getting up and going to the foot of the bed. She turned slowly and stiffly onto her back, watched me silently as I cranked up the head of the bed. "Would you like some water?"

She tried to speak, but her voice caught. She coughed, winced, and croaked, "Yes, please." I held the cup and straw for her as she sipped. "Thanks," she said. "Hi, Greg."

"Hi, Bobbi," he said.

"I heard you talking about my dad. He's okay?"

"He's fine," Matthias said.

"How long have I been here?"

Matthias didn't answer. I looked at him. He nodded. "Almost a week," I said.

"A week? What day is it?"

"It's Monday."

She absorbed the information slowly, expression incredulous. "What happened?"

I let Matthias take that one. "You were attacked," he said.

Her eyes grew wide. "Attacked? Shit, you mean like — raped?"

"No, you weren't raped. Last Tuesday night you were beaten up and thrown into False Creek under the Burrard Street Bridge. You've been in a coma since you were found by an off-duty paramedic."

"Was I mugged?"

"No, we don't believe it was a mugging. Do you remember anything at all?"

She rolled her head back and forth on the pillow. "No," she said. "The last thing I remember, I think, was talking to Tom in the office about the move. God, if I've been here a week ..." Her voice trailed off. "Sorry."

"Don't worry about it," I said.

"Anything else?" Matthias said.

She rolled her head again. "No, that's ... Wait. I

remember a blonde woman. She was getting onto the elevator as I came into the studio. She wanted pictures of her boat, you told me. You thought she was cute." She paused, closed her eyes for a moment, then opened them again. "I remember someone reading to me."

"That was me," Matthias said. "Earlier this evening, just before you woke up." He held up the book. She smiled weakly.

"The doctor said you might be hungry when you woke up," I said. "Are you?"

"Hungry? I dunno …" Her eyes widened. "Christ, yes. I could eat a goddamned rhino, horn and all."

"Would you settle for chicken soup?" Dr. Sandra said from the door.

chapter fourteen

Bobbi managed to eat half a cup of chicken broth and a couple of spoons of green Jell-O before proclaiming, "I guess I wasn't as hungry as I thought," then closed her eyes and went to sleep again.

"I guess we aren't very stimulating company," Matthias said.

It was past nine. Dr. Sandra said Bobbi would most likely sleep through the night, so we left. There was a different cop on the door. Matthias told him to stay in the room with her and that if she woke up, to write down anything she said.

When I got home half an hour later, the message light on my phone was flashing. I logged into my voice mail. There was one message.

"Mr. McCall, it's Anna Waverley. It's seven o'clock Monday evening. Please, could you come to my home as soon as possible. There's something I urgently need to tell you. Don't worry about the time; I seldom go to bed before midnight." She paused, then added, "I'll be waiting."

It was almost ten o'clock. I didn't have her telephone number, nor did the phone's call display show it, so I went back up to the parking lot, got into the Liberty, and drove to Anna Waverley's house in Point Grey. The freakish weather had worsened. A cold, heavy fog had rolled in off Burrard Inlet and it was like driving through watery milk. Despite my eagerness to know what Anna Waverley had to tell me, I took it easy and was almost rear-ended twice by less cautious drivers. It was ten-thirty when I parked beside the Volvo in the wide drive-way. The fog swirled around the coach lamps bracketing the front door as I rang the bell and waited for an answer that was not forthcoming. Except for a dim glow from within, visible though the etched-glass bricks on either side of the door, the coach lights were the only lights that appeared to be on. I peered up at the little video camera above the door, to see if the red light was on. It wasn't. I rang again and waited some more. Still no answer.

Perhaps she'd had a few too many glasses of wine waiting for me and had fallen asleep. Foregoing the bell, I rapped on the door. I could hear music through the mail slot. Classical piano. Bach, I thought, mainly because Bach was the only classical composer whose music I could recognize — sometimes — just as chardonnay was the only wine I could identify by taste — sometimes. I knocked again, harder, but still she did not answer.

Whatever she had to tell me would have to keep, I thought, as I turned and started to walk to my car. Then, on some unfathomable impulse, I went back to the door and tried the handle. The polished brass lever was cool and slick with condensation. Unexpectedly, it turned. Why was the door unlocked? I wondered, as I pushed it open. Feathery fingers brushed the back of my neck as the cool night air wafted into the house.

"Mrs. Waverley?" I called, leaning through the door-way. "It's Tom McCall. Hello?"

No answer. In retrospect, I should have closed the door, driven to the nearest phone, and called the police, but I stepped into the dark vestibule and closed the door behind me.

"Mrs. Waverley," I called again. "Anna? Are you decent? It's Tom McCall."

Inside the house, the music was louder, but not so loud that she shouldn't have been able to hear me, unless she was wearing headphones or had taken a sleeping pill, both of which seemed unlikely if she was waiting for a visitor. The music, as well as the only apparent light in the house, was coming from the short hallway to my left that led to the day room we'd talked in on Saturday, before moving to the immaculate, under-utilized kitchen.

My footfalls made almost no sound on the thick Oriental carpets as I moved along the hallway toward the source of the music and the light. If she couldn't hear me, I didn't want to sneak up on her, startle her.

"Anna? Mrs. Waverley? Are you here? It's Tom McCall. Hello?"

I hadn't noticed it on my previous visit, because it had been open, but the day room had a sliding wood panel door, which now mostly closed. Dim yellow light leaked through the gap.

I knocked on the door. "Mrs. Waverley?" I said through the gap. "It's Tom McCall. Are you there?"

No answer. I slid the door open an inch or two more. "Mrs. Waverley?"

She still didn't answer. I slid the door fully open.

In the muted glow of a small halogen lamp on the ornate Victoria dining table, I could see her standing motionless in the middle of the room.

"Mrs. Waverley?" I said, as I stepped closer.

Was she standing on a chair or the coffee table? I wondered, because she seemed to be a good eighteen inches above the floor. She was wearing a T-shirt and shorts that looked like men's boxers, facing away from me, her head oddly cocked.

"Anna?"

Slowly, she turned toward me, her face coming into the light. I took another step toward her, wondering stupidly what was wrong with her face. It was a strange colour, her mouth was partly open, and her tongue protruded slightly between her teeth. Then the realization struck me like a massive blow from a gigantic fist.

She wasn't standing on anything at all.

I leaped forward, wrapped my right arm around her bare thighs and lifted her, at the same reaching up with my left hand and trying to loosen the noose around her neck. The flesh of her neck was stiff and cool where the heavy-duty orange extension cord had bitten deep. The other end of the cord was looped around a thick cedar beam. Supporting her weight, I clawed at the noose, fingernails gouging her flesh, until I finally managed to loosen it and slip it over her head, all the while remotely aware of the fact that while her body was still warm, it wasn't quite as warm as it should have been.

Lowering her to the floor, I tilted her head back, and blew into her mouth, but her tongue was stiff and distended, blocking her airway. I pulled her jaw down and out, pressed her tongue to the base of her mouth with my finger, and tried again. Her chest expanded. Kneeling over her, I clasped my hands together and pressed the heels hard on her breast bone, once, twice, three times. At the count of ten, I leaned over and blew into her mouth again. I repeated the cycle, then repeated it again. I knew it was too late, though; she was dead and had been for some time. Nevertheless, I continued to try to revive her until I was bathed in sweat and dizzy from hyperventilation.

I climbed unsteadily to my feet, pushing off on a fallen chair, until I realized that it must have been the chair she'd been standing on. I jerked my hand away. Too late, of course. I'd surely left fingerprints, contaminating the crime scene. Was suicide still considered a crime? I wondered dimly. Probably not, at least according to civil law. Nevertheless, I didn't want to contaminate the scene more than I had already. Not that I was planning on going anywhere.

There was a cordless telephone on the dining table, next to her laptop, atop its stack of books. I started to reach for the phone, but decided I would call 911 from another one. There was one in the kitchen, I recalled.

The Bach was coming from the mismatched stereo system in the entertainment unit. As I stood looking at my reflection in the dark glass of the sliding doors to the patio, Anna Waverley's body at my feet, the CD ended and the room was plunged into sudden, deathly silence. I staggered as my vision blurred. I braced myself against the big Victorian dining table, sucking in lungful after lungful of air through my mouth. Some hero, I thought, and I took myself away from her and went to the kitchen to call 911.

When I hung up the telephone, my hand was shaking and the edges of my vision flickered with random flashes of light and darkness, like movement in my peripheral vision. I found a bottle of Scotch in a sideboard, poured myself a stiff jolt, and sat down to wait for the police, trying not to think about Anna Waverley's cooling body in the day room, how beautiful she was, even in death, and the sad, lonely manner in which she had died.

It was almost one in the morning when the police were finally finished with me. I was exhausted and sick from telling my story a half a dozen times, to the first cops on the scene, the medical examiner, to Constable Henshaw, to a woman from the coroner's office, and twice to Sergeant Kovacs, who hadn't been the least bit pleased to see me.

"Goddamn it to bloody hell," he'd said tiredly. "What the fuck did you think you were doing? I should bust your meddlesome ass for obstruction or interfering with a police investigation." He took a breath. "What the hell were you doing here, anyway?"

"She called me at seven," I'd told him. "She left a message on my voice mail. She said she had something to tell me."

"Any idea what?"

"No."

"You came to see her on Saturday night. Why? You told me you didn't know her."

"I didn't. I came to see if she could tell me anything about what happened to Bobbi and we spent most of the evening together." His expression soured. "Just talking. She was a very lonely lady."

"Okay," he'd said then. "Go home. Stay there. We'll be in touch."

The wind came up as I drove home, shredding the fog to thread-like tendrils that whipped and undulated through the tunnel of light ahead of the Liberty. I felt empty and cold, as if my insides had been scooped out and replaced with dry ice. I could still feel the waxy coolness of her lips against mine, the staleness of the air expelled from her lungs as I'd pressed on her chest. My thoughts seemed to come from a great distance, thin and hollow, spoken by a ghost. Anna Waverley's lonely death saddened me and angered me and left me feeling as though I'd failed her somehow. I didn't like the feeling at all and wished it would go away. It didn't.

I lay awake in my bed for a long time, despite my exhaustion, and when I finally did sleep, I was awakened by dreams I'd rather I didn't remember, but did. Early in the morning I awoke from a particularly disturbing one, sweating, heart pounding, and mouth dry. I'd been making love with Anna Waverley on her big Victorian dining table, when she'd fallen overboard and slowly sank out of sight into the cold and dark water.

It was 4:30 by the clock on the dresser. I knew I wouldn't be able to sleep without dreaming, so I got up, got dressed, and went downstairs. The house was cool and quiet, which wasn't unusual, but it was unusual for me to be aware of it. I was also aware of the almost imperceptible motion as the house rocked gently on the tide and in the wake of passing boats. I turned on the radio in the kitchen to catch the news, but immediately turned it off again, afraid of what I'd hear. I started coffee, and fixed a bowl of cereal, ate two mouthfuls before scraping the rest into the garbage disposal. When the coffee was ready, I poured a cup, put on a jacket, and went up to the roof deck and sat under the awning to wait for the sun to rise over the coastal mountains, even though it likely wouldn't be visible through the cloud cover and fog, anyway.

What had she so urgently wanted to tell me? It must have had something to do with Bobbi's attack — what else could it have been? Surely she hadn't been involved, but perhaps she had witnessed it? Or perhaps, when she'd been at the marina, she'd seen someone else on the boat besides Bobbi. Or perhaps, more circumstantially, she knew who'd posed as her to hire us to photograph the boat. There were any number of possibilities.

None of which explained why she'd killed herself.

I played back her phone message in my head, which was the only place I could play it back, since I'd erased it from my voice mail, to Sergeant Kovacs's chagrin. Her voice had sounded urgent, but not desperate. For a moment I couldn't recall if she'd said that there was something she'd urgently needed to tell me or if she'd said she urgently needed to speak with me. If the latter, perhaps it had had nothing at all to do with Bobbi's attack and everything to do with her suicide. I was fairly sure, though, that she'd said she had something she needed to tell me. Which brought me full circle back to where I'd started, wondering what she'd wanted to tell me. I would likely never know.

"You must think I'm a very foolish woman," she'd said to me as we sat in her kitchen and drank tea after she'd almost single-handedly polished off two bottles of wine. "You'd be right," she'd added before I could reply that I didn't think she was foolish at all. "Foolish and useless. I'm not stupid, if I do say so myself — I have degrees in art history and English — but what do I do with my time? I mope around this damned *warehouse* all day feeling sorry for myself, drinking too much, and doing endless research for a book I'll never write, about a subject no one cares about, which even if I did publish, no one would read, anyway."

"Maybe you just need to get out more," I said.

A smile flickered at the edges of her mouth, but she raised her teacup, almost as if it embarrassed her to smile, that she needed to hide it. "What an unusual man you are, Mr. McCall."

"I'm sorry," I said. "I didn't mean to sound flippant."

"Oh, don't apologize," she said, almost snappishly. "You were simply being honest. And you're right. I do need to get out more. Do you sail?"

"A little," I replied.

"I love sailing, but my husband, well, he's never been an especially competent man, physically, that is. I'm the one who insisted on having a sailboat. He wanted a motor yacht. They are less demanding and require somewhat less skill to operate than a sailboat. You live at Granville Island. Do you live on a boat? No, you said you owned a house."

"I live in a floating home," I said. "Which requires no skill at all to operate."

She smiled. It was a distant, fleeting smile, but a smile nonetheless. "It's been ages since I've enjoyed the company of a man without sex being involved," she said. She looked at me, her cheeks flushed. "That didn't come out quite the way I meant it to."

"Don't worry about it," I said. "Happens to me all the time."

"I used to enjoy the company of my husband," she said. "Quite a lot. And I think he once enjoyed mine. Now he prefers the company of the limber and long-legged Doris." She shook her head, mouth pinched. "She's very sweet. And quite bright. As I said, I've no idea what she sees in Sam. I hope she enjoys his company. I never really enjoyed the company of many of my lovers. Most of them tried too hard to impress me. You don't know how refreshing it is to be with someone who doesn't feel the need to impress."

"You mean me?" I'd replied, with mock astonishment. "Right now, if I thought it would impress you, I'd stand on my hands and recite love poems from *The Rubaiyat of Omar Khayyam*. That is, if I could stand on my hands or knew any of the love poems from *The Rubaiyat of Omar Khayyam*."

She'd laughed then. "I've got a copy around here someplace."

"Shit," I said, sitting in my chair on the roof deck of my house, as the rain began to fall.

chapter fifteen

At nine the following morning I left Mary-Alice and Wayne to mind the store and drove to the hospital. I hadn't told Mary-Alice or Wayne about Anna Waverley's death. It wouldn't mean anything to them, anyway. Naturally, they were pleased to hear that Bobbi was awake, and asked me to give her their regards, tell her that they'd come visit soon.

"The move went all right, then," Bobbi said, after I passed on the well wishes from Mary-Alice and Wayne.

"It went fine," I said. It was the third time she'd asked. She was still having trouble with short-term memory, which the doctor had told me was to be expected.

"Ask them to bring me a pizza when they come," she said. Her appetite had returned, but hospital food left something to be desired, to say the least.

"I will," I said.

"Jeanie Stone came by," she said.

"She said she might."

"This is a horrible thing to say, but when I first met

her, I thought she was a lesbian. She isn't, though."

"How do you know?" I said. "Did you make a pass at her?"

"I'm not a lesbian," she said seriously.

"I know you're not a lesbian, Bobbi. I was trying to make a joke."

"Oh." She smiled unevenly. "Of course you were. Sorry. My brain still isn't working properly, I guess."

"If it ever did."

"Haw."

"Has your father been by to see you?" I asked.

"No," she said. "My mother called, though."

"Oh, crap, I forgot all about your mother. I'm sorry. I should have called her." Bobbi's parents had been divorced for years. A year or two before, her mother, who once upon a time had been a nurse in that very hospital, had moved to Nanaimo with her second husband. Or was it her third?

"It's all right. Greg called her. Don't worry about it. She likes him better than you, anyway. Or did, at least."

"I know your father doesn't like me, but I thought your mother did. What did I do wrong?"

"Mom got it into her head that we should be married. I told her you didn't want to marry me and I certainly didn't want to marry you, but that didn't seem to make any difference to her. And now that Greg's decided to go and raise horses with Isabel, he's in her bad books, too."

"Well, at least I have company. What did you mean you 'certainly' didn't want to marry me? Some women might even consider me a good catch."

"It'd help if I was in love with you, or you with me, wouldn't it?"

"Mm, I guess."

"You're good company, though. Most of the time."

"Thanks," I said, reminded of my conversation with Anna Waverley.

"What's wrong?"

"Nothing," I said.

"C'mon. I know you. Something's wrong. What is it? Oh, shit. You've broken up with Reeny, haven't you? You have that look. I'm really sorry."

"Thanks," I said, and shrugged it off. "Have you remembered anything about the attack?"

She shook her head. "No, not really. I get little flashes of things, a boat, being in the water, a face hovering over me, probably the guy who gave me CPR. I don't remember anything about being beaten up."

"Any idea of when they're going to let you out of here?"

"Couple of days, Dr. Sandra said. God, doesn't she have the most fabulous eyes?"

"She does indeed," I agreed.

"The rest of her ain't bad, either," Greg Matthias said from the door, Dr. Sandra at his side, a huge smile on her face. He beckoned to me. "Tom, can I speak with you for a minute?"

"Sure," I said and went out into the hall with him.

"How are you doing?" he asked.

"I'm all right. Spooked, though. I have the strangest feeling that the world is a very different place than it was yesterday, I just can't pin down how it's changed, even though I know how it's changed."

"Understandable. I want you to tell me everything you remember about last night, from the time you got Anna Waverley's message till the police arrived."

"Again? Now? Here?"

"Let's go get a coffee."

I agreed. He told Bobbi we'd see her in a little while, then we went down to the coffee shop, picked up two coffees, and found a quiet corner. When I was finished telling my story for the seventh time, he said, "The door was unlocked?"

"Yes," I replied. I hesitated, then said, "She didn't kill herself, did she?"

"No," he said. "The ME saw right off it wasn't suicide. There were ligature marks on her throat inconsistent with hanging, and her hyoid bone was fractured, indicating that she'd been manually strangled before the noose was put around her neck and she was strung up to make it look like suicide. And there were marks on the overhead beam where it was scored by the extension cord as she was hauled up."

That was more than I really needed to know, but he wasn't done.

"She had a moderately high level of alcohol in her blood, but a lot more in her stomach. Ante-mortem bruising indicates she may have been forced to ingest it before she was killed."

I closed my eyes and saw the empty wine bottle on the dining table, and the two wine glasses next to it, which I hadn't remembered until that moment.

"There was no sign of forced entry, so she probably knew her killer. Or killers. Let them in, anyway. The lengths he — or they — went to to make it look like suicide were pointless, really, given the state of the art of forensic science these days. But," he added, with a shrug, "in the real world most killers are stupid and think cops are even stupider."

"If this is the real world," I said, "you're welcome to it." Then something quite unpleasant occurred to me. "I'm not a suspect, am I?"

"No. The TOD — time of death — was between eight and nine. You've got a good alibi. Me. You didn't leave the hospital till after nine and a neighbour puts your arrival at Anna Waverley's house at ten-thirty."

"Do you have any suspects?"

"I can't really discuss it with you, Tom. I've already told more than I should. You're not a very popular guy around Major Crimes right now. Kovacs wants you charged with interfering with an ongoing investigation. He'll calm down eventually, but I'd stay out of his way for a while. He's still handling Bobbi's case. I've caught Anna Waverley's only because we're a bit short-handed at the moment. If we can show a reasonably conclusive connection between Bobbi's attack and Anna Waverley's murder, I'm out of it, though."

"The connection seems pretty conclusive to me."

"Yeah, it's a good bet, but so far there's nothing but coincidence to connect them. Except for you, of course."

My guts twisted into an icy knot. "Do you think Anna Waverley was killed because I went to see her?"

"There was something she needed to tell you, you said. Urgently. She was killed shortly after leaving the message on your phone. Odds are that whoever killed her didn't want her talking to you again, perhaps afraid of what she might tell you about Bobbi's attack."

"If that's what she wanted to talk to me about," I said. A cold feeling came over me. "Uh, do you think my phone or my house may be bugged? Or hers?" It was easy enough to do, with gear you could by at almost any electronics store or off the Internet.

"I doubt it," Matthias said. "It's more likely that she mentioned your visit to someone. But we'll check, if you like."

"I don't know," I said. "You're probably right about her talking to someone else. I'll let you know."

"When you were at her house the other night, did she say anything that implied she knew who attacked Bobbi or who else may have been on the *Wonderlust* the night of the attack?"

"No."

"She drank almost two bottles of wine. How drunk did she get?"

"Hard to say. She became fairly talkative, but she

didn't slur her words or lose track of the conversation. I'm not sure two bottles of wine was necessarily a lot for her."

"Are you saying she was an alcoholic?"

"No, but it's a definite possibility."

"How much did you drink?"

"Not much. A glass and a half, maybe."

"How certain are you that she had a lover at the time of her death?"

"Reasonably certain. Sixty, seventy percent."

"Any idea who he might be? Whoever he is, he's at the top of our list right now."

"Sorry. She didn't mention a name or tell me anything about him."

"We'll need to fingerprint you to eliminate your prints from the scene."

"No problem. Just tell me where to go."

He did, asking me to go there as soon as I could, and I promised I would, then we went back upstairs and visited with Bobbi for a while longer. He left before I did. I left when Bobbi started to yawn. She still tired easily, she said. I drove back to Granville Island, but I didn't go to the studio, going home instead. I wasn't in the mood to face Mary-Alice's nagging or Wayne's good-natured eagerness. I wished my friend and neighbour Daniel Wu were around, as I could have used someone to talk to, but he was in Montana or Manitoba or someplace for most of the month, overseeing the final stages of the construction of a public library he'd designed. I was supposed to be looking after his plants while he was gone. I'd been neglecting them lately, so I got his keys and let myself into his house, directly across the dock from mine. Maggie Urquhart was also away, on a book-signing tour — Maggie was a retired professor of anthropology who wrote bestselling books about modern urban mythology and spirituality that had made her more than moderately wealthy — and I was supposed to be neglecting her plants, too, so when I'd done with Daniel's, I took care of Maggie's. It was a good thing she'd boarded Harvey, her Harlequin Great Dane, or he'd have starved to death, among other things. Then it was lunchtime. I made a toasted tomato-and-cheddar-cheese sandwich, ate half of it, then wrapped the rest in Saran and left it in the fridge to be thrown out at a later date.

When I got to the studio at a few minutes past two, Mary-Alice said, "Where have you been?" as if she were married to me and not my little sister and junior partner.

"Visiting Bobbi," I said, stretching the truth.

"I tried to reach you. Bobbi said you left before lunch."

"I must've fallen into a time warp," I said, eliciting a scowl. "Why were you trying to reach me?"

"Walter Moffat's office called."

"Is that right? What did they want?"

"He's changed his mind —"

"And this is news? He's a politician. They change their minds as often as I change my socks. Maybe oftener. What exactly has he changed it about?"

"What do you think?"

"He's going to join the Green Party."

She sighed. "He's changed his mind about the exhibition catalogue. He'd like to meet with you to discuss it."

"Okay. When?"

"As soon as possible."

"I take it he isn't interested in coming to us."

"No, of course not. Should I call his secretary and make an appointment?"

"I suppose."

"Try to be a little more enthusiastic. What's going on with you, anyway?"

It was wishful thinking to hope that Anna Waverley's

murder, with all the gory details, possibly including my involvement, wouldn't be all over the news before too long, so I took a breath and told Mary-Alice how I had found Anna Waverley's body. I kept it short and simple, but by the time I was finished my voice was ragged and I wanted to run away and hide somewhere.

"God," Mary-Alice said when I'd done. "You do manage to get yourself into some fine messes, don't you?"

"Not exactly by choice," I said.

"What were you thinking? Or perhaps I should ask, 'What were you thinking *with*?'"

My patience ran out. "Goddamn it, Mary-Alice," I snapped. "Stop treating me like I've just run down the next door neighbour's dog with my bike. I'm not a little boy and you're not my mother, for Christ's sake."

"You don't have to shout at me," she retorted hotly.

"I'm not shouting," I shouted back.

"You are too!"

Wayne stood up from the computer to which the digital studio camera was attached. "Anyone want a coffee?" he asked, but almost ran out the door without waiting for an answer.

"How well does David know the Waverleys?" I asked Mary-Alice.

"What?" she asked. I repeated the question, to which she replied, "What makes you think he knows them at all?"

"He told me at the party that he'd met them both. He's also purchased art from Samuel Waverley's gallery."

"So what? I buy fish at Fisherman's Wharf. That doesn't mean I know the fishermen. Anyway, even if he did know them, what could it possibly have to do with her murder?"

"Nothing at all," I said. "I was just thinking he might be able to tell me something about her, who her friends were or if she had a lover and who he might be."

She glared at me. "What is that supposed to mean?" she demanded.

"Pardon me?"

"Are you implying that David was her lover?"

"What? No. For god's sake, Mary-Alice. All I asked was how well he knew her or her husband."

"Sorry," she said, deflating. "It's just that — well, never mind."

I knew better than to ask, so I didn't. Mary-Alice's marriage was a little like Dr. Schrödinger's boxed cat: as long as you didn't look inside the box, a state of quantum uncertainty existed, but as soon as you checked to see if the cat was dead or alive, the uncertainty collapsed and the cat died — or not. I didn't want to be the one to collapse Mary-Alice's marital uncertainty.

More than once Mary-Alice had told me that she'd suspected David of having an affair. My typical response had been to dismiss it, write it off as her imagination getting the better of her. But while Mary-Alice was prickly and a little insecure, she was, as Anna Waverley had put it, far from stupid. Me, I'm not so sure of. Until Mary-Alice had brought it up, the possibility that her husband had been Anna Waverley's lover had been the farthest thing from my mind. However, the "Six Degrees of Separation" theory postulates that we are never more than six people away from anyone in the world — you know someone who knows someone and so on a maximum of four more times until you get to someone who knows me — so the possibility that David Paul and Anna Waverley had been lovers may not have been so far-fetched at all. Until the day that faux Anna Waverley had walked into my office, I'd never heard the name Anna Waverley, but I'd been only one degree — David Paul — away from knowing her. Unhappily for her …

Mary-Alice must have smelled something burning. "What is it?" she asked, peering intently at me.

"Nothing," I said. "Are you going to make that appointment with Walter Moffat?"

"Of course," she said.

Something else occurred to me then: if I'd been only one degree of separation away from Anna Waverley, it seemed likely that I wasn't many more degrees of separation away from the faux Anna Waverley.

chapter sixteen

The ex-Honourable Walter P. Moffat did not live in the riding he'd once represented, although he did, as I later learned, maintain a pied-à-terre in the West End, which his former riding encompassed. His principal residence was a big, ramshackle old stone house that squatted on a rocky promontory jutting out into Howe Sound a few kilometres north of the ferry terminals at Horseshoe Bay. A brass plaque affixed to a moss-encrusted stone pillar at the entrance to the grounds identified the house as the headquarters of the Josiah E. Bridgwater Foundation, established in 1927 for an unspecified purpose. The Liberty jounced along the winding potholed drive between overgrown cedar hedges, wild gardens, haphazardly mowed lawns, and unkempt woods. Whatever the purpose of the foundation, it didn't waste money on groundskeeping.

I parked at the end of a row of eight other cars parked facing the dripping woods along the edge of a weedy gravel apron in front of the house. There were six Japanese compacts of varying makes, models and vintages, one battered, rusting Chevy pickup, and a relatively recent Dodge Caravan with the name of the foundation in discreet lettering on the front doors. The other vehicles likely belonged to house staff or foundation employees; I couldn't imagine the ex-Honourable Walter P. Moffat being caught dead in any of them. His car was probably tucked safely away in the three-car garage of the coach house next to the crumbling mansion.

There was another plaque bearing the name of the foundation under a doorbell button beside the massive oak doors. I pressed the button, but didn't hear a chime and had no idea if the bell worked at all. The general condition of the house wasn't reassuring. As I wondered if I should knock, one of the doors swung open on creaking hinges.

Half expecting an ancient foot-dragging hunchback to appear, I was pleasantly surprised to see a lovely dark-eyed woman with thick, wavy hair the colour of dark-roasted coffee beans and a complexion like coffee with a touch of cream, who said, "Mr. McCall, come in, please," in a voice that was as smooth and warm and sweet as melted milk chocolate. Mellifluous didn't begin to describe it.

"Thank you," I said, as she stood back then closed the door behind me. She was barely five feet tall, wearing snug-fitting jeans and a dark wool V-neck sweater. I pegged her age at twenty-five, more or less.

"This way, please, Mr. McCall," she cooed sweetly, and started up the broad, curved staircase. I followed, trying without much success not to stare at the beguiling twitch of her sumptuous rump. It was right there, not quite in my face, but at eye level. What was I to do? At the top of the stairs she stopped, turned, and said, "This way, please, Mr. McCall," gesturing down the long upstairs hall. She fell in beside me, the top of her head an inch below the level of my shoulder. She smelled delicately of vanilla. The edible woman, if you'll pardon the allusion.

The walls of the long hall were dark wood panelling above wainscotting, the kind of place where one expects to see rows of ornately framed oil paintings of ancestors, red-coated gentry riding to hounds, rolling farmland dotted with cows and sheep, or ancient churches and dilapidated castles. However, there was not a single painting on the walls, no marble statuary lurking in shadowed corners, no vases with or without wilting flowers in the niches, no decoration of any kind save heavy drapery over the high mullioned windows. The Josiah E. Bridgwater Foundation, I surmised, did not support the arts.

My guide stopped at a door at the end of the hall and knocked gently. The door was opened immediately by Mrs. Elise Bridgwater Moffat.

"Thank you, Maria," she said to the girl. Of course her name would be Maria. "That will be all."

"*Gracias, señora*," Maria said, with a bright, dimpled smile. Was she one of Mrs. Moffat's Children in Peril? I wondered.

"Mr. McCall," Mrs. Moffat said to me as I watched the lovely Maria walk back down the long hall toward the stairs. "Thank you for coming. Come in, please. My husband will be with you shortly."

"Thank you," I said.

If the big downstairs foyer and the drab upstairs hallway looked like something out of a Gothic horror movie, the rooms into which Mrs. Moffat led me were decorated like a 1960s movie set, with chunky upholstered sofas, loveseats, and matching easy chairs, a leather La-Z-Boy recliner, vaguely Swedish/Danish casual tables and chairs. There were frilly table lamps and stately floor lamps, Oriental carpets over wall-to-wall broadloom, a blond wood console TV and hi-fi in one corner, and a beige brick fireplace in which a log fire burned behind a chain curtain spark screen. A painting hung over the fireplace, an English countryside scene with thatched-roof cottages and fat black-and-white cows. There were other paintings on the walls, too, some old, some less so, all figurative landscapes or still lifes, none even remotely impressionistic or abstract or modern.

"Let me say how pleased we were to hear of your partner's improvement," Mrs. Moffat said.

"She isn't out of the woods quite yet," I said. "But thank you."

"Has she been able to provide the police with any information about her attacker?"

"Not so far."

"I'll remember her in my prayers."

I wondered if she'd heard about Anna Waverley's death. Probably not. I'd heard a report on the radio on my way there, but the police hadn't released Anna's name, pending notification, et cetera, so the only way Mrs. Moffat could have known was if someone had told her — assuming, of course, that she hadn't killed Anna herself, which I considered improbable in the extreme.

"Uh, Mrs. Moffat, the other night at my sister's house you said that you knew Anna Waverley."

"Did I?" Mrs. Moffat said, a little nonplussed. "I am acquainted with her, of course. She's a generous contributor to the Children in Peril Network. She and her husband both. Why do you ask?"

So she hadn't heard. She would soon enough, though, either from the police, an acquaintance, or the news.

"What is it, Mr. McCall? Why did you ask me if I know Anna? Has — has something happened to her?"

"I'm afraid so," I said. *Oh, hell.* "She's dead."

She went pale and wobbled slightly on her feet. "Dead?" she whispered, clutching at the heavy silver crucifix on her breast.

"I'm sorry," I said.

"How?" she asked, steadier on her feet, voice firmer, but still shaky.

"She was murdered," I said.

"Oh, dear Jesus."

"I'm very sorry," I said.

"Pardon me, Mr. McCall," she said, collecting herself. "I am not normally so faint-hearted. Anna — Mrs. Waverley — was a good person, much closer to God than she was prepared to admit. It's a horrible shock to have someone you know … Well, of course, you understand, don't you?"

"Yes," I said. "I do."

She clutched her big silver crucifix, rubbing it rapidly between her thumb and index finger. She glanced down, seemed surprised to catch herself in the act, and dropped her arm to her side.

"You must excuse me now," she said. "My husband will be along momentarily, I'm sure."

And she fled, leaving me there, waiting amid the ordinary furniture and conventional paintings. I didn't have to wait long, though, before another door opened and the ex-Honourable Walter P. Moffat strode into the room.

"Sorry to keep you waiting, Mr. McCall," he said. We shook hands.

"No problem," I said. "I've been admiring the decor."

He smiled. "Most of the house is occupied by my wife's foundation," he explained. "These apartments were my father-in-law's when he was alive. A bit drab, aren't they? They are much the way they were when he died. Except for the paintings, of course. Like his father, my father-in-law did not believe in art. Fortunately, my wife does not share her father's attitude, although her taste is somewhat, shall we say, conservative. Come though to my office."

I followed him into the other room, a very utilitarian office — for 1960. There was even an old Royal manual typewriter on the credenza behind the desk, although there was a laptop computer on the desk itself.

"Can I offer you something to drink, Mr. McCall? I have some excellent Scotch."

"Thanks," I said. I wasn't sure I really wanted a drink so early in the day, but I didn't want to appear unsociable.

He went to a tall cabinet that looked as though it was made from veneered plywood and opened a door to reveal a meagre collection of liquor bottles. "If you want ice, we'll have to get some from the kitchen."

"Straight up is fine," I said.

"Straight up it is, then." He uncorked a bottle of Chivas Regal and poured a centimetre or two into each of a pair of mismatched cut-glass tumblers. He handed one to me. "Cheers."

"Cheers," I replied. His idea of excellent Scotch wasn't mine, but as blended Scotches went, Chivas wasn't bad.

He tossed back half of his drink in a single gulp. I sipped mine.

"Please," he said. "Sit down."

I sat in an easy chair. It was like sitting on an upholstered rock. He lowered his elegant frame onto a sofa, which didn't look much more comfortable. We stared at each other for a few seconds.

"By the way," he said, "how is your partner? Bobbi?"

"Yes. Much better," I said. "She regained consciousness on Saturday. She doesn't remember anything about the attack, though."

"Perhaps that's a good thing," he said.

We stared at each other for a few more seconds. I wondered if he'd heard about Anna Waverley's death.

"I'm afraid I upset your wife," I said.

"Oh?"

"Perhaps you've heard. Anna Waverley is dead."

"Yes, I had heard," he said, shaking his big head mournfully. I wondered how, and why he hadn't told his wife, but he didn't give me time to ask. "Shocking," he went on. "Simply shocking. Murdered in her own home. Her husband will be devastated. I didn't know her well, of course — my wife knew her better than I — but she was a charming person."

"Yes, she was," I said.

He speared me with a look of suspicion. "Pardon me, but when we spoke at your sister's home, I had the impression that you did not know her. Was I mistaken?"

"I just recently made her acquaintance," I said. If I spent too much time with Moffat, I would end up talking like him. "I found her body."

"You did? My heavens, how horrible."

"It wasn't pleasant," I agreed.

"No, I'm sure not." He drank the rest of his Scotch and stared at me some more.

"How did you hear about Mrs. Waverley's murder?" I asked.

"My manager, Mr. Getz, told me," he said.

"How did he learn about it?"

"I've no idea. He has numerous contacts in the media. Perhaps one of them. It's his job to keep abreast of anything that might adversely affect my campaign, directly or indirectly." He got up and poured himself another two centimetres of Chivas. I shook my head when he held the bottle in my direction. He put the bottle back and resumed his seat. "Shall we get down to business?" he said.

Why not? I thought. "Mary-Alice tells me you've decided to go ahead with the exhibition."

"Not precisely," he said. "I would, however, like to document my collection onto a CD-ROM, which I may make available for sale. I haven't decided yet. CD-ROM? Is that the correct term?"

"It is," I said. "Generally, just referred to as a CD."

"You could do this?"

"Certainly. How many pieces are we talking about?"

"Not quite a hundred. Ninety-seven, to be precise."

"Where are they?"

"In my private gallery downstairs. Why don't I give you a quick tour? That way you can get a better idea of what you will be working with."

He tossed back his drink, and I did likewise, then we left the apartment by another door from his office and went down the back stairs, probably once used by servants, perhaps still. Emerging into the main hall, I followed him toward the rear of the house. He stopped before a sturdy door, took a card out of his wallet, and inserted it into a slot above a keypad beside the door. When he removed it, a green light glowed beneath the slot and the door locks thudded. It must be some collection, I thought, as he pulled the door open. Inside, as the door swung shut, he punched a code into a keypad in an alarm panel.

The room was about thirty feet long and twenty feet wide. It could have been in any gallery in the city, with fifteen-foot ceilings, track lighting running the length of the room, plain flat-white walls. The walls were lined with framed oils, watercolours, and drawings of varying sizes, few larger than about thirty inches square, most smaller. Down the centre of the room stood a row of pedestals upon which were displayed a number of bronze sculptures, figures ranging in size and shape from just a few inches to a couple of feet. The one closest to me was a small standing nude, about the size of a wine bottle, a sturdy little thing that made me think of Maria. Two of the pedestals held painted vases or urns.

Moffat beamed at me as I slowly walked the length of the room. I wasn't really looking at the subjects of the sculptures or the paintings and drawings. I was thinking about lighting, glare off the polished surfaces of the bronzes, the varnished surfaces of the oils, whether I would shoot them in situ or set up a seamless backdrop and lights at the end of the room and shoot them all there. The paintings and drawings were all small enough to remove from their frames, place on a low table, and shoot from above using a camera suspended beneath the big tripod, which was equipped with a levelling bubble that would ensure the paintings were absolutely parallel to the focal plane of the camera.

Then it hit me, everything suddenly jumping into focus, as if I'd been looking at one of those weird computer-generated squiggly abstracts popular in the 1990s called autostereograms, out of which another image would magically appear if you stared at it long enough with your eyes crossed or unfocused. My jaw literally dropped.

The ex-Honourable Walter P. Moffat had a thing for tits. Art Nouveau, Victorian, and Edwardian tits. Every one of the oil paintings, watercolours, drawings, and bronzes in Moffat's collection depicted women with bared breasts. Even the painted vases. Naked nymphs in limpid pools or cavorting topless in wooded glens. Women climbing into or out of old-fashioned bathtubs or sitting at dressing tables. Ethereal figures draped in diaphanous veils. There was a woman on horseback brandishing a long spear, naked but for a plumed helmet and a short skirt of leathery armour. There was a painting that looked like an early Maxfield Parrish, before the Golden Age of Illustration, but it wasn't labelled or signed. Nor was the one that resembled a Vargas *Playboy* pinup. And none of the figures was naked below the waist. Just tits. Hundreds of tits. The whole thing was so astonishingly cheesy it took my breath away.

Except for the Maxfield Parrish and the Vargas, I didn't recognize any of the paintings, or the artists' names or styles, although some seemed vaguely familiar. Many of the oil paintings reminded me of the paint-by-numbers kits my mother had given Mary-Alice and me for Christmas when we were kids, except that none of them had featured nudes. I might have been more interested if they had.

"It's one of the finest collections of its kind in the country," Moffat said proudly.

"I can believe it," I said.

"It's taken me years to put it together," he said.

"I'm sure it has," I agreed.

"You might find these interesting," Moffat said, directing my attention to a small grouping of photographs in the corner by the door.

I moved closer. There were half a dozen small monochrome prints, all late nineteenth and early twentieth century, nothing more recent — by the 1920s women were baring their breasts at the drop of a camisole, I supposed. Not surprisingly, I recognized some of the photographers' names, if not the photographs themselves. There was a small sepia-toned print of a nude standing in a pool or stream, which was labelled as being by Julian Mandel, circa 1920. It wasn't bad, I conceded. Next to it was a photograph from the same period by Arundel Holmes Nicholls of a half-naked girl sitting demurely on a beach. She wasn't bad, either. But the remaining four were of the anonymous "Dirty French Postcard" school of erotica, better than average, perhaps, but typical.

"It's not erotica for the sake of erotica, you understand," Moffat said. "Although many people mistake it as such. It's a celebration of the female form, that which makes a female, well, female."

"It's quite, um, remarkable."

"It is, isn't it?"

It was all I could do to keep from choking. Was he serious? Of course he was. It was written all over his face as he gazed upon the works on display in his little gallery. I couldn't wait to tell Bobbi about it. I wondered, too, how Mrs. Moffat felt about her husband's obsession. I couldn't imagine her approving. Perhaps she was behind Moffat's decision not to exhibit the collection to raise money for her foundation.

"Will you be able to work here?" he asked.

"Shouldn't be a problem."

We discussed the details of the job. We would set up once and photograph each object on the same display stand, which would be faster than moving the lights and setting up for each object. I told him I wasn't comfortable about handling such valuable objects, though.

"Of course," he said. "Caroline will assist you."

"Caroline?"

"She's interning, so to speak. She's a major in art history and conservation at UBC. I don't know where she's got to. She was supposed to join us today. No matter. She will be available to assist."

We discussed cost. Ninety-seven items, at fifteen minutes to half an hour for each, it wouldn't be cheap. He didn't bat an eye when I gave him a ballpark estimate of three to five days work, me and an assistant, which would run about eight hundred a day. I wondered how much his collection was worth, but thought it would be rude to ask.

"Have you seen enough?"

"Yes, thanks."

As we left the gallery, he entered a code into the alarm system. The door locks thunked behind us.

"Thank you for coming so promptly, Mr. McCall. And who knows, perhaps my wife's foundation might also have a need for your services from time to time. Let me walk you to the door."

"Sir," I said, as we walked down the long wide hall toward the front of the house. "You're the only person

I know, besides your wife and my brother-in-law, who knew Mrs. Waverley." I hesitated.

"Yes?" he prompted.

"Do you know anything about her personal life?"

"No, I can't say that I do. The only times I ever saw her and her husband socially was at my wife's fundraising events. They do not share my political views."

"So you wouldn't know if she was having an affair or with whom."

"I would not, sir," he said stiffly.

"You know how Anna and her husband met, don't you?"

"I believe she once worked for him," Moffat said.

"That's right. She was his assistant twenty-five years ago. She had an affair with him. He evidently has affairs with all his assistants."

"I wouldn't know anything about that," he said. "And if I may offer some free legal advice, sir, I'd be careful about to whom I made such allegations, if I were you."

"I meant no disrespect to Mr. Waverley or his wife. It was Mrs. Waverley who told me about it."

We'd reached the foot of the main staircase, where the scrumptious Maria was waiting.

"As I said, Mr. McCall," Moffat said. "I know nothing of the Waverleys' private life." He held out his hand. "Thank you again for coming so promptly. We'll speak soon."

He went up the stairs, taking the steps two at a time, while Maria showed me the rest of the way to the door.

As I reached for the door handle of the Liberty, someone called out to me, "One moment, Mr. McCall, please." I turned to see Moffat's campaign manager, Woody Getz, striding toward me across the weedy parking apron. He did not look happy. I wondered if I'd somehow violated protocol. Perhaps I'd used his parking space.

"How are you, Mr. McCall?" he said, holding out his hand, his lacquered comb-over immobile despite the stiffening breeze off the sound.

"I'm fine," I replied, gripping his hand briefly. "How are you?" He was flushed and slightly out of breath.

"Oh, you know how it goes," he said.

"Is there something I can do for you?" I asked.

"I was just wondering how your meeting with Walter went," he said.

"Quite well," I said.

"What do you think of Walter's collection?"

"It's very interesting," I said. "I've never seen anything quite like it."

"I'll bet," he said, without cracking a smile. "What else did you talk about?"

"Pardon me?"

"I'm not asking to be nosy," he said. "Just doing my job. And part of that is to control — or at least try to control — the flow of information. To avoid unpleasant surprises. You understand."

"We didn't talk politics," I said.

"It's not politics that concerns me," he said. "Do you follow politics at all?"

"Not if I can help it."

"Well, if you did, you'd know that as often as not the success of a campaign doesn't come down to the issues but to the personalities. Walter can hold his own on the issues, but I'd like to keep his private life out of it. You understand."

"You can relax, then. We didn't discuss anything of a personal nature, either, although he did ask after my partner. And we briefly discussed Anna Waverley's death."

"Yeah, I heard. Elise — Mrs. Moffat — must be taking it quite hard. She and Mrs. Waverley were friends. I understand the police are treating it as a home invasion or robbery gone bad."

"Could be," I said.

"Well," Getz said. "Let's hope they catch whoever did it. Anyway, look, I hope you won't think I'm being a control freak or anything here, but in future, if you need to talk to my — to Mr. Moffat, I'd appreciate a heads-up. You understand."

"Sure," I said. "No problem. Why not?"

"Good," he said. "Oh, and how's your friend doing, anyway? Has she been able to tell the police anything about what happened?"

"Not yet," I said.

"Well," he said, sticking his hand out again. "I'm sure I'll see you around. In the meantime, take it easy."

"Likewise," I said, as he turned and strode purposefully away, a man on a mission.

chapter seventeen

Traffic was as terrible as usual on the Lions Gate Bridge and it was after five by the time I got back to Granville Island. Mary-Alice was still at the studio. I filled her in on my meeting with Walter Moffat. She wasn't particularly surprised when I told her about the nature of his art collection.

"I had a feeling it was something like that," she said. "Although she never came right out and said so, Elise implied that his collection made her uncomfortable. At least it isn't child pornography." Her eyes narrowed. "It isn't, is it?"

"No," I said. "The wood nymphs look a bit like sexually mature little girls, but there's nothing even remotely pornographic about them. Even the early twentieth-century photographs, which were probably considered pornographic in their day, are tame by modern standards. You see more nudity on cable TV."

"Still, you can't blame her for being upset by it," Mary-Alice said. "The Bridgwater Foundation is extremely conservative. Its supporters, too."

"Does it do anything else besides rescue children in peril?" I asked.

She shook her head. "These days it's dedicated exclusively to the Children in Peril Network."

"Which does what, exactly?"

"It sponsors orphanages and foster homes in Central and South America, as well as providing medical supplies and educational materials to hospitals and schools. David and a number of his colleagues donate a week or two of their time once a year, going down there and working with the local doctors. Originally, the foundation ran group homes all over the province for Christian girls in peril, which was a polite way of saying unwed mothers. Josiah Bridgwater was Elise's grandfather …" She hesitated, then said, "Did David tell you about her, how she ran more than a little wild when she was a teenager?"

"Yes, he mentioned it. Something about a jazz musician." I looked at her for a moment. "Are you saying that she was one of the foundation's girls in peril?"

"She may have been," Mary-Alice said. "During the last election one of Walter's opponents started a rather nasty whisper campaign that when she was fifteen she had a child, which was put up for adoption. Elise has never denied that she had some fairly serious problems as a teenager. In fact, on the foundation's web site she describes how, 'with God's help,' she turned her life around. There's nothing in her bio about her having had a child, but it might explain her dedication to helping children in the Third World."

"So might a number of things," I said.

"I suppose."

"How did her grandfather make his money?" I asked.

Mary-Alice smiled. "You're going to love this. He made his first fortune from mail-order sales of women's undergarments. He made even more money after expanding into hardware, farm equipment, and cleaning supplies, but he went to his grave known as the Corset King of the Pacific Northwest."

"Seems somehow fitting then that Walter is obsessed with breasts."

"He's following the Bridgwater family tradition in more ways than one," Mary-Alice said, a worried expression replacing the smile. "He didn't ask you to donate your time, did he?"

"No. In fact, money didn't seem to be a problem. Why?"

"According to Elise, Walter's almost as tight with a dollar as her grandfather was. She says the old man turned miserliness into an art. His only indulgence was the house, which he built for Elise's grandmother, who was apparently as mortified by the nature of the goods her husband sold as Elise is by Walter's collection."

"They certainly don't waste any money on the house or the grounds," I said.

"I don't think there's much of the old man's money left. Elise's father wasn't really very interested in running the foundation, except that it let him mingle with the upper crust. Walter told David the house is literally falling apart around their ears. He thinks the foundation would be better off selling or developing the property and renting offices someplace, but Elise won't hear of it. She's launching a fundraising campaign to do repairs. That's why Walter was going to exhibit his collection, I suppose, to donate the proceeds to the foundation. I guess Elise talked him out of it."

"His campaign manager, Woody Getz, may have also had a hand in that," I said.

I went home, washed down the soggy second half of the toasted tomato-and-cheese sandwich I'd made for lunch with a Granville Island Lager, then drove to the hospital. The cop on the door was gone. Bobbi was sitting up in bed, playing cribbage with Wayne. The medical monitors and the IV pump stood idle in a corner and the urine bag no longer hung from the side of the bed. Bobbi's colour had improved, but she still looked as though she had gone three rounds with Mike Tyson, except that both ears were intact.

"I went to the bathroom on my own today," she said proudly. "Saw myself in the mirror. Not as bad as I expected, but I guess I'm never going to make the cover of *Cosmo* any time soon."

"Y-you're s-still b-beautiful," Wayne stammered, face blazing.

She grinned lopsidedly, grimacing as she stretched the stitches in her mouth. "Thanks, D. Wayne," she said. Ever since Wayne had started working for us, Bobbi had called him D. Wayne, running it together, like Duane with two syllables, Duh-Wayne. He never complained when Bobbi did it, but he didn't like it when I or Mary-Alice did it.

"A Sergeant Kovacs came to see me," Bobbi said, as Wayne counted his points and moved his pegs on the board, still flushed. "He was disappointed when I told him I didn't remember anything about being attacked. He showed me a photograph of a woman with dark red hair and asked me if I'd seen her anywhere. I didn't recognize her. Who is she?"

"Has Kovacs or Greg told you anything about what happened the night you were attacked?" I looked at Wayne as I asked. He shook his head.

"Not much," Bobbi said. "I was beaten up and was thrown or fell into False Creek under the Kitsilano end of the Burrard Street Bridge. The van was dumped and torched and the gear was stolen. That's about it."

"Do you remember the woman who came to the studio last Tuesday and hired us to photograph a boat called the *Wonderlust*? You were coming in as she was going out. Thirty-ish. Blonde. Artificially augmented, you said."

"I think I do remember something like that," Bobbi said. "You said her name was, ah ..." She shook her head. "I can't quite get it. I'm sure it wasn't her in the photograph Sergeant Kovacs showed me."

"It wasn't. Although the woman who came to the studio said her name was Anna Waverley, she wasn't Anna Waverley. And the *Wonderlust* didn't belong to her."

"So who was the woman in the photograph? The real Anna Waverley?"

"Yes. She and her husband, an art and antiques dealer in Gastown, also have a boat at the marina, but it's a sailboat."

"Why did he show me her picture if she wasn't the woman who hired us?"

I took a breath. "She's dead," I said, throat tight. "She was murdered in her home last night."

Her eyes widened. "Oh."

"I found her body."

"You what? Jesus, Tom, what's going on?"

"Damned if I know. Whoever killed her tried to make it look like suicide."

"It can't be a coincidence," she said. "I've been around cops long enough to know that."

"You're probably right, but so far there's not much to link her to your attack. The police are working on the theory that someone wanted to set me or you or both of us up. You haven't pissed anyone off enough lately to want to do this, have you?"

"Not that I can think of. Except maybe that Loth guy. But I think I'd remember if it was him who did this to me."

I wasn't so sure, but I refrained from saying so.

"How did you come to find Anna Waverley's body?"

Bobbi asked. "I don't recall you ever mentioning her name before she came to the studio."

"I met her for the first time on Saturday night," I said. "Then last night she called and left a message on my voice mail asking me to come over, that there was something she wanted to tell me. When I got there, she was dead. I think she may have known who attacked you."

"And someone killed her to keep her quiet? Jesus, Tom, you're getting to be a dangerous guy to know."

"If it was set up," I said, "you've no idea how much I wish I'd gone instead of you."

"It's all Mary-Alice's fault," Bobbi said.

"Eh? How do you figure that? Ah. If Mary-Alice hadn't got Jeanie Stone's shorts in a knot, Jeanie wouldn't have insisted on meeting with me and I'd have gone to meet the fake Anna Waverley on that boat instead of you."

"I'm kidding, you know. Don't you? It really wasn't Mary-Alice's fault."

"Nevertheless, I wish I'd gone instead of you."

"Well, don't beat yourself up about it," Bobbi said. "If you'll pardon the expression. Maybe you wouldn't have been as lucky as me. Maybe you'd have been killed."

"When you put it that way," I said.

She grinned and grimaced again. "I wish I could remember what happened."

"The doctor says your memory will return in due course. Then you may wish it hadn't."

"It's scary, not remembering. Like there's a hole in my life. I've read about people who had gaps in their memories and when they were hypnotized it turned out that they believed they'd been kidnapped by aliens. Now I know how they felt."

"I wish you had been kidnapped by aliens," I said. "I don't recall that Scully ever got the crap beaten out of her by the aliens."

"Mulder d-did though," Wayne said. "And Scully got p-pregnant."

"All things considered," Bobbi said, "I'd rather be beaten up by an alien than impregnated by one."

Bobbi and Wayne finished their crib game, Wayne skunking Bobbi, who claimed her powers of concentration hadn't yet fully recovered. After he left, Bobbi and I played a game, and she beat me by a good margin. By eight she was yawning and so was I. I said good night.

When I opened the door, I saw the cop was back.

"Tom?" Bobbi said. I paused in the doorway, looking back at her. "Thanks."

"For what?"

"For, well, you know."

"You're welcome."

Although I'd been yawning in sympathy with Bobbi at the hospital, by the time I got back to Granville Island I was wide awake. I didn't feel like sitting around an empty house, and I was hungry, having eaten nothing but the sandwich since breakfast, so I parked at Sea Village, then walked back the length of the island to Bridges, all of half a kilometre.

"Twice in a week," Kenny Li, the manager, said. "Better be careful, Tom. Might get to be a habit."

"The week's still young, Kenny." Phil, the bartender, drew me a Granville Island Lager and I ordered a burger. I took my beer to an out-of-the-way corner and nursed it until my burger came.

I was finished my burger and most of my beer when Greg Matthias dropped into the chair across the table from me. He had a fresh pint in his hand so I assumed he wasn't on duty. He looked tired. I wondered where he lived. In the time I'd known him, he'd never said. Nor had Bobbi. So I asked.

"Burnaby," he said. "Just east of Boundary Road, near the Chevron tank farm."

"Mabel Firth lives around there, too, doesn't she?" I said.

"Yeah. She and her husband live a couple of streets over. There're a few cops in the neighbourhood. Misery likes company." He drank some beer. "Did you see Bobbi tonight?"

"Yeah. She's doing fine. They might release her in a day or two. Kovacs went to see her," I added, "but she wasn't able to tell him anything."

"He thinks she's holding out on him, that she remembers more than she's telling."

"Why would she do that?"

"Good question."

"Perhaps he just has a suspicious mind."

"It helps in this business."

"You don't think she's holding out, do you?"

"It's not my case."

"Is that a no?"

"Yes. No, I don't think she's keeping anything back. Kovacs probably doesn't, either. He's just letting his frustration show. This is one of those cases that shouldn't be that hard to solve. Given the time of day and location of the attack there should be witnesses coming out of the woodwork. Just our bad luck, or the perp's good luck, that when he bundled her into the Zodiac and took her out into False Creek, everyone was looking the other way. By the way, the Marine Squad found a Zodiac adrift in English Bay. Good bet it belonged to the *Wonderlust*." He drank some beer. "Anna Waverley's murder has complicated things, too."

"Are you still on that case?" I asked.

"For now."

"And …?"

"You know I can't talk about it."

"Has anyone been in touch with her husband?"

"Not yet. According to the woman looking after his gallery, he's supposed to be in London this week, but he's not at the hotel he normally uses, and the London cops haven't managed to track him down."

"Could he have sneaked back into the country and killed her himself?"

"Not if he arrived by air. He'd have had to show his passport and we've alerted customs to be on the look-out for him. On the other hand, if he flew to Seattle and drove up from the States, he wouldn't necessarily have had to show his passport or even identify himself to Canada customs." He looked at his watch, downed the dregs of his beer, and stood. "It's one of the possibilities we're considering," he said, and left.

I went to the bar and paid my tab, then found Kenny Li and arranged for Art Smelski and his wife to have drinks and dinner on me. The cobbled streets of Granville Island were quiet as I left the pub. Intending to swing by the studio, I took the roundabout way home, along the Foreshore Walk past the Broker's Bay Marina. I found myself wondering what Reeny was up to, over in Germany, with her new fiancé, whom she was sure I'd like. I hoped things worked out for them. I also wondered how Jeanie Stone's meeting with her thesis advisor had gone. Perhaps I should call her, I thought. I could tell her I was no longer spoken for.

The lights on the docks of the marina were ghostly in the night, shimmering off the inky water. The docks were deserted, most of the boats dark. Another big motor yacht occupied the *Wonderlust*'s slip. I wondered if the police had had any success tracking down the *Wonderlust*'s owners. How hard could it be? Even if they had, though, they weren't likely to tell me about it. I scanned the marina, looking for Anna Waverley's beloved sailboat, *Free Spirit*. It was supposed to be berthed about halfway along the dock next to the *Wonderlust*'s, but I had trouble locating it. No wonder. I wasn't looking for a boat with the interior lights on. Then I saw movement as a figure emerged from the hatch into the cockpit.

My first thought was that unbeknownst to Greg Matthias, Anna Waverley's husband had returned from overseas. But Samuel Waverley had been described to me as medium height and portly, while the person that stepped from the boat onto the finger dock was small and slim. A woman. Stooping, she picked up a box or carton, which appeared to be heavy, and carried it aboard the boat and down into the cabin.

The marina gate was still propped open, so I went down the ramp and walked along the dock to the *Free Spirit*'s slip, then out the narrow finger dock toward the boat's stern. The ports were open and I could hear pop music playing softly, but no voices. I stepped up onto the gunwale and down into the roomy cockpit. The Sabre 386 was a good-sized boat and barely registered my weight. The hatch was open. I looked down the companionway into the cabin. A woman stood at the counter that separated the galley from the main salon, her back to me as she removed groceries from a cardboard carton. She had short, dark hair, wide shoulders and slim hips, which swayed gently in time with the music, a woman singing in a smooth, smoky contralto about twisting in her sobriety.

I rapped on the hatch combing. The woman at the galley counter jumped and turned, eyes wide with alarm.

"Sorry," I said.

She stared up at me. "Oh, shit," she said. "What the fuck are you doing here?"

I knew instantly who she was.

chapter eighteen

"I could ask you the same thing," I said, descending into the cabin. I stood by the foot of the companionway, though, blocking her main avenue of escape. "You do know whose boat this is, don't you?"

"Of course I do," she said in her sandpapery voice. Her eyes were a pale, limpid blue, but they'd been green when she'd came to the studio; she'd worn coloured contacts, I presumed, or she was wearing them now. "It's my boat. And I don't remember giving you permission to board, so get the hell off before I call the police." She took a cellphone out of the back pocket of her jeans.

"Be my guest," I said. "Call the police. I'm sure they'd like to talk to you, too. Here," I added, taking out my wallet and finding Sergeant Kovacs's card. I held it out to her. "Here's the number."

Ignoring the card, she smiled thinly, acknowledging that I'd called her bluff. "What do you want?" she said.

Although I should have probably called the police myself, I didn't have a cellphone, and I didn't think she'd be likely to lend me hers, so I put the card back into my wallet and my wallet back into my pocket.

"What do you think?" I said.

She answered with a shrug.

"Let's start with your name," I said.

"My name is Anna Waverley," she said, unwilling to completely give up her charade. "As you sodding well know." I thought I detected a faint trace of a British accent to go along with the British slang.

"Let's try again," I said. "What's your name? Your *real* name."

"I told you," she said, still sticking to her story, but there was slightly less confidence in her voice. "It's Anna Waverley."

"No, it's *not*," I said roughly. "Anna Waverley is *dead*."

"What?"

"You heard me," I said. "She's dead."

"Bullshit," she said, eyes narrowing. "You're lying."

"I wish I were," I said.

She stared at me for a moment, realized I wasn't lying, and sagged back against the galley counter. "Goddamn it," she said. She squeezed her eyes shut. "*Goddamn it*," she said again, with more emphasis. "Fuck." Her distress seemed genuine.

"I'm sorry," I said.

She moved by me into the main salon and slumped onto a cushioned built-in berth that looked more comfortable than my living room sofa. She sat with her elbows on her knees and her face in her hands. There was a shrink-wrapped twelve-pack of single serving plastic bottles of mineral water on the butcher's block cover over the galley sink. I broke the shrink wrap and freed a bottle. Twisting off the cap, I went into the salon and handed her the bottle.

"Thanks," she said absently, but she did not drink.

I sat down on the edge of the berth against the opposite bulkhead, facing her across the hardwood deck, ready to intercept her if she made a break for the hatch. "Are you all right?"

"Yeah, sure."

"You and Anna Waverley were friends," I said.

"You could say that. How —" Her voice caught and she coughed. She raised the bottle and took a sip of water.

Anticipating her question, I said, "She was murdered in her home last night. Strangled. Whoever did it tried to make it look like suicide by stringing her up with an electrical extension cord. I found her body."

"Shit," she said.

"I know exactly how you feel."

"I doubt it," she said.

"All right," I said. "Let's start at the beginning. What's your name?"

Her eyes flashed and for a moment I thought she was going to refuse to tell me, but she said, "Chrissy. Chrissy Conrad."

"Well, Chrissy Conrad, if that really is your name, what are you doing on Anna Waverley's boat?"

"She lets me stay here when I need a place to crash."

"Were you here last Tuesday evening?"

She shook her head. "No."

"Where were you last Tuesday evening?"

"And how is that any of your business?"

"You damned well know how it's my business," I said angrily. "I'm not in the mood to play games with you. My partner was attacked on the boat you hired us to photograph."

"I don't know anything about that," she said.

She had dropped her cellphone onto the berth beside her. I reached over and picked it up. "Screw it," I said. "If that's the way you want to play it, we'll let the police sort it out." I flipped open the phone. "What will it be?

Are you going to answer my questions or shall I call the police?"

"Knock yourself out," she said, with a mocking smile. "It's locked."

I pressed a button on the phone's tiny keypad. The screen lit up, instructing me to enter a password. Closing the phone, I gestured toward the navigation station at the forward end of the cabin. "I'm sure there's a phone in the electronics locker. Ship-to-shore radio, anyway. Why don't I just give the Coast Guard a buzz and ask them to put me through to the police?"

She stared at me for long moment before saying, "All right, fine. The whole thing has turned to shit, anyway. First, though, you have to promise me two things. One, that you'll hear me out and, two, you'll wait at least twenty-four hours before telling the cops you talked to me, give me a chance to get out of Dodge."

"Why would I promise you anything?"

"Do you want me to answer your questions or don't you?"

"Okay," I said. "I'll hear you out."

She waited for me to continue. When a few seconds had passed and I hadn't, she said, "Shit," her raspy voice defeated. "I need a cigarette."

"I don't smoke."

She gestured toward the galley. "There's a pack on the counter."

I got up and went to the galley, where I found a pack of Player's Light and a matchbook on the counter. I handed them to her and resumed my seat. She lit up and blew smoke upwards, where it was caught by the gentle cross-breeze through the open ports above the berths.

"Anna doesn't like me smoking on her boat," she said. "I don't suppose that matters now." Her hand shook as she raised the cigarette to her lips. She pulled hard on it, cheeks hollowing, then drew smoke deep into her lungs. I suppressed the urge to cough. "No one was supposed to get hurt," she said, smoke spilling from her mouth, thickening her words. "I'm sorry about that. Really. I was sick when I heard about it. At first I thought it was you who'd been hurt. Then I found out it had been a woman. I'm really sorry."

"Tell that to my partner. She'll be getting out of the hospital in a day or two. Do you know who attacked her?"

"No. I don't. I — all I wanted was some pictures of that boat. I didn't know there'd be anyone on it. Really, I didn't." She tapped cigarette ash into the palm of her hand. "You believe me, don't you?"

"I don't know," I said. "Your track record with me isn't good."

"Yeah, okay. But I'm telling the truth now."

"Why did you want pictures of that boat?"

"I really did have someone who was interested in buying it."

"It's not your boat to sell."

"I've never let little details like that bother me. I once sold a house I didn't own. A couple, in fact. You'd be amazed how easy it is." She smiled again, a bit predatorily, I thought. "Some free advice. Always let the local plods know you're going on vacation. Not that it's likely to do any good."

"Okay, so you were conning someone into buying the *Wonderlust*. Why pass yourself off to me as Anna Waverley?"

She shrugged. "It seemed like a good idea at the time."

"Not good enough," I said.

"Tough." She drew hard on the cigarette.

Chrissy Conrad was about five feet five inches tall and wiry, probably didn't weigh more than a hundred and twenty pounds — Bobbi had been right; most of the

superstructure she'd displayed at the studio had been artificial. Anna Waverley had been an inch or two taller
and a few pounds heavier, but I didn't think Chrissy
would have had any trouble hoisting her up with the extension cord.

"How do I know you didn't kill her so you could
steal her identity and her boat?" I said.

"We're even, then," she said coolly. "How do I know
you didn't?"

"I have an alibi," I said. "A good one, as a matter of
fact. Where were you last night?"

"None of your fucking business."

"Okay," I said. "I guess it's time to call the police."

I stood up and crossed to the navigation station.
The electronics locker over the chart table did indeed
contain a ship-to-shore radio. It also contained the compact stereo system upon which the smoky-voiced singer
was currently lamenting the slicing up of a poor cow.
A CD jewel case on the chart table identified the singer
as Tanita Tikaram. I vaguely remembered her from my
early twenties. Chrissy Conrad would have been barely
in her "tweens." The disc must have belonged to Anna
Waverley.

"Hang on a minute," Chrissy said. Standing, she
reached through the open port over the berth and tossed
her cigarette and palm full of ashes overboard — or
at least onto the portside deck. "All right, look," she
said, dusting her hands. "I knew Anna, okay? We were
friends. Sort of. I worked for her husband. That's how
we met. Anyway, well, we had a bit of a row over … it
doesn't matter. God, don't look at me like that. I didn't
kill her." She took a breath. "Christ, what a fucking
cock-up." I wondered if she really was British or whether the faint accent and the quaint colloquialisms were
just part of her act, picked up from too many episodes of
Coronation Street.

"This row," I said. "Was it because you were having an affair with her husband?"

"Eh?" she said, surprised by the question. She regrouped quickly, though. "Not exactly. Sam has affairs with all his assistants. I was just one in a long line. No, it was because she refused to leave him."

It was my turn to be surprised. "Just what kind of 'sort of' friends were you?"

"We weren't lovers, if that's what you're thinking. We're both straight. I am, anyway. Reasonably sure she was, too."

"What was it, then? You wanted Sam Waverley for yourself?"

"Christ, no. Sam's a bastard. But I liked Anna. If I weren't straight, I might have —" She broke off with a shake of her head. "There's no point in thinking about that now, is there? In any event, she talked a lot about leaving Sam, just never got round to doing anything about it. It pissed me off." She shrugged, as if that were reason enough for friends to fall out.

"That's why you used her name when you came to my studio last week," I said. "Because you were angry with her."

"No, although I suppose it was part of the reason I set up a scam to sell this boat."

"This boat?" I said, pointing at the deck. "Not the *Wonderlust*?"

"Yes. No. My original plan was to run the con with this boat, but when I hooked a mark who wanted a fixer-upper motor yacht, I had to act fast. The *Wonderlust* was a perfect fit, but I needed photos and I didn't have time to create a new false ID. But I never meant for your friend to get hurt. Or Anna."

"You were supposed to meet me on the *Wonderlust* at eight that night. Were you there? Did you see what happened to Bobbi?"

"No. I was nowhere near here that night. I never intended to meet you, which is why I gave you the key and told you to use it in case I was late. I was going to call the next day and get you to email the photographs directly to my — client."

"Who really owns that boat?"

"I haven't any idea. Some corporation, is all I know."

"And you've no idea who may have been on it that night."

"No. I knew it was rented out for parties, but I called the agency that handled the bookings to make sure it wasn't booked that night."

"Your 'client,'" I said. "Could he have caught on to your scam and laid in wait for you? Maybe he mistook Bobbi for you."

"Not a chance. He's pissed that I haven't sent him the photos yet."

"Does he know what you look like?"

"No. But it wasn't him. He's still hot to buy the damned thing. Look, you've got to believe me. I never intended for anyone to get hurt."

"It really doesn't matter what you intended," I said. "The reality is that Anna Waverley is dead and my friend was damned near killed."

"What makes you think Anna's murder has anything to do with me or your friend getting hurt?"

"Anna called me last night and told me there was something she needed to tell me, but by the time I got there, she was dead."

Chrissy looked as though she was going to be sick. She gulped water.

I wasn't sure I believed everything she'd told me. In fact, I was damned sure I didn't. I had no idea, though, what part of what she'd told me was the truth and what part of it was fiction. Perhaps, I thought, just to be on the safe side, I should consider everything she'd told me to

be a lie. Starting with her claim that she hadn't been anywhere near the marina when Bobbi had been attacked.

"Why did you choose the *Wonderlust* to base your
scam on?" I asked, figuring that a roundabout approach
might work better than a straight-on assault.

"Like I said," she replied. "It was exactly what my
mark wanted. Anyway, what difference does it make?"

"Humour me. How did you get the key you gave
me?"

"I crashed a party the week before I came to see you
and swiped it from the guy who was throwing it."

"When was the last time you were onboard?"

"The night I swiped the key. Look, I know what
you're thinking, but, I told you, I wasn't anywhere near
that boat the night your friend was hurt."

"Where were you?"

She looked at me for a long moment before replying.
"I was working," she said at last. "Setting up another
score, if you must know. And that's all I'm going to tell
you."

"And last night?"

"Same answer."

"Do you know if Anna had a lover?"

"No. Not for sure, anyway. Probably. It wouldn't
surprise me. Yeah."

"I don't suppose you know his name, then?"

"No."

"When was the last time you saw her?"

"Six weeks ago or so. I don't remember exactly."

"How long did you work for her husband?"

"Not long. A year, maybe a bit more."

"When?"

"Until last fall.

"And you became friends with Anna Waverley even
though you were having an affair with her husband?"

"Is that so weird? I dunno, maybe it is. Anyway, we

met a couple of months after I started working for him and we hit it off right away. She was smart and funny and interesting, but she was the unhappiest person I ever met. I don't think I saw her smile more than once or twice, and even then they were sad smiles. I don't know how she dealt with it. I'd probably have killed myself." She shrugged.

I looked at her for a moment, then said, "I think you should go to the police with what you know."

"It'd just be a waste of time," she said. "Theirs and mine. I don't know anything more than what I've told you. I don't know who hurt your friend and I don't know who killed Anna. And how can you be sure Anna's murder had anything to do with what happened to your friend? Maybe it was something else."

"Such as?"

"How the hell should I know? Look, I'm sorry, I really am. I never meant for anyone to get hurt, but it'll just jam me up if you turn me over to the police." Did I detect a hint of desperation in her voice?

"Give me one good reason why I should give a damn if you get jammed up?" I said.

"Well," she said. "Maybe I could make it worth your while."

"I'll probably regret asking," I said, "but what do you have in mind?"

"I could cut you in on the deal I'm working on."

"Your next scam, you mean. Thanks, anyway."

"All right, look," she said, "I might know someone who could tell you who really owns the *Wonderlust*. What would that be worth to you?"

"Who?"

"I'll take you to him," she said. "But only if you'll agree to leave me out of it."

"Where is he?"

"Not far," she said. "Is it a deal?"

"Let's hear what he has to say first."

"Okay, fine," she agreed petulantly.

I watched as she closed and dogged the ports. She fetched a waist pack from the galley, from which she took a set of keys, and into which she stuffed her cigarettes, matches, and phone. She gestured for me to precede her up the companionway to the cockpit. I did, but I was careful to keep an eye on her, lest she attempt to brain me with the small fire extinguisher affixed beside the door to the head. In the cockpit, I watched again as she locked the main hatch.

"He lives on a boat in the Harbour Authority marina," she said, putting the keys into her pack and strapping it on.

The *Free Spirit* was moored bow in between the two narrow finger docks. As we stepped onto the dock, she pointed toward *Free Spirit*'s stern, and said, "I don't really know much about boats. The rope at the back came loose and I don't know if I tied it properly. Would you mind checking it?"

I went to the end of the finger dock and looked at the stern line tied to the dock cleat. "It looks o—"

Suddenly, I was in the air.

I should have seen it coming. Chrissy Conrad may not have known much about boats, but she knew something about leverage. With a quick thrust, she'd sent me sailing out over the end of the dock. I hit the water with a curse and a resounding splash. By the time I sputtered and spit to the surface, she was halfway to the ramp. By the time I pulled myself out of the water onto the dock and pelted after her, she was at the top of the ramp, where she kicked the prop out from under the gate and slammed it shut. By the time I got to the top of the ramp, she was long gone. That's when I discovered you needed a key to get out of the marina as well as into it. Cursing, I clambered over the ramp railing, managed to get onto the quay without falling into the water again, and began the long squelch homeward.

The first thing I did when I got home was to strip out of my wet clothes and shower the scummy salt water of False Creek out of my hair. The next thing I did was call Greg Matthias's cellphone number. The call was picked up by his voice mail. After the beep, I said, "Greg, it's Tom. Call me ASAP. It's urgent. Thanks." I hung up and poured myself a generous shot of Bowmore Legend. It was a decent enough Islay, and less pricey than Lagavulin, Laphroaig, or the older Bowmores, but I hadn't quite made up my mind about it. I was just about to pour another shot when Matthias called back.

"What's up?"

I told him about my encounter with Chrissy Conrad. As I repeated what she'd told me, I realized that it distilled down to very little of any real value. And how much of it could be believed was anyone's guess.

He said he'd send someone to check out the boat, then said, "Any reason to think anything she told you was the truth?"

"No," I said. "I'm not even sure she told me her real name."

"What about her relationship with Anna Waverley?"

"She was probably lying about that, too. At least about being friends. She might have been telling the truth about working for Sam Waverley, though."

"At least that gives us a place to start tracking down her real identity."

"She was also probably lying about not being at the marina when Bobbi was attacked. She may have even been on the boat. I doubt she's personally responsible for Bobbi's beating, unless she had help, but I'm sure she knows who is. She may also know who killed Anna Waverley, but I'm not quite so sure about that. I'd give you odds she knows the identity of Anna Waverley's lover, though."

"Too bad you let her get away."

"Yeah."

"All right," he said. "We'll circulate her description. Do you know what kind of vehicle she might be driving?"

"No, sorry. Have you been able to track down the ownership of the *Wonderlust*?"

"I couldn't say. Why?"

"Everything seems to revolve around that boat. It's obvious Bobbi's attack is tied to it, but Anna Waverley's murder may be, too. Then there's Chrissy Conrad's scam to sell it. Joel Cairo was asking about it, too."

"Who?"

"The slippery character who came to my studio last week and who tried to get into Bobbi's hospital room. I call him Joel Cairo because he reminded me of Peter Lorre's character in *The Maltese Falcon*."

"I've never seen it," he said. Was he kidding? "But you may be right," he added.

He hung up and I went to bed without brushing my teeth; Crest and single malt whisky do not mix.

chapter nineteen

I spent the following morning finishing the estimate for Walter Moffat's CD catalogue, then emailed it to the address he'd given me. There was still a lot to do to get the new space in shape for the official opening two weeks hence, so after sending off the quote, I went downstairs to lend a hand. Mary-Alice was standing at the new glass-topped display counter that we hadn't yet decided where to put, talking on her cellphone. Her face was set and her back was rigid.

"All right, fine," she said coldly, and closed the phone with a hard, plastic snap. She threw it onto the countertop.

I recognized the tone of her voice — I'd heard it often enough from Linda, my former spouse — and assumed she'd been talking to her husband, so I kept my mouth shut. The last place I wanted to be was in the middle of their marital no man's land.

"I sent the quote to Moffat," I said, figuring it was a safe enough topic.

"Did you?" she said. "Bully for you."

"I decided to donate our time to the foundation after all."

"Fine. Whatever. You're the boss."

"I'm joking, Mary-Alice."

"Fine. Whatever." She began viciously stripping bubble-wrap from framed examples of my and Bobbi's work that had hung on the wall of the old studio.

I picked up one of the photographs Mary-Alice had unwrapped. It was a shot of a pair of bridge workers dangling by their safety harness from the underside of the Lions Gate Bridge. I'd told Anna Waverley about the award I'd won for the photograph of the man rescuing the six-foot marijuana plant from the burning house, because I'd hoped it would make her smile. The photo of the dangling bridge workers had also earned me an award of sorts. I'd shot it from Wes Camacho's helicopter. I'd been hired to take aerial photographs of the harbour area and had subcontracted Wes and his whirlybird. We were about to call it a day due to high winds and head back to the heliport when we saw the bridgeworkers' scaffolding come apart and plummet into the water two hundred feet below. We hovered under the bridge while the wind beat at the chopper and Wes radioed information to the rescue workers and I snapped pictures. Wes had deserved the citation for bravery from Vancouver Fire and Rescue we'd shared, but as for me, I'd been scared half to death and had simply kept shooting as a distraction from my terror. Maybe Anna Waverley would have found that story worthy of a smile, I thought, as I stacked the photograph with the others.

Mary-Alice was sitting on the floor, a half-unwrapped photograph in her hands, staring at nothing.

"Mary-Alice?"

She looked at me. "What?"

"Is everything all right?"

"Of course. Why wouldn't it be?" She went on with her unwrapping.

I knew it was pointless pressing her, and likely to just make her angry, but I said, "I've been through it, you know. It isn't easy, but you'll come out of it okay. You're strong."

She surprised me. "I appreciate your concern, Tom, but I'd rather not talk about it. Not right now."

"Reeny called the other night," I said.

"Oh. And how is she? Will she be coming home soon?"

"She got engaged. She says I'll like him."

"Oh, Tom." She stood. "Are you okay?"

"Of course. Why wouldn't I be?"

She surprised me again when she smiled and put her arms around me. "We're a pair, aren't we?"

"We are indeed."

After lunch I told Mary-Alice that I had a couple of errands to run, that I'd be back in an hour or so. A few minutes later I was standing on the quay by the Broker's Bay Marina. The gate was propped open again and a line from a Dire Straits song about security being laid-back and lax rattled through my brain. The *Wonderlust*'s slip was empty once more. While I was reasonably certain that Chrissy Conrad had been lying about knowing someone who knew who owned the *Wonderlust* as a ruse to lure me onto the dock so she could tip me into the water, I thought it couldn't hurt to ask around.

I jumped when someone came up behind me on the quay and clapped a hand onto my shoulder. I spun to face Skip Osterman.

"Christ almighty, Skip." I saw that Connie was with him. "Uh, sorry, Con."

"The Lord has a thicker skin than that," she said with a smile. "Otherwise Skip would've been struck dead ages ago." Connie Osterman was five feet tall, tough as a juniper root, but every inch a lady. "How's Bobbi?" she asked.

"Good," I said. "She'll be coming home any day now."

"Praise Him," she said.

"What's up, Tom?" Skip said. "I got your message. Don't know as we can be much help, but we'll do what we can."

"You probably know most of the people who own these boats. They'll open up to you, tell you things they wouldn't tell the police. Or me."

"Maybe," he said carefully.

"Mrs. Waverley was killed on Monday night," I said. "Murdered in her home."

Connie gasped.

"Heard on the news about a woman gettin' killed in a home invasion," Skip said. "Her body was found by a friend. That was her?"

I said it was. Skip was the second person to mention the home-invasion theory, the other being Woody Getz. I supposed the police were deliberately misinforming the media to lull the killer or killers into a false sense of security. Keeping certain details of the murder under wraps also helps to weed out the crazies who'll confess to anything, just for the attention. I was grateful, too, that they hadn't released my name to the media. I liked Skip and Connie, they were good people and good friends, and would be sympathetic and understanding, but I didn't want to have to relive the events of that night over again.

"Do you think her murder has something to do with what happened to Bobbi?" Connie asked.

"It looks that way," I said. "It's complicated."

"An' we're just simple working folk," Skip said,

without rancour. "Oof," he added, when Connie jammed a fist into his ribs.

"Sorry," I said. "What I meant was, it's kind of hard to explain."

"Then save it for some evening over a couple of beers," Connie said. "What can we do to help?"

"It's not that I think anyone would wilfully withhold information from the police about Bobbi's attack or Anna Waverley's murder, but you know boat people, especially the ones who live aboard. They can be an independent, cantankerous bunch. Present company excepted, of course," I added.

Not to mention that living full-time on a boat in most marinas around Vancouver not zoned for living aboard was illegal. For one thing, they weren't equipped with waste disposal hook-ups. Sea Village had a vacuum-operated waste extraction system, but it was for the floating homes only, owned and maintained by Sea Village Inc. — that is, me and my independent, cantankerous neighbours. You could stay on your boat, as long as you had an onshore address and didn't live on the boat for more than thirty days at a stretch. Many boat people had onshore addresses, those who could afford to, but many didn't. Generally, the former usually stayed put in one marina, technically living ashore one day a month, while the latter tended to move from marina to marina. Neither group liked attention.

"So you want us to ask around, is that it? Sure. No problem."

"Just put out the word that anyone who knows anything that might help find the person who attacked Bobbi shouldn't be afraid to talk to the police. The police aren't interested in busting them for living aboard. But if they really don't want to talk to the police, they can talk to me. They have my word I won't reveal their identities. I'll only pass on the information they provide."

"That shouldn't be a problem," Skip said. "Most regulars know who you are, especially after your house nearly sank. Some might even trust you. What exactly is it you want to know?"

"It's a safe bet that someone was on board the *Wonderlust* the night Bobbi was attacked, either the woman who hired us or Anna Waverley or both. There may have also been one or more men on board, too; I don't think it was a woman who beat Bobbi half to death. The police haven't been able to find anyone who will admit to seeing anything unusual that night."

"Maybe no one did," Skip said.

"No one admits to seeing anything at all."

"I'm just sayin' …"

"What?"

"People around here mind their own business."

"Bobbi was almost killed by whoever was on that boat, goddamn it."

"I know, but —"

"They may have also murdered Anna Waverley."

"It's all right, Tom," Connie said. "We'll do what we can. It's the least we can do."

"Sure," Skip said. "I didn't mean … well, you know. It's just, I …" Connie put her hand on her husband's arm. He stammered to a halt.

"I really appreciate it, you guys. And, um, sorry about the language, Con."

"I've heard lots worse," she said. Skip smiled self-consciously.

I spent an hour talking to people in the marina, as well as many who worked in the shops, restaurants, and cafés in the vicinity of the marina. I was acquainted with some of them by name, and I knew many more of them by sight, and many of them knew me the same way. The police had spoken to most of them already, either Mabel Firth and Baz Tucker, the detectives, or both, but those with whom the police hadn't spoken weren't able to add anything useful. No one had seen anything out of the ordinary the night Bobbi had been attacked. A number of people recalled seeing Anna Waverley in the marina on a regular basis, although not that night, and a few had seen her husband around, too. Some had even seen activity on the *Wonderlust* at various times, but not on that particular night. The boat seldom left the slip, and then usually just to go over to the civic marina for fuel or to empty its holding tanks. Almost everyone I talked to reported seeing strangers on the docks, but that wasn't unusual; there were numerous charter and tour companies that operated out of the marina, two or three boat rental companies, as well as a number of boat brokerages. Between part-time sailors, browsers, tourists, and gawkers, at any time of year there were always strangers coming and going. One or two more weren't going to stand out.

Almost the entire southern shoreline of False Creek, from west of the Burrard Street Bridge, where the civic marina and the coast guard station were located, to well east of Granville Island toward the Cambie Street Bridge, was lined with marinas, often so close together they appeared to be one continuous marina. One of the busiest lay between the Burrard Street Bridge Civic Marina and the Broker's Bay Marina. The False Creek Harbour Authority was a co-operative owned by the commercial fishermen who worked out of the marina, although it rented recreational moorages as well, permanent and transient. At a few minutes past 2:00 I walked along the seawall from Granville Island, past condominiums with decorative gardens and ducks paddling in artificial tide pools, to the False Creek Harbour Authority, where I went into the office underneath the promenade ... and almost collided with the malodorous mountain of flesh that was Loth. He stood just inside the entrance, broad back to the door. His powerful body odour filled the small office. Jimmy Young, the marina manager, stood behind the counter, round cheeks and high forehead red with anger. The rest of his face was covered with a bristly grey beard. Behind Jimmy, slightly taller, stood a handsome, middle-aged woman with dark, wavy hair, silvered with grey at the tips, and bright blue eyes. A thin, barely visible line of old scar tissue slanted across the top of her cheek below her left eye. She looked vaguely familiar; I'd probably seen her around, but I didn't know her name. She looked frightened but defiant.

"... ain't gonna t'row me outta my home," Loth was saying as I tried to duck around him. "I jus' a sick old man, ain't got no other place to go." He swung ponderously toward me, leaning on the handle of his sturdy wood cane.

I backed against the counter. "I believe you," I said, holding my hands up, palms out.

"That boat isn't your home," Jimmy Young said. "Mr. Duckworth may let you stay on it, but we don't allow full-time living aboard. Mr. Duckworth knows that."

"I got rights," Loth said to me, ignoring Jimmy. "Tell 'em, mister man."

"Sure you do," I said agreeably. "Absolutely. You've got rights. Plenty of rights."

Jimmy's scowl was scorching. "He's been flushing the holding tanks into the harbour. And he's made filthy comments to Barb," he added, turning his head toward the woman standing behind him. Her cheeks coloured, causing the thin furrow of scar tissue below her eye to stand out white against pink. There was another scar running along the left edge of her jaw, longer, slightly deeper, but just as old.

"I din't mean nothin'," Loth whined. "I'm jus' —"

"Yeah, I know," Jimmy said. "A sick old man."

"Tell 'em, mister man," Loth said to me. "I ain't hurt no one. No one." He lumbered out of the office, leaning heavily on the cane. It bent so much under his weight I expected it to snap at any moment. Fortunately, it held; it would have taken block and tackle to get the huge old man onto his feet again.

"It was just words, Jimmy," the woman said when Loth had gone. "Crude, but I've heard worse." She leaned toward him, kissed him tenderly on the cheek. "But thanks, you're a gent." He flushed and she smiled at me. "Hello, you're Tom McCall, aren't you? I'm Barbara Reese." She held out her hand. Her handshake was warm, dry, and strong.

"How do you do," I said. "Um, have we met?"

"No, not really," she said. "But I do volunteer work at the community centre and you and a young lady gave a demonstration of digital photography for the kids this spring."

Mary-Alice's idea. Goodwill advertising, she'd said. It hadn't generated any work that I was aware of, but it hadn't cost us anything but a little of our time, and it had been fun.

Jimmy cleared his throat. I didn't know Jimmy Young well, but he was a regular at Bridges, liked to talk fly-fishing, about which I knew next to nothing. I'd asked him once if he ate all the flies he caught or was he a catch-and-release fly fisherman. He'd actually laughed, as if he hadn't heard it a thousand times.

"Cops came around asking about you," he said. "Did we know anyone who had it in for you? That sort of thing. I told 'em I didn't know you well enough, just to jaw with in Bridges sometimes. They asked a load of questions about last Tuesday night, too, did we see anything unusual going on. People runnin' along the seawall or the path under the bridge. Someone dumping some-thing out of a Zodiac."

"Did you?"

"Couldn't very well. Can't really see much of the promenade from here," he added, pointing to the ceiling. "Even if we could, we weren't workin' that night. Patsy and Roger were on. They didn't notice anything, either. Real sorry about your friend, though. Hope she's goin' to be all right."

"Thanks. She's going to be fine. There's something I'd like to ask you, though. Do you know who owns the boat Bobbi was attacked on? It's called *Wonderlust*."

"Couldn't say."

"What about Anna Waverley and her husband, Samuel?"

"Name rings a bell," Jimmy said.

"You remember, Jimmy," Barbara Reese said. "They came in a few months back looking for a berth for their sailboat, but we didn't have anything available. She was very quiet. About forty. Pretty. Reddish hair. He was older. Drove a Mercedes. You called her a 'trophy wife' because she was younger than him."

"Yeah, I remember now."

"She was murdered the other night," I said.

"Oh, dear," said Barbara.

Jimmy said, "What's that got to do with us?"

"Nothing," I said. "Except that she may have been on the *Wonderlust* the night Bobbi was attacked. You can see the slip where it was moored from here. Even better from the dock nearest Granville Island," I added, pointing to the map on the wall behind the counter that showed the five docks of the marina jutting out into the shallow curve of Broker's Bay. The easternmost dock was only twenty metres or so from the where the *Wonderlust* had been moored. "Maybe someone in one of the boats on that dock saw whoever was on the *Wonderlust* Tuesday evening."

"Maybe," Jimmy said. "I couldn't tell you."

"We could ask," Barbara said. "There's usually a few people on those boats at night." She came out from behind the counter. She had a voluptuous figure and her jeans fit her nicely. I'd always thought there was something alluring about a mature woman wearing jeans, as long as she wasn't too mature. "Come on, Mr. McCall, I'll take you out and introduce you."

We left Jimmy in the office and went out into the sunlight. The breeze off the water was cool, smelling of fish, salt, and iodine, as we walked down the ramp onto the easternmost of the five docks. A dozen fishing boats of various sizes were moored two deep along both sides of the dock. On the side facing Granville Island, two big, rough-looking men at least twenty years apart in age sat on the centre hatch cover of the middle outside boat, smoking and drinking beer from cans.

"Matthew, John," Barbara called across the inside boat.

"Hey, Barb," the older of the two said as they both stood. They threw their cigarettes into the water, then made their way across the intervening boat and stepped down onto the dock. Close up they looked even bigger and rougher, but both wore friendly, open smiles.

Barbara Reese introduced me to Matthew and John Ostrof, father and son. I shook hands with them. Their hands were like warm blocks of gnarled hardwood. "You heard about that girl who was attacked on that boat over in the Broker's Bay Marina?" she said to them.

"Yeah," Matthew Ostrof said. His son nodded. "That lady cop and a detective told us about it."

"She was Mr. McCall's friend. He wants to ask you a couple of questions about what you might've seen that night."

"Like we told the cops," Matthew Ostrof said, "we didn't see nothin'. Sorry."

"Yeah," John Ostrof added. He was in his late twenties, muscular and ruggedly handsome. I'd seen him in Bridges, playing darts for beer. He didn't buy very often. Bobbi had commented on how delicately he'd held the darts in his hard, powerful hand, how effortlessly he'd flicked them at the board. She'd thought he'd make an interesting subject, wanted to photograph him, but had been too shy to ask.

"The boat she was assaulted on is owned by a company that rents it out for parties," I said. "You must have a front row seat."

"Pretty close," Matthew Ostrof agreed. "But there was nothin' happening on Tuesday that we saw, was there?" His son shook his head.

"What about other times? Do you know any of the people who have been to the parties?" Both men shook their heads. "Do you know Sam or Anna Waverley?"

Matthew Ostrof shook his head again, but John Ostrof said, "She's the one they were talking about at Bridges, Dad. The one that got killed in Point Grey. She bought fish from us a couple of times," he said to me. "Owns that blue Sabre over there," he added, pointing.

"The runner with the nice —" the elder Ostrof said.

"That's her," his son said.

"Did you ever see Mrs. Waverley at one of the parties on the *Wonderlust*?" I asked.

"Nope," John Ostrof said. "I wouldn't expect to, either. They're more like business meetings than parties. You know the kind, a half a dozen middle-aged guys, booze, and a couple of 'professional' women" — he made quote signs in the air — "as entertainment." He shrugged. "It's a good, solid boat, but kinda neglected. Looked her over a few weeks back. Heard she might be for sale."

"What do you want a fancy boat like that for?" his father said disapprovingly.

"Thought we might do charters, Dad. We talked

about this, remember? It's getting too hard to make a living fishing."

"Humph," Matthew Ostrof opined.

"When Mrs. Waverley bought fish from you, was she alone?"

"Yup."

"You've never seen her with a man?"

"Nope, sorry," Matthew Ostrof said.

But John Ostrof said, "I remember seeing her one day a couple of weeks back. I was heading over to Bridges and she was on the quay by the marina entrance talking to some guy."

"This man," I said. "What did he look like?"

"Just an ordinary guy," John Ostrof said with a shrug. "Tall as you, maybe, but a bit heavier and a few years older. Kept patting his head, like he was making sure his hair was still there."

"Could it have been her husband?"

"I suppose."

"Did you hear what they were talking about?"

"Nope," he replied. "She looked upset, though, like maybe they were arguing about something. When he put his hand on her arm, she jerked it away, then turned and walked away from him. He looked pretty angry, too." He looked thoughtful for a moment, then said, "Now that you got me thinking about it, I might've seem him a time or two on that party boat."

I thanked them for their time. They said they were sorry they weren't more help, and clambered back across the intervening boat to their own vessel.

There was no one aboard any of the other boats moored along the dock. I walked Barbara Reese to the marina office, thanked her, then headed back along the seawall to Granville Island.

chapter twenty

As I walked beneath the Granville Street Bridge along Anderson onto Granville Island, I spotted Mabel Firth and Baz Tucker on the boardwalk by the Broker's Bay Marina. They were confronting Loth. Curious, and not wanting to feel left out, I joined the small crowd gathering on the boardwalk to watch the action unfold.

"Mr. Loth," Mabel said. "We don't want any trouble. You just come quietly, okay, we'll get it all straightened out."

"I ain't goin' nowheres wit' you," Loth replied plaintively, waving his stout cane to emphasize his point. "I jus' a sick old man, mind my own bidness, don't bother no one 'less they bother me. That Jimmy Young, he wanna t'row me outa my home." He shook his head. "It ain't right. Them people's lyin'. I ain't hurt no one. No one. It jus' lies."

"If you'll just come with us, please, sir," Mabel said. "We'll get it all straightened out. And, if you wouldn't mind, maybe you could stop waving the cane around.

We don't want anyone to get hurt."

Loth shook his great balding head and repeated his familiar refrain, "I ain't going nowheres. I ain't hurt no one. I'm jus' a sick ol' man."

Baz Tucker had his nightstick out and seemed more than ready to use it on the old man.

"Put that away," Mabel said to him. "I've called for backup. Let's wait for it, all right?"

Baz Tucker slid his nightstick into his belt loop. "All right folks," he said to the crowd. "Go on about your business. Nothing to see here."

Grumbling, the onlookers began to disperse.

Loth saw me, bulled between Baz and Mabel.

"You, mister man," he said, lumbering toward me. "You tell 'em. What they want to bother a sick old man for, who ain't never hurt no one? You know I ain't hurt that one on that boat. That Bobbi. I ain't never done nothin' for her to call me bad names for. I ain't never hurt no one. Not her. Not that other one, either."

"What other one?" I asked.

"The whore that sucks on men's dicks for money on that ol' boat. I tol' her I give her money if she suck on my dick, but she said no, go away, like my money ain't good enough, like she was better 'n' other whores. A whore is a whore is all what I know. I seen her with them mens, sneaking onto that boat to get their dicks sucked on for money."

"What men?" I asked.

"Mens. You maybe, too, mister man. She suck on your dick too, eh? You suck on her, eh? Fuck her in the bum hole?"

I bit back on my disgust. "When did you see these men?"

"All-a-time. Seen her with womens, too. She fucks with womens, I bet." He shook his cane in my face. "That ain't right, no."

"What women?" I demanded. "When did you see these women?"

"Tom," Mabel Firth said sternly. "You're only making things worse."

"All-a-time," Loth said. "She jus' a whore. All womens's whores. That Barbara. Her, too. She sucks on that Jimmy Young's dick, lets him fuck her in the bum hole. Thinks no one knows. But I seen 'em. I seen that whore on her boat too, fucking with mens." He waved his cane. "Go away. I ain't talkin' to no one no more."

He lumbered off along the boardwalk toward Anderson Street, waving his cane at the crowd, scattering it like a flock of ducks, ignoring Mabel Firth's commands to stop.

"We can't just let him go," Baz said, drawing his nightstick again.

"What're you gonna do, Baz? Whale on an old man with your stick? Besides, where's he gonna go? Wait for backup."

"Why are you trying to take him in?" I asked her. "What did he do?"

She looked at me, and I realized the width of the gulf that lay between us, cop and civilian, despite our friendship. Then her expression softened. "Besides a couple of dozen complaints about indecent behaviour," she said, turning her attention back to Loth as he limped along the boardwalk, "he's in violation of the conditions of his release. He's supposed to report for weekly tests to make sure he's taking his medication. He hasn't reported for almost a month."

"Medication for what?" I asked.

"Your guess is a good as mine," Mabel said. "Which would be schizophrenia, but —"

A woman cried out as Loth struck her with his cane.

"Hey!" a man shouted. Loth whacked at him with his cane. Blood sprang from the man's cheek.

"Aw, crap," Mabel said. She ran to the man, helped him to a bench, while Baz called for paramedics on his radio as he jogged to intercept Loth, who was standing on the boardwalk between Granville Island and the Kitsilano mainland, swinging his cane at passersby.

"I'm all right," the man said, waving Mabel off. A woman sat beside him, handed him a wad of tissues, which he pressed against his cheek.

Mabel drew her stick. She looked frightened. "This is going to be bad," she said to me. She looked around. "Shit, there must be a dozen fucking video cameras in this crowd."

In the four years I'd known her I'd heard her swear mildly a few times, under stress, but I'd never heard her say "shit" or use the fuck word in any of its myriad variations.

"Wait for your backup," I said, as Loth took a swing at a man on a mountain bike, sending him crashing into one of the massive concrete piers of the Granville Street Bridge. He flipped off his bike onto Anderson Street where, fortunately for him, traffic had stopped to watch the fun.

"Shit," Mabel said, as she moved after Loth and Baz.

She was right. It was bad. In fact, it was a disaster. She and Baz Tucker tried to persuade Loth to get into their squad car, first with pleas, which he ignored, then with physical restraint, each on an arm damned near as big as my leg, which he also ignored. When he shoved Mabel in the chest, almost sending her reeling off the causeway into Broker's Bay, Baz whacked him on the back of the legs with his nightstick, aiming for thick muscle, scrupulously avoiding joints, spine, internal organs. He might as well have been hitting a sack of sand for all the apparent effect it had.

The backup arrived then, three male officers and one female, in two squad cars. They all piled on, trying to force the old man to the ground and get cuffs on him. Loth shook them off like a rhino shakes off tick birds. They surrounded him, drew their sticks. He struck out with his cane. The female constable shattered it with her nightstick. Meanwhile, in the crowd, video cameras whirred and cellphone cameras chirped.

"They need a fucking Taser," someone near me said.

"Or a tranquilizer gun," someone else said.

"Or one of them loops they use to catch stray dogs," another added.

"Just shove him into the fucking water," suggested a fourth.

"Fuck it," contributed a fifth. "Just shoot the great ugly bastard." I glared at him. "Just tryin' to be helpful," he said with a shrug.

"Fucking pigs," differed an overweight man with long, ratty hair strung with coloured beads.

"Shut up, asshole," a bystander growled at him.

"Why you doon this?" Loth bellowed as he lumbered along the boardwalk and the cops flailed at his legs and buttocks with their sticks. "I ain't done nothin'. I ain't hurt no one."

He grabbed one of the cops, lifted him off his feet as though he were a child, and threw him over the edge of the causeway into the bay. He hit the water with a bellow and a spectacular splash. One of the other cops leaped onto the huge old man's back, jamming his nightstick under his chin, trying to incapacitate him with a choke-hold. Loth heaved and rotated his massive shoulders and the cop lost his grip, went flying, and almost ended up in the drink himself.

"Loth, stop it!" Mabel shouted at him. "Please. We don't want to hurt you!"

"I ain't goin' nowheres with you. I ain't done nothing. I ain't goin' back to jail. I ain't goin' to no hospital, neither."

"Fuck this shit!" Baz Tucker roared. He lowered his head and charged at Loth, throwing himself at Loth's knees like a football guard protecting the quarterback from a blitz. Loth staggered, but did not fall, fortunately for Baz, upon whom the gigantic old man would surely have landed. One of the other male cops slammed his shoulder into Loth's thick gut, while Baz clung to Loth's massive legs. With a roar, Loth toppled backwards, landing on his broad rump, half sitting on Baz. He rolled over and tried to stand, but the rest of the cops, wet and dry, piled onto him. The one who'd gone into the water managed to get one bracelet of his handcuffs onto Loth's thick right wrist, used it to lever Loth's arm back while kneeling on his spine. Mabel snapped another cuff onto Loth's left wrist, then they linked the free bracelets. Loth bellowed and thrashed, but with his arms manacled behind his back he was as helpless as a beached whale. He gave up the struggle and went limp, face red and breathing heavily and rapidly.

Mabel stepped back, gulping air, cap missing, dark blonde hair loose around her face. She caught her breath, then spoke into the microphone clipped to her shoulder, calling for more paramedics. Loth didn't seem to be in distress, was breathing more or less normally and muttering about having done nothing to warrant such treatment, but Mabel wasn't taking any chances. A man stepped out of the crowd of onlookers, pressed close, aiming a video camera at Loth and the cops surrounding him. Baz Tucker stepped in front of the camera. The aspiring videographer tried to manoeuvre around him. Baz, his face blazing with anger, ripped the camera out of the man's hand, cocked his arm, and threw it like a quarterback going for the desperate long bomb.

"Son of a bitch!" the man shouted, as he watched his camera arc out over Broker's Bay and drop into the water almost halfway to Fisherman's Wharf.

"Aw, geez, Baz," Mabel said.

"Fuck this shit!" Baz shouted at no one in particular, while from a safe distance a Chinese girl with black-and-orange hair aimed her cellphone at him.

It was after four by the time I got to the studio. The door was locked and Mary-Alice and Wayne were nowhere to be seen, so I went home, got a beer out of the fridge, and took it and the cordless phone up to the roof deck. I phoned the hospital and spoke to Bobbi for a few minutes. Wayne was bringing pizza, she told me, did I want to join them? I said thanks, maybe I'd drop by later. We chatted for a minute more, about nothing of any real consequence, then rang off. I realized I'd forgotten to ask her if she remembered anything more about her attack. I supposed she'd have mentioned it if she had.

There was a heaviness in my chest that seemed to go well with the sense of detachment I felt, a disconnection from the world and the people around me. The hinges of my jaw ached and I realized I was clenching my teeth. I forced myself to relax, took a drink of beer. It tasted vaguely foul, as if it had turned skunky. Or I had. I took another swig and felt nausea clawing at the back of my throat.

Had Loth been talking about Anna Waverley when he'd claimed to have watched a woman having sex with men on a boat, which I presumed to be the *Wonderlust*? I didn't want to think so, but it hardly mattered what I thought; the universe would unfold as it would, irrespective of what I wanted. It always had. And so what if Loth had spied on Anna Waverley having sex with men on the *Wonderlust*? As Mabel had said, perhaps Anna met her lover on that boat, rather than on her own, because she didn't want to violate a bed she shared with her husband, whom she had professed to still love. Did that make her a bad person? No, of course not. It made her human.

On the other hand, if Loth were indeed schizophrenic, as Mabel thought, he wasn't a particularly reliable witness.

I took another mouthful of beer.

Who was the man John Ostrof had seen Anna arguing with, and who he thought he might have seen on the *Wonderlust*? Was it her husband, her lover, or just "some guy," as he'd said? I made a mental note to tell Matthias, who might want to sit John Ostrof down with a sketch artist.

I went downstairs, where I dumped the rest of the beer down the sink. It was not quite 5:30, a little too early to think about dinner, but the emptiness gnawing at my gut felt like hunger, so I scrounged through the fridge for something to eat. I thawed some slightly freezer-burnt spaghetti sauce in the microwave, boiled some pasta, and ate it a little too *al dente* with a salad and a couple of glasses of red wine. It was not quite seven when I finished washing up. I took another glass of wine into the living room, put a Renee Fleming compilation on the stereo, and lay down on the sofa. Listening to Renee Fleming's pure, soaring voice reminded me of Reeny. Not only because of the similarity of their names, but because it had been Reeny who'd introduced me to opera, particularly sopranos. Until then, most opera, sopranos in particular, had sounded to me like a cat with its tail caught in a door. Some still did. But thanks to Reeny I had developed an appreciation for Renee Fleming, Cecilia Bartoli, Dawn Upshaw, and Kiri Te Kanawa, to name the few I'd collected so far. I was going to have to work harder to like tenors; they weren't nearly as pretty.

I wondered if Reeny's new fiancé liked opera, but I didn't wonder about it for long. I fell asleep halfway through the disc and didn't wake up until a couple of minutes past eleven. Feeling masochistic, I turned on the television to catch the remainder of the eleven o'clock news ... and there was Baz Tucker, in living colour, rifling the tourist's video camera out over Broker's Bay. I stabbed the remote and went up to bed.

chapter twenty-one

Greg Matthias came by the studio at 9:00 Thursday morning. "They're releasing Bobbi this afternoon," he told me. "I'm going to pick her up, if that's all right with you."

"Why wouldn't it be?"

"Just checking."

"Well, it's fine with me. I've got plenty to do around here." I waved toward the machine. "The coffee's fresh. Cups in the cupboard."

He poured himself a cup of coffee, slurped it noisily, pronounced it drinkable. Then he said, "Is your sister around?"

"She's upstairs. What's up?"

"I need to ask her some questions about her husband's relationship with Anna Waverley."

"He'd met her and her husband at some fundraising events. I think that's about the extent of it."

"I still need to talk to her."

"Should I get her?"

"In a minute." He drank some more coffee, then said, "Firth and Tucker are in some serious hot water over what happened yesterday."

"I don't doubt it."

"The other cops, too, but mostly Firth because she was senior officer on the scene and Tucker because he did what thousands of cops have wanted to do since the Rodney King fiasco."

"They coped the best they could with a bad situation," I said. "That old man is strong as a truck. And he's more than a little bit crazy to boot. They may as well have tried to catch an elephant with a butterfly net." I told him what Mabel had said to me just before it had gone bad.

"Yeah, and Loth's lawyer, some grandstanding civil rights hotshot who specializes in wrongful imprisonment cases, is going to do everything he can to see that she pays for it. I just hope the bosses don't hang her out to dry."

"They won't if they call me and some of the other people on the quay as witnesses. Not just the tourist whose camera Baz Tucker chucked into Broker's Bay."

"Don't count on it. Another thing. Have you seen Norman Brooks lately?"

"Not since the night of his run-in with Loth outside Bridges. Why?"

"Bobbi's worried about him. He hasn't been to see her since she woke up."

"I hate to say this, but maybe he's gone on a bender."

"Let's hope that's all it is," Matthias said. "He's been making a nuisance of himself since Bobbi was hurt. He still has connections and it looks like he may have used them to get access to the case files. But he's been more than a little out of control lately and it's possible he's stirred up something he couldn't handle." He drank some more coffee, then speared me with a look. "Speaking of nuisances, I understand you've been playing detective, asking around about Anna Waverley."

"Yeah …?"

"Learn anything useful?"

"I don't know. Probably not." I told him what John Ostrof had told me about the man he'd seen arguing with Anna Waverley on the quay.

"Lovers' tiff?"

"Or marital."

"Could it be the guy who came to your studio?"

I shook my head. "I don't think so. The description doesn't fit."

"Any idea who it does fit?"

"No. It was a bit vague. But he also said he thought he might have seen him at parties on the *Wonderlust*."

"Would he be willing to sit down with a police artist, see if we can come up with a reasonable facsimile?"

"I think so. You might also try talking to Loth again. If anything he says can be believed, he's apparently been spying on people in their boats. Maybe he'll make more sense when he's back on his medication."

"Loth's a peeper? It's hard to imagine a guy that size creeping about and peering through portholes."

"Who's peering into whose portholes?" Mary-Alice asked as she came down the stairs from the office. She dimpled at Matthias. "Hi, Greg."

"Uh, hullo, Mrs. Paul," Matthias said, standing.

Mary-Alice's eyes narrowed. "Mrs. Paul?" she said warily, glancing from Matthias to me and back to Matthias again.

"I'm here on official police business," he said.

"Okay …?" she said.

"I understand your husband knew Anna Waverley," he said.

"He's purchased a couple of *objets d'art* from her husband's gallery," Mary-Alice said. "And Mrs.

Waverley was a supporter of Elise Moffat's Children in Peril Network, as is David. I wouldn't say David knew her, though, except very casually."

"We examined the Waverleys' phone records," Matthias said. "There were a number of calls placed during the evening from the Waverleys' home number to your home number last month, as well as two calls to your husband's office number."

"Maybe Mr. Waverley was just trying to sell David more art."

"That would explain it," Matthias agreed. "Did you speak to Mr. Waverley when he called your home?"

"No."

"Were you acquainted with Mrs. Waverley?"

"No. I'd never met her. Although I'm sure we were at a couple of events together."

"All right, thanks — Mary-Alice."

"Are you going to be speaking to David?" she asked.

"Yes," Matthias replied.

Mary-Alice nodded curtly and went back up the stairs to the office.

Matthias gulped down the dregs of his coffee. "Duty calls," he said.

I walked him to the door. "David isn't a suspect, is he?"

"Just about everyone who knew her is a suspect. That's how it works."

"I knew her," I said.

"But you appear to have neither motive nor opportunity. Anyone who has both is automatically moved to the top of our list." He paused, then said, "I'm picking Bobbi up around two. She wants to go home, but I'm not sure she should be on her own right now. She may still be at risk. We can post a car outside her apartment house and a police officer inside, if she'll let us, but it'd be a lot easier if she could stay with someone till she's ready to come back to work. She won't stay with her father. I don't blame her. Nor does she want to go to her mother's in Nanaimo. I suggested she could stay with Isabel in Pemberton, but she just accused me of trying to start up a harem. Could she stay with you?"

"Sure," I said. "It wouldn't be the first time she's bunked with me. She might not agree, though. We work together all right, but living together is another thing altogether. Evidently I'm not the easiest person to live with."

"I'm sure she can put up with you for a while," Matthias said dryly.

Claiming she didn't want to be a burden, Bobbi had Matthias take her home rather than bring her to my place. She agreed to the cops leaving a car outside her building, but she adamantly refused to allow a police officer to stay with her. I was disappointed she'd chosen not to stay with me; I could have used the company. As it happened, it was a fortuitous decision.

At eight that evening, while I was taking a week's worth of clean dishes out of the dishwasher, the phone rang. I lifted the cordless handset off the wall cradle, held it between my chin and shoulder as I continued emptying the dishwasher.

"Hello?"

"McCall?" a man said.

"Yes." The voice had a familiar ring, but I couldn't quite place it. "Who is this?" I stopped putting the dishes away.

"It isn't important who I am," he said. "It's what I know that's important."

"And what's that?" I recognized the voice then. It belonged to "Joel Cairo."

"For one thing, I know who killed Mrs. Waverley," he said. "And who beat up your girlfriend."

My heart thudded and my skin prickled. "Who?"

"I'll tell you. But not on the phone. Meet me in the parking lot of the Safeway at 4th and Balsam in an hour. Alone. Don't call the cops. I see any cops, or anyone else at all, I'm out of there."

"How do I know this isn't some kind of trap? How do I know it wasn't you who beat up Bobbi and killed Anna Waverley?"

"Meet me or not, it's up to you. But if you don't, you'll never know, will you? It's eight-ten now. I'll wait exactly an hour. Not a minute longer." He hung up.

It took three tries to put the phone back into the cradle, my hand was shaking so much. My first impulse, originating in the ancient reptilian part of my brain, scaly and savage, was to go, find out who had hurt Bobbi and killed Anna, so I could avenge them both. The Safeway at 4th and Balsam was less than ten minutes away by car, maybe twenty on foot. Then the kinder, gentler mammalian part of my brain shrieked, *Don't be stupid!* My mammalian brain was right. I was being stupid. I had no idea what I might be walking into. I should call Matthias. Surely the police could shadow me, cover me in such a way that they wouldn't be seen. If they even let me keep the appointment. They might not be willing to put a civilian at risk. Which was just fine with me.

I found Matthias's card and called his cellphone.

"Matthias," he growled after the second ring.

"Greg, it's Tom. I just got a call from someone who claims to know who killed Anna Waverley and beat up Bobbi. I think it was Joel Cairo. He wants me to meet him in an hour."

"Where?" he asked. After I told him, he said, "All right. Sit tight. Don't do a thing. We'll handle it."

"Okay," I said.

I hung up just as someone knocked on the door. I went to the door and peered through the peephole I'd had installed to avoid unwelcome surprises. I couldn't see anything. I checked the switch by the door that controlled the porch light, but it was in the on position. The bulb must have burned out, I thought, as I opened the door.

Dumb move.

A horse kicked me in the chest. At least that's what it felt like when "Joel Cairo" jabbed stiffened fingers into my solar plexus. I fell backwards, diaphragm temporarily paralyzed, unable to speak, fight back, barely able to breathe. He stepped into the foyer and closed the door behind him.

"You called the cops, didn't you?" he said, standing over me. "I figured you would. It doesn't matter. Here, let me help you up." He helped me to my feet. His hands were hard and he was extraordinarily strong. "Sorry about that," he said, brushing non-existent dust from my non-existent lapels. "I wanted to make sure I had your attention. It's amazing how pain focuses the mind, isn't it? Here, let me give you another demonstration."

He gripped my elbow, steely fingers probing. Pain lanced though my arm, as if every nerve ending from my armpit to the tip of my second finger was on fire. My hand cramped into a claw and felt as if a spike had been driven though my palm. The pain was so intense my mouth gaped, but the only sound that escaped was a strangled squeak. He released me and I collapsed to the floor, arm tingling painfully, eyes burning, body bathed in cold sweat, breath ragged in my throat.

"Have I got your attention?" he asked, squatting in front of me. "Have I? Answer me!"

"Yes," I croaked, trying to sit up.

"Good. Now listen carefully. Are you listening? Shit, you're not listening, are you?"

He drove the heel of his hand into my left chest just below my heart. My vision went black and I thought my heart had imploded. Feeling as though my chest were being squeezed between the jaws of a steel vice, blinded by tears of pain and fear and anger, I crawled away from him, flopped like a stranded fish down the two steps from the hall into the living room, and lay gasping and shuddering on the cold, hard wood of the living room floor.

Something blunt and hard prodded my ribs. "Sit up." A harder prod. "Sit up!"

Pain shooting through my chest, certain I was having a heart attack, I rolled over and clawed myself into a sitting position, back against the end of the sofa. I breathed in short, shallow gasps that hurt. He squatted on his heels in front of me, face close to mine.

"I have a message for your girlfriend," he said. His cologne was sharp and his breath smelled of peppermint. "Are you listening?"

I didn't have to be asked twice. "Yes," I rasped. "I'm listening."

"Good. Here's the message. She keeps her mouth shut about what went down on that boat. She keeps her mouth shut or everybody she cares about — her old man, her mother, you, your sister, the guy that works for you, everyone — will feel pain ten thousand times worse than what you just felt. Tell her I'll hurt them so bad they'll beg me to kill them. And when I think they've begged enough, I'll oblige them. Then I'll come see her and kill her. I'll have some fun with her first, though." He slapped me. Not hard. Just lightly. Flicking the tips of his fingers across my face. "Do you understand?"

"Yes," I ground out between teeth so tightly clenched my jaw creaked and my teeth ached.

"Tell me what I just said."

Rage and terror waged war within me and I could not speak. I knew, though, that if I didn't speak, that if I didn't do exactly what he told me to do, he would hurt me again. So I choked the words from my throat, forcing them through my teeth. Each word burned like acid. And as I spoke, repeating what he'd said, I knew for the first time in my life what it felt like to want to kill someone. I wanted to kill this man, needed to kill this man, to choke the life out of him, smash him to a pulp, stomp him into a grease spot, erase him from existence. But I couldn't move a muscle.

"If she talks … you'll kill everyone … she cares about. Then you'll … kill her."

"That's the gist of it," he crooned softly, gently stroking my cheek. "But it lacks nuance, don't you think? It will have to do, though. I don't have any more time to waste on you. Goodbye, Tommy-boy. Here's a little something to remember me by."

His hand dropped to my crotch and he squeezed once, sharply and horribly. A scream locked in my throat as the pain exploded though my groin. I convulsed as though I'd been hit with a massive electrical current. He left me folded in a fetal ball on the floor of my living room, hands clamped between my thighs, breathing in short guttural grunts, any previous pain he'd inflicted forgotten in the exquisite agony that pulsed through me.

I don't know how long I lay there before I slowly and carefully unfolded myself, gasping and nauseated, straightening first one leg, then the other, until I lay on my back, breathing through my mouth, breath catching at the start of each exhalation. After a few minutes, I rolled over onto my stomach and levered myself up onto my knees. I sat on my heels for a while, bracing myself on the arm of the sofa as a wave a dizziness washed over me, almost making me vomit. The pain diminished somewhat; it felt as though I'd been struck by only a small truck. Shakily, I got to my feet and hobbled into the kitchen, walking as though I had a soccer ball between my knees. I took a hot/cold gel pack out of the freezer compartment and almost suffered actual cardiac arrest when I shoved it down my pants and cupped it beneath my inflamed gonads. The relief was immediate, albeit not complete. I lifted the cordless telephone off the wall cradle and took it into the living room. Lowering myself carefully onto the sofa, I found Matthias's cellphone number in the phone's redial memory and speed-dialled it.

"Matthias," he answered.

"It's Tom. Where are you?"

"I'm just about to leave Bobbi's and go to meet your friend. What's up?"

"I just had a very unpleasant visit from him. Very unpleasant indeed."

"Are you all right? You sound funny."

"I don't feel funny. I feel bloody awful."

"What happened?"

"In simple terms, he beat the stuffing out of me."

"I'll be there in fifteen minutes. Do you need paramedics?"

"No, I don't think so. A bag of frozen peas should do the trick."

He disconnected and I put down the phone. I laid my head back and tried to find a more comfortable position on the sofa. The effect of the frozen gel pack was wearing off and a dull throbbing ache was spreading through my lower abdomen. I thought about getting up and taking a couple of Tylenol, but it seemed like too much trouble, and they probably wouldn't have done much good, anyway. I must have fallen asleep then, because no sooner had I decided it was too much trouble to find the Tylenol than Bobbi was leaning over me, hand on my shoulder.

"Tom?"

"Umph," I said as I sat up, gritting my teeth in anticipation of the pain I knew the sudden movement would cause. I was profoundly relieved when all I felt was a distant achy discomfort.

"Are you all right?" she asked. She gaped at my crotch. "Holy shit, you're all swollen."

"Oops," I said, reaching into my trousers and extracting the warm gel pack. "Pardon me," I added as I cautiously rearranged myself in my trousers.

Greg Matthias stood in the hallway, his cellphone to his ear, listening. "All right," he said, and flipped it closed. He looked so smooth and cool as he did it I thought I should get one. "You don't look any the worse for wear," he said, descending the steps into the living room.

"He did things that inflicted a godawful lot of pain," I said, "but didn't leave any marks or do any lasting damage." I giggled. "I hope."

"You sure you're all right?" Matthias asked.

"Uh, I think so. Feeling a bit giddy, though. Like I've had a bit too much to drink. Which I haven't. Yet." I started to get up.

"I'll get it," Bobbi said. "Scotch?"

"Please. Lots."

She went to the little cabinet I use as a bar and poured me a large shot of the Bowmore. As she handed it to me, there was a knock on the door, then a pair of uniformed cops came in, both beefy males in their thirties. I didn't know either of them. Mabel Firth and Baz Tucker's replacements, I presumed. They conferred briefly with Matthias, standing close and keeping their voices low so I couldn't make out what they were saying. He nodded and they left.

Matthias took the report. Bobbi grew wide-eyed and pale when I repeated the message the man had wanted me to give her. When I finished, I tossed back the Scotch and held out the glass for more.

"Motherfucker," she said angrily, pouring me another big shot. "I wish I could remember what happened."

"You will," Matthias said. "And when you do, we'll nail this nasty prick, don't worry about that."

"I just hope I remember before anyone else gets hurt," Bobbi said.

"I don't get it," I said. "If this is the guy who attacked Bobbi and killed Anna Waverley, what does he think he's doing? First he comes to the studio and demands to know who hired us. Then he tries to get to Bobbi in the hospital. Now he attacks me and threatens to kill us all if Bobbi reveals what happened on the boat. It's like standing on a street corner shouting, 'Here I am, I did it, catch me if you can.' Even if Bobbi can't identify him, I can. Does he really think that he can scare us into keeping quiet?"

"He scares me," Bobbi said. "And after what he did to you, aren't you scared?"

"Bloody right I'm scared," I said. "But I'm more angry than scared."

"Of course you're angry," she said. "Anyone would be. He beat the shit out of you." She shook her head. "He more than beat the shit out of you. He, well, humiliated you."

"Funny. I don't feel humiliated. Much." I thought about it for a moment, then said, "I'm not ashamed that someone with martial-arts training beat the shit out of me, any more than I'm ashamed that Yo-Yo Ma can play the fiddle better than I can."

She stared at me for a couple of beats, then smiled slightly. "Yo-Yo Ma plays the cello," she said.

"Which is just a fiddle on steroids. My point is, my self-esteem isn't based on my ability, or lack thereof, to fight or withstand pain." I gritted my teeth as a brief flicker of residual sensitivity rippled along the nerve endings in my groin.

"You're a lover, not a fighter," Bobbi said, in a gently mocking tone.

"You said it, not me."

"All right, so why are you angry?" she asked.

"Because he invaded my home, violated my sanctuary, and threatened to hurt people I care about. Oh, yeah, and beat the living shit out of me. I guess what makes me most angry, though, is that I opened that fucking door." I took a mouthful of Scotch and looked at Matthias. "Does he seriously believe threatening to kill us is going to stop us from talking?"

"Speak for yourself, fella," Bobbi said.

"He probably does," Matthias said. "He seems like a classic sociopath. Impulsive, reckless, and narcissistic, with no real grasp of consequences. He's probably reasonably bright, but thinks the rest of us are idiots." He smiled self-consciously. "Criminal profiling 101."

"You make it sound simple," I said. "Like you can just go out with a big net and bag him."

"Would that it were so easy. We've got to find him first. His prints are probably in the system. We'll dust ..."

I shook my head, eyes closed, visualizing Joel Cairo's hand as he stroked my cheek.

"What?" Matthias said.

"He wore gloves," I said.

"He isn't totally crazy, then," Bobbi said.

Matthias shook his head. "As I said, he's probably reasonably bright, maybe even a bit brighter than average, but you wouldn't necessarily know it from his behaviour. From our perspectives, his actions are those we tend to associate with stupidity. Reckless and irrational. From his perspective, his actions are completely normal. We're on totally different wavelengths, which makes it difficult to anticipate what he'll do next."

"Maybe he'll move to Venezuela," I said.

Matthias stood up. He looked at Bobbi. "What are you going to do?

"I'll stay here."

"Good," I said. "I need all the protection I can get."

"We'll leave a car on the quay," he said to me. He turned to Bobbi. "I'll arrange to have someone take you home in the morning to pick up your stuff."

"Thanks," Bobbi said. She walked him to the door, where they spoke quietly for a moment, then she gave him a quick, sisterly kiss on the cheek and he left. She came back into the living room.

"You sure you're okay?"

"Yeah. I'm sore, but I'm all right. The Scotch is helping. How about you?"

"Tired. And my stitches itch." She ran the tips of her splinted fingers along the line of tiny stitches where her eyebrow had been shaved off.

"There's a spare toothbrush in the upstairs bathroom," I said. "And I think the bed linens in the spare room are clean. Clean enough, anyway."

She smiled, said good night, and went upstairs. I levered myself off the sofa without too much discomfort, a bit wobbly and head buzzing with the Scotch I'd drunk too quickly. I made the rounds, checking that all the windows and doors were locked, even the door to the roof deck. I rarely locked the door to the deck. Getting into the house via the roof would necessitate, in order of descending probability, scaling the exterior wall, leaping across the twelve-foot gap from Daniel's roof, landing by parachute, or jumping from a hovering helicopter. But the world felt a lot less safe, secure, and predictable than it had as hour earlier. It wasn't a good feeling. I'd had guns pointed at me, I'd been physically threatened, even manhandled, but I'd never been rendered so utterly helpless and vulnerable as I had that night. Despite the brave front I'd put on for Bobbi and Matthias, Joel Cairo scared me. The next time I saw him I either wanted a hell of a good head start or one of Skip Osterman's shark pikes in my hands. Of course, I'd just as soon never lay eyes on him again, under any circumstances, no matter how well-armed.

chapter twenty-two

"You sure you'll be okay?"

It was Friday morning. Bobbi and I were in the kitchen, eating breakfast. Rain rattled against the kitchen window, wind moaned softly in the eaves, and the house quietly creaked and groaned as wavelets lapped gently against the hull.

"He isn't going to try anything in broad daylight in a public place," I said, even though it was possible he might do just that, given Matthias's description of sociopaths as impulsive and reckless. Truth be told, the man I called Joel Cairo had spooked me more than I cared to admit. I felt an urge to check behind every door before I walked through. I might never be able to watch *The Maltese Falcon* again.

"I can come with you, if you like," Bobbi said. "Strength in numbers."

"I'll be fine," I insisted. "Besides, Wayne's coming with me. And Jeanie Stone will be there."

Bobbi snorted, then coughed and grunted with pain,

pressing her left hand to her rib cage. "Well, I'm worrying for nothing then, aren't I?"

"What about you?" I asked.

"I talked to Greg while you were in the shower. He's arranged for Mabel to come by to take me home to pick up some stuff. Then, well, I thought I'd visit my dad."

I yawned and stretched, trying to work out the ache that was like an overstretched bungee cord across the top of my back. Fortunately, I didn't seem to be suffering any obvious ill effects from my encounter with Cairo, save for a bruise on my chest and a little residual soreness in my nether regions. I hadn't slept well, plagued by dreams I didn't remember, but which nevertheless awakened me sweating and tangled in my sheets, to lie staring into the darkness for a long time before falling back asleep, only to dream again. I'd have said to hell with it and stayed in bed for a week, except that at ten that morning Jeanie Stone, Wayne, and I were scheduled to go to Stanley Park to scout locations for the calendar shoot, set to begin Sunday at dawn. That is, if the rain ever let up.

The streets were quiet as I walked through the rain to the studio. First to arrive, as usual, I put on the coffee. I was working on my second cup when the door buzzer jangled and Mabel Firth came in wearing a wide-brimmed Tilley hat and a waxed-canvas Australian stockman's coat that hung to her ankles. She stood by the door as she removed her hat and shook the rain from the tips of her dark blonde hair.

"I'm dripping all over your floor," she said.

"It's concrete," I said. "It won't notice." I poured her a cup of coffee while she took off her coat and hung it from a hook by the bottom of the stairs to the office. "What's up?" I said, handing her the coffee.

"Matthias told me what happened. I just thought I'd stop in and see how you were doing. You've had a rough week."

"I've had better."

"If you need to talk to someone, I can recommend a couple of people who specialize in working with victims of violent crime. I'm going to give them to Bobbi, too."

"I appreciate your concern," I said. "But I'm okay. No obvious ill effects, physical or psychological. How about you? Greg told me you and Baz have got yourselves into some trouble over what happened with Loth the other day."

"We'll both get reprimands in our jackets, but we'll be okay. One of the tourists' videos clearly shows Loth whacking the guy with his cane, sending the bicyclist into the bridge pier, and throwing a cop into the bay. And Baz replaced the camera he threw into False Creek with a far better one."

"This won't jeopardize your chances of becoming a detective, will it?"

"I might miss out on the next round of promotions," she said. "I can live with that."

The door buzzer buzzed again as Wayne came into the studio. Water dripped from his yellow rubberized poncho, his sneakers squished and squeaked on the anti-skid floor paint, and his jeans were soaked below the knees. Jeanie Stone was behind him, carrying a gigantic golf umbrella. Before coming inside she closed the umbrella and shook it off. Despite the umbrella, her leather jacket was beaded with rain and her coal-black hair glistened with moisture.

"Wet?" I said.

"Some," she said, combing her fingers through her hair. "The CIA must be messing with those Russian scalar things again."

Wayne took off his glasses and wiped the lenses with a soggy tissue.

"We can put off checking out locations till the weather clears," I said.

"What, because of a little rain?" Jeanie said. "You won't melt, will you?"

"Just shrink a bit," I said.

She smiled, glancing at Mabel. "But if you're busy …"

Mabel looked at me. "We're supposed to scout locations for a calendar featuring female forestry workers," I explained. "Jeanie is Miss October."

"Ah," Mabel said. "Well, don't let me keep you."

Jeanie and Wayne went back out into the rain. I handed Mabel her coat and hat, then took my squall jacket from the hook.

"By the way," she said, as she put her long coat on. "I know it goes against your nature, but it might be a good idea for you to keep your head down for the next little while. A couple of years, say."

"Why? What have I done now?"

"Jim Kovacs is on a tear. He's angry that Matthias talked to you about the Conrad woman rather than letting him handle it. Likewise, your assault. Not unjustifiably, either; Bobbi's assault is Kovacs's case, not Matthias's, and your assault is obviously connected to Bobbi's. He also wants Matthias off the Waverley case. Chrissy Conrad was on Anna Waverley's boat, and admitted to knowing her, which is compelling evidence that there's a connection between your and Bobbi's assaults and Anna Waverley's murder."

"Greg is homicide," I said. "Kovacs is just robbery and assault."

"He's handled homicides before," Mabel said. "He's more than qualified. Besides, he seems convinced that Matthias is covering for you because of your friendship and his relationship with Bobbi."

"That's nuts. Greg's a good cop. Besides, we aren't all that close. Anyway, there's nothing to cover me for. Hell, I'm a victim myself."

"Whatever, there's a definite conflict of interest.

Apparently, the you-know-what really hit the fan yesterday when Kovacs thought he was being shut out of Matthias's interview with Samuel Waverley."

"So he's back?"

"Didn't Matthias tell you?" She looked worried, as if she'd said something she shouldn't have.

"No," I said, as we left the studio. "But it's unlikely that Mr. Waverley had anything to do with his wife's murder, isn't it, given that he was out of the country? Unless he hired someone to do it. He didn't, did he?"

"Matthias doesn't think so," she said, rain dripping from the rim of her Tilley hat. "He was apparently pretty badly shaken by the news of his wife's murder."

I put my hood up and locked the door. If the bizarre weather kept up, I thought, we were going to have to think about installing an awning over the studio entrance. Or pontoons. Jeanie and Wayne waited in Jeanie's truck, a bright red Ford Escape Hybrid, idling silently at the curb.

"Listen, Tom," Mabel said. "Kovacs is looking for any excuse to bust your balls, pardon my French, and push Matthias out of both investigations. The only reason Greg hasn't been pulled is that he outranks Kovacs and Major Crimes is short-handed at the moment. Stay out of trouble, all right?"

"I'll try," I said.

"Try harder," she said.

It didn't take Jeanie, Wayne, and me long to find suitable locations for the calendar shoot. There was still some equipment left over from the Stanley Park clean-up that we could use as props. Jeanie pointed out some of the areas where she had worked in the immediate aftermath of the windstorm. "You really shouldn't operate a chainsaw with tears in your eyes," she said.

Afterwards, I had Jeanie drop me off at Sea Village, where I got into my Jeep Liberty, which seemed inordinately noisy and smelly after a couple of hours in Jeanie's hybrid, and drove to Samuel and Anna Waverley's house in Point Grey. The house was dark and there was no one home, so I got back into my noisy, smelly Jeep and headed back toward Granville Island. Instead of going to the studio, however, I crossed Burrard Street Bridge to the West End, then worked my way through the heart of the city to Gastown, the historic site of Vancouver's beginnings. The most popular legend is that Gastown was named after a Yorkshire steamship operator turned saloon keeper named John "Gassy Jack" Deighton, but the less poetic claim the name derives from a pocket of natural gas that erupted to the surface. How Gassy Jack acquired his nickname may also be disputed, but his likeness stands atop a whisky barrel at the corner of Carral and Water Streets, the original location of his first saloon.

Waverley Art and Antiques was farther west along Water Street, jammed between a travel agency and currency exchange office. A bell tinkled as I went in. The shop — calling it a gallery was being overly generous — was long and narrow, musty and gloomy, and crammed to the rafters with enough heavy furniture, ornate lamps, brass bed-ends, knick-knacks, sculptures, and old paintings to fill a couple of dozen houses like the one in Point Grey. There was even a collection of taxidermy, dusty, moth-eaten and glassy-eyed: half a dozen different kinds of raptors, a couple of red foxes, and a badger. *Where was PETA when you needed it, eh, guys?* I silently asked.

"Can I help you?" someone asked out loud. A head appeared above a tall bureau. It belonged to a woman, blue haired and wrinkled, who must have been eighty years old — and at least seven feet tall.

"I'm looking for Mr. Waverley," I said.

The head disappeared and a moment later the entire

woman emerged from behind the bureau. She wasn't seven feet tall at all. She was barely five feet tall. She was still eighty years old, though. "He isn't here," she said. "There's been a death in the family. Mr. Waverley's wife. Such a tragedy. I'm Mrs. Martini. How can I help you?"

"I was acquainted with Mrs. Waverley and I'd like to express my condolences to Mr. Waverley. He isn't at home, though. Do you know where he is?"

"Yes," she said. "He has a cabin near Garibaldi. You know where that is, don't you?"

Garibaldi was about halfway between Squamish, at the head of Howe Sound, and the resort town of Whistler. There wasn't much there, not even a gas station. It was really just a jumping-off point for hikers, backpackers, and climbers heading into Garibaldi Provincial Park.

"Yes," I said. She seemed to expect more, so I added, "It's on the Sea-to-Sky Highway on the way Whistler."

"That's right," she said, smiling. She had a full set of perfectly straight, brilliantly white teeth. If they were her own, I wanted the name of her dentist. "But there's no phone or cellphone service, I'm afraid."

"Do you think you could tell me how to get there?" I said.

"Oh, goodness, no," she said. "I've never been there myself. I do have a little map that Samuel drew, though."

"Could I have a copy?"

"I only have one."

"Perhaps I could take it next door and make a photocopy."

"I don't see why not." She disappeared behind the big bureau again, climbing onto a two-foot-high platform that supported a small office area. She rooted through a desk drawer, found what she was looking for, then descended to hand me a three-by-five index card upon which a rough map had been drawn. "You'll bring it right back," she said.

"Of course," I said, and went next door to the travel agency, where a young woman with enormous grey eyes and a lovely lopsided smile made a copy. She refused to take any money, but gave me a handful of business cards and asked me if I wouldn't mind handing them out. I said I'd be happy to. I returned to the antique shop, thanked Mrs. Martini for her assistance, then walked through the rain to my noisy, smelly car.

When I got to the studio I was more than a little surprised to see Chrissy Conrad perched, legs crossed, on a high stool by the glass-topped display counter, drinking coffee with Mary-Alice. Chrissy was wearing a jean jacket and a skirt that showed off her very nice knees — and a good deal of her very nice thighs as well. The tips of her hair were curled from the damp. There was a backpack on the floor by her feet. I shook the rain from my squall jacket, hung it up, then crossed to the coffee machine.

"Is something wrong?" Mary-Alice asked. "You're walking kind of funny."

"Am I?" I said. "It must be the gravitational anomalies. I find they're always stronger on Friday." Mary-Alice frowned. I smiled at Chrissy Conrad. "Don't you agree?"

"Um, sure."

"Well, if you'll excuse me," Mary-Alice said. "I have a couple of calls to make." She smiled at Chrissy Conrad. "Thanks for the muffins." Then, to me, "I'll talk to *you* later," spoken in the same tone of voice my mother had used when she'd said, "Wait till your father gets home." Once again, I wondered what I had done.

Mary-Alice went up the stairs to the office. I poured a cup of coffee. There was a box of fat bakery muffins beside the coffee machine. I hesitated a nanosecond or two before taking a blueberry.

"The police are looking for you," I said to Chrissy, slurping my coffee and munching my muffin.

"They found me," she said. "A charming fellow

named Kovacs grilled me for an hour, but lost interest when he finally got it through his head that I really didn't know anything about what happened on that boat or about Anna's murder."

I slurped more coffee and munched more muffin. I looked at Chrissy. She was looking at the map to Sam Waverley's cabin. "Did you know that Sam Waverley was back?" I asked.

"Yes. I spoke to him yesterday morning." She unhooked the heels of her western boots from the crossbar of the stool and stood up.

"Really. Why?"

She moved away, closer to the door, maybe getting ready to run again, except that she hadn't picked up her backpack. "It isn't important," she said, with a shrug. "Just business."

"Did you tell him about Anna?"

"He already knew," she said. "The woman who looks after the shop when he's away told him. Do the police know he's back?"

"Yes. They interviewed him yesterday. He's been cleared of any involvement in Anna's death."

"You're very well informed," she said.

"I have friends in the VPD."

"Convenient."

"Not really."

She circled back to the counter and pointed to the map. "This is a map to Sam's cabin. What are you doing with it?"

"I was thinking of paying him a visit."

"Why?"

"Just to pay my respects."

"You don't know him."

"I knew his wife," I said.

She looked at the map again. "I've been to the cabin. You'll never find it using that."

I picked up the card. Though crudely drawn and not to scale, the map clearly showed the Sea-to-Sky Highway from Vancouver to Whistler, with the town of Squamish located about halfway between. And halfway between Squamish and Whistler was a turnoff to the left onto what was identified as Lake Lucille Road. It crossed some wavy lines representing the Cheakamus River and hatched double lines that I took to be the BC Rail tracks, before meandering past a blob labelled Lake Lucille toward a smaller blob named Lake Freeman. An X marked a location at the end of a short line jutting out from a sharp bend in the Lake Lucille road, midway between the two blobs. The map included distances, as well as the turnoff to the Black Tusk access road a kilometre and a half beyond the Lake Lucille turnoff.

"Seems clear enough to me," I said.

"Sam drew that for me a couple of years ago," Chrissy said. "You'll get lost if you follow it. I know I did."

"Yet you've been to the cabin."

"I was lucky."

"I'll be fine," I said. "I drive a Jeep."

"Um, look, why don't I go with you?"

"Why would you want to do that?"

"Maybe I want to pay my respects, too."

Right, I thought.

"In the meantime," Chrissy said, "I was wondering if there was anything I could do around here to earn a couple of bucks. I'm a bit short of cash and … what?"

"You're joking, right?"

"C'mon," she said, a hurt expression on her face. "Cut me a break, all right. I know a little about photography, which end of a camera is which, anyway, and a fair amount about retail. Plus, I'm not afraid to get my hands dirty. Your sister —" She paused.

"My sister what?"

"Well, she said you could probably use some help till

your partner comes back to work."

"My insurance company is upset enough as it is, without me inviting the fox into the henhouse."

"Hey, it was just an idea," Chrissy said, an edge of anger in her voice.

Mary-Alice came down the stairs from the office. "Did you ask him?"

"Yeah," Chrissy said glumly.

"And …?"

Chrissy shook her head.

"We could use some help, Tom," Mary-Alice said. "And someone who knows something about retail might prove useful."

"Do you know who this is?" I said to Mary-Alice.

"Yes," Mary-Alice said. "She told me. She made a mistake, Tom."

"Explain that to Bobbi." Mary-Alice looked at me as though I had just kicked her puppy, if she'd ever had a puppy. Chrissy Conrad just looked prettily woebegone. "All right, fine," I said, relenting. "Find something for her to do. But she's your responsibility. Just don't leave her alone with anything of value."

I left Mary-Alice to work out the details with Chrissy, put on my jacket and went out, without any idea where I was going, succumbing to an urge for random motion.

chapter twenty-three

W here I went was home. I had something to eat, then went back to the studio. The rain had let up, but the sky remained threatening. I found Chrissy in the darkroom with Wayne. Tom Petty and the Heartbreakers blasted from Wayne's CD player and they sang along to "Mary Jane's Last Dance" loudly and off-key while they applied a coat of matte black paint to the walls. She'd changed from her skirt to jeans, presumably from her backpack.

"Still feel like taking that drive?" I said to her.

"Um, sure, I guess." She looked at Wayne.

"I can finish up here," Wayne said.

"I'll get cleaned up," she said.

Fifteen minutes later we were in the Liberty heading north through Stanley Park toward the Lions Gate Bridge. Chrissy sat quietly beside me, staring into shadowy green forest that pressed close on either side of the road. Was she having second thoughts? I wondered. Was I?

Anna Waverley's description of Samuel Waverley had left me with the impression of a selfish and self-centred man, a serial philanderer who did not want children, who did not like home-cooked meals, and who had encouraged his wife to take lovers. Why had he married her in the first place? I wondered. Had he ever intended to be faithful? Perhaps, but, as Anna has said, it simply wasn't in his nature.

"What is Sam Waverley like?" I asked Chrissy.

"He's a bit of a cold fish, I guess," she said. "Particularly where people are concerned. He doesn't relate to them very well, emotionally speaking. He probably regards Anna getting herself killed as a terrible inconvenience."

"You don't like him much."

"No, I guess I don't. I liked Anna, and he treated her like shit."

I hadn't got the impression from Anna Waverley that she'd thought her husband had treated her badly, that he'd been inconsiderate or unkind, just that he'd been somewhat emotionally detached.

"You don't like him, but you'll do business with him," I said.

She gave me a "You know how it is" shrug.

"Can you think of a reason why Sam Waverley would want her dead?" I asked.

"No," she said. "Because I can't think of one doesn't mean he didn't have one, I suppose, but even if he did, he wouldn't have a clue how to go about hiring a hit man."

"What about his girlfriend?"

"Boudica? Please."

"I thought her name was Doris."

"It is. Boudica's just what I call her." At my blank look, she explained, "Formerly known as Boadicea, the Queen of all the Celts. Wait till you meet her. You'll see why."

"How about you?" I said.

"Pardon me?"

"Would you have a clue how to go about hiring a hit man?"

"I might," she said. "More than Sam or Boudica, anyway. But I didn't."

A voice in the back of my mind told me I was being reckless trusting Chrissy Conrad, or believing anything she told me. I tried to ignore it, but it wouldn't be silenced. *Why did she offer to come along?* it asked. *For all you know, boyo, she's luring you into the middle of nowhere to thump you on your pointy noggin and bury you in the piny woods.* It was a possibility, I supposed, although not a very likely one. She knew more about Bobbi's attack and Anna Waverley's murder than she was letting on, but how much more, I couldn't begin to guess. However, while I may not have been the world's best judge of character, my instincts told me she wasn't a killer, although it was certainly conceivable that she was an accessory, before or after the fact. I felt, though, that if she were an accomplice to murder and attempted murder, she was an unwilling one, perhaps even an unwitting one. There was a better than even chance that she was as far in over her head as I was. Nevertheless, it might pay to be vigilant, I decided, and avoid turning my back on her.

"If Anna Waverley had a lover," I said to her, as we motored north along the edge of Howe Sound toward the town of Squamish, "what sort of man would he be?" The road was called the Sea-to-Sky Highway, except that there wasn't much sky, just a lot of low, dark clouds that periodically dumped buckets of rain on us.

"How would I know?"

"You knew her fairly well, didn't you?"

"Not that well. Anyway, what difference does it make?"

"She described her husband as something of a wimp, not very physically competent, she said."

"Well, he's no Lovejoy, that's for sure," Chrissy said.

"Who?"

"*Lovejoy* was a British TV series about a shady, crime-solving antiques dealer," she said. "Sam's a bit on the shady side, I suppose, but that's where any resemblance to Lovejoy ends. What's your point? If you're worried about him roughing you up, forget it. Sam wouldn't hurt a fly. He never laid a hand on Anna, or even raised his voice to her. He just wasn't very, well, attentive."

"Would she take the kind of lover who was likely to physically or psychologically abuse her?"

"I doubt it. No. Definitely not."

"Which is it?"

"She wouldn't put up with any kind of abuse."

I wasn't so sure about that. Being ignored was a kind of abuse in my books. Maybe the worst kind.

"Look," Chrissy said, "why do most people have extramarital affairs? To get something they aren't getting at home, right? What Anna wasn't getting at home was any kind of intimacy. If she had a lover, it would be with someone who satisfied her need for intimacy. Not just sex, but sex would be part of it, too, probably. Sam's pretty boring in bed, which might explain why he's had so many lovers: they get tired of him, not the other way around."

"And you've no idea who Anna's lover might be?"

"No," Chrissy replied, with a sigh in impatience.

"I hope you won't be too offended when I tell you that I think you're lying through your almost-perfect teeth."

"I might be offended if I gave a fuck what you thought," she shot back.

"Ouch," I said.

She smiled thinly. "Besides, if I knew who Anna's lover was, why wouldn't I tell you?"

"I don't know. It's in your nature?"

"I think I've had enough of this crap," she said. "Turn around and take me back to Vancouver."

"We're past the point of no return," I said.

"I'll have you charged with kidnapping."

"Wayne will testify you came willingly. We're just a few klicks from Squamish. I'll let you off there, if you like. You can catch a bus back to Vancouver."

"Forget it." She slumped in her seat, arms folded across her chest like a petulant child.

The Sea-to-Sky Highway dropped down to sea level one last time just before Squamish. I thought of Jeanie Stone. I was undoubtedly romanticizing, but she seemed like such a refreshingly straightforward, uncomplicated person, until I remembered that she was taking a doctorate in geology. Everybody has hidden depths. Even me. I just wasn't quite sure how deep mine went.

After Squamish, the Sea-to-Sky Highway lived up to its name as it snaked along the Cheakamus River gorge, climbing into the Coast Mountains toward Whistler. Due in part to construction on the highway in preparation for the 2010 Winter Olympics, but mostly because Chrissy insisted the map was wrong and we had to backtrack from the Black Tusk turnoff, it took longer than I thought it would to find Lake Lucille Road. When we finally found it, I was soon very glad that I had a four-wheel-drive vehicle; after the first kilometre the road was rutted and muddy and so steep and rocky in spots that the Liberty had difficulty maintaining traction, especially since it wasn't equipped with off-road tires.

"This is ridiculous," Chrissy said more than once. "We're never going to make it. We should go back."

It took over an hour, but we finally made it to the turnoff to the cabin, which was set a few hundred metres back in the trees along an even rougher track. A mud-spattered Mercedes sedan was parked haphazardly about halfway up the track. I was amazed it had got this far, until I saw that it was a 4Matic all-wheel-drive model. Even so, it must have been a difficult drive, particularly for someone who had been described as physically inept. I said as much to Chrissy as I parked the Jeep behind the Mercedes.

"Boudica probably drove," she said.

We got out of the Jeep and picked our way up the track through the gloomy, dripping woods, our breath smoking in the cool pine- and cedar-scented mountain air. Sam Waverley's cabin was a rough-hewn log structure with a high, steeply pitched corrugated steel roof, better to shed the nine or ten metres of snow the area received every winter. The roof overhung the front door by a metre or two, supported by thick timber posts. Under the overhang, quarter cords of split firewood were neatly stacked two deep along the exterior walls on both sides of the front door. Wood smoke wafted gently and aromatically from a large stone chimney that protruded from the peak of the roof, as well as from an external insulated steel chimney at one end of the cabin. The windows were modern double-glaze, and glowed warmly in the shadowy afternoon gloom. There were no power lines that I could see, but a generator thrummed quietly somewhere nearby. It took a long time for anyone to respond to my knock.

"Who's there?" a woman's voice called through the door. Boudica, I presumed, a.k.a. Doris Greenwood.

"My name is Tom McCall," I replied. "I'd like to speak to Mr. Samuel Waverley about his wife's death."

"Are you the police?"

"No."

"Go away, then. We aren't interested in talking to the media."

"I'm not a reporter," I said. "I'm here with Chrissy Conrad. I was a friend of Mrs. Waverley. So was Miss Conrad. She's also a former employee of Mr. Waverley."

"I know who she is," the woman said. "Go away."

"For Christ's sake, Doris," Chrissy said. "Let us in."

"No. Please go away."

"Not until I've talked with Mr. Waverley," I said. "Is he here?"

"Yes, he's here ..."

"Then I need to speak with him. Please."

After a moment a latch rattled and the door swung open. Standing on the threshold was a tall, raw-boned woman with shoulder-length unruly red hair. She was about forty, with a long, strong face, awash in freckles. Definitely of Celtic stock. She was barefoot and her simple cotton housedress hung on her rangy frame like an afterthought.

"Hello, Doris," Chrissy said. "Nice to see you again."

"Hello, Chrissy," Doris replied stiffly. The smell of fresh coffee wafted from the warm interior of the cabin.

"May we come in?" I asked.

Silently, Doris stepped back. I went in first, tried wiping the forest muck off my shoes on the mat inside the door, then gave up and toed my shoes off. Chrissy followed, removing her boots. Doris closed the door behind us.

The room into which we stepped was the living room, occupying the full width of the cabin and the middle third of its length, dominated — almost overwhelmed — by a square fieldstone fireplace in the centre of the room. The ceiling of the living room was peaked, supported by thick, rough-hewn beams, and the walls were cedar plank, decorated with framed wildlife prints and drawings, as well as the obligatory old-fashioned snowshoes, wood skis, and bamboo ski poles. The floor was pegged oak, worn smooth and dark with years of waxing. The furniture was appropriately rustic. A wood and fieldstone counter separated the living room from the kitchen/dining area at one end of the cabin. I guessed the bedrooms were through the doorway at the other end. Ladder-like stairs led to lofts over both the bedrooms and the kitchen area.

A man stepped out from behind the fireplace. He was medium height, plump, and grey. His hair was grey. The jogging suit he wore was grey. Even the skin of his face had a sickly grey tinge. He did not have the look of a well man.

"Hello, Sam," Chrissy said.

"Hello, Christine," Samuel Waverley said, his voice dull and grey. He looked at me.

"Sam," Chrissy said. "This is Tom McCall."

"How do you do, Mr. McCall. Did I hear you tell Doris you were a friend of Anna's? I don't recall her ever mentioning your name."

"I only met her recently," I said. "I'm very sorry for your loss."

He cleared his throat. "Yes, well, thank you." He had the good grace to look embarrassed, accepting condolences on the death of his wife in the presence of two women with whom he'd also shared his bed.

"He's the one who found Anna's body," Chrissy said. I shot her an angry glare, which she ignored.

"Ah," Waverley said, as if he weren't really interested. "That, um, couldn't have been very pleasant."

"You're right about that," I said.

He nodded toward the redhead. "Doris has just made coffee. There's probably enough for the four of us. Doris, why don't you bring it." Silently, Doris withdrew to the kitchen. As she passed in front of the fire, the skirt of her flimsy housedress was momentarily translucent. Her legs were long and strong and straight. She reminded me of Reeny Lindsey, with a little more mileage on her.

"Why don't we sit down," Waverley said, gesturing toward the long, rustic wood-frame sofa against the wall facing the far side of the fireplace. Without waiting for a reply, he sagged into a matching armchair. "How well did you know my wife, Mr. McCall?" he asked.

"Not well," I said, sitting at the end of the sofa nearest his chair. "I met her just a couple of days before she died." Chrissy sat beside me, perched on the edge of the sofa, hands on her knees. Her jeans were spattered with dried black paint.

"Were you …?" he began. "Did you …?" he tried again. Finally, he said, "What was the nature of your relationship with her?"

"It was too soon to tell," I said.

"I see," he said. "How did you come to meet her?"

"Her name came up in connection with an incident in which a close friend of mine was badly hurt," I said diplomatically.

"Incident? What sort of incident?"

"My friend and business partner was attacked while attempting to photograph a boat called the *Wonderlust*."

"The *Wonderlust*? But that's …" He paused, then said, "How could Anna possibly have been involved in your partner's attack?"

"I don't think she was."

"I don't understand."

"*Someone*," I said pointedly, "posing as your wife, hired us to photograph the *Wonderlust*." Chrissy gave me a hard look. "My partner was beaten and thrown into False Creek under the Burrard Street Bridge. Your wife may have witnessed the attack. She left me a telephone message the night she was killed, saying that she had something to tell me, but by the time I got to your house, she was dead."

Doris came out of the kitchen carrying a tray with four coffee cups, sugar, and creamer. She had tied her unruly hair back, which accentuated the length and strength of her face. She placed the tray on the table beside Waverley's chair.

"Help yourselves," she said, taking one of the cups and folding herself into another armchair at the far end of the sofa, tucking her long legs under her, arranging her skirt over her knees.

"I'll be mother, then, shall I?" Waverley said. "I know Christine takes hers black." He handed me a cup. It was only slightly more than half full. I passed it to Chrissy. "How do you take yours, Mr. McCall? It's only milk, I'm afraid."

"Black will be fine," I said.

He handed me a cup. "That was easy." He added sugar and milk to the fourth cup, stirred it in with two strokes of a spoon. After he'd tasted it, he nodded, set it down, cleared his throat, and said, "So, you were explaining why you went to see Anna the night she was killed. She had something to tell you, you said. What was it?"

"I don't know," I said. "She never got the chance to tell me."

"Yes, of course." He picked up his coffee cup and saucer and, holding the saucer in one hand, the cup in the other, delicately pursed his lips on the rim of the cup and sipped. He returned the cup to the saucer and put both down again. "The police told me a man visited Anna at our home on Saturday evening, and stayed for over two hours, but that he was not a suspect in her murder. Was that yourself?"

"Yes."

"And yet you deny you were having an affair with her."

I hadn't denied it, because he hadn't asked. I said, "I went to talk to her about my partner's attack."

"About which you yourself said she knew nothing."

"That's what she told me."

"You didn't believe her?"

"I don't know. No, I don't think I did. I think she

was killed by the same person who attacked my partner."

"The police gave me to believe that it was likely a home invasion gone wrong," Mr. Waverley said.

"Whoever killed your wife tried to make it look like suicide, Mr. Waverley, as if she'd hanged herself from a ceiling beam."

"That's absurd," Waverley sputtered, face reddening. "Anna would never ..." He hesitated, shaking his head, his expression uncertain. "She'd been depressed lately, but ..." He shook his head again, as if trying to dislodge an unwanted thought. "No, I can't ..."

"You're not listening," I said, a little more harshly than I'd intended. "I said her death was made to *look* like suicide. Why would a home invader bother to do that?"

"Uh, yes, of course. My apologies. I'm very upset." He picked up his coffee cup, took three small, noisy sips, then set it down again, his composure seemingly restored, although he still looked like death warmed over. "How is it that you were the one to find my — Anna's body, Mr. McCall? What were you doing in my house at that time of night? Were you having an affair with her?"

I felt the heat rise in my face, along with the frustration. How many times was I going to have to explain the nature of my relationship with his wife before it stuck? "No, sir," I said. "I was not having an affair with your wife."

"Again, my apologies," Waverley said. "I'm not tracking very well. The shock, I suppose."

"I understand," I said.

"You don't know what it was she wanted to tell you?"

"Not specifically," I said. "I'm sure she was killed to prevent her from telling me who was responsible for the attempted murder of my partner, though."

"Did you not say that it was someone posing as

Anna who hired you, not Anna herself?"

"Yes, that's right," I said.

"Then how could Anna have known anything about your partner's attack?"

"She was at the marina around the time of the attack."

"She's often there. The marina is on her running route. Also, we keep our sailboat there."

"It's also possible she was on the *Wonderlust*?"

"The *Wonderlust*?"

"The boat my partner was attacked on," I said, trying without much success to control my impatience.

"Yes, of course. Both Anna and myself have been on the *Wonderlust* a number of times. Surely you're not suggesting that Anna was present when your partner was attacked."

"I think she was."

"Well, you're wrong, I'm sure."

"I don't think I am," I said. "I think that's why she called me the night she was killed."

His eyes narrowed. "Are you certain it was Anna who called you?" he asked. "Could it not have been the same person who impersonated her to hire you to photograph the boat?"

"No, it was Anna."

"How can you be so positive?"

I looked at Chrissy. "Do you want to tell him?"

She shook her head. "Go ahead. You're doing fine."

I turned back to Sam Waverley. "It was Miss Conrad who posed as your wife to hire us to photograph the *Wonderlust* as part of a fraudulent sales scheme."

From her chair by the far end of the long sofa, Doris laughed. It was not a pleasant sound. Chrissy glared at her. "Sorry," Doris said, but she didn't seem the least bit contrite.

Waverley stared at Chrissy in silence for a long

moment, before saying, "Anna was right about you, wasn't she?"

Chrissy replied with a shrug.

"Can you think of any reason your wife would be on the *Wonderlust*?" I asked.

"We've both been on it as guests of the owners," Waverley said.

"Do you know the owners?"

"Of course. It's owned by a charitable foundation Anna supported. I, ah, don't recall the name. Something to do with children. It's headed by …" He hesitated.

"Elise Moffat," I said.

"Yes, that's right. However, surely it's common knowledge that Mrs. Moffat's foundation owned the boat. After all …" He paused, looking at Chrissy. "You certainly knew."

"I did not," Chrissy denied vehemently.

"In any event," Waverley said, "what reason would Anna have to be on the *Wonderlust* the night your partner was attacked?"

"I think she was meeting her lover. I think Bobbi interrupted them, and your wife's lover attacked her."

"Her?"

"My business partner is a woman."

"I see." He leaned forward and reached for his coffee cup. His hand shook slightly as he picked it up, took a sip, and made a face. It rattled in the saucer as he put it down. "An interesting theory," he said. "But what makes you so certain Anna even had a lover?"

"She told me you encouraged her to take lovers," I added, glancing at the silent and watchful Doris. "To assuage your own guilt."

"Assuage," he said, undoubtedly impressed by my vocabulary.

"Do you know your wife's lover's name?" I said.

"What? No. Of course not."

"Because if you do, the police would be very interested in knowing it." As would I, I added to myself.

"I don't even know for certain that Anna had a lover."

"With all due respect, Mr. Waverley —" I began.

"That's bullshit," Chrissy Conrad concluded.

"You know damned well your wife had a lover," I said.

"So do I," Chrissy said.

Waverley waved his hand in front of his face. "Who cares what you think?" he said. "You are nothing but a thief and a whore."

"Hey," Chrissy protested. "I am not a whore."

Did Doris frown? I thought I caught the glowering of a frown, but she hid it behind her coffee cup, a gesture that was painfully reminiscent of the way Anna Waverley had hidden her smiles.

"Perhaps it's time you left," Samuel Waverley said. "Before it gets too dark to drive back down the mountain."

"I came here because I hoped you would be able to help me figure out who tried to kill my partner and who killed your wife. I get the feeling, though, that you aren't really interested in who killed your wife."

He looked as though I'd sucker-punched him. "That's preposterous," he protested.

"You know who her lover was, don't you?"

"No, I don't," he sputtered.

"Why are you protecting him?" I demanded. "There's a good chance he killed her."

"No, I —"

"Goddamn it," Chrissy said, jumping to her feet. "You hired someone to kill her, didn't you, you bastard." She was singing a different tune than she had earlier, when she'd said she didn't think Waverley would know how to hire a hit man.

"What? No. That's ridiculous," Waverley said, his voice weak and rasping.

"Sure you did, you son of a bitch. She was going to divorce you, wasn't she?"

"No ..."

"And if you didn't give her everything she wanted, she was going to tell the police how you'd been fiddling provenance for years, ripping off your clients with fakes and reproductions and student copies."

"Please, Mr. McCall," Waverley pleaded. His colour was even greyer and perspiration beaded his upper lip. The fireplace threw a fair amount of heat into the room, but I didn't think that was the reason he was sweating. "Don't listen to her. She's nothing but a —" He gasped for air. "She —"

Doris unfolded herself from her chair and went to him. "Sam?"

"Are you all right?" I asked, suddenly worried. He was sweating profusely and the flesh of his face was splotched with red.

"Help him," Doris said to me.

"I think we should get him to a doctor," I said.

Chrissy snorted with disgust. "The bastard's faking. There's nothing wrong with him."

Waverley staggered out of his chair. His eyes rolled up into his head. And he fell to the floor as though he were a marionette and someone had just clipped his strings.

chapter twenty-four

"Sam!" Doris cried, throwing herself onto her knees, crouching over him.

"Oh, fuck," Chrissy Conrad said.

"Sam!" Doris cried again. "Oh, god, Sam!" She rolled him onto his back. His face was a ghastly grey-green and his lips were beginning to turn blue.

I knelt beside her, pressed my fingers to Waverley's throat. I actually felt a pulse — amazing what you can learn from the Discovery Channel — but it seemed thready and irregular.

"Does he have heart-attack medicine?" I asked Doris.

"What? No. Oh, god. A heart attack. We've got to get him to a hospital."

"Is there a phone?" I asked, before remembering that the woman at Waverley's shop had said there wasn't. Chrissy had her cellphone out. She pressed buttons. "No service," she said, closing it.

I pulled Doris to her feet, looked at her flimsy housedress. "Get some clothes on. Bring some blankets. We'll take him in my car."

While Chrissy and I donned our respective footwear, Doris put on a long, down-filled coat and green rubber wellington boots and slung a purse across her shoulders. Then we lifted Sam Waverley to his feet and half carried, half dragged him out of the cabin. It was raining again, light but steady, and thin tendrils of residual fog hung in the trees. Waverley was a dead weight as we manhandled him down the muddy track to the Liberty. Doris opened the back door, then went round to the other side. Between the three of us we got him into the car. Doris climbed into the back with him and wrapped him in the blankets.

"You're going to have to fasten his seat belt," I said to her as I got into the car. "It's going to be a rough ride."

Rough didn't begin to describe the drive down the mountain on that miserable excuse for a road. The Liberty shuddered and banged and tilted alarmingly as it careened along the old logging road, bouncing over rocks and splashing through ruts and skidding round switchbacks, while Chrissy braced herself against the dashboard and Doris held on to Sam Waverley, who flopped like a rag doll in her arms. It was all I could do to maintain a grip on the steering wheel. At times I thought it was going to come off in my hands. As we rounded the final switchback, Doris cried out and Chrissy said, "Oh, shit," as the Liberty heeled over onto two wheels like a sailboat running close to the wind. It slammed down again with a horrendous crash, fishtailed sickeningly as I fought for control, then straightened with a frightful bang and a gut-wrenching lurch.

"Christ," Chrissy said, but she was grinning broadly.

"I'm glad you're having fun," I said through clenched teeth.

It had taken more than an hour to get from the highway to the cabin. It took less than half an hour to make the return trip. When we reached the highway, I had to almost pry my hands from the steering wheel to shift into two-wheel drive. Twenty minutes later, I pulled into the emergency bay of Brackendale Community Hospital in the town of Squamish, where Sam Waverley was pronounced dead on arrival.

"I'm sorry," the young Native doctor said. "There wasn't anything we could do. You did the best you could to get him here, but even if he'd had the heart attack next door, we might not have been able to save him, it was that massive."

"Oh, god, did we kill him?" Chrissy moaned when the doctor had left.

I was about to say we probably had, but Doris shook her head, her mane of wet red curls fanning, falling across her face. "It wasn't your fault," she said softly, almost to herself. Her eyes were red-rimmed, but dry. "It's as much my fault as anyone's," she went on. "Before you arrived we'd been arguing about — well, I'd told him two weeks ago that when this trip was over, I was going to leave. He was very hurt and angry. Added to the stress of travel and the shock of learning of Anna's death …" She shook her head. "He'd been having chest pains for some time," she added.

Chrissy did not look comforted.

Doris looked at me. In the hard, hospital lighting, her freckles stood out starkly against the paleness of her skin. "With Anna dead, too, who's going to make arrangements for him?"

"Did he have any other family?" I said.

She shook her head. "He has a sister, I think, but I don't know where she is."

"She's in a nursing home in Toronto," Chrissy said.

"Then there's no one," Doris said.

"He must have a lawyer," I said.

"Yes, he does. Of course. Thank you. I'm not thinking

very clearly right now. I'll get in touch with him when I get back to the city. Thank you."

"Do you need anything from the cabin?" I asked her. I didn't relish the drive. It was still raining and the thick cloud cover had turned day to night.

"No, nothing. Oh, except the car. And I suppose someone will have to go back and close it up. But I've no way of getting back to Vancouver."

"We'll take you," I said.

"Would you? That's very kind of you."

It was the least we could do, I said to myself, after killing her boyfriend.

Doris told the admissions clerk someone would be contacting them about arrangements for Sam Waverley's body, then we went out to the parking lot.

"Christ," Chrissy said when she saw the Liberty. The rain had washed most of the mud off, revealing numerous dents and gouges in the side panels, doors, fenders, and rocker panels. Not a square centimetre of the bodywork seemed unscathed. Branches were caught in the grill, one tail light was broken, and the passenger side rear-view mirror dangled on the internal control cables. But all four wheels were still round and pointed more or less in the same direction and the engine started without a problem. When we were underway I noticed a few unusual rattles and odd noises, but it ran and handled normally. For some reason, the radio no longer worked. Fortunately, the windshield wipers still did.

Doris sat in back. "Poor Sam," she said after ten minutes of silence.

Beside me, Chrissy grunted softly.

"He did love her, you know," Doris said, adding, "Anna," in case we didn't know whom she was talking about. "With his other women it was just — well, I was going to say it was just sex, but it wasn't, was it? He lost interest in sex quickly, didn't he?"

I recognized the question as rhetorical, but Chrissy said, "He wasn't very good at it, either."

"I suppose that depends on one's expectation," Doris replied. "I'm surprised he had an affair with you. Or that he even hired you in the first place."

Chrissy turned in her seat at glared at Doris. "What's that supposed to mean?"

"You're so attractive," Doris said. "All his other affairs were with women who were more like me, homely and awkward, grateful for the attention of any man. He didn't like women who were more intelligent than him, either. Don't take offence, Christine, but most of Sam's lovers, me included, weren't particularly bright."

I thought she was selling herself short, both physically and intellectually. "Do you know who Anna Waverley's lover was?" I asked her.

I watched the rear-view mirror as she shook her head. "No," she replied.

"Did he?"

"Yes, I'm sure he did," she said. "I don't understand why he was so reluctant to tell you his name."

A reasonable possibility occurred to me. If Anna's lover had indeed killed her to prevent her from talking to me about Bobbi's attack, Waverley could very well have been afraid for himself, less concerned about seeing his wife's killer brought to justice than for his own skin. If Anna's lover was the man I called Joel Cairo, I could hardly blame him. I couldn't imagine Anna Waverley being in love with either a coward or a psychopath, but that likely said more about my lack of imagination than her choice in men.

From the back seat, Doris said, "Christine —"

"Chrissy."

"Sorry. Chrissy. You don't really believe Sam hired someone to kill Anna, do you?"

"I guess not," Chrissy said. "I was just trying to,

well, shake him up so he'd tell us who Anna's lover was. I guess I came on a little strong."

The rain beat down and the wiper blades batted back and forth. "What did he mean when he said Anna had been right about you?" I asked her.

"Got me," Chrissy said, with a shrug so theatrically nonchalant it was hard to believe she was a successful con artist.

"Shall I answer, then?" Doris said. I looked at her in the mirror, but her face was masked in shadow.

"Oh, here we go," Chrissy said.

"If you'd rather … No? Well, when Christine — Chrissy — was Sam's assistant she began forging provenance documents and passing off worthless junk to some of Sam's clients behind his back. Anna found out about it —"

"I told her about it," Chrissy interrupted. "I didn't think she'd care. Stupid."

"Anna told Chrissy to stop or she'd tell Sam," Doris went on, ignoring Chrissy. "When she didn't, Anna told Sam what Chrissy was up to. Sam wasn't above taking advantage of his more gullible or less-informed clients — he had nerve calling you a thief."

"And a whore," Chrissy added.

"Yes, well. What does that make me, eh? In any event, Sam was a strong believer in 'buyer beware.' If a client was well informed and did his homework, Sam was scrupulously honest. However, if the opportunity presented, Sam wasn't completely immune to temptation himself. Some collectors can be incredibly easy, um, what's the word …?"

"The word you're looking for is marks," Chrissy said.

"Yes. Marks. The problem was, Chrissy wasn't as cautious as Sam and Sam was afraid it would eventually come back to him."

I looked at Chrissy. "That's the real reason you fell out with Anna, then. Not because she wouldn't leave her husband, but because she ratted you out to him."

Chrissy shrugged. "What can I tell you?"

Doris lived in New Westminster. The most efficient way to get there from the North Shore was to stay on the Upper Levels Highway and take the Second Narrows Bridge into Burnaby. However, as we approached the Taylor Way exit for the Lions Gate Bridge, Chrissy said, "Could you drop me off first?"

"Where?" I asked.

"Granville Island," she said. "The marina."

"It's all right," Doris said. "I can take the SkyTrain home."

"No," I said. "I said I'd take you home and that's what I'm going to do." Besides, I wanted a chance to speak to her without Chrissy around.

I detoured across the Lions Gate Bridge and dropped Chrissy off at the Broker's Bay Marina. Then Doris Greenwood and I continued east on Broadway toward Kingsway, which would take us to New Westminster, the former capital of what was to become the Province of British Columbia. Doris had moved into the front seat. With her unruly hair, long, sad countenance, bulky coat, and wellingtons, she reminded me somewhat of the woman who'd used to sit for hours on the bench in the little park at the eastern tip of Granville Island, feeding gulls, pigeons, and squirrels from a huge bag of popcorn. I hadn't seen her in a year or so and I wondered what had become of her.

"You don't have to do this, you know," Doris said.

"I know," I said. "A promise is a promise."

"Thank you."

"You're welcome. But I have an ulterior motive."

"Oh?"

"Just how bent was Sam Waverley?" I asked.

"Bent?"

"Crooked. How big a crook was he?"

"Not very."

"Define 'not very,'" I said.

"Let's put it this way," she said. "He wasn't any-where near as 'bent,' as you put it, as Christine."

"Ah."

"It depended on the client. In fact, if it weren't for the fact that some of his clients were 'bent' themselves, I doubt Sam himself would have been. He was a basically honest person who succumbed to temptation."

"Like most of us."

"Yes. I consider myself honest as well, but I looked the other way when Sam 'adjusted' a work's provenance. More than once, I'm afraid."

The rained had stopped, but the fog had moved in again. "What would happen if it became public knowl-edge that he was doctoring documentation or selling fakes?"

"He'd be ruined," Doris said. "And charged with art fraud, of course. But I'm sure you know that. What's the point of your question?"

"How much did Anna know about his business?"

"Everything there was to know, I suppose. She helped him research provenance from time to time. She was extremely knowledgeable. Perhaps even more so than Sam."

"So she knew about his shady deals."

"Of course. All his assistants did. It could hardly be otherwise."

"Would she have told anyone?"

"I doubt it. Ah. You're thinking she might have told her lover. Whoever that may be."

"Could he have been one of the clients Sam ripped off?"

"It's possible," Doris said. "I couldn't really say."

"Was one of Sam's clients a slim, swarthy character with slicked-back oily black hair, too much cologne, and a nasty disposition?"

"I don't recall anyone like that," Doris said. "But I haven't met all of Sam's clients."

"Was there one client in particular who Sam fleeced especially badly?"

"Sam had no respect for any collector who didn't know what they were doing, but there was one he was particularly contemptuous of. He'd been selling him junk for years. I don't know his name — Sam tended to play things close to the vest — but I got the impression from Sam that he was easy to fool because he was too arrogant and egotistical to think he could be fooled."

"Do you know anything at all that would help identify him?"

"Only that he liked breasts."

"Beg pardon?"

"Sam told me that if an eighteenth-, nineteenth-, or early twentieth-century work had a bare female breast or two in it, he would buy it, no questions asked."

Oh, hell.

Built on the hills overlooking the Fraser River, New Westminster was the oldest incorporated city in Canada west of Winnipeg. Doris lived in a townhouse from which the broad brown ribbon of the river would have been just barely visible between intervening structures if it hadn't been for the fog. I parked on the street and walked her to her door in her wellies and long coat. She shook my hand and thanked me for my trouble. I handed her a business card.

"What's this for?" she asked.

"If you need anything," I said.

She smiled, thanked me again, and went inside. I got in my car for the long drive back home.

It was almost seven by the time I pulled into the lot in front of Sea Village. I had to park in one of the spaces reserved for students and employees of the Emily Carr Institute because all the spaces reserved for Sea Village residents were occupied. I recognized all but two of the vehicles as belonging to my neighbours. I was in a lousy mood, so I jotted down the plate numbers of the unfamiliar cars, then went down to my house to check on Bobbi. But Bobbi wasn't there. Perhaps she was still visiting with her father, I thought. I checked the spare room, but didn't find any evidence that she'd moved in yet, no clothing or personal items. Bobbi travelled light, but not that light.

The message light on the phone in the kitchen was blinking. When I retrieved my messages, there was only one. "What did you say to Walter Moffat?" Mary-Alice's voice demanded. "His secretary called and told me they wouldn't be needing our services after all. She was very cold, almost rude. What happened? I thought everything had been settled. Was I wrong? Call me."

I deleted the message, put on my jacket, and left the house, taking a roll of duct tape to mend the Liberty's broken side mirror. The fog was so thick I could barely see the door of Daniel's house on the other side of the dock. It was cool and clammy on the skin of my face and hands and it gobbled the light from the lamps along the floating docks and in the parking lot, not to mention the headlights of the Liberty. Once I got off Granville Island, the traffic inched along at a speed that made a snail's pace feel breakneck, but it moved steadily; Vancouver drivers were accustomed to fog, but usually only in winter. Which is not to say that a few of them didn't play bumper cars with one another. However, I managed to get across the Lions Gate Bridge without adding to the damage the Liberty had already sustained that day. The fog thinned at higher elevations and the traffic moved almost normally on the Upper Levels Highway, until it dropped back down to sea level at Horseshoe Bay and the fog closed in again. It took me three passes to find the turnoff to the Bridgwater Foundation estate.

chapter twenty-five

T he Liberty's abused suspension groaned alarmingly as the wheels jounced through the potholes in the winding driveway, which seemed even narrower in the fog. There were no lights along the drive, nor in the parking area in front of the house, which was empty but for the foundation's Dodge Caravan. I parked by the front steps and turned off the engine. When I turned off the headlights, the darkness was almost claustrophobic. The only light came from a pair of coach lamps that glowed feebly on either side of door, fitted with low-wattage compact fluorescent bulbs. The rest of the house was dark, hunched in the misty gloom like something out of a bad horror movie. I opened the car door and the interior lights went on, but I was plunged into semi-darkness again when I closed the door.

I pressed the rusty doorbell button beside the massive wood doors and waited. After thirty seconds or so, I pressed it again and waited some more. Still no one answered. I pressed it again, holding the button, wiggling it. Then I tried knocking, rapping my knuckles on the door. The dark, ancient wood was like rock. I closed my fist and hammered.

"Hello," I called, voice seeming very loud in the stillness. "Anybody home?" I hammered again, and was about to hammer a third time when I heard the rattle of the lock. I stepped back.

The door creaked open a few inches, a narrow band of dull, yellow light spilling onto the stone steps, and the lovely dark-eyed Maria peered through the gap.

"Is Mr. Moffat here?" I asked her.

"It is late," she replied in her sweet, syrupy voice, regarding me without expression.

It was just a few minutes past nine. I said, "Yes, I'm sorry, but I need to speak to him."

"It is late," she said again and started to close the door.

I put my hand out and held it. "Please," I said. "I need to speak with him. It's important. Tell him — tell him I've spoken to Samuel Waverley." She stared at me as though she didn't understand a word I was saying. Perhaps she didn't really speak English at all, but just knew a few well-rehearsed phrases by rote. Then she nodded and opened the door.

I stepped into the gloomy foyer and she closed the door behind me. Her thick, dark hair was tangled and she was wearing baggy, shapeless sweats that looked sizes too large for her. Early to be in bed, I thought.

Maria escorted me into the entrance hall. "Wait," she said, pointing to a worn spot on the old Oriental carpet. She ran up the wide stairs, fleet as a deer.

I waited, staring at the worn spot on the carpet. There wasn't much else to look at. The hall contained not a stick of furniture and the wood-panelled walls were completely bare but for a few sconces that also contained compact fluorescent bulbs, none of which were lit, except one at the bottom of the staircase and another at the top.

A figure appeared at the top of the stairs and began to descend. It was Mrs. Moffat.

"Can I help you?" she asked, as she stopped at the third step from the bottom of the stairs. She looked down at me. She was wearing slacks, a prim blouse buttoned to her throat, and a shapeless cardigan sweater with sagging pockets.

"I'm sorry to intrude like this, Mrs. Moffat, but I need to speak to your husband."

"I'm afraid my husband isn't accepting visitors, Mr. McCall."

"He's here, though?"

"Yes, he is. But, as I said, he doesn't wish to be disturbed."

"Can you give him a message?"

Her expression tightened. "What sort of message?" she asked.

"Tell him I've spoken to Samuel Waverley."

"And why would he be interested in that fact?" she asked.

"Just give him the message. Tell him I need to talk to him about — well, I need to talk to him."

"No, I'm afraid I can't do that."

"Mrs. Moffat. I don't want to be impolite, but I need to talk to your husband."

"You can insist all you like, Mr. McCall, and be as impolite as you think necessary. It won't make any difference."

Now what? I wondered. How certain was I about Moffat? Not very. What if I was wrong? I'd be making a complete fool of myself, although it wouldn't be the first time, or likely the last. On the other hand, what difference would it make? To hell with it, I thought.

"Excuse me," I said to Mrs. Moffat, brushing past her and starting up the stairs. As I passed her, she took something out of the pocket of her cardigan. I hoped it wasn't a gun. It wasn't. It was a phone. It beeped quietly.

"Walter," I heard her say as she followed me up the stairs. "I'm sorry to bother you, dear, but Mr. McCall is on his way up to see you ... Yes, I told him you did not wish to be disturbed. Shall I call ...?" She paused, then said, "Very well." The phone beeped again, and she turned and retreated down the stairs.

The long upstairs hall was even more dimly lit than the entrance hall. I walked to the door at the end of the hall and knocked. A few seconds later, it opened and Walter Moffat stood silhouetted against the light. He was wearing a dressing gown cinched tight across his trim middle and leather slippers with tassels. His breath smelled of Scotch when he asked me to come in, but he didn't appear to be drunk.

I went in. He closed the door behind me. The room looked exactly as it had the first time I'd seen it, still like something out of a 1960s television family drama. I don't know why I expected it to have changed, but I did. Something about the atmosphere of the whole house seemed different somehow.

"I assume that you have come to talk to me about why I have changed my mind about engaging you to catalogue my collection," he said, still talking as though he were paid by the word. At least that hadn't changed. "I regret to inform you that a situation has arisen that renders the entire exercise moot. There is no longer a collection to catalogue."

"What do you mean?"

"Last night thieves broke into the gallery and stole the entire collection."

"You're kidding," I said.

"I am not, sir," he said stiffly. "Would that I were. It is gone. Every last piece of it." I thought he was going to burst into tears at any moment.

"Why on Earth would anyone want to steal a collection —" I managed to stop myself before I put my foot in it. I had been going to say, *a collection of worthless junk.* "Um, I mean, it's very difficult to sell stolen art, isn't it?" I said instead.

"Whoever stole it has no intention of *selling* it," he said.

Then why bother stealing it in the first place? I wondered. Unless ...

"They are holding it for ransom," Moffat said. "They've threatened to destroy it if I do not pay."

"Ah," I said. "Well, that's what insurance is for, right?"

"Have you any idea what it costs to insure an art collection, Mr. McCall? Particularly one as valuable as mine?"

"Um. No."

"More than I could afford, I'm afraid. Despite what you might think, sir, I am not a wealthy man. Neither is my wife a wealthy woman. And if I can't afford insurance, I can hardly afford to pay the ransom."

"I'm very sorry for your loss, Mr. Moffat, but I didn't come here to talk to you about your art collection."

"No? Why are you here, then?"

"I spoke to Samuel Waverley today."

"Did you? His wife's death must have been a terrible shock to him. How is he holding up?"

"Not very well," I said. "He's dead."

"Pardon me?"

"He's dead. He had a massive heart attack in his cabin near Lake Lucille. We tried to get him to the hospital in time, but he didn't make it."

"I see," he said, with a politician's cool. "I'm very sorry to hear that."

I'd decided to fib a little, keep it simple. "Before he died, he told me that you were having an affair with his wife," I said, looking him the eye.

"I'm sure he told you nothing of the sort," he said, looking me straight in the eye back.

"You're denying it, then?"

"Of course I'm denying it," he sad.

"You weren't Anna Waverley's lover?"

"No, I wasn't," he said patiently. "Frankly, Mr. McCall, under other circumstances, I might find your allegations amusing. The whole idea is quite absurd." He turned away, as if looking for his glass, which was on the coffee table, and I knew he was dissembling, and trying to cover it up. "Perhaps you haven't noticed, sir — she doesn't flaunt it, after all — but my wife is an exceptionally attractive woman," he added, casually picking up his glass and walking to the bar. "Would you care for a drink? You've been through a lot recently. Perhaps you are suffering from a form of post-traumatic stress." He poured a centimetre of Chivas into a glass, and held it out to me.

I couldn't argue about the stress, but I said, "No, thanks."

He shrugged and poured it into his own glass. "Well, then," he said, "if you don't mind seeing yourself out, there are more pressing matters that require my attention."

"With all due respect, Mr. Moffat," I said. "I know you're lying. You were having an affair with Anna Waverley and you were on the *Wonderlust* with her the night Bobbi was attacked. I don't believe for a minute that Mrs. Waverley attacked her, so that leaves you. What was it? Did you panic because you were terrified that your political career, such as it is, would be ruined if it became public that you were having an affair with your art dealer's wife?"

"Mr. McCall," he said with a heavy sigh, as if dealing with a recalcitrant child. "You really are trying my patience. If you persist in these ridiculous allegations, I will be forced to call the police. I think you should leave at once."

"Go ahead," I said. "Call the police. They'll be very interested to learn that your wife's foundation owns the *Wonderlust*, which you neglected to tell me when we first met."

"It was hardly relevant. It has been years since I or my wife have been on her father's boat. It was my understanding that it had been sold some time ago. In fact, if I'm not mistaken, and I'm certain I'm not, it was sold to a film production company. Whoever told you that my wife's foundation still owns it is obviously misinformed."

"It was Sam Waverley," I said. "Just before he died."

"At the risk of sounding callous, Mr. McCall, that hardly makes him a reliable source."

If he was lying, he was very good at it. As a politician, he had better be. The problem was, I found myself half believing him. Maybe more than half. Did I have him figured all wrong? Maybe he hadn't been Anna Waverley's lover. Jeanie Stone had told me that he'd been a perfect gentleman when he'd spoken at the meeting of female forestry workers, despite the best efforts of some of her colleagues. And he was certainly right about his wife being an attractive woman. But so had Anna Waverley been, and that hadn't stopped Sam Waverley from wandering. I was as certain as I could be that Anna had been on the *Wonderlust* when Bobbi had been attacked. If Moffat hadn't been on the boat with her, who had been? I was back at square one, without a clue as to my next move. So I winged it.

"Why haven't you called the police?" I asked.

"If you aren't out of my house in two minutes, I shall do just that."

"I mean about the theft of your collection."

"If you must know, I was told not to involve the police or they would destroy it."

"They're going to destroy it, anyway," I said, "since you can't pay the ransom. If you call the police, at least there's a chance you'll get some of it back. Maybe even all of it."

"That may be so," he replied flatly. "However, it is no business of yours. Now, please go."

"How did Sam Waverley react when you told him you wanted to send your collection on tour to raise money for your wife's foundation?"

"What do you mean? He was as excited as I at the prospect."

"I'll bet he was excited," I said. "It would have ruined him."

"Don't be absurd."

"I hate to be the one to break this to you, Mr. Moffat, but most of the so-called art you bought from Sam Waverley was worthless junk. If you'd exhibited it, the whole country would have realized he'd been selling you crap for years. His reputation would have been destroyed. And yours — as a collector, anyway."

"That's ridiculous," Moffat said. "It's one of the finest collections of its kind in the country."

"That may be so," I said, "but I have it on good authority that it's mainly rubbish."

"Whose authority?"

"Mr. Waverley's assistant told me that Waverley has been ripping you off for years. I expect his wife knew about it, too, as well as a former assistant or two."

"You do not have the slightest idea what you are talking about, Mr. McCall. Samuel Waverley was of exemplary character, one of the most respected art dealers in the country. Your opinion means nothing to me. Less than nothing. You are a narrow-minded cultural barbarian. Despite your so-called profession, you do not have an artistic bone in your body. You are a cretin, sir, and beneath my contempt." I'd obviously hit him where it hurt the most.

"Okay, fine," I said. "Maybe I wouldn't know a Picasso from a pizza. I didn't come here to discuss your taste in art. Your collection could be worth millions, for all I care. All I care about is who tried to kill my friend and killed Anna Waverley and seeing that he's fittingly punished."

"How may times must I tell you that I know nothing about Anna Waverley's murder or the attack on your friend?"

"This might surprise you," I said, "but I think I may actually believe you."

"Imagine my relief," he said sarcastically.

"But I'm sure you're connected in some way to Bobbi's attack and Anna's murder. Where were you the Tuesday before last?"

"Why should I answer that?"

"Why wouldn't you, if you have nothing to hide?"

"Very well. If it will get you out of my house. I'd have to check my calendar to be sure, but I was here, working. My assistant will confirm it, if necessary."

"And last Saturday night? The night Anna Waverley was killed?"

"I had a strategy meeting with my campaign manager, Mr. Getz, whom you met at your sister's house. His staff was there as well. The meeting lasted till well past midnight."

"Were you aware that Anna Waverley had a lover?"

"I was not."

Oops. Something shifted in his eyes. He wasn't as good a liar as I'd thought, perhaps because until now he'd been mostly telling the truth. He also realized that I wasn't buying it and tried to recover.

"But it's hardly surprising, is it, since her husband is a well-known philanderer."

"Do you know who her lover was?"

He was ready for that one. Too ready. He looked me straight in the eye and said, "If I was unaware that she had a lover, how could I possibly know her lover's identity?"

It was so obvious he was lying that I couldn't help but laugh. "Walter," I said. "You'd better pray that you don't become anything more than an obscure back-bencher, because you are one bloody awful liar."

I had to give him credit, though; he didn't ruffle easily. "Be that as it may, I have no intention of continuing this conversation. Good night."

"What can you tell me about a man a little shorter than me with slicked-back black hair, an olive complexion, and too much cologne?"

"Nothing at all," he said. "Good night, Mr. McCall. You can find your own way out." He opened the door.

What could I do? I left.

chapter twenty-six

When I reached the bottom of the main staircase, the delectable Maria was waiting for me, standing on the worn spot on the Oriental carpet, hair brushed to a gleaming ebony lustre, but still dressed in her baggy sweats.

"This way, *señor*," she cooed softly. "The *señora* would speak to you."

I assumed "the *señora*" was Mrs. Moffat. "Then I would speak to the *señora*, too," I said.

I followed Maria down the gloomy hallway toward the rear of the house. We passed darkened rooms lined with crowded bookshelves and filled with tall file cabinets and ancient wood desks upon which sat silent computers almost as old as Maria, some possibly older. Maria knocked on a door at the end of the hallway, opened it, and ushered me into a bright and somewhat more modern office. Elise Bridgwater Moffat sat behind a blond oak partners desk the size of a snooker table, the top piled high with file folders, printouts, and what appeared to be dozens of photo albums. The wainscotted walls were covered with hundreds of colour eight-by-tens of wide-eyed brown children ranging in age from toddler to teen. Mrs. Moffat's Children in Peril, I presumed, although all looked happy, healthy, well-fed, and clean. Post-peril, perhaps.

Mrs. Moffat stood and came around from behind the big desk. "That will be all, Maria," she said. "*Gracias*."

"Very good, *señora*," Maria said, and withdrew, closing the door behind her.

"Thank you for seeing me, Mr. McCall," Mrs. Moffat said. "Sit down, please." She indicated one of a pair of worn and cracked leather wingback chairs facing the desk. I sat down. The chairs were more comfortable than they looked. Certainly more comfortable than those in her husband's upstairs study. "Would you care for something to drink?" Mrs. Moffat asked. "Tea? Whisky?"

I'd refused her husband's offer of a drink, but I accepted hers. "Uh, whisky, thank you."

She took a bottle of Glenmorangie from a cabinet against the wall by the door. Her taste in Scotch was better than her husband's, and she was more generous as she poured two fingers into a squat, heavy glass, which she handed to me. She sat in the other wingback chair.

"I won't join you, if you don't mind," she said, in response to my look. "I rarely drink alcohol. But, please ..."

I sipped self-consciously. "I apologize for my behaviour earlier," I said, as the whisky diffused warmly across my palette.

Nodding her acceptance, she said, "What did you need so desperately to see my husband about?"

"Perhaps you should ask him that," I said.

"Mr. McCall," she said patiently. "As you may have realized by now, my husband is ... well, not to put too fine a point on it, but if by some miracle Walter does somehow manage to get elected again, he won't be the least intelligent man in Parliament, but he won't be the most intelligent, either. Nevertheless, despite his faults, he is a good man, relatively speaking. While he may not do much good in Ottawa, he won't do any harm, either. Pray that if he is elected, and his party remains in power, the prime minister is himself intelligent enough to realize that Walter is not cabinet material."

"Why are you telling me this, Mrs. Moffat?"

"Your sister thinks very highly of you, Mr. McCall. So does Dr. Paul."

"Mrs. Moffat," I said. "While your husband may not be the brightest bulb on the tree, your bulbs are loose."

She smiled. It made her look ten years younger. "Mary-Alice told me that that would be your reaction."

"She's brighter than the average bulb," I said.

"Yes, she is, isn't she?" Mrs. Moffat said. "I like her very much."

"She'll be please to hear that." I sipped my Glenmorangie.

"Are you enjoying your whisky, Mr. McCall?"

"Yes, thank you, it's very good," I said, taking another sip.

"Is it better than the whisky my husband offered you?"

"In my opinion, yes."

"Do you know why he offers his guests the kind of whisky he does?"

"Presumably because he likes it himself," I said.

"A reasonable assumption," Mrs. Moffat said. "But incorrect. He offers his guests Chivas Regal because someone once told him it was good whisky."

"Many people like it," I said.

"Many people evidently like poutine, Mr. McCall. Would you serve it to your guests?"

"I don't know what that is."

"It's a Quebec dish consisting of French fries, cheese curds, and brown gravy."

"Mrs. Moffat, please," I implored.

She smiled again. "The point I'm trying to make, Mr. McCall, is that while my husband is an essentially good man of average intelligence, he's also easily influenced. Too easily, I'm afraid, especially by individuals possessing particularly strong personalities."

Such as yourself, I thought. "Liking Chivas Regal," I said, "or poutine, for that matter, is hardly ..." Then the light dawned. "Are you talking about his art collection? Someone, presumably Sam Waverley, told him such art was good, is that it? Believe me, Mrs. Moffat, that's not why I came to see your husband tonight. I had nothing to do with the theft of his collection."

"I'm sure you didn't, Mr. McCall."

"You're not sorry it was stolen, though, are you?" Another flash. "Mrs. Moffat, please don't take offence, but when you couldn't talk him out of exhibiting his collection to raise money for your foundation, did you hire someone to steal it?"

"No, I did not. As much as I find many of the pieces in my husband's collection mildly objectionable, it is his pride and joy, and evidently quite valuable. I do love my husband, Mr. McCall. I would never knowingly do anything to hurt him, nor would I stand by and do nothing to prevent others from hurting him. As I said, he is a fundamentally good man."

"With questionable taste in art," I said. *But very good taste in wives*, I added to myself.

"Perhaps," she agreed. "However, it wasn't his taste in art I was referring to. I was referring to his campaign manager, Mr. Charles Getz."

"Charles?"

"*Woody* is a nickname," she said, her distaste for the man evident in the set of her mouth as she spoke his name.

"You consider him a bad influence on your husband?" I said.

"Do you know what he did before he became my husband's campaign manager? He produced pornographic films." Which explained how he knew Kenny "Mr. See-em-sweat" Shapiro, the former director of *Star Crossed*, Reeny's sword-and-sex sci-fi series, which some people, especially those with a staunchly conservative mindset, might consider soft-core porn. It might also explain how he'd acquired his nickname. "And before that," Mrs. Moffat went on, "he owned a dozen used-car dealerships."

"Pardon my cynicism," I said, "but being a pornographic film producer or a used-car salesman doesn't necessarily disqualify him from running a political campaign."

"Perhaps you're right," she said. "However, I don't believe he has my husband's best interests at heart."

"It may be my cynical streak showing again," I said, "but I agree it's unlikely he's in it for anyone's good but his own. I'm sure your husband is paying him very well for his services. And, if by some miracle, as you say, your husband should win, I'm sure Mr. Getz expects to be amply rewarded. One way or another. Seems to me they both want the same thing for their own reasons. It's a marriage made in heaven, if you'll pardon the expression."

"I don't believe it matters one way or another to Mr. Getz if my husband wins or loses. He isn't in it for the long haul, as they say, whereas my husband is."

"This is very interesting," I said. "And I'm enjoying your whisky. But what does any of it have to do with me? To be honest, it doesn't matter to me either if your husband wins or loses."

"It matters to me," Mrs. Moffat said emphatically. "What is more important, it matters to the foundation and the thousands of children it helps. The foundation is everything to me, Mr. McCall. It's important to my husband, as well. If Walter should win a seat in Parliament, he will be a powerful advocate for the children of the Third World. Even as a backbencher, his voice will be heard. Nevertheless, I am a realist. I know the likelihood of his winning is not great. However, I will do whatever I can to ensure that the odds against him do not get any worse than they already are."

"Okay," I said. "I see what you're getting at. You want me to stop stirring things up over my partner's attack, is that it?"

"What happened to your partner was a regrettable accident, Mr. McCall. I prayed for her recovery and my prayers were answered. I understand that she was released from hospital yesterday. Perhaps you should just be thankful she is recovering and get on with your lives."

"Is that what your husband told you?" I said. "That it was an accident?"

"My husband knows nothing at all about what happened to your partner," she said, with such complete conviction that I was inclined to believe her.

"Someone was on that boat with Anna Waverley the night Bobbi was attacked," I said. "If it wasn't your husband, who was it?"

She regarded me, cool green eyes reflecting calm, total control. "Anna Waverley wasn't on the *Wonderlust* that night, Mr. McCall. Neither was my husband."

"Bobbi will eventually remember what happened," I said. "What then?"

"She will confirm that neither my husband nor Anna Waverley was involved."

"What about Anna Waverley's murder?" I said. "I'm certain she was killed because she knew something about Bobbi's attack."

"My husband told me that Anna was killed during a home invasion."

"The police often deliberately keep certain details of a crime from the media to weed out false confessions and to give themselves an edge when interviewing suspects," I said. "Home invaders wouldn't bother to make it look like suicide."

She paled. "I—I didn't know," she said. She clutched at the crucifix on her breast. "How is it that you know her murder was made to look like a suicide?"

"I found her body," I said.

"You …" She paused. "So she …" She paused again.

"So she what, Mrs. Moffat?"

She straightened her shoulders and took a deep breath, still holding onto the crucifix. Calm restored, she said, "Anna told me about your visit, Mr. McCall. She liked you and regretted having to lie to you, but she was protecting me, you see."

I thought about it for a second, then said, "You were on the *Wonderlust* the night Bobbi was attacked, weren't you?"

"Yes, I'm afraid I was."

"With Anna?"

"No."

"Who, then?"

"I'm afraid I can't tell you that, Mr. McCall."

"Why? Who are you protecting?" I waited for the obvious answer. When it wasn't forthcoming, I said, "Your husband was on the boat, after all."

She shook her head. "No."

"All right," I said. "Tell me what happened."

"I'm afraid I can't do that, either."

We were at an impasse. Then a telephone chirruped. She stood and excavated a cordless handset from the stacks of files on her desk.

"Yes, Maria … Oh, Mr. Getz." Her mouth compressed. "What is it?" she asked, voice chilly. She looked at me. "As it happens, he is." She listened, still looking at me, expression darkening, then said icily, "Very well. We'll be right up." She pressed a button and laid down the phone.

I stood. "What's going on?"

"Come with me," she commanded.

I followed her out of her office into the long hallway. "Is something wrong?" I asked, as we headed toward the front of the house.

"My husband apparently wishes another word with you."

"What about?"

She didn't answer. I followed her up the wide staircase to the second floor and along the hall to the door of the private apartments. She knocked on the door. It opened almost instantly.

"Come in, Mr. McCall," Woody Getz said, standing aside. I went in. "Thank you, Elise," he said, and closed the door in Mrs. Moffat's face. The last glimpse I had of her, her eyes were like cold, green laser beams drilling holes in Woody Getz. He didn't notice.

"Where's Mr. Moffat?" I asked.

Woody Getz smiled his weaselly, fish-eating smile. "He'll join us in a moment. We have a few things to discuss first, you and I."

"I can barely contain my curiosity," I said.

"You've been making quite a nuisance of yourself."

"Thank you."

"You seem to be under the impression — or perhaps the delusion — that Mr. Moffat is somehow involved in the attack on your partner and the death of Anna Waverley."

"Well …" I said.

"You're treading on dangerous ground," Getz said.

"Well …"

"I'm sorry your partner was hurt," he said. "I truly am. I understand she doesn't remember anything about the attack."

"Not yet," I said.

"I hope her memory does return. When it does, she'll tell you Walter had nothing to do with her attack. Let's say, for sake of argument, she does tell the authorities Walter was on the *Wonderlust* that night. He wasn't, but public figures are fair game these days, aren't they? He'll be forced to defend himself. How credible a witness will she make? Any halfway decent lawyer will tear her testimony to shreds, suggesting she's delusional as a result of permanent brain damage from the attack, lack of oxygen, or the subsequent coma. Or maybe that someone — knowingly or unknowingly — contributed to her recalling something that never happened, like those people who claim to remember childhood abuse or being abducted by aliens, but which turn out to be false memories implanted by suggestion, wishful thinking, misguided hatred, or the need to blame someone else for their failings. You don't want your friend to go through that, do you? No, of course you don't. But that's exactly what'll happen if you continue to poke your nose where it doesn't belong."

"The police might be interested to know that Mrs. Moffat's foundation sold the *Wonderlust* to a film production company. You own a film production company, don't you, Mr. Getz?"

"You'll have to do better than that," Getz said.

"All right. What about Anna Waverley? Who murdered her? And why?"

"I have no idea," Getz said. "It certainly wasn't Walter. The police won't find his fingerprints in her home; he never visited her home. However, they'll find yours, won't they? Maybe you killed her. She was a very beautiful woman. Maybe you made a play for her and she blew you off, so you killed her in a fit of rage? Yes, yes, I know. You're going to tell me you have an alibi for the time in question. But perhaps the medical examiner was wrong about the time of death. Forensics is an imprecise science, not at all like on television. You see how it can go, don't you?"

"You seem to know a lot about the case."

"The Waverleys were acquaintances of the Moffats. I made it my business to learn what I could about Mrs. Waverley's murder, if only to make sure the police were doing all they could to apprehend the individual responsible."

"And protect your investment in Walter Moffat."

"Of course," Getz said, patting the top of his head, as if checking that his lacquered comb-over was still in place.

"Oh, shit," I said, remembering what John Ostrof had told me about the man he'd seen talking to Anna Waverley on the quay, who he'd also seen at the parties on the *Wonderlust*, that he had patted the top of his head, as if afraid his hair might blow away.

"Don't take it too hard," Getz said, smiling as though he had a fishbone in his throat. "Win some, lose some. That's just the way it goes sometimes."

I didn't know why Elise Moffat had lied to me about being on the *Wonderlust*, but she had. It had been Anna Waverley on the boat after all. Not with Walter Moffat, though; with Woody Getz. Woody Getz was Anna Waverley's mysterious lover. Well, I told myself, not without some disappointment, there was no accounting for taste.

"What happened, Woody?" I said. "Did Bobbi stumble into the middle of something she shouldn't have? Did she catch you and Anna Waverley together? Maybe you thought she was a spy for the opposition and tried to take her camera away from her. She wouldn't have given it up without a fight. Was she hurt in the struggle? Is that what happened? It is, isn't it? I can see it in your face. You thought she was dead, that you'd killed her. You panicked and forced Mrs. Waverley to help you load Bobbi into the Zodiac and dump her under the bridge."

"This is very entertaining," Woody Getz said. His

hand twitched at his side, as if, like Dr. Strangelove's arm, it had a mind of its own and he was barely able to prevent it from swinging up and patting the top of his head.

"That's what Anna was going to tell me before she was killed, wasn't it? I bet I know who killed her. That nasty character who looks like Joel Cairo from *The Maltese Falcon*. Trouble with people like that, Woody, is that when they get caught, and they almost always are, they're quick to roll over on their employers in exchange for a reduced sentence."

"It's not what you believe that's important," Getz said. "It's what you can prove. Utter a word of this bizarre fantasy to the police or the press, I'll sue you within an inch of your life. I'll take you for everything you own and everything you or your children and their children will ever own. You're fucking with the wrong guy, McCall."

"Oh, yeah."

"But I'm a firm believer in positive reinforcement," he went on, patting the top of his head again as he sailed into familiar territory. "I'm in a position to send a substantial amount of business your way. Nothing too big — we're always under a certain amount of scrutiny — but what would you say to three thousand a month, give or take?"

He should have quit while he was ahead. Until that moment I'd been ready to admit defeat and slink away with my tail between my legs. He was right. I might be able to make things a little hot for him, but I couldn't prove anything. Moreover, as he'd pointed out, even a middling competent lawyer would tear Bobbi apart on the stand. However, men like Woody Getz aren't satisfied until they own your soul. Any doubt about his involvement in Bobbi's attack or Anna Waverley's death, or how far I was willing to go to see him punished, evaporated in a puff of foul smoke with his next words.

"I can't guarantee you'll be able to retire to the Bahamas in five years," Getz said, "but what was it Humphrey Bogart said at the end of *The Maltese Falcon*? 'This could be the beginning of a beautiful friendship.'"

"That was *Casablanca*," I said. "And I'd rather be sued."

"Is that right?" someone behind me said. "How do you feel about dead?"

chapter twenty-seven

Walter Moffat stood in the doorway to his office. There was blood on his face from a gash under his eye, startlingly red against the sickly paleness of his complexion. It hadn't been Moffat who'd spoken, though. The man I called Joel Cairo stood behind him, smiling nastily. He had a revolver in one hand and held Bobbi's elbow in the other. Her wrists were duct-taped together in front of her, and there was another length of tape wrapped around her head and across her mouth. Her eyes were round with fear, but when she saw me, hope blossomed. I only hoped it wasn't misplaced.

Cairo prodded Moffat in the back. Moffat took two stumbling steps into the room. "That's far enough," Cairo said. Moffat jerked to a halt, as though he had reached the end of an invisible tether.

"Kittle," Woody Getz said. "What the hell are you doing here? I told you to leave town."

"I will," Cairo — or Kittle — said. He thrust Bobbi toward me. She stumbled and I caught her. "As soon as I clean up a few loose ends. Starting with these two."

"You know this guy?" I said to Getz.

Getz ignored me, turning to Moffat, who seemed dazed and confused. "For god's sake, Tony," Getz said. "Did you have to hit him in the face?"

Moffat looked at Getz, as if uncertain where he was. "Woody?" He raised his hand to his head, touched the blood, brought his hand down and looked at the blood on his fingers. "Woody. What's going on? I'm bleeding. I need to sit down." Getz helped him to a chair. He almost fell into it. "Elise?" he said plaintively, glancing around the room, looking for her. "Where are you?"

"Hmmm-mm," Bobbi hummed through her nose, shaking her head, trying to claw the tape from her mouth. I started to help, plucking at the end of the tape with my fingernails.

"Leave that," said the man Getz had called Tony Kittle, waving his gun for emphasis. I left it.

"Mm-hmm," Bobbi hummed again, growling deep in her throat and scowling fiercely, the stitched cuts on her face livid.

"What's she going to do?" I said. "Scream? Who'd hear her?"

"I said leave it," Kittle snarled, pointing his revolver at me. I'd had guns pointed at me in the past, but never by someone as coldly and frighteningly malevolent as Tony Kittle. I had the feeling he'd just as soon shoot me or Bobbi as look at us. Bobbi became very still.

"Tony," Getz said, with strained reasonableness. "For god's sake. Put that thing away before you hurt someone."

I'd made a very bad mistake not returning Mary-Alice's call and telling her where I was going, but there was no reason anyone else had to know that. "People know I'm here," I said. It sounded lame, even to me.

"So what?" Kittle said. "I'm not planning on hanging around after I've taken care of business." He moved the revolver in Getz's direction. "Speaking of which, where's the money?"

"What money?" Getz said, staring at Kittle's gun.

"Don't shit me," Kittle said. "You know what money. Your slush fund."

"What are you talking about?" Getz said, eyes shifting to Moffat then quickly back to Kittle. "What slush fund?" It was obvious he knew exactly what Kittle was talking about.

"Jesus Christ," Kittle said. "You should go back to selling cars or whatever the fuck it was you did before you discovered politics was an even better sucker's game." He waved his gun in Moffat's direction, who stared blankly into space, oblivious to what was going on around him. "You're almost as fucking dumb as he is," Kittle said. "And we both know how dumb that is, don't we? You've been skimming money from Wally's campaign contributions from day one." He leaned toward Moffat. "Feel that, Wally? That's you being fucked by your campaign manager."

"Goddamn it, Tony," Getz said.

"He's been fucking your wife, too," Kittle continued, his tone at once both mocking and cruel. "Figuratively speaking, of course. He's been using her stupid foundation to wash the money he extorted from your pals with videos of them getting it off with hookers on that boat." He turned back to Getz, deadly serious. "Where is it?"

"All right," Getz said. "Take it easy. It's in the safe in Walter's office."

"That's more like it." He waved his gun in the direction of the door to Walter Moffat's office. "Let's go."

Getz helped Moffat to his feet and Kittle herded us all into Moffat's office. He stood by the door as Getz settled Moffat into a chair. Getz then went to the credenza behind Moffat's desk and opened a cabinet to reveal a small, incongruously modern safe with a glowing keypad lock. He punched six digits into the keypad, opened the door, and peered into the safe.

"Oh, fuck," he said.

Oh-oh, I thought, squeezing Bobbi's arm. *This isn't good*. Bobbi looked at me, then at Kittle standing by the door.

"What's wrong?" Kittle said.

"It's gone," Getz said.

"What to you mean, gone?" Kittle said.

"Gone," Getz said. "As in *not there*. Have a look for yourself? Shit."

Keeping his gun on me and Bobbi and Moffat, Kittle went behind the desk, waved Getz out of the way, and looked quickly into the safe.

"What the fuck is this?" Kittle shouted, spittle flecking his lips. He wiped his mouth with the back of his gun hand as he looked into the safe again, just to be sure. "What are you trying to pull? Where is it?"

"I don't know," Getz said worriedly.

Kittle came around from behind the desk. His movements were spasmodic, random, as if his body and his brain weren't quite in synch. He waved the revolver about, pointing it at me and Bobbi, at Moffat, at Getz, as if trying to decide which one of us to shoot first. He wiped the back of his gun hand across his mouth again and seemed to regain some semblance of control.

"Who else knows the combination?" he shouted at Getz. "Who?" His face was livid and the smell of his cologne filled the room, intensified by the heat radiating from his body.

"No one," Getz said. "I changed the combination. Not even Walter knows it."

"What about his old lady?" Kittle said.

"No," Getz said. "Only me."

"Either someone else knows the combination," Kittle

said, "or you took the money." He smiled savagely, as if impressed by his powers of deduction.

"Oh, shit," Woody Getz said. "Caroline."

Caroline, I remembered, was the art history major who was interning for Moffat and whom he'd said would help us photograph the collection. At the mention of her name, Moffat raised his head. I supposed, since the collection has been stolen, she was out of a job.

"What the fuck would you give her the combination for?" Kittle said.

"I didn't," Getz said. "But she was in the room the other day when I opened the safe. She must have — I didn't think she was paying attention. She was talking on her cellphone."

Kittle laughed. It was an ugly sound. "You goddamn moron," he said. "Who doesn't have a fucking video phone these days? She recorded you punching in the number, you dumb fuck. Shit. I thought there was something hinky about her." He thought for a moment, eyes shifting from Moffat to me and Bobbi to Getz, but the revolver pointed unwaveringly at me and Bobbi. Then his eyes locked on Getz. "Well," he said. "I guess you're just gonna have to owe me."

Kittle took a roll of duct tape out of his pocket. Not your usual large diameter roll, but a smaller roll that looked like a few feet of tape wrapped around a short length of dowel. He tossed it to Getz, who fumbled it. Kittle sneered with contempt as Getz picked it up, but he didn't take his eyes — or his gun — off me. My hand was still on Bobbi's arm. She was as stiff as a statue, breathing hard through her nose.

"Tape him up," Kittle said.

"You can't get away with this," I said.

Getz looked at Kittle. "Don't do it here, for god's sake. Take them up into the mountains. Use his car. Kill them and bury them in the woods so no one will ever find them. Then dump the car in the sound."

"Are you all completely out of your minds?" I said. "You can't just kill us."

"I deeply regret the necessity, believe me," Getz said. "Make sure no one sees you leaving the house with them," he added to Kittle. "Go down the back and around."

"Wait a goddamned minute. You'd kill two people, just like that, in cold blood?"

Kittle stared at me, as if he couldn't believe what he was hearing. "My ass is on the line if Slim here talks," he said, pointing his gun at Bobbi. "His, too," he added, nodding at Woody Getz.

I looked at Moffat, slumped in his chair. "Mr. Moffat, you can't let them do this."

Kittle snorted. "I wouldn't count on any help from him," he said.

"You can't possibly believe you're going to get away with this," I said desperately. "Bobbi's father and boy-friend are both cops. You think they're aren't going to figure out what went down here?"

"Cops don't worry me," Kittle said, with a shrug. "Besides, her old man's a drunk. Isn't he, Slim?"

Bobbi glared daggers at him. "Mmmm," she hummed, struggling against her bonds and wagging her head back and forth. I tightened my grip on her, afraid she was going to go after him.

Getz began unwinding tape from the makeshift roll.

"Walter!" I shouted. "Snap out of it! Your wife says you're a decent guy. You'd trade the lives of three people — four, if you count Sam Waverley — to save your bloody career?" Moffat raised his head and looked at me.

Kittle snorted. "He'd trade his fucking soul. Already has. Only he's too fucking dumb to know it."

"Hold out your hands," Getz said. I kept them at my

sides. Bobbi huddled against me, mewling softly through her nose.

"No," Moffat said, speaking at last. He stood. "No."

"Stay out of this, Walter," Getz said.

"I can't let you do this."

"It's too late, Walter," Getz said. He nodded at Kittle.

Kittle picked up a cushion from the sofa, held it over the muzzle of his pistol, a makeshift silencer, pointed at me. "Hold out your hands or I'll shoot you right now."

"No," Moffat snapped, some of the strength returning to his voice. "Mr. Kittle, put that gun away. Woody. Remove the young lady's bindings."

"I can't do that, Walter."

Kittle aimed his cushion-silenced gun at Bobbi. "Put out your hands or I'll blow one big fucking hole in her."

"Mr. Kittle," Moffat said. "Woody. You both seem to forget that you are my employees."

"Fuck it," Kittle said. "Consider this my resignation." He swung the pillow toward Moffat.

"No!" Woody Getz shouted.

There was a muffled *whump* and the cushion burst, spewing smoke and fragments of scorched foam rubber. Moffat said, "Oof," as if someone had punched him in the stomach. He staggered backwards and fell, blood pumping from a hole in his chest. Then it stopped.

"Oh, fuck," Woody Getz said. Kittle swung the cushion toward him. Getz bolted for the sitting room. The sound of the gun was louder through the ruined cushion, but Kittle missed, blowing a chunk out of the door frame instead of Woody Getz.

Kittle stood in the door to the sitting room, taking aim at Getz's back. I dove at him as Getz yanked open the front door and ran out of the apartment. Kittle ducked aside, stepping into the sitting room and swinging his gun toward me. No longer muffled by the cushion, the gun went off with a sharp bang. Something exploded behind me as I tried to grab his arm. He slipped out of my grasp. Bobbi had ripped the tape from her mouth and, with a startling shriek, threw herself at Kittle, diving, pivoting on her bound hands, slamming her hip into his knees. Again, he danced aside and she ploughed into me. She rolled, kicked, and the gun flipped out of Kittle's hand. It spun across the sitting room carpet.

Kittle went after the gun and I went after Kittle, throwing myself onto him and dragging him to the floor. He writhed like an alligator in a neck snare, rolling, lashing out with his elbows and knees. I grabbed a handful of his oily black hair. His elbow slammed into the side of my head as he slid out from under me. Bobbi somehow managed to get her arms over his head and around his neck. The tape binding her wrists stretched across his throat, but he rotated in her embrace until he faced her, then ducked his head, slipping free. She clamped her legs around his hips while I clung to his arms, but he wriggled away and slithered across the floor toward the gun. I pounced onto his back, but he rolled under me, flipping me aside. He kicked at me, the heel of his shoe clipping my cheek. I fell back as he threw his arm out to grab the gun. I struck out with both feet, striking his elbow. The gun slid away from him, skittering under the big sofa.

Then he was on his feet, crouched, hands cocked, fingers crooked like claws. "I don't need a gun to take care of you two," he snarled. I believed him.

Bobbi spun and kicked, but he flitted aside and she fell, off balance. I grabbed a table lamp, threw it at him. He dodged and it crashed against the wall. I threw a piece of heavy marble statuary, but that missed too, bouncing and rolling across the carpet and through the office door until it came to rest against Moffat's body. I flung a tall blue vase with Chinese figures on it. Kittle caught it and threw it back at me. I ducked and it smashed against the old console TV. Bobbi was on her feet by then and charged him, but he side-stepped and kicked her feet out from under her. It was not going well.

I grabbed her, hauled her to her feet, and together we ran out the door and into the hall. Kittle didn't waste any time trying to find the gun, came after us instead. He hit me in the middle of the back. I staggered and pitched forward onto my face. Bobbi skidded to a stop, tried to help me up, but Kittle was on her like a panther. She fell, tried to scrabble away from him. He leaped at her, kicking. She rolled into a ball, trying to protect her head with her arms. I ran at him, but he flicked aside, grabbed me, sent me spinning toward the top of the stairs. If I hadn't fallen, I would have plunged down the stairs. He came at me.

There was a flash and an explosion. A section of dark wall panel splintered, exposing the lighter wood beneath the varnish. Kittle froze. Elise Moffat stood in the hall not ten feet from him. She held Kittle's revolver in both hands, her left hand cupped under her right hand, like a cop on television. Smoke drifted lazily from the muzzle.

"I missed deliberately," she said. "I didn't want to shoot you in the back, Mr. Kittle. I wanted you to see who it was that killed you."

"Mrs. Moffat," Kittle said.

"You killed my husband," she said. She took a step toward him. The muzzle of the pistol did not waver. "And you killed Anna."

"No, no," Kittle said, holding his hands out, as if they could stop a bullet. "It was Getz's idea, not mine."

"You are about to die, Mr. Kittle," Mrs. Moffat said. The pistol flashed and roared. Kittle flinched as the bullet plucked at the sleeve of his jacket. It seemed even I could hear the slug whiz by. I scrambled out of the line of fire, pulling Bobbi with me.

"Please, Mrs. Moffat," Kittle pleaded, backing away from her. He glanced quickly over his shoulder toward the stairs. It was his only avenue of escape.

"Don't run, Mr. Kittle," Elise Moffat said. "It's so unbecoming."

Kittle whimpered and sank to his knees.

"Please," he sobbed. "Please. Don't kill me."

She stepped closer to him.

"Don't get too close to him," I warned her.

She stopped five feet from him, pointing the pistol at his face.

"You won't shoot me," Kittle said. "You'd go to jail. Think about it. Who would save all those little kids?"

"I am thinking about them, Mr. Kittle. Without Walter the foundation may not survive. You haven't just killed my husband, you may have sentenced thousands of little children to a life of endless suffering and poverty." She took a step toward him, the muzzle of the pistol less than a foot from his face.

"I'm sorry," Kittle blubbered, trembling, tears streaming down his face, mucous running from his nose. "I'm sorry."

Her knuckle whitened on the trigger.

"Don't kill him, Mrs. Moffat," I said.

"Why not?" she asked, not looking at me, not taking her eyes off Kittle.

"Because it's a much more fitting punishment that a man like him will have to live with the memory that he cried like a baby and begged you for his life in front of people he terrorized."

"Listen to him," Kittle cried. "He's right. I'm begging you. Oh, please, I don't want to die." Then he laughed and slowly straightened until he was poised in a half crouch. "Screw this," he said, grinning. "You're out of bullets."

She took a step back, arm and eyes steady.

"I counted the shots," he said. "I fired four times and you fired twice."

"Let's find out, shall we," Elise Moffat said. Her finger tightened on the trigger.

Kittle leaped …

… and died as the gun roared and the sixth bullet tore out his throat.

"Stupid prick," Bobbi said flatly, looking at Kittle's body, sprawled in a bloody heap halfway down the main staircase. "If you're gonna play *Dirty Harry*, at least count the fucking shots right."

"I think he knew he'd only fired three times," I said. "He was just trying to rattle her."

Bobbi looked at Elise Moffat, sitting on the straight-backed chair Maria had brought from another room and placed for her on the worn spot on the Oriental carpet. Maria stood beside the chair, her hand resting protectively on Mrs. Moffat's shoulder. "I don't think she rattles that easily."

"She's tough stuff," I agreed.

"I remember what happened on the boat," Bobbi said.

"What? Poof, suddenly it's all there?"

She shook her head slowly. "No. It's weird. It's like it's always been there, which it has, I guess. But it's like I don't remember not remembering." She shook her head again. "It's a very strange feeling."

"So what happened? If you feel like talking about it, that is."

She'd got to the boat a few minutes after eight, she told me. Using the key Chrissy Conrad had given me, she let herself into the main salon and began setting up the remote flash units. She heard a sound from below and assumed it was Ms. Waverley, but as she test-fired the strobes, a man appeared in the hatch leading to the forward staterooms. It was Woody Getz, although Bobbi didn't know it at the time.

"Who the bloody hell are you?" Getz demanded.

Bobbi's first thought was, *Aw, Christ, I'm on the wrong fucking boat.* The key had worked, though. Getz came toward her.

"Look," Bobbi said. "I don't know what's going on. I —"

A woman's face appeared in the hatch, behind Getz, but Bobbi didn't recognize her, either.

"Give me that camera," Getz said, reaching for the camera Bobbi had slung around her neck. He grabbed the strap and pulled.

"Hey," Bobbi said, pulling back. "I didn't take any pictures."

"Bullshit. I saw the flash."

"Mr. Getz," the woman said. "Leave her alone."

Getz pulled harder. So did Bobbi. Then the strap broke and Bobbi fell.

"I must've hit my head," Bobbi said. "I don't remember. The next thing I knew, I was in a Zodiac. It was dark. I was wrapped in a blanket or a sleeping bag and something was pressing into my back. My head hurt like hell. I tried to roll over and sit up, but whatever was pressing into my back just pressed harder. I started to yell. Something hit me in the head, banging my face onto the deck. I managed to get free of the blanket. I saw a man. Him, I guess," she said, indicating Kittle's body, "but I couldn't really say for sure. He kicked me in the face. I fell into the bow of the boat and he came after me, hitting me and kicking me, stamping on my hands as I tried to crawl away from him. I remember falling, or jumping, and then being in the water. I don't remember passing out, but I must have. Then I woke up in the hospital with you and Greg sitting beside the bed." She reached over, placed a hand on mine. It was cool. She squeezed, then let go. "Thanks for being there, by the way."

"No problem," I said. "The woman on the boat. It was Anna Waverley?"

Bobbi shook her head. "No. It was her." She nodded toward Elise Moffat.

I looked at Elise Moffat in her chair at the foot of the staircase. Her eyes followed me as I went down to her. She hadn't been lying after all.

"What were you doing on the *Wonderlust* with Getz?" I asked her.

"I went to get proof that he was blackmailing people into contributing to Walter's campaign by video-taping them consorting with prostitutes," she said calmly. "He used similar tactics to get them to invest in his films. He must have followed me."

"The police impounded the boat," I said. "As far as I know, they didn't find any recording equipment."

"Mr. Getz removed it after Miss Brooks was — he told me you were dead," she added to Bobbi. "He called Mr. Kittle to dispose of your body. Mr. Getz and I left when Mr. Kittle arrived. I'm so sorry."

"Why didn't you call the police?" I asked.

"Mr. Getz also had recordings of me," she said softly. "He threatened to post them on the Internet. It would have destroyed any chance Walter had of winning the election."

"You wouldn't be the first politician's wife to have an affair with another man," I said.

"Walter's supporters are quite conservative," she said. "Traditional family values are very important to them."

"Still …"

"Must I spell it out for you, Mr. McCall? It wasn't a man Mr. Getz recorded me with."

"Oh," I said, as it hit me. "You were Anna Waverley's lover."

She nodded. "Yes," she said softly, sadly, tears filling her eyes. "We were lovers. It was a new experience for both of us …" Maria's hand tightened gently on her shoulder. Elise reached up and placed her hand on

Maria's. "Like me, Anna also still loved her husband, but it was not an emotionally satisfying relationship," she said, tears spilling over.

"Still," I said again, "if you were to have come out, if you'll pardon the expression, how much damage would it really have done to your husband's campaign? I mean, given that he had almost no chance of winning, anyway."

Her back stiffened. "I told you earlier, Mr. McCall, that I would do nothing that might jeopardize his chances, as slim as they might have been. However, I also had the foundation to consider. Its principal supporters are even more conservative than Walter's." She smiled weakly. "Walter said they made his supporters look like liberals."

"Did your husband know about you and Anna?"

"Yes," she said. "Our relationship did not have a sexual component. Despite the nature of his art collection, Walter wasn't interested in the messier aspects of sex. It was — convenient."

I heard distant sirens. "One more thing before the police arrive," I said. "Do you know a woman named Christine Conrad? Goes by Chrissy. Early thirties. Brunette. Clear blue eyes. Not quite as tall as Bobbi. It's possible you know her by a different name."

"No," she said, shaking her head. "I don't believe I know anyone answering that description, by any name." I didn't need the look on the lovely Maria's face to tell me that Elise Moffat was lying; she was as bad a liar as her husband had been.

chapter twenty-eight

"Let's go through it one more time, all right?" Sergeant Jim Kovacs said for the fourth or fifth time in the two hours since the police had arrived. "Just to make sure I've got it straight."

"If you haven't got it by now," I grumbled, half under my breath, "you're never going to get it."

"That kind of attitude isn't going to help," he growled.

"Sergeant Kovacs," said the burly RCMP staff sergeant from the Squamish detachment. "We called you as a courtesy, and at Mr. McCall's suggestion, I might add. It's been a long night. We're all tired. We've got everything we need from Mr. McCall and Miss Brooks for now. I think we can let them go."

"Just one more question," Kovacs insisted.

"Whatever it is," the staff sergeant said sternly, "it will keep. Do you need a ride home?" he asked me as Kovacs glowered.

"No, I have my car," I replied.

He signalled to a constable. "We'll be in touch if we need any additional information."

The constable escorted Bobbi and me out of the house, which was crawling with police and crime-scene investigators, even though most of the action had taken place in the upstairs apartments and in the hallway. Moffat's and Kittle's bodies had been removed. The paramedics had checked out Bobbi and me, repairing some of Bobbi's stitches, re-splinting her fingers, and pronouncing my bullet wound superficial — a diagnosis with which I had to concur, since I hadn't even been aware I'd been grazed just above my right hip until Bobbi noticed the blood on my shirt. The paramedics had also treated Elise Moffat for shock, although she'd remained very calm and in control until the police had arrived. An alert had been issued for Woody Getz.

"Do you think they'll charge Mrs. Moffat with anything?" Bobbi asked me as we climbed into the Liberty. If she noticed the duct-taped side mirror and the other damage, she didn't say anything.

"No, I don't think they will."

"She saved our lives, you know."

"I know."

The fog had lifted and less than forty minutes later I pulled into the lot in front of Sea Village. Bobbi woke up when I turned off the engine.

"Sorry," she said, yawning and rubbing her eyes. "Did I sleep all the way?"

"I dunno," I said, catching her yawn. "I was asleep most of the way myself." With a shiver of horror I realized I had no memory at all of driving across the Lions Gate Bridge.

We got out of the car, staggering with exhaustion as we made our way down the ramp and along the dock to my house.

"I'm going to have a Scotch or six," I said when we

were inside. "Do you want anything?" She didn't answer. I turned to find her staring at me. "What is it?"

"We've never made love," she said.

"What? Jesus, Bobbi. What the hell …?"

"I thought I was going to die tonight."

"Me, too," I said. "But look, maybe you're in shock or something. Post-traumatic stress whatever."

"Maybe," she said. "But when that crazy bastard was pointing his gun at us I really thought we were going to die, right there and then, and all I could think about was that in the ten years we've known each other we've never made love. I realized that I didn't want to die without ever having made love with you."

"For god's sake, Bobbi."

"Is the idea so awful?"

"Hell, no. It's just that, well, you're my friend. It would almost be like making love with my sister."

"You said 'almost.'"

"Yeah, well, you aren't my sister, are you?"

"Pour your Scotch," she said, smiling with a wattage I hadn't seen in a while. "You look like you need it more than ever."

While I was pouring my Scotch, she got herself a Granville Island Lager from the kitchen. When she came back into the living room, we sat side by side on the sofa, feet on the coffee table.

"So," I said. "When would you like to do it?"

"Oh," she said. "Sometime before I die."

"Good. I'm a little tired tonight. I don't think I could do a proper job of it."

"Me either," she said. "And my stitches hurt."

We clinked, glass to bottle, then simply sat there, shoulders touching, not talking, until we were both struggling to stay awake. Bobbi's eyelids fluttered, drooped, then lifted.

"Go to bed," I said.

"I think I will," she said, getting up from the sofa with a sofa grunt of pain. She leaned over and kissed me on the forehead. "G'night, boss."

After she had gone upstairs, I sat for a few minutes longer, finishing my Scotch. Then I got up, made certain the doors and windows were locked, and went up to bed. Surprisingly, I slept dreamlessly until I awakened at eight o'clock Saturday morning to the smell of coffee.

I spent most of Saturday going over the plans for the calendar shoot with Bobbi, Wayne, Mary-Alice, and Jeanie Stone, details such as props, costumes (such as they were) and accessories, a tent for the ladies to change in, movable privacy screens, as well as our own gear. Bobbi tired quickly, but did her share of the work, maybe more. Greg Matthias came by in the middle of the afternoon, asked her if she felt up to talking about what she remembered about her attack, and took her for coffee when she said yes, she'd be grateful for the opportunity to sit down. When she returned half an hour later, she was a little preoccupied, which wasn't surprising, but soon rallied. Every so often, though, she tended to stop what she was doing or saying, like a wind-up toy running down, and slowly drift off to somewhere else in space and time, perhaps one of Anna Waverley's alternate timelines.

When I least expected it, the realization that I'd witnessed the deaths of three people in less than a single day kept creeping up on me like a speeding cement truck, leaving me feeling empty and cold inside, breathing hard and heart pounding, desperately wishing that I could slip away to an alternate timeline myself. This reality had taken on a strange and disturbing perspective, as if I were living in a world with too little depth of field, as if my world were compressed into a very narrow band of focus, like one of Toni Hafkenscheid's whimsical landscapes, minus the whimsy. I didn't like it at all. Surely there was a parallel universe somewhere in which Walter Moffat was still enjoying his paintings of half-naked ladies, Woody Getz was selling used cars and making cheesy porn with Mr. See-em-sweat, where Sam Waverley and Doris Greenwood snuggled in front the fire in Sam's cabin in the mountains, and Anna Waverley found a lover she liked in Elise Moffat.

Bobbi's father came into the studio at a little past five. Everyone else had gone.

"Got a minute?" he said.

"Depends on what you have in mind," I said.

"I came to say thank you," he said. Neatly dressed in a suit and tie, freshly shaved and barbered, he looked like a different man. I was willing to bet he was sober, too.

"For what?" I said. "I almost got your daughter killed. Again."

"Yeah, she told me what happened. She told me you saved her life."

"She was exaggerating."

"Goddamn it," he growled. "I'm trying to do the right thing here. Save the smart remarks, okay?"

"I'm sorry," I said. "But Mrs. Moffat is the one you should be thanking, not me."

"The way Bobbi tells it, if you hadn't jumped Kittle when you did, he'd have killed both her and you."

"Maybe," I said. "Bobbi jumped him at the same time I did."

"That's not what she says. Anyway …" He held out his hand.

"Okay," I said, as we shook hands. "You're welcome."

"I'm sorry I've been such an asshole, too."

"Don't worry about it," I said. "I understand."

"I haven't been handling retirement very well," he

said. "That's no excuse, though. Believe it or not, I was a good cop, but I was a truly lousy husband and father. There's not much I can do about the former, except treat my ex and her husband with more respect, but I intend to do everything I can to make up for being a lousy father."

"Bobbi will like that," I said.

"We'll see," he said. He looked at his watch. Bobbi had told me she was meeting him for dinner, some place where she wouldn't frighten children. "Gotta go."

"Good luck," I said.

"Are you okay?" Bobbi said, as we sat on the roof deck later that evening, nursing a pair of Granville Island Lagers.

"Yeah," I said. "It's just, well, every so often I realize how close I came to being shot."

"You were shot."

"It's all right, ma'am, it's only a flesh wound," I drawled. "I mean really shot," I added. "Dead."

"Yeah," she said. "I try not to think about it."

"Me too."

"Does it work?" she asked.

"Not really," I said.

"Me either."

"You told your dad I saved your life …"

"Well, you did. Sort of."

"It's hard to find good help these days," I said. "What about the other thing?"

"What other thing?"

"What you were thinking when you thought we were going to die. Did you tell him about that?"

"No, of course not."

"Good," I said. "Because I was thinking that maybe I'd like to make love with you too before I die, but not so soon."

"Am I going to regret telling you that?"

"Probably."

The calendar shoot was scheduled to begin at dawn Sunday morning, which, a few days before the summer solstice, was at the unconscionable hour of 5:10 a.m., so we said good night and headed for our respective beds. I didn't think I'd get to sleep, but I must have, because the next thing I knew it was four o'clock in the morning and Wayne and Jeanie Stone were pounding on the front door. Figuratively speaking, leastways; Bobbi was already up and had made a thermos of coffee, which we took with us to the studio to pick up our gear.

"What happened to your car?" Jeanie wanted to know, eying the duct tape around the stem of the broken side mirror as we loaded our gear into the back of the Liberty — some of it was already stowed in Jeanie's yellow Ford Escape Hybrid.

"It had a rough night," I told her. "I'll tell you about it someday."

Jeanie, a.k.a. Miss October, posed on one of the pieces of logging equipment left in the park after the windstorm cleanup, something called a "feller/buncher" that could bite off a tree up to four feet in diameter. She stood on the massive jaws, wearing nothing (apparently) but a hardhat and work boots, peeking out from behind the strategically positioned blade of a huge chainsaw standing on end. In reality, she was also wearing a tiny string-bikini bottom — we'd Photoshop out the bikini strings on her hips later to make it look as though she really were completely naked behind the saw. By 5:00 p.m. we were all exhausted, but we had managed to shoot Misses May through October — we'd shoot Misses November through April in the studio and

Photoshop in the appropriate backgrounds. Although the other "models" left as soon as their sessions in front of the camera were over, Jeanie hung in for the whole day, helping Bobbi with the heavy lifting.

"Thanks for your help," I said, as we unloaded gear from the cargo area of her Escape back at the studio.

"It was fun," she said. "When do you want to do the rest of the months?"

"Let's see what we've got so far," I said. "We might want to redo Miss May in the studio. How about I call you late tomorrow or early Tuesday?"

"Okay. Once we've done the rest, we can decide where you're going to wine and dine me."

"Oh. Right."

"Not having second thoughts, are you?"

"Heck, no. I'm looking forward to it."

"Good. Me, too." She climbed into her Escape and waved as it hummed away, the tires making more noise on the cobbles than the hybrid engine.

"How did it go?" Mary-Alice asked when I went into the studio.

"It went great," I said. "Jeanie and the other girls worked their — worked very hard. It's going to be a fun calendar. I think they're going to raise a lot of money for the park restoration fund."

"At least it's all for a good cause," Mary-Alice said.

I tidied up a few loose ends, then told Mary-Alice I'd see her later. Five minutes after that I was standing on the quay overlooking the Broker's Bay Marina. My timing couldn't have been better. The tide was out, the ramp down to the docks steeply sloped, and Chrissy Conrad waddled slightly as she descended to the dock, carrying a heavy paper bag of groceries in each arm. Her hair was blonde again, and even shorter. I caught up with her at the bottom of the ramp.

"Let me help you with those," I said.

"Oh," she said with a start. "Hey. It's all right, I've got it."

I relieved her of a bag, anyway. "Taking a trip?"

She looked at me for a beat or two before answering. "Yeah, I guess you could say that."

"This is too much boat for someone to handle on their own," I said as we approached the *Free Spirit*. "Especially someone who doesn't know much about boats."

"I'll manage." She set her bag of groceries on the gunwale beside the cockpit. "Thanks for the help," she said, reaching for the other bag.

"I don't suppose the fact that you don't own it is going to stop you from taking it." I held onto the groceries as I stepped aboard the boat. The hatch was open. I peered down the companionway into the cabin.

"Sam and Anna aren't going to need it, are they?"

"No, I suppose not. Awfully cold, though."

"Look, I appreciate your help, but I can take it from here."

"So, Chrissy — or should I call you Caroline? — whose idea was it to steal Walter Moffat's art collection? Yours? Or Woody Getz's?"

"Gimme a break," she said. "Woody doesn't have that much imagination. Or the balls."

"Yours, then. But you must've known most of it was junk. You must've also known that Moffat couldn't afford to ransom it back."

"It wasn't all junk," she said. "There are a couple of bronzes that are worth three or four grand apiece. And an early Maxfield Parrish that Sam sold to Walter by mistake. He thought it was a copy, but it turned out to be the real deal. It'll fetch at least fifty grand at auction, maybe more. There's a Franz von Stuck 'Amazon' that might be real, too. It just needs a little better provenance."

"What about the rest of it?"

"Threw it into a skip." I could almost hear poor old Walter spinning in his fridge at the morgue.

"What if Mrs. Moffat reports the theft?" I said.

"How likely is that? She'd have to admit that her husband collected tits. And even if she does, I've got bills of sale dated from before the robbery."

"Forged, no doubt."

"So what? By the time anyone gets around to checking, I'll be long gone."

"Did you take the money from the safe, too?"

"What money?" she said archly. "Oh, you mean the illegal campaign contributions and the proceeds of Woody's blackmail scheme? It never existed, did it?"

"And the boat?"

"It was a gift from Anna."

"You don't really expect me to believe that, do you?"

"I don't care what you believe."

"Did you know that Kittle was going to abduct Bobbi and kill her — and me?"

"Shit, no."

"When I asked Elise Moffat if she knew you, she lied. Why would she do that? Why would she protect you?"

She shrugged. "Maybe because she thinks I'm her daughter."

She'd be the right age to be the baby Elise had put up for adoption. And there was a superficial resemblance. But I didn't believe for a minute that Chrissy — or Caroline — was Elise's daughter. "You aren't, though, are you?"

"What do you think?"

"I think you are one cold-hearted piece of work," I said.

"Yeah, well ..."

"Four people are dead because of you."

"How do you figure that? All I did was try to run

a simple little scam that backfired through no fault of mine. Like I told you, no one was supposed to get hurt. And if Woody hadn't panicked when your friend showed up, no one would've been. Stupid bastard."

"But people did get hurt, didn't they? Maybe you aren't directly responsible, but you set a number of balls in motion that resulted in Bobbi's near drowning and the deaths of Anna and Sam Waverley, Walter Moffat, and Tony Kittle. Not to mention the likely collapse of the Bridgwater foundation."

"Not my problem. Anyway, what's the most the police could charge me with, even if there was any proof, besides your word, that I was the one who hired you to photograph the *Wonderlust*?"

A sun-bleached young man came sauntering along the dock, a bulging backpack slung over one muscular shoulder. I'd seen him around Bridges and the marinas, but I didn't know his name. Your basic boat bum. Chrissy had close to ten years on him.

"Hello, sir," he said pleasantly as he climbed aboard the *Free Spirit*. He dropped the backpack to the cockpit deck. "Are you a friend of Lucy's?"

"Hey, baby," Chrissy said, leaning into him, kissing him on the mouth. "He was just helping me with the last of the groceries. You all set?"

"All set."

Chrissy said to me, "Well, thanks for all your help."

I looked at the boy. "I wouldn't go with her on this boat, if I were you," I said.

Predictably, he said, "You aren't me, though, are you?" I mouthed it along with him, which seemed to annoy him.

"Why don't you cast us off, baby?" Chrissy said. "We've still got a couple of hours of light."

"Sure, Luce," the boy said. "You'd better go ashore now, sir."

I stepped over the gunwale onto the dock. "Well, good luck to you," I said to him. "You're going to need it."

I watched as he cast off and Chrissy/Caroline/Lucy started the engine. I was still watching as they motored out of the marina into False Creek and turned toward the Burrard Street Bridge and the open water of Burrard Inlet. Then I went home and made a couple of telephone calls. The first one was to Elise Moffat. I told her what "Caroline" had told me, that while most of her husband's collection was junk, some of the items were quite valuable and that she should immediately report them stolen.

The next call was to the Coast Guard, to report a stolen sailboat.

The End

acknowledgements

Thanks to Alan Annand and Marc Casinni for their support, encouragement, and invaluable comments on early drafts; Toni Hafkenscheid for his wonderful cover photo; Dr. Judith Paterson for suggesting the title of Jeanie Stone's thesis; Stuart Ramsey for correcting my geographical and topographical blunders — all errors are my own; the folks at Dundurn Press for a stellar job, as usual. And to Pamela Hilliard, without whose love, patience, and understanding, writing — and life — wouldn't be nearly as much fun.